BOOK
ONE

A CROWN FORGED

IN FLAME

J.M. WALLACE

A Crown Forged in Flame

Copyright © 2024 by J.M. Wallace

Cover Art by GetCovers

All rights reserved.

This book is a work of fiction. The names, characters, and events in this book are the products of the author's imagination or are used fictitiously. Any similarity to real persons living or dead is coincidental and not intended by the author.

ISBN (Print) 979-8-9901901-0-8

www.jmwallaceauthor.com

For the horse girls who dreamed their ponies had wings.

Contents

N
W
E
S
Solaris
Astarfall
Festiri

Pronunciation Guide

Adalina: a(ă)-duh-lee-nuh
Alfie: al-fee
Alistair: al-iss-tair
Astarfall: a(ă)star-fall
Bellamy: bel-luh-mee
Calida: kaa-lee-duh
Callum: k(ă)-l-uhm
Elettra: eh-leh-trah
Erabelle: air-uh-bell
Festiri: fest-eerie
Gwendolyn: gwen-duh-lin
Heely: heel-lee
Lina: lee-nuh
Seraphine: sera-feen
Solaris: sol-air-is
Uthred: ooh-th-red

One

Family legacies were a blessing and a curse. Adalina knew better than most about both the honor and the excruciating pressure that came with having to live up to them. Tonight just happened to be more pressure than honor. The fire in her veins would arise soon and she would need to tend to the flame. If everything went right, the reward would be well worth the trouble.

For now, all she could do was wait. Adalina held a sewing needle between her teeth. With her free hand, she reached down to flip to the next page in her book: *Histories of the First Men*. The linen shirt in her other hand could wait just a moment, but the story about the bonding of dragons and men—one she had completely thrust herself into—could not. She sensed her mother's looming presence behind her. The soft-spoken woman gazed over Adalina's shoulder; no doubt to check whether she had mended the torn sleeve yet.

Adalina plucked the needle from her mouth and set it down. "Yes, Mother?" she drawled with suppressed irritation.

"Just checking, dear. You really should have finished that by now."

"Surely, Councilman Heely will survive another hour without his favorite shirt." Adalina bit her tongue to keep from saying more about the overzealous man. The one who had been sticking his nose into her business for far too long.

His irritatingly optimistic voice was in her ear more often, the older she got. *It's time you marry like the other young ladies, Adalina. Or perhaps the magic in your veins is just not strong enough.*

She bit back a growl. Nothing ever seemed to be enough. Perhaps, though, her bitterness came from the fear that had taken root in the last few years. A voice in the back of her mind—that to her irritation seemed to mimic Heely's—saying he was right. That the dragon would not wake because Adalina did not possess the power or ability to perform the ceremony.

"Nosy dolt," she grumbled under her breath.

Her mother's honey sweet voice took on a chiding tone. "He only wants what's best for you. We all do."

"I don't see why he should be so invested. Someone should get that man a hobby. Sewing perhaps?" Adalina shot her a sly grin.

Her mother swatted playfully at her. "The council simply wants to see the young women of this town happy and settled. Honestly, Lina, it's not like they're forcing you into anything."

As the granddaughter of a dragon warrior, Adalina had no interest in the council or their plans. Her grandmother had chosen her own path with no say from anyone else. Was it really so scandalous for Adalina to want the same opportunity?

She opened her mouth to speak but was cut off as the door swung open to reveal her father. His skin was tanned from hours spent in the field and he left a smudge of dirt behind as he wiped his brow and removed his hat. He greeted her mother first with a kiss, then set his sights on Adalina. His warm smile tipped into a frown when he noticed the book she was balancing beside her as she worked.

"At it again, eh?" was all he said as he pulled his boots off and placed them by the door.

Adalina set the shirt down and grabbed the book defensively. She glanced at the page she'd been reading.

In the beginning, darkness filled the land. Neighbors fought over food, property, and even the shirts on their backs. They were nearly as vicious as the fearsome beasts who stalked them in the dead of night. Basilisks who gnawed their prey with curved teeth and naga who slithered between realms were amongst the many monsters who threatened the vulnerable. But the dragons changed all of that. They were birthed from the fiery depths beneath the earth, and with them, light, safety and power followed.

With a resigned sigh, she marked her page before closing the book. Her father might not agree, but their histories were a treasure that should be shared and remembered. Adalina knew the stories by heart. Not because she had lived them. No. Things never worked that well in her favor. Instead, she devoured every story possible, hoping her inherited magic would grant her the power she needed to live up to her grandmother's legacy. From the time she could walk, she was consumed with curiosity about the great winged beasts who roamed the land side by side with her people for a millennium. She was envious of those who had reaped the benefits of being bonded by ancient magic and a unique understanding between one another.

"Our history is how we learn and grow..." She started using the rehearsed excuse. The one that helped cover up just how selfish her motivations actually were. But before she could go any further, she was abruptly interrupted by intense heat spreading through her chest. It burned and clawed at her, and she dropped the book on the floor.

Her mother was beside her in an instant. Her large blue eyes widened into saucers, and she placed a cool hand on Adalina's forehead. In a voice that would have been perfect for commanding armies, she ordered Adalina's father, "Fetch some water and the rags. She's burning up again."

"I'm fine," Adalina mumbled.

She'd known this was coming, but there was no way to prepare herself. It was the same each time. She wasn't fond of this feeling. Her clothes clung to the sweat beading all over her body. Even her vision betrayed her, growing hazy at the edges. It would only get worse the longer she waited. It filled her with a sense of urgency and anxiety. But hope and wonder always accompanied it, as well, giving her the rush of energy she needed to get up and move. And at that moment, she couldn't stop a small part of her from welcoming it like an old friend.

Her father quickly did as her mother bid. He dipped the rag into the water and pressed it against Adalina's temples. Although he used a gentle, fatherly touch, his words were heated as he said, "If you do not pay any heed to it, it will fade. Your mother's fits stopped by nineteen. You're twenty-two. There's no reason you should still be experiencing this."

Adalina spoke with more bite than she intended. "Ignoring it is what makes it hurt. Besides, it's not as if I ask for this."

That was a fib, of course. Since she was a child, she had embraced the familiar call each month; seeing it as her chance to begin a new chapter in her life. She winced as another shot of fiery heat blazed through her. Now it reached down to the tips of her toes. It was time to go. If she ignored the discomfort, the draw to the cave where her grandmother's dragon, Elettra, slumbered would only grow.

Why was it that they still couldn't understand? As Adalina grew up, she had worshipped her grandmother and the stories about her being the only woman to perform the Great Bonding. She was everything Adalina wanted to be. Independent, a force to be reckoned with... If Elettra were to awaken, it would show everyone that she was all those things too. That the legacy of the dragon warrior lived on. That she could do so much more than mend people's favorite shirts.

Her father passed the rag off to her mother and wandered to the kitchen to pour himself a drink. Adalina glared at him and leaned away from her mother, who had taken to fussing over her. Then she stood from her seat, abandoning the day's work, and grabbed the bag she'd already packed that morning. Without another word, she swung it over her shoulder and took her shawl off the hook.

Her father lectured, "If you would set aside your ambitions and focus on the present, then perhaps this madness would stop. It's time to stop living with your nose in those books and your head in the clouds. You need to accept the hand you've been dealt."

Easy for him to say. He wasn't expected to spend hours in the shop sewing garment after garment. There was no one to tell him where to go or the proper way for him to behave. Nor had he ever experienced the call. Dreams were all she had to her name, and she wasn't ready to give them up.

There was just one problem. Her dreams were buried under dirt and sediment. They were close, yet always out of reach. If she could fly away from the dress shop, from her father's judgmental gaze, and the council's heavy rule, then she would.

He spoke again as she reached for the door. "What if the dragon did wake? What then?"

Adalina gave an exasperated sigh. She wanted to say that she would fly, of course. That it was all she had ever dreamed of doing, and that it was reason enough to keep trying. But they'd had this conversation so many times before. She knew whatever answer she gave him wouldn't be enough. Not when he wanted her to accept the hand that she'd been dealt and find contentment like her mother.

And maybe he was right. But in that moment, all she knew for certain was that there was no ignoring the fire that raged around her heart with each new moon. He seemed to take her silence as a triumph. The last thing she saw before she slammed the door behind her was the smug look on her father's face.

Adalina hurried up the hill to her grandmother's cottage. But she wasn't on her way there for a visit. If anything, she would need to stay out of sight to avoid the pitiful stares from both her grandparents. They, like her father and the council, had little faith in what she was about to do.

The heat—a sign of the remnant of magic that ran through her veins—spread to her face. She tugged at the collar of her dress. The fever was in full swing. To distract herself, she recalled the histories and the beautiful, monstrous beasts who filled them. As she walked, she tried to imagine shimmering scaled wings beating heavily above her. But all she found was a flock of exceptionally fat geese heading south for the coming winter.

She shivered and pulled her wool shawl tightly around her as she approached the large, sturdy cottage. The fever was fading the closer she came to her destination. Her grandparents, Calida and Bellamy, had lived on the highest hill in their village since she could remember. The garden was as tidy as ever, with rows of vegetables lifted off the ground by wooden planters to keep the critters out. In late summer, she always admired the towering sunflowers that reached for the sun. There weren't any now, of course. Not with snowy days on the horizon.

She veered away from the front door to peer around the cottage. Far beyond the home, nestled into a cluster of trees, Adalina spotted the dark cave that held her greatest treasure. The last remaining evidence of a gift that her people had earned through courage and kindness. A remnant of what they had lost. Of what *she* hoped to gain one day.

She stopped in her tracks and shut her eyes. A cool, late autumn wind drifted past, blowing her wild, fiery hair into her face. If she listened closely—blocking out the noise of everyday life in the village—she could trick herself into believing she heard the rumbling snores of the sleeping dragon tucked peacefully in that cave.

It had been a tedious day in the dress shop, but despite the needle pricks in her fingers and the ache in her neck, she needed to take advantage of the new moon. Otherwise, she would have to wait for an entire moon cycle to pass before trying again. It would mean another month of listening to her father and Heely conspiring to find her a husband, and weeks of people whispering about the girl who wasn't as strong or fierce as her grandmother. She shifted, adjusting the heavy bag on her hip. If she was quick enough, her grandparents wouldn't notice her ducking into the mouth of the cave.

Adalina inched around the side of the cottage and crept below the windows so no one would spot her. When she reached the back, she sprinted toward the cave. The mouth was opened wide, with icicle-shaped deposits hanging from the top and jutting from the ground. Her pulse quickened at the sight. She imagined it was similar to the great gnashing teeth of the dragons.

Heat tugged at her chest. The discomfort was gone, replaced with a steady rhythm of warmth. The magic that had been passed down through generations crackled in her arms like a dying fire in the coals. It was a familiar feeling. One she was met with every time she came to the cave. And no matter how many times she experienced it, she felt nothing but awe and excitement.

Was it the sleeping dragon calling to her? Or was it just the remnant of old dragon magic lingering in her veins—calling her to perform the ancient rites of her people? Gingerly, she stepped between two of the teeth-like stone structures, which were nearly as tall as her. Inside, the cave was dark and damp. The musty scent from the water pooling at the foot of the walls made her nose wrinkle.

Cool air swept out of the depths and bit into her face. She trembled, unnerved by the strange sensation that the cave itself was breathing. After taking a few steps inside, Adalina glimpsed the mound. It was roughly the size of a longboat she had seen when she'd visited the southern ports. A shiver ran up her spine and she willed her eyes to adjust to the darkness. If she stared hard enough, she hoped she might see the rise and fall of the dragon's breath.

At first glance, it appeared to be nothing more than a bump on the cave floor. Just an abnormality created by water trickling through the earth. But she knew what was hidden beneath. The one thing that could save her from living under the thumb of her father and the other men who acted as guardians of Solaris.

Adalina inched toward the mound and knelt before it. Scattered around the cave floor were an array of trinkets. It was a treasure trove of items that Adalina had collected over the years. There were tiny dolls carved messily from oak and toy swords from her childhood. As she matured, she began collecting second-hand jewelry from the market and precious gemstones from the river. All of them were spread out in an offering to the sleeping dragon. Each one was evidence of her failed attempts.

Adalina pressed her forehead to the ground in humility. She owed it to the dragon who slumbered in this cave—the one who once belonged to her grandmother. Years after the great war, the other dragons had died either from old age, or battle. Even the remaining dragon eggs had hardened; fossilizing without their mothers to breathe their life-giving fire into them. Elettra was the only one of her kind left.

Adalina ran a hand over the curved head of the mound. Horns longer than her arms could still be seen, though they were now covered in stone and crystals. Her heart ached for her grandmother, imagining how she must have felt the day she returned from the village to find Elettra sound asleep in the cave.

It hadn't been unusual for dragons to sleep for long bouts of time when it grew too cold for them. But when spring came and the frost began to melt from the trees, Elettra still didn't wake. Adalina knew it had devastated her grandmother, but as time went on, she started a family of her own, and the heartache became manageable. Whenever

Adalina asked why she didn't try to re-perform the bonding ceremony, her grandmother would simply state that her time with Elettra had passed. And because of that, she did her best to live the remainder of her life to the fullest, taking comfort in knowing that her dearest friend was nestled peacefully in her nest.

It might be selfish for Adalina to not share that same sentiment. But for years, she had clung to the stories and the hope that Elettra had rested enough. That there was a reason for the discomfort that returned each month. And if she could just complete the ritual, the dragon would wake.

She sat up, ready to begin the rites that had once been performed by the warriors amongst her people. It had begun with the First Man and was then carried on through the generations, including her grandmother's. As she opened her bag and laid out the month's offerings, she spoke out loud as if telling the sleeping dragon a bedtime story.

"With these gifts, we honor the Great Bonding between man and dragon. A gift for a gift."

She recited the words passed through generations of her people word for word, never missing a beat as she set a locket and a hand-carved heart at the dragon's foot.

Adalina inhaled deeply. She crept over to the ivory torch that was placed deep in the ground. It rose above her, standing as tall and proud as the day it had first been erected. She reached up and used the flint she'd brought to light it.

Then, she continued, "Light to replace the darkness."

The fire blazed to life as if excited by her words. Adalina raised her chin, reveling in the heat of it. Steadily, she removed a small thread cutter from her bag and pricked her finger. She squeezed it over the fire until the blood dripped down. And she recited, "Blood for blood. May these offerings honor the strength and connection we share."

Her stomach fluttered as the flame grew higher and higher, giving light to the entire cave. Crystals glimmered, casting an orange and red glow on the sleeping dragon who was still hidden by years of sediment and rock.

The heat from the flame spread through the cave, sending the tingling sensation of magic through Adalina's fingers and toes. It pulsed faintly. Just out of reach. For a moment, the fire burned hotter and brighter, snuffing out any remaining shadows. It rose and with it, so did Adalina's hope, but just like always, it sputtered and returned to normal.

Though the fever subsided completely, and her chest was free of the striking heat, there was no rumble of an awaking dragon. Just a bitter chill and unbearable darkness. Another refusal. Another rejection.

She wanted to scream or break something. Why taunt her with the call to perform the ritual if it wasn't going to work? Why torture her with another failure? She could practically hear the fates laughing at her.

"Please," she pleaded. "Please, Elettra."

Adalina knelt beside the dragon's head. She trailed her fingers over the rough earth that had grown overtop and tried to imagine how smooth Elettra's scales must have felt.

Her voice cracked as she grew more desperate. "This can't be our fate."

Was she to remain in the village until she, too, grew tired and returned to the earth? Was she wrong for trying to pull Elettra from her peaceful slumber? Her father's smug face flashed in her mind. He wasn't a bad man. Not at the core. But order mattered to him. Even if it meant telling his only daughter to ignore the power that pulsed in her with each new moon. He, like the council, expected her to ignore the deep, aching call to complete the Great Bonding, just as her mother had obediently done.

A hot, angry tear drifted down her cheek and she clenched her fists tight to keep the despair at bay. Every new moon she had come to this cave. She had scraped together pennies to buy the offerings and had spent hours searching for beautiful treasures to bring to Elettra. And yet, each time, the dragon refused to wake. The magic in Adalina's veins did not seem to be enough. The council theorized that it had simply faded as the years flew by, or that perhaps her grandmother was meant to be the only female rider. But Adalina refused to believe that. She would wake the dragon even if it meant being denied month after month. She would find a way.

Two

Adalina stepped back from Elettra with a deflated sigh. The fiery presence of magic ebbed away, leaving her with the faintest tingle on the tips of her fingers. It was like an echo of the power that was within her grasp only moments ago. If she reached deep enough, she might find its heat once more, but what was the point? She wouldn't be able to perform the ritual again until the next new moon. So instead, she resigned herself to yet another month of finding warmth by her family's hearth rather than beside a dragon's belly.

When she reached the mouth of the cave, the back door to the cottage creaked open and her grandmother called out to her with a slight scolding. "Lina, by the fire, what are you doing out there? Get your behind in this house before you catch a chill."

Adalina laughed lightly. "Yes, Grandmother."

Although Adalina was a woman of twenty-two, her grandmother still treated her as if she were a child. Maybe it was because she remained unmarried and living in her father's home. Part of her often wondered, though, if it was because, at her age, her grandmother had seen battle. Had wielded a sword atop the last dragon and defended her people from dangerous magic-wielders known as the *frost breathers*. It was one of Adalina's favorite stories. The one about exiled men from the south who came to claim her land and her people, just to be met with the only female dragon warrior in history.

Adalina greeted her grandmother with a kiss on the cheek and stepped into the toasty cottage. Fire was raging in the large hearth. The heat would have bothered most people, but despite the sweltering flame, her grandmother was unphased without even the slightest hint of a flush.

She was a petite woman with silvery white hair that was once the same fiery red shade as Adalina's. At nearly seventy-five, she didn't look a day over fifty. But her eyes, which were also the same sea-green blue as Adalina's, gave away the strife she had experienced. They were the eyes of someone who had seen more in her lifetime than most and made you feel as if she were staring into the darkest depths of your soul. It unsettled some villagers, who were too young to remember what she had done for their people, which was why she and Adalina's grandfather isolated themselves on the hilltop.

Her grandfather grumbled at her grandmother from the sofa. "Calida, you'd think that damned council would choose to meet before the sun goes down. It's colder than a yeti's arse out there."

Adalina's snicker and her grandfather's complaining were promptly cut off with a stern look from her grandmother. The no-nonsense woman tossed the scarf that Adalina's mother had knitted in his direction. It was made from rough woven wool and had no trouble keeping the evening air's bite away.

Her grandmother sniped at them both. "Get yourselves together. The night market is beginning and *you*, Bellamy, can't miss the meeting. Heely is eager to reveal more about his trip in the south and our family needs you to be there when he does."

"What's on the agenda for tonight?" Adalina asked.

Ignoring the question, her grandmother handed her a heavy cloak. "Wear this or you'll catch your death."

Once her grandmother turned her back, Adalina rolled her eyes, and her grandfather clasped a strong hand on her shoulder. He winked at her. "Best not to resist."

Her grandmother shook her head as she laced her old brown leather boots. "There's more at stake tonight than just a few local grievances."

With a strange look at Adalina, she cleared her throat and said to her husband, "You need to be there to represent this family."

Adalina wasn't privy to the inner dealings of the council. Their meetings were closed to the women of Solaris. But whatever was happening, it seemed to have her grandmother in a particularly fitful mood.

As capable as the councilmen were, Adalina would have had more faith in them if they allowed her grandmother into their ranks.

In a near mumble, she said, "If they would let one of their most experienced warriors join them..."

Her grandmother strode to the kitchen and grabbed a basket for the night market. Dishes clanged around, echoing through the cottage. Adalina eyed her, surprised she didn't want to discuss her exclusion from the council as they so often did. Tonight, her grandparents seemed to be avoiding anything she had to say altogether. Something was going on. Something, as they said, concerned their family's interests.

She was about to ask when her grandmother returned, carrying three baskets and a canvas bag. The lines on her forehead were creased into a frown until Adalina's grandfather took the baskets from her and said, "Let's go, little flame."

Her grandmother's face softened at the use of his pet name for her, but she threw an exasperated hand in the air, anyway. Then she announced, "Alright, my loves, let's go." To Adalina's grandfather, she added, "Make sure you find a seat in the front where you can see their pompous faces clearly."

Adalina smiled to herself. Her grandmother didn't appreciate the council's rule any more than she did. For years, she had been trying to get placed amongst the elders, but some old rules seemed too deeply rooted in their history to be changed. Only the eldest son from the oldest families received a council chair.

Her grandparents walked slightly ahead of her, whispering to one another with worried faces. Assuming it was a lovers' quarrel, Adalina tuned them out, instead looking down at her hands intently while she walked down the dirt road. Now that she had a quiet moment to herself, she couldn't stop thoughts of the failed ritual from creeping in. Why hadn't it worked? She knew it was pointless to wonder. No one had an answer for her, only speculations. The magic was there. That she was sure of. But it didn't seem to be enough. Or was it *she* that wasn't enough? Did Elettra find her unworthy of waking for?

It didn't take them long to reach the village going downhill on the hard dirt packed road. By the time they reached the town square where the market was in full swing, a few groups had already gathered. They were split apart, talking amongst themselves in excited whispers. It was like this every month during the peak of the new moon. People flocked to the stands, peddling expensive trinkets. It was the one time a month that the villagers were most likely to treat themselves.

Food and drink were popular items as well. Her grandmother exchanged some coin for a bottle of mulberry wine and placed it in one of her baskets. Adalina's mother waved to them from a stand selling soaps and bath salts. Beside her, Adalina's father crossed his arms, and his steady gaze weighed heavily on her. Too ashamed to face him so soon after their fight—and her ultimate failure of a ritual—she wandered in the opposite direction.

She danced on her feet to keep warm when someone caught her eye in the crowd. His brown eyes seemed to darken, and a frown tugged at his lips before he turned back to his friends. Adalina spun on her heel, pretending to be suddenly very interested in an old cart parked beside her.

Harold was the butcher from the village who always gave Adalina the best cuts. Not so long ago, he'd been eager to give her a bit more than that, too. She blushed at the heated memory. He was quite the eligible suitor, according to most of the women in town. And for a time, Adalina saw nothing wrong with a little flirtation, kissing, and... things of a more carnal nature. But it wasn't long before the council involved themselves. Soon Harold was throwing around words like *courting* and *marriage*. Things her father and the council had been encouraging in their typical overbearing manner.

Adalina had promptly cut him off after that. Perhaps that was why he currently refused to meet her eye. Part of her felt sorry for the way she had treated him. There was nothing wrong with being a butcher's wife, but Harold was dreadfully dull when it came down to it. He was charming and kind, but there was no spark that set her heart on fire. He also didn't challenge the council's heavy hand in any way and, in that sense, a life with him might have meant bending to yet another man's will.

And he certainly didn't look at her with the same light in his eyes that her grandfather looked at her grandmother with. Theirs was a marriage to be envied. Her grandparents had *chosen* each other. No one had pushed for them to be together. If anything, her grandmother had ignored naysayers and decided to do what she wanted. To be with the man that her *heart* chose.

Adalina firmly believed it wasn't fair for anyone to make life choices for her. Especially not when all they wanted was for her to be settled and content. And more importantly, not when she spent so much time envious of the grand adventure her grandmother had experienced. The one that had brought her and Adalina's grandfather together, no less.

A few murmurs in the crowd caught Adalina's attention. She glanced at the longhouse where men of the council were already gathering. A few wore worried frowns with their brows knitted together.

Adalina strayed from her grandparents and inched closer to do some eavesdropping. Pretending to be interested in an arrangement of roses, she caught a few excited whispers from the younger members.

"I don't understand why Heely is calling a meeting now."

A young man's voice shook with anticipation. "Something big must have happened."

"I hear the King of Astarfall has made a request," another said.

"But the attacks haven't yet reached us here in Solaris. It's not our problem to worry about," said an older man with a mean set of his jaw.

"It would be foolish to wait until the problem reaches our borders," replied the younger man.

The older gentleman's gaze pinned her down, and she clumsily reached for coins to pay for the flowers she was pretending to be interested in. A few dropped to the ground, and she hurried to pick them up, but her grandmother reached them first.

"What's going on?" Adalina hissed in a whisper. When she glanced back at the men, they were gone; already slipping through the doors to the longhouse.

Her grandmother handed the coins and flowers to her and ushered her away from the stand. Adalina couldn't imagine what attacks they were referring to. There had been a longstanding peace in Solaris.

With a sigh, her grandmother said, "The council is voting on ways to strengthen Solaris tonight."

"Strengthen us against who?" Adalina wracked her brain for potential enemies. There had been a few cattle thieves in the past, but beyond that, they had a good relationship with the neighboring kingdoms. In all her life, she couldn't recall a time when there had been any true danger to their wellbeing. Thanks to her grandmother, no one had dared challenge Solaris.

"There has been word from Astarfall. Raiders are sweeping through their western borders." Hastily, her grandmother added, "I do not want to worry you. Your grandfather is dealing with it."

What help could Adalina's grandfather be? Although he was born and raised in Astarfall, he had left them behind to be with her grandmother. He had chosen to put his allegiance and interests with Solaris. Besides, Astarfall—the kingdom to the south of Solaris—was one with unmatched strength. They didn't need dragons or foreign armies to protect them like Solaris once did. Instead, they had magic of their own. Power that was not to be trifled with. Anyone who tried to raid their lands would have to be insane. Or incredibly powerful in their own right.

As they walked through the crowded street, Adalina asked, "Has anyone been hurt?"

Her grandmother bit her lip. "According to their king, the latest raid has left several injured or dead."

Adalina's heart hurt for them and their families. But still, she couldn't understand why Solaris would trouble themselves when the border in question was so far south. Unless Astarfall's king, Alistair, was asking for Solaris' help...

Adalina's heart sped. "There's more. Something you're not telling me. I noticed it in the cabin."

Her grandmother cast her eyes downward. "Lina, your grandfather will handle it."

"Not good enough." Adalina stopped walking. She stood her ground as she asked, "Is King Alistair asking for Solarian soldiers to help him?"

Her stomach twisted in knots as she waited for her grandmother to answer. The people of Solaris were no longer warriors. Those who had fought the frost breathers hadn't picked up a sword in over fifty years. And their children and grandchildren had enjoyed the long-lasting peace, honing their talents for hunting and farming. Surely Astarfall needed soldiers, not farmers.

Her grandmother opened her mouth to speak, but Adalina's father interrupted them. His face was blanched and with urgency, he said, "Calida. You need to get in there. What they're asking... It's outrageous."

Adalina stared wide-eyed at her father. He rarely disagreed with the council. Whatever they were asking, it must have been bad.

Something seemed to snap in her grandmother. She set her shoulders back and raised her chin. Then, with an air of authority, she strode right past the men at the longhouse door and into the council meeting.

Three

A jolt of anxiety and confusion set Adalina in motion. She dodged her father, who held out a hand to stop her and followed her grandmother. Trying to emulate that same sense of authority, she passed through the doors. Men from various families were seated at a table in the grand hall. Some of the lesser known, less powerful men—like the young one she'd overheard outside—pressed against the man next to him in an attempt to get a better look at the dais where the heads of the council were already presiding.

Adalina halted behind her grandmother, just a few paces away from where her grandfather was standing defiantly. He appeared to be in the midst of an argument with Heely, who stood at the head holding a piece of parchment with the Astarfallen royal seal on it.

Her grandfather stepped aside to allow his wife and Adalina to stand beside him, but the council did not even honor the women with a quick glance. Instead, they spat heated words at one another. Adalina caught only bits and pieces.

"Out of the question—" her grandfather started.

"Best to solidify our precarious alliance," said one elder.

"Saying no to Astarfall could come back to haunt us," Heely stated in a solemn tone.

Her grandmother said, "Gentlemen, if you please."

Adalina glanced around to find that the crowd's anticipatory gaze fell on her grandmother, who wore a fierce expression on her face. The council, however, led by Heely—a man who was fairly young for his position—paid no attention. They continued to argue. Their voices were so boisterous that Adalina was having trouble figuring out what they were disagreeing on.

Her grandmother raised her chin and tried again, "Esteemed Councilmen, I implore you to—"

There was an uproar on the dais, drowning out her interjection.

The man beside Heely raged. "It would be unwise to deny such a powerful ally!"

Adalina had never considered Astarfall an ally before. They were useful for trade, that much was true. But in the past, they had failed to come to Solaris' aid when they needed it the most. She stepped forward and attempted to sort out what was happening. The men were still ignoring her grandmother. Her grandfather tapped his foot, a sure sign that his patience was wearing thin. So was Adalina's now. Her face warmed. If Solaris' governing body was truly as worried as they appeared, then they should be listening to one of their most renowned warriors. It did not matter that women couldn't have a seat on the council. This discussion clearly concerned them all.

Seemingly unable to stand it any longer, Adalina's grandfather spoke. His voice was so thunderous it seemed to quake the entire meeting house. It was in brief moments like this that she was reminded that he, too, had been a warrior.

Silence fell over the room as he said, "I don't want to hear it. None of it. Let Astarfall settle their own disputes as they made you settle yours."

Heely's eyes widened. "Bellamy, you of all people should understand this predicament. For it was you, an Astarfallen, who decided to stand with us when your own people would not."

Adalina's grandfather balled his hands into tight fists. Her grandmother placed a hand on his shoulder, and it seemed to give him a sense of calm. At the least, it was enough for him to hold his composure and not march up to punch Councilman Heely in the face.

It was her grandmother who spoke next. "Bellamy chose for himself. You are trying to make decisions for others. That is unacceptable."

Adalina's frustration rose with each passing second. Did Astarfall want them to send an army south? What exactly were they asking? She swallowed the bitter taste in her mouth. Did her grandparents really think her so incapable that they had decided to keep whatever this was to themselves? It was as if she was trying to solve a puzzle and everyone else in the room was holding the missing piece behind their backs where she couldn't see.

Heely argued, "Astarfall's borders are being tested. If those lines are breached, then what's stopping these invaders from coming north?"

She knew her grandfather well enough to realize he was shaking with pent-up frustration. She reached up to pat his arm, to remind him that someone was on his side. His honey-brown eyes shined when he smiled down at her. But the moment he looked back at Heely, his scowl returned.

Her grandmother stepped closer to the dais and Adalina noted a few council members shoot nervous glances at one another. The woman was a force to be reckoned with and it was times like this where they were reminded of it.

She folded her hands in front of her, but stood tall. "What *exactly* is Astarfall suggesting?"

Adalina narrowed her eyes at the tone her grandmother used. She had a sneaking suspicion that she had already guessed what Astarfall truly wanted.

Heely glanced around nervously. "With all due respect, your husband is here to represent your family. We recognize your standing in Solaris, Calida, but you should not be here."

"Yet here I stand."

Heely twisted the hat in his hands and his eyes darted to Adalina so quickly, she almost thought she imagined it. Then he said, "Astarfall wants to know if the dragon..." he trailed off as if afraid to finish the sentence.

Adalina's heart leaped into her throat. Elettra? Why were they bringing her into this? This should have been a matter of whether to raise a defensive force, not a discussion about her family's dragon. Just hours ago, she had unsuccessfully tried to wake Elettra. The council knew of the failed attempts. What changed?

Adalina's grandfather shifted, and Heely shrank away. Her grandfather was deadly calm as he said, "You may want to reconsider what you're suggesting."

Another councilman interjected. He'd been her grandfather's friend for many years; playing cards with him at the tavern and taking lazy strolls on Sundays. But now he fumbled as he said, "Bellamy, if they wake the dragon, it benefits all of us."

Her grandfather growled. "Hasn't our family sacrificed enough? Raise your guard. Build a wall around Solaris if you must. My granddaughter has tried every month for years to wake Elettra. It does not work."

Adalina winced but she knew her grandfather meant no malice with his words. It was a simple truth.

The councilman gritted his teeth. "But—"

With a hand on her hip, Adalina's grandmother asked, "There was more to it than that, wasn't there? What did their correspondence really suggest?" She posed a question, but the way she asked told Adalina that she already suspected the answer.

Heely's gaze flitted around to each of them, but Adalina's grandparents stood their ground.

The councilman placed his hat on the table and announced, "Emotions are clearly high. I have given Bellamy Astarfall's terms. You may take the night to confer and return tomorrow with your answer."

Adalina tapped her booted foot on the floor. Astarfall was in a position of power. They had access to the best ports, land nearly as prosperous as theirs, and a royal family that had been in power for centuries. More than that, they had magic of their own. Granted from the very heavens above. Powerful, ancient magic that was much stronger than the power Solaris had been gifted by the dragons. Surely, they could fend off a few cutthroat thieves.

Angry, excited muttering spread through the crowd like wildfire. Her grandfather took the parchment Heely had been holding and handed it to her grandmother. After reading it, she shook it in her fist and said, "Why wasn't this sent directly to us?"

Adalina's grandfather shrugged. "Perhaps because of the history between you and King Alistair's father. Maybe he hoped the council would have better luck in persuading us."

Adalina tried to peer at the parchment to read it, but her grandmother folded it angrily.

The council members scurried away through the back of the longhouse while the crowd began to disperse. Adalina remained still with a coil in her stomach. With a sigh, she tugged at her grandfather's sleeve and whispered, "What's going on? What am I missing?"

"The council needs to mind their business. That's what's going on." He crossed his arms and sneered at the back of Heely's head as the man ducked out the door.

Adalina eyed her grandfather warily. His beard had grown longer than he usually kept it, and there were dark circles around his eyes like he hadn't slept well. Meanwhile, her grandmother stood with her arms crossed and her lips pressed into a thin line.

"Grandfather, we've never kept things from each other before. Why start now?" She nudged him playfully, but it didn't bring a smile to his face.

Instead, her grandmother spoke. "King Alistair has sent a personal request. One that the council has deemed themselves worthy of speaking on rather than allowing us to handle it."

Adalina furrowed her brow. Maybe Astarfall didn't have things under control like she'd thought. Whatever they were asking of them was big enough to elicit this sort of reaction from her grandparents. If it was simply a matter of waking the dragon, why were they so worked up?

Adalina was happy to continue trying to make the ritual work. She wanted to wake Elettra more than anything else. And if it meant doing so would protect Solaris, then all the more reason for her to do anything in her power to complete it.

They moved to the door, where the last of the villagers were trickling out into the cool night. Her parents were waiting for them silently as her grandmother came to a halt. She set her shoulders back in a hard, unmoving stance.

There was a hint of something fierce in her eyes as she said, "King Alistair wants our dragon to defend his lands."

Although Adalina had gathered that by now, heat flared in her chest and she said, "He's got some nerve. How can he ask for our help when his own father refused our people when we needed him?"

Her grandfather snorted. "Alistair seems to have inherited his father's balls—"

"Bellamy," her grandmother hissed, "that's quite enough of that." Amusement sparked in her eyes briefly, despite the chiding she'd just given him. Then she sighed and stepped up to a torch that had been placed beside the door to give light to the longhouse entryway. The flames cast a golden glow on her and for a moment, Adalina glimpsed the warrior who had summoned fire from deep within her dragon's belly. The woman who had sent thousands of men to their knees in surrender.

"As I was saying, King Alistair wants you to wake her—"

"But Elettra refuses to wake," Adalina said, then winced at the shadow of sadness on her grandmother's face at the mention of it. "I'm sorry, but if she will not wake for me, then she certainly will not do it for another."

Her grandparents were as silent as the sleeping dragon in the cave. They stared at one another with a look that Adalina had seen often. The sort that only couples who were truly meant for each other exchanged. One that made it seem as if they were reading each other's mind, heart, and soul.

Adalina wrapped her shawl and cloak around her tightly. "What aren't you telling me?"

Her grandfather forced a soft smile. "He believes there could be two reasons that your magic has not woken the dragon. Either it is because you are a woman," he held up a calming hand when Adalina opened her mouth to argue, then he continued, "or that it has been so long since the First Man performed the ceremony gifting our people with the dragon magic, that it no longer burns as strong as it once did. That there is a chance your power is like a dying flame that simply needs to be fanned."

Her grandmother handed her the crumpled letter and added, "His solution is one that hasn't been used in centuries."

Adalina grabbed the parchment. Although it was light, there was a weight of expectation that came with it and settled into her hands. The knots in her stomach twisted tighter like a snake trying to squeeze the courage out of her.

Her grandmother's gaze was soft and sympathetic. There was a hint of regret as she said, "King Alistair wants to invoke the binding rites."

Adalina vibrated with nervous energy. The binding ritual was not the same as the one she performed each new moon on her own. Rather, it was a ceremony between their two realms—Solaris and Astarfall—rooted deeply in the ancient magic of their lands. And it hadn't been performed in ages. Not in her lifetime, her mother's, or even her grandmother's. There had been no need for it with peace between the neighboring realms. At least, not until the frost breathers attacked. And even then, King Alistair's late father had denied the request to perform it—declaring that they would not get involved.

At Adalina's stunned silence, her grandmother continued, "King Alistair holds on to the hope that the binding rites would grant the couple enough power that they might wake Elettra."

"But she belongs with *our* family. Another woman in the village could not wake her—if it's even possible—and even if she did, she wouldn't be able to ride her."

Dragons were loyal to familial bonds. They honored those who rode them by extending that loyalty to their ancestors. Adalina shared her grandmother's blood. If Elettra had not gone into her deep slumber, she would have allowed Adalina to ride her.

"You are correct. Another in the village would not." Her grandmother gave her a pointed look. The kind that she always used when she was attempting to teach Adalina a valuable life lesson and was waiting for her to catch on.

Adalina's heart raced, beating so rapidly she could hear it in her ears. It muffled out the sounds of the night market. If King Alistair wanted to perform the ceremony between one of his people and a woman from Solaris in order to use their dragon, then the woman would have to be unwed. Unwed *and* in Calida's family.

It all clicked into place. The reason her grandfather had been furious at the mention of their dragon. Her grandmother's apologetic frown. And the tension that was growing, sucking the air from Adalina's lungs.

She clenched her fists tightly. "It would be me. I would have to marry an Astarfallen."

"Yes." Her grandmother took her hands and squeezed them tight. "Your power is the dying flame and an Astarfallen husband's power would be the fan to grow it."

A weight settled in the pit of Adalina's stomach.

All this time, she had hoped and wished for the dragon to wake again. They were presenting her with a sliver of possibility. But she knew better when it came to the Astarfallen and their so-called *rites*. Marriage in any set of circumstances meant power, but it most certainly was never tipped in the woman's favor. They were dangling her dream of waking the dragon in front of her and stripping away her freedom in the same breath.

Heat bloomed across her face, spreading down to her chest, and making her itch. If the combined power of Solaris and Astarfall was strong enough to complete the ritual, then she would get the one thing she'd always wanted. Elettra would wake. But it was a double-edged sword. Would she want Elettra to wake if she wasn't going to be the one to ride her? If it was to be an Astarfall man to take that honor? More than that, someone else would be choosing the man she gave herself to for the rest of her life. What great love could come from an arrangement like that?

"Who is it? Who am I to marry?" she demanded.

No one would look her in the eye. It was her father who answered. "Bindings by tradition are only allowed to be with someone from the royal line. Their magic is naturally stronger. And they would not risk placing this sort of power in just anyone's hands."

Adalina's mouth went so dry she wasn't sure she'd be able to spit out her next words. "The Prince?"

Her grandfather nodded solemnly.

If Adalina could breathe fire, she would have at that moment. The council had not even given her the respect to approach her directly. Instead, they had held this horrid meeting. All this time they were planning to vote on *her* fate and future with no regard to what she wanted. And now she was meant to lie down for a man she had only met once? One who, as far as she was concerned, she couldn't stand. Adalina dug her nails into the palm of her hands to keep from saying what she was thinking. *Damn them to the fiery depths.*

Four

King Alistair was officially at the top of Adalina's shit list, along with the pompous Astarfallen ass of a prince he planned to marry her off to. Her protests had been met with indifference. Heely was quick to reassure her that she would not be *forced* to do something she did not want to do, but that felt more like placating than anything else. The rest of the council insisted that the least she and her family could do was go south to assess the urgency and danger for themselves and hear the royal family out before giving an answer one way or the other.

Which explained why Adalina was now squished into a carriage beside her mother, while her grandmother sat across from her, wearing an interesting scowl on her face. Adalina supposed it was because she wasn't looking forward to setting foot on Astarfallen territory any more than she was.

Long-standing peace between Solaris and Astarfall meant they couldn't outright deny the King's request. At least, not from the council's perspective. However, it was not the same courtesy Astarfall's late king afforded them. It seemed her grandmother was not quick to forget, nor to forgive.

The carriage bounced roughly, slamming Adalina into the side panel. She cursed under her breath and grumbled, "This is ridiculous."

"*This*, my dear," her mother drawled, "is our duty."

"We owe them nothing." Adalina cast a pleading glance in her grandmother's direction. "Where were they when you needed *them*? When their own discontented people came into our land to claim it for themselves?"

The men her grandmother had fought—known as the frost breathers for the icy magic they wielded—had been exiled by the late King of Astarfall. They had been unruly and believed their power should be revered above all others in their kingdom. And when they were banished from their homes, they'd come in search of another. They had come for Solaris.

Her grandmother's eyes darkened at the mention of them. Adalina supposed she was recalling the memories of having to clean up Astarfall's mess as she said, "While I admit I'm not thrilled about this, I do not want to behave the way they did back then."

Adalina crossed her arms, then quickly uncrossed them, realizing she must look like a pouting child. With a curt shake of her head, she said, "We need to figure out a way to talk them out of it. With time, I could try to wake Elettra again on my own."

Her grandmother pursed her lips. "From the sound of it, they don't have time."

Gritting her teeth, Adalina tried to think of another way out of it but came up short. Instead, her voice broke as she admitted, "They'll take everything from me. A chance at love... and Elettra."

Her grandmother laughed. "Would you relax? We're not selling you off to them. I won't let anyone strong-arm you into anything you don't want to do. No matter how hard they try. This is nothing more than a courtesy." With a tense inhale, she added, "The council is right about one thing. We can't afford to risk trade with Astarfall. Their access to the ports is too valuable." An unreadable mask of emotion fell over her face as she leaned against the window. "Besides, Elettra has slumbered for far too long. There is no guarantee these rites would wake her. No man in his right mind would be willing to marry a stranger without these certainties."

Adalina's mother huffed and crossed her arms. The similarity between her and Calida was always strongest when they were in one of their moods. Now, they each wore mirrored scowls with their lips pressed tightly. Adalina stifled a scoff with the back of her hand.

Her mother lifted her chin in the air and said, "They wouldn't have even proposed it if they weren't desperate. I fear things are worse than the stories we've been hearing."

Adalina's chest tightened. Her mother had a point. Why ask for the rites if they weren't truly afraid? Still, it didn't have to fall to *her* to fix their problems. Worse, what would happen if the rites didn't work? She would be trapped in a marriage to a stranger. And an Astarfallen at that. One that she would be bound to in matrimony until death. The ceremony was unique in the sense that it connected their magic, but it was a wedding ceremony, nonetheless.

Soon, the city rose into view. Its sandstone towers shone under the sun and the sea sparkled in the distance. It was almost like a mirage—distant and out of reach. It was so stunning it was hard to believe it was real.

Despite her objections to the trip, she popped her head out the window to get a better look. She had been to Astarfall only once before when she was very young. Her grandfather had been invited back to his homeland for a wedding. Some cousin of a cousin or something of that sort.

Adalina hadn't been more than eight at the time, but she remembered the trip as if it were yesterday. More than that, she remembered the children she had been forced to play with. While the port city was a stunning sight to behold, the other children had been rude and haughty. They had shown off their magic, flicking it at geese to make them honk loudly or using it to grow a carnivorous plant from the ground that nipped at Adalina's toes.

The prince had been the worst of them all. He was an arrogant little fool who had insisted she call him *Callum the Courageous*. And when she refused, a vicious smile crossed his face.

"*I'm the Crown Prince, so you have to do exactly as I say,*" he had said before sticking his tongue out at her.

She'd had half a mind to pinch that tongue. Instead, she had argued, "*I'm Solarian. You're not my Prince.*"

To which he had responded by shoving her off the dock. *That* was who they expected her to marry. It was outrageous. She sat back now with a huff; her anger about her current predicament fueled by that memory.

The people of Astarfall had heaven granted magic. They were born with power. It was woven into nature itself, leaving the wielders intertwined with the world around them. It would be foolish to say it wasn't a remarkably beautiful sight to see.

But it also made the Astarfallen acutely aware of their advantages. Giving them an air of superiority around outsiders. They had not had to bargain and trade, or jump through hoops for their power, as her people had done with the dragons and their offerings. That made the Astarfallen pompous and sure of themselves. *Especially* the Prince. It made her sick to her stomach just thinking about coming face to face with him again after so long. He probably wouldn't even recognize her or remember what a bully he had been to her.

They entered the city through two towering columns crafted of the smoothest white marble. They rose high above Adalina's carriage in the shape of seagulls taking flight. Their wings were the size of a dragon's, and the similarity made her heart flutter.

That is until they pulled through the entrance and onto the crowded street. The carriage jolted to and fro, even though her grandfather slowed it significantly to avoid hitting anyone who might stray from the crowd.

Some people cheered and waved merrily. Sparks flew from their fingertips like little fireworks as they drew power from the sun. Others clapped and blew gusts of wind into people who were blocking their view. The attention and their eagerness only made an uncomfortable blush bloom across the bridge of Adalina's nose. She sank back into her seat and slumped low enough that no one could spot her in the window.

Her grandmother chuckled. "It seems word in Astarfall spreads as fast as I remember."

Her mother tapped Adalina on the leg gently and scolded, "Don't slouch."

Her grandmother tsked at her daughter. "Let the girl be. She doesn't owe them a show."

Adalina's mother folded her arms across her chest and turned toward the window nearest to her. Her grandmother, seemingly unphased by her daughter's pouting, patted Adalina on the knee. It brought no comfort, though, as the carriage came to a stop.

Councilman Heely's voice boomed as he greeted someone outside. "Uthred, a pleasure to see you again, old chap! How is that beautiful wife of yours? No little broods running around yet?"

Adalina rolled her eyes. *There he goes.* It wouldn't take long before he started trying to charm King Alistair's court. After all, making Solaris look good in the eyes of the mighty Astarfall was the only reason he'd accompanied them. That and to keep an eye on her. The council appeared to be under the impression that Adalina wasn't going to go into this willingly. She snorted to herself. And they'd be right about that.

The carriage door opened, and her grandfather was there to help them down. Her grandmother went first, followed by Adalina, and then her mother. The men stopped speaking and turned to bow at the women.

Adalina shifted uncomfortably under the studious gaze of a handsome man with hair as dark as the night sky. A man she could only assume was Uthred since Heely was standing shoulder to shoulder with him like they were old friends. The man clasped his hands together and said cheerfully, "Ah, this must be the lovely Lady Adalie."

"*Adalina,*" she corrected him boldly.

The man paused in a brief moment of stunned silence, then recovered as he said, "My apologies. I'm afraid we're all a bit out of sorts here since the attacks began, you understand?"

She made no indication that she did. Instead, she found a rather interesting spot on the nearby beach to look at, ignoring him completely. Heely laughed and said something about women tiring on lengthy journeys, to which Uthred said he absolutely understood.

Uthred ran a tanned hand through his hair and faced her family. "We are honored that you decided to consider our offer. As we all well know, the binding ceremony is an ancient rite. Pooling together magic from our two kingdoms to make it one is a great honor. To have a dragon..." His eyes grew hungry as he drifted off.

Meanwhile, the crowd was closing in, each onlooker trying to get a better view of the Solarian girl whose dowry came with a dragon.

A *sleeping* dragon, she wanted to emphasize to them. Would they all be staring at her with hope and fascination if they knew how many times she had tried to wake Elettra only to fail?

More likely, they already knew, but were too confident in the power of their royals to believe that the marriage ceremony would not work. She twisted her fingers into the heavy fabric of her skirts and wished she had worn clothing more appropriate for the southern heat. Sweat was already beading down her back, but she did her best to ignore it. She was Solarian and she would wear their garments proudly for as long as the humidity—and Councilman Heely—allowed.

Her grandmother raised an eyebrow. "We are still only *considering*. Ultimately, it will fall to *Adalina's* discretion."

Heely forced a nervous laugh, and his eyes darted between her grandmother and the welcoming advisor.

Uthred blushed. "Of course. But you, Calida, rider of dragons, know better than most that sacrifices must be made when darkness befalls a kingdom. If I recall, you once came to us with the same offer that we are coming to you with."

"Yes, I do know better than most. If I recall, your king at the time did not agree."

Uthred seemed unbothered by the point. "It is a new regime. Times have changed. I do hope that you will not allow a muddied past to affect the future. Our men are trained warriors. And with a dragon, Prince Callum should have no trouble crushing this nasty issue. For the good of both our countries."

Adalina clenched her fists and tried to hide them behind her skirts. Giving the prince, of all men, authority over her and her dragon made her feel as if she were being thrust under a wave in the sea. As per tradition, he would have the ability to invoke his rites to ride and command the dragon. To share the bond with Elettra. But it hadn't been done in centuries.

Yet, the way Uthred was talking, handing the gift over to the prince was exactly what they intended. She'd be lucky if she even got to sit on Elettra for a moment.

Heely chuckled uncomfortably. "Let's not discuss these matters here in the street. Surely, we would all be more open to listening to one another after we've changed from our travel clothes. Perhaps later over a spot of tea. Or better yet, brandy."

Uthred laughed boisterously. "But of course! Let us retire to the oceanic estate. King Alistair has set up lovely accommodations for you overlooking the sea. He thought you might appreciate some time to recuperate from the tiring journey and hopes you will join him tomorrow for a special luncheon to welcome you all here."

Adalina glared at Heely, who was swooning over the delights of being guests of the King and whispered to no one in particular, "Social climber."

The men were already lost in conversation and didn't hear her. But her grandmother raised her eyebrows. Adalina shrugged. Everyone knew Heely was an ambitious man and a suck up. It was how he'd gained enough favor in Solaris to rise at lightning speed in the council.

Uthred would be harder to figure out, though. At first glance, he seemed just as eager to charm, but there was an alertness in the way he looked at her and each of her family members. Like he, too, was sizing them up. Perhaps not everyone was so keen on a foreign princess.

Her grandmother looped an arm through hers and drew her away from the men who were chatting idly now. She patted Adalina's hand and said, "Don't let them see that they're getting to you, Lina. It is important that we show a united front."

"I'm hardly united with Heely," she scoffed.

"Even so, we are here to represent Solaris as a whole. We cannot afford to show weakness or discord amongst ourselves. Please trust me on this."

A few dock workers tipped their hats as the women passed by. Up ahead, Adalina caught sight of young men and women wandering in and out of storefronts on the cobblestone street. They were sun-kissed and appeared utterly happy. Strange, considering the stories of the attacks on their borders.

Her grandmother stopped and put both hands on Adalina's shoulders so that she had to face her. "I think all you need is some space to clear your head." She winked and nodded toward the bustling street. "Maybe see what Astarfall has to offer. It might surprise you."

"Doubtful," Adalina grumbled. "How am I supposed to relax when tomorrow I'll be faced with my shackles?"

Her grandmother laughed. It was like a wind chime—free and lovely. "My dear, you certainly are my granddaughter with all those dramatics. A husband is not the same thing as shackles."

"It is when it means the one thing that I have always dreamed of having—that is *rightfully* mine—will go to said husband. To a total stranger."

"Marrying your grandfather was the greatest adventure of my life."

"You didn't have to sacrifice Elettra in exchange, though. And you *chose* him. You cannot compare my situation to yours."

Her grandmother bit her lip thoughtfully. "No, I suppose I can't. But if they try to pressure you, then I will stand by your side. I am here to support you, whatever you decide to do. Except, now, I think you should go over there. No sense in sulking in the palace and getting into tiffs with your parents."

Adalina eyed the troves of people gathered around an inn with a large balcony overlooking the water. The sign on the door read, *Drinks, Music, and Board.* Then she peeked over her grandmother's shoulder to see Heely signaling for their attention. Her grandmother ignored him, then whipped back to Adalina.

"This is the part where you run." She winked.

The eagerness on Heely's face was enough to convince Adalina.

"Don't wait up," she said as she kissed her grandmother on the cheek.

Then, before she could lose her nerve, she spun on her heel and took off down the street. Someone shouted something behind her, but no one followed. She smiled to herself as she sidestepped a woman wearing what almost looked like a sheet wrapped around her body.

True, Adalina would rather be home where the rolling emerald green hills stretched as far as the eye could see. But if she was going to be dragged away from everything she'd ever known and trotted before a foreign kingdom like a prized pony, she could at least have a little fun first.

She grinned ruefully. Only fate and time would tell if she ended up engaged to Callum the *Chump* tomorrow. Tonight, she would revel in whatever freedom she could take for herself. And although she'd be discreet, she was going to make sure it was scandalous enough that Heely would keel twice over if he ever found out.

Five

The Dew Drop was nothing like the inns back home. Adalina found herself in a spacious lobby, brightly lit by the sunlight drifting in through massive open windows. Beyond the innkeeper's desk, she had a generous view of the glittering sea. The inns and taverns in Solaris felt like cozy little caves, whereas this one was more invigorating.

"Hello traveler," piped an enthusiastic man around her age with blond hair so light that it was almost translucent.

He, like most in the city, had an ethereal beauty about him. Much like the Fair Folk in story books. It was startling and suddenly—surrounded by so many Astarfallen—Adalina felt rather dull and drab in comparison. The only solace found was that there were no other Solarians in the inn to keep watch on her. She was free to do as she pleased for the time being.

"Hello," she said uncertainly.

"Here for a room or a drink?" he asked, flipping through a stack of parchments.

"A drink," she stated decidedly. There would be no need for a room since King Alistair had oh so graciously accommodated her and her family. As if a waterfront view in his grand palace would help to convince her that she should tie herself to his odious son.

Her thoughts continuously drifted back to the prince. It was possible he had changed since they met as children. It *had* been a long time. Maybe she should give him the benefit of the doubt...

The man smiled broadly and gestured behind him. "We have seating inside, or you may enjoy the deck. My name is Alfie. If you need anything, please don't hesitate to ask."

"Thank you." Adalina slipped away as an older couple stepped up to the desk to check into a room. Alfie paid no mind to her as she strolled onto the deck.

The view certainly was breathtaking, giving a clear line of sight to the water and beaches below. Off to the side, ships sailed lazily into the harbor. The shouts of dockworkers and sailors ending their busy day echoed on the soft breeze.

Adalina chose a small table for two near the edge of the balcony and sat back with a heavy sigh. The salty air clung to her skin and once again she was reminded that she was poorly dressed for the weather. Solarian fabric was heavier, guarding against the coming cold and snow. But in Astarfall, they enjoyed mild, warmer temperatures even at the height of winter.

Adalina glanced around at the scantily clad women. They glowed in the warmth on the deck and seemed to be cooling themselves with sparkling, bubbly drinks. Men trickled in now, dressed in clothing practical for a day's work.

At the table nearest to her, she overheard someone mentioning Solaris.

The woman's voice was high with intrigue. "The Solarians have arrived. Did you get a look at her?"

Her companion, a woman with round, rosy cheeks, leaned in as if to whisper. But her voice carried loudly as she said, "I couldn't get a good look through the carriage. But I hear she's beautiful with hair that looks like flames."

A blush crept across Adalina's face. She had half a mind to thank the girl, but held her tongue, hoping to catch some gossip.

"I hear she's been working as a seamstress in her mother's shop."

Word certainly did travel fast in Astarfall. Surprising considering the massive size of the city.

The other girl chimed in, "Imagine having to rely on another in order to get your power to work."

Adalina winced. Should she really have been surprised at the woman's snide tone, though? Adalina felt as if she were eight years old all over again and back on that dock with the Princeling and his friends.

The woman continued, "I wonder if she'll be able to handle his royal highness. Can you imagine him with a Solarian?"

The women fell into a fit of giggles that grated on Adalina's nerves. As they placed their coin on the table and left the deck, Adalina leaned back with a huff. Could she handle the prince? The real question was, could he handle *her*? Even if she agreed to the match, she wasn't willing to be an obedient little wife. Just because the ceremony would give him control over the dragon didn't mean he would have control over Adalina.

A breathtaking woman—one of the inn's waitresses—with eyes the color of the deep sea, deep brown skin, and tight golden-brown curls cascading down to her waist glided over to the table. Adalina had to do a double take to make sure her feet were, in fact, touching the ground. She'd never seen someone move so gracefully that they appeared to be floating.

"Can I get you anything?" The waitress gave her a warm smile. "Sun tea? Or perhaps a summer ale? We have quite a few options. My favorite is the dragon fruit."

Fruity ale? Adalina fought against raising her brows in skepticism in fear of offending the woman. "That sounds good," she said. Besides, *dragon* fruit seemed fitting for the occasion. A dragon was, after all, the only reason she'd agreed to the extravagant trip.

The waitress glided away in that same strange movement—or lack thereof—and Adalina squinted in her direction, trying to figure out how someone could move with such grace.

She hummed to herself but was interrupted by the gravelly voice of a young man that said, "She's a wind-wielder."

Adalina jumped slightly and turned to find a man not much older than her with a disarming grin splayed across his face. He brushed a light golden-brown hand through his hair, which was a darker brown than most others from Astarfall. But as he plopped into the seat across from her, the sun highlighted golden threads in the strands.

As if explaining magic to a child, he added, "She can manipulate the wind. It helps give her that sort of floating appearance."

Adalina narrowed her eyes at his impetuousness. She hadn't invited him to join her, yet here he was, propping his feet up on the deck railing with his hands behind his head as he relaxed back in his seat.

He mused, "I didn't realize Solarians enjoyed lazing about in the heat."

The laughter in his voice made her chest buzz with irritation.

"How do you know I'm Solarian?" she countered.

As soon as the question slipped from her lips, his dark blue, roving eyes made her regret it. He sat up, gaze flitting from her chest to her waist, which was visible over the table. There was a grimace on his face, as if her clothing offended him.

She shifted and tugged at the bodice. "Right." Was all she could think of saying.

"I assumed you came in with the wedding party. A few carriages arrived yesterday, and I passed more on my way here."

Adalina gulped. She knew a few prominent families from the village who could afford to leave their work for a small holiday were coming to Astarfall; as well as a few other council members. The curiosity was too much to resist. Many of them were likely coming to see if she would indeed be auctioned off like prized livestock.

"I wouldn't call it a wedding party," she corrected. She hadn't agreed to anything yet. Even if she had no choice but to say yes in the end, she was going to draw it out as long as she could. She would hold on to any semblance of free will she still had left.

"Oh really? Is the girl not here to be betrothed to the Crown Prince?"

Adalina's heart leapt into her throat at the mere mention of him. She was at the inn to forget about him and the entire ordeal. This was intended to be a night to forget her troubles. She was tempted to say, *No. Absolutely not. Over my dead body.* Instead, she took a steadying breath, refusing to let this stranger see her sweat any more than the sun was already causing her to.

"Nothing has been decided. Unless there is something I have missed?" she said casually.

Had King Alistair announced an *engagement* to the entire city? It would be rather presumptuous of him and only furthered Adalina's preconception of Astarfall and the royals who ruled it. Was her *choice* in the matter nothing more than an illusion meant to placate her until she caved under the pressure and gave them the answer they wanted?

The man shrugged. "I suppose he expects your people will see sense and do the right thing."

The last bit of his sentence came out rather sarcastically, and she wondered if maybe he, too, thought the whole thing was ridiculous. For some reason, that was irksome. It was one thing for *her* to be annoyed. After all, she was the one who was being matched. But Prince Callum would be the one benefiting and gaining the most from their union. In turn, so would his people. If the ceremony worked, that is. What did this man have against Solaris?

She sized him up. He was dressed in typical Astarfall fashion—fitted linen pants and a shirt with fabric so thin his taut muscles showed through it. It resembled the style the dockworkers and sailors were wearing. Their clothing must have been made to last a day of labor. For a moment, she wondered how in the world their seamstresses were able to work with such enduring, yet delicate, fabric. Was it easy to mend? Or did they just toss the shirts away and buy themselves new ones like it was of no consequence? Astarfall was a successful kingdom, the people prospered from trade and lived comfortably.

The man interrupted her thoughts and asked, "So, do you know the lucky bride to be?"

She scoffed at the word *lucky*.

"Yes," she paused, studying the man.

He was ridiculously good looking with that same ethereal quality as Alfie, the inn keeper. And apparently, he had no inkling of who she was. Perhaps for tonight she *could* be just another guest passing through. Maybe this man's company was a blessing in disguise.

A man wearing a gardening apron walked by the table with a pipe in hand. Dirt caked his fingernails as proof of a hard day's work.

Adalina's new companion held out a hand to stop him and gestured to the pipe. "Need a light?"

The gardener placed the pipe in his mouth and leaned forward with a grateful smile. Her companion snapped his fingers casually over the bowl of the pipe, casting small sparks into it. Smoke rose, and the gardener tipped his head in thanks before walking away. Adalina stilled, not wanting to give an Astarfallen the satisfaction of seeing her in awe of his magic. But in awe, she was. He was a light-wielder... if she had to choose a favorite of Astarfallen powers, it would be that one. The ability to create fire by utilizing the sun, moon, and stars was the closest to dragon magic as an Astarfallen could get.

Her companion cracked his knuckles and said, "Tell me, is the bride to be as stiff and uptight as I hear most Solarians are?"

Laughter danced in his eyes. Was he trying to goad her? Perhaps she was to be his entertainment for the night, as he was hers. She relaxed back in her seat. She was there for a good time. Possibly her last. If he wanted to get a rise out of her, then two could play at that game.

With her nose stuck slightly in the air, she said, "Tell me, is the Crown Prince your typical arrogant, indulgent Astarfallen?"

This time, he laughed freely. "Well played."

The waitress returned carrying two drinks. She set the dragon fruit ale in front of Adalina, then handed the man an ale topped with a bright orange slice. He beamed up at the woman, but her eyes were darting between him and Adalina. When her gaze fell back on him, she chuckled and rolled her eyes.

"Enjoy your night, you two," she said as she sauntered away.

Adalina's cheeks burned at the implication. A few women glanced at them and whispered behind their hands to one another. It filled Adalina with a sudden sense of gratification that she had been the one to catch his attention. Despite his brashness, she was enjoying the way all the other women in the room were staring at him. It was as if she had caught the prized fish. What better way to pass the night than with an unfairly beautiful man who had an air of strength and confidence any woman would swoon over?

The man took a long swig of his drink and said, "I'm sorry, I didn't catch your name."

Adalina tensed. If word had spread through the city about her arrival, her name might have as well. Careful not to give herself away, she licked her lips and teased, "Where's the mystery and fun in exchanging names?"

His brows rose in surprise. But the smile that slowly spread across his face told her he was into this particular sort of game.

He raised his glass. "To mystery and intrigue. And to the soon to be happy couple. May their bed always be warm."

Adalina rolled her eyes as she raised her glass and drank deeply. It was surprisingly light and refreshing. Nothing like the ale they brewed back home which was dark, stout, and strong enough to warm you on even the coldest northern night.

The man, who was apparently there to stay, made idle chit chat about the state of the waters and what it meant for the sailors coming in and out of port. From the way he spoke in reverence about sailors and the sea, Adalina guessed he did in fact work on or near the docks, but she didn't care enough to ask.

Throughout the next few hours, ale kept appearing before them. The waitress was quick and attentive, floating in and out like a soft breeze on the ocean. It was something Adalina appreciated, because the more she drank, the more relaxed in the overconfident stranger's presence she became.

He grew more curious about Solaris, stating that he had never had the opportunity to visit the hilly countryside. Adalina was happy to indulge him, telling him about the beauty of her land. When she brought up the stories she'd read as a child and the mysteries held in their forests, he listened with attentive fascination.

Soon the sun was setting, giving her some relief from the sticky heat. She lounged back lazily and ran her fingers around the rim of her nearly empty glass. She felt the man's gaze on her. When she met his eye, there was a familiar hunger there. The sort that Harold used to get when they rendezvoused in his father's barn. If this stranger wanted her, then she would be quick to return the sentiment. A smile tugged at her lips.

He leaned forward, resting his elbows on the table. "Admit it. This place isn't so bad."

"I never said it was."

"Ah, but you were thinking it. I could tell by that scowl on your face when I sat down."

She leaned forward, meeting his steady gaze. "Did it ever occur to you that the scowl was directed at you and not this city? You *did* sit down uninvited."

The corner of his mouth tipped up and she found herself reveling in that dimpled smirk.

He chuckled, seemingly unphased. "So, you've told me about the beasts that used to haunt your lands. The customs in which your people celebrate and how you deal with the snowy winters. But it strikes me as odd that you haven't spoken at all about the dragons."

In truth, Adalina hadn't mentioned the dragons because she was afraid it might give away who she was and why she found herself sitting in an Astarfall tavern.

She shrugged. "The dragons are a deeply rooted part of our history. The same way that your magic is a part of you, so is the connection to our dragons. But whereas your magic has grown in strength throughout the centuries, ours has begun to burn out."

"Except for the girl here to marry the prince." The way he said it made it seem more like a statement than a question. Was their king really so sure that she was the answer to their problems? Had they not even considered that, even with Astarfall's magic, it might not be enough?

"Perhaps."

He tilted his head slightly and became very solemn. "I personally don't see the appeal."

Adalina furrowed her brow. How could anyone not want to experience the power and greatness of a dragon?

Then he caught her off guard by asking, "Do you wish that your family had a dragon? I've wondered lately if there is jealousy amongst your people that only one family still has one."

Adalina's mouth became as dry as the sand on the beach below. She could lie. But the man struck her as the observant sort, and she wasn't ready to give her true identity away.

She stalled by finishing off the rest of her ale. "Is there a restroom nearby?"

His face was unreadable as he leaned closer. When his leg brushed against hers, delightful shivers shot up her spine. With bated breath, she froze, allowing him to push his knee between her thighs. It was bold. And attractive. Her head spun. Then, as quickly as he was there, he drew back and pointed over his shoulder.

She leapt to her feet. "I'll be right back."

Ducking into the restroom, she took a moment to relieve herself and went to the basin. There was a copper pipe that ran fresh water into it. A waterfall erupted from it when she turned the nozzle and she smiled. What an interesting system. She washed her hands with soap that smelled of honeysuckle and then splashed water onto her flushed face.

The humidity had done a number on her untamed hair. And the ale had given her pale cheeks a pinkish glow. Or was it the man's advances? She had never been with a complete stranger before. And maybe she was reading his signals all wrong, but part of her longed to be wanted by him. If this was her last night of freedom, then didn't she owe it to herself to do something she had never done before?

Once she was finished, she slipped back into the hallway that led to the deck, but the man was already there waiting. He stepped up to her, closer than she would normally let a stranger get.

His voice was husky as he said, "I was thinking you'd like to see the beach? In the evening, it's easy to spot moonglass in the sand."

He was at least a head taller than her, and she had to crane her neck to look up at him. There was power and strength in the way he carried himself and for a brief moment, her heart leapt at the prospect of feeling his body pressed against hers.

She taunted, "How do you know I don't already have somewhere to be?"

"Because it's nearly nightfall and you haven't mentioned it." He took a step closer to her, and she welcomed it as butterflies fluttered wildly in her stomach.

What would Heely say if he could see her now? It would certainly horrify the council if she were to let this stranger kiss her. To encourage him to take her right there and then. If she did find herself engaged tomorrow, then this would make for a brilliant last rebellion.

This man was a stranger. Just someone who was looking for some fun with an out of towner. He'd probably done so a dozen or more times, judging by the exchanged look between him and the waitress.

He leaned in, and the heat of his body blanketed her. With one hand pressed firmly against the wall by her head, he brushed a stray strand of hair from her face with the other. He practically purred as he said, "It's just a walk... I'll understand if you do have somewhere else to be, or someone waiting for you—a lover, perhaps?"

Fire licked in her veins. *Not yet*, she wanted to say. She was tethered to no man. At least not tonight. Instead, she chose to answer with action. With a subtle shake of her head, she lifted her chin and parted her lips invitingly. Surprise flickered in the man's eyes, but he didn't hesitate as he pressed his mouth against hers. Adrenaline coursed through her entire body, making her braver as she twisted her fingers in his hair, drawing him closer.

This was a man who didn't control her. He was not part of the council who dictated the course of her life. Or the King who had gotten her there with a simple letter. The stranger had no hold over her. Had demanded nothing from her. She was tired of letting men tell her what to do. She'd had enough of that over the last few days. They could all go to the fiery depths.

The man pressed his body against hers, and her back met the wall. A weight seemed to lift off her shoulders as she channeled all her frustration into that kiss. His hands found her hips, drawing her into him hungrily. Heat spread between her thighs, and it was at that moment that she made her choice. After all, a little spiteful sex never hurt anyone.

Six

B reathlessly, Adalina pulled away from the embrace. Her voice was hoarse, betraying her lust as she said, "It's getting late."

"Perhaps we should call it a night." He raised an amused eyebrow. More formally, he straightened and said, "I could escort you to your room."

"My room?" Adalina asked shakily, still soaring a little from the kiss.

"Here at the inn? I'm sorry. I assumed you would be staying here."

Adalina suppressed a groan. Of course he did. She was supposed to be there as a wedding *guest*, not as the potential bride to be. Recovering quickly, she said, "I didn't have a chance to check in."

He gave her a curt nod and clasped his hand around hers, leading her back to the lobby. It was so informal of him that anyone passing by might guess they were two old friends or lovers. She glanced around nervously for anyone she might know from Solaris. But there was no one else there. No one was there to witness her going up to a room with this stranger other than the innkeeper. And something told her Alfie wasn't the type to spread gossip all over town. Not if he wanted patrons to continue visiting his inn without worrying their business would be shared with the entire city.

The man drew her to the front desk, which seemed to be left unattended. He then leaned comfortably against it and called out, "Alfie! This lovely young woman is in need of a room."

There was a bang under the desk and then Alfie popped up from underneath with disheveled hair. There was a smear of red lipstick on his face, and he adjusted his linen shirt hastily. "Ah, yes. A room."

Adalina tried to peer over the desk with the sneaking suspicion that he hadn't been down there alone.

The nameless man chuckled. "You have a little something there." He pointed to Alfie's lipstick-stained cheek.

A woman giggled from under the desk beside Alfie's legs.

Adalina's companion leaned over it and said, "Enjoying your night, Seraphine?"

"Yes," a familiar voice squeaked out. When the woman stood, Adalina recognized her as the waitress. Her lipstick was the same shade of red that was smeared on Alfie's face. She waved her thin manicured fingers and with a shimmer of magic, a gentle wind ruffled Alfie's hair back into order.

Adalina pressed her lips together to keep from grinning. It seemed she and her new friend weren't the only ones giving into temptation tonight. Alfie shuffled through his papers without the same air of decorum that she was met with when she first arrived at the inn. Then with an "ah ha" he pointed to a number and said, "Room five. It's all yours."

Adalina's new friend snagged the key from Seraphine and said, "Put it on my tab."

Adalina shook her head. She wasn't about to let him pay. "No, I can get my own room. Thank you."

"First night is on me."

The man, still holding her hand, began to pull her from the desk, but she froze for a moment.

He laughed awkwardly. "Consider it Astarfallen hospitality."

When he winked, her knees buckled. Fates be damned, he was handsome. And so... free. This was a man who knew what he wanted and didn't back down. Images of what would happen if they went into that room together flashed in her mind. What would it be like to feel him—all rippling muscle against her own softer body...

Her gaze dropped to the key in his hands. Heat bloomed across her cheeks, and she fought the urge to drag him out of the lobby so they could be alone. Her mother would give her an earful in the morning when she noticed her bed had not been slept in. Lucky for Adalina, she knew her grandmother would cover for her. After all, she was the one who told her to go out. And Adalina *had* warned her not to wait up. Besides, she was new to Astarfall and Councilman Heely would surely agree that a woman should not be wandering the streets alone at night. She suppressed a laugh. If only he knew the truth. She'd love to see the look on his face.

Satisfied, she squeezed her companion's hand and allowed him to tug her toward the hall leading to the inn's rooms. He paused at the door to room five and asked, "Did you have luggage?"

"It's with the carriage," she blurted. "I'll retrieve it later."

The ale was still making her body buzz in that way that made her feel invincible, and she didn't want to waste time talking about mundane things. Not to mention, her belongings were already unloaded in the palace. Not that she could say that without giving herself away.

The man pushed the door open to reveal a gorgeous room with baby blue painted walls and fine golden details traced in the pattern of waves. The bed had a canopy which flowed in the soft breeze that was drifting through the open balcony. Beyond that, stars were beginning to twinkle in the darkening sky, shining down and reflecting off the water.

Now *this* she could get used to. As much as she loved the lush green lands of Solaris, she couldn't deny that Astarfall lived up to its name. It was as if the very stars were reaching down to bless their waters.

Her friend lingered in the doorway. "I suppose I should thank you for allowing me the pleasure of your company tonight."

"You're not coming in?" Adalina frowned. Had she been reading his signals all wrong? Mocking his tone from earlier, she said, "What? Do you have someone waiting for you? A lover perhaps."

He drew in a heavy breath as if trying to muster any bit of self-control he could. It made his firm chest puff out which in turn only depleted the little self-control *she* still had. She desperately wanted to see that chest unhindered by his shirt. But she could see a war brewing in his eyes. Did he think she was indecent for suggesting that he stay? He didn't seem to find her advances offensive only moments ago.

Finally, with a dimple showing in his cheek, he said, "I wouldn't want to impose."

"You wouldn't be. No more than you were when you invited yourself to drink with me this evening," she joked. More seriously, she added, "No strings attached. I just want to enjoy the night." She swept an arm toward the magnificent view and breathed in the salty air.

He placed two fingers under her chin, drawing her attention back to him. His dark blue eyes bore into hers. She could have drowned in those eyes; she was certain of it. Like a sailor sinking into the mysterious depths of the sea.

"You're absolutely certain?" he asked with more sincerity than she'd seen from him thus far.

"I am," she said with the same seriousness.

Without further hesitation, he stepped inside the room. The door clicked shut behind him and she sucked in a sharp breath when the man tugged at the collar of his shirt. He flashed her a dazzling smile and heat crept down her neck. Only mischief danced along his face now, and there was no doubt he knew the effect he was having on her.

Hoping it wouldn't ruin the moment—but needing to settle her nerves before continuing—she said, "The waitress and the inn keeper..." She needed to choose her words carefully. There must be a way to ask without drawing suspicion. "They won't say anything about this?"

"Not a word. Alfie is my closest friend. We grew up together. They're both discrete I assure you."

It was all she needed to hear. Part of her wondered if the answer had even mattered. She had already made up her mind. And so what if the prince and his father found out about her little escapade? They didn't own her. Not yet.

The rebellion of it all sent giddy jitters down her arms and legs. She tugged at the laces on the front of her bodice. He waited patiently, not moving from his place until she gave him the cue. With a summoning motion of her finger, his grin widened.

She noticed his arched eyebrow when he stepped closer. Like he was surprised that she was actually following through. If he was, though, he didn't mention it out loud. Instead, he tugged her top down until her dress fell into a crumpled heap on the floor. Beneath it she wore a light blue slip that nearly matched the walls. It was as if fate had known she would find herself there with the man tonight.

He released a pleased groan as his eyes snaked over her greedily. Still, he did not go any further. Not until she pulled the slip off. She stood fully naked with only him and the blanket of stars blinking through the window as witness.

This was quite possibly one of the wildest things she had ever done. It made her feel powerful and in control, and she loved it. Tomorrow they would part just the same as they met. As total strangers. No ties to one another. Nothing owed between the two of them. If only the same could be said for the rest of the men in her life. For the prince who was expecting both her hand and her dragon.

Her fingers lingered over the man's shirt. The hesitation must have made it seem like she was second guessing herself, because he teased, "Nervous?"

With a flare of her nostrils, she replied, "Just taking my time. What's the rush?"

"Just making sure you haven't changed your mind."

"Now, why would I do that?" Adalina wrapped her fingers around the fabric of his shirt.

He growled hungrily in response, summoning the feral side of her. She gripped the shirt and tore it. Buttons clinked onto the floor, but the man didn't flinch. Instead, he groaned and drew her into him roughly. His skin was golden and sun-kissed, a stark contrast to her own. Her fingers itched to run along each outline of muscle, to see if it was as smooth as the marble at the gates of his city.

As if sensing her wishes, the man grabbed both of her hands and placed them on his chest. She trembled slightly when he let go. But not because she was afraid or nervous. No, it was because she was trying to grapple with the carnal instincts that were clouding her mind. She wanted this man to take her. To make her forget all about the council and the prince and their plans for her. To forget about the heartache of not being enough to wake the dragon on her own.

Tonight, she was not herself. No longer Adalina of Solaris, grand-daughter of the great dragon warrior. Instead, she was merely another woman passing through the city of starlight. There to watch *another's* fate be decided. She was a girl, tipsy on sweet ale, who had found enjoyment in a stranger's company.

The man bit his lip, and it nearly made her lose her mind, imagining what else that mouth could do. Then he spoke. "Who knew Solarian women were so…"

Placing a finger over his lips with a soft smile, she said, "It might be better if we don't talk during this part." The last thing she wanted to think about was what a good Solarian woman should be doing or what doubts were stirring in his mind. She especially didn't want to dwell on what *she* should be doing—or rather, not doing.

Magic shimmered from his hands, casting a soft glow around them like candlelight. She trailed her fingers down his chest, stopping at his waist. He placed a hand on the back of her head and drew her in gently for a kiss. She leaned in harder, nipping lightly at his lip. He groaned deeply in response and wove his fingers through her tangled mass of hair.

Lost in the kiss and desperate for more, they stepped clumsily toward the bed. She laid back on the pillows, which were as soft as she imagined clouds would be. He leaned over her but didn't go further. Instead, they took their time, desire building as they continued to kiss.

This was far from Adalina's first time with someone. But never in a million years did she imagine finding herself in the thralls of a man from Astarfall. One whose name she hadn't even bothered to ask.

But it didn't matter. Because this was her decision. Something she was taking for herself. And when the man's lips grazed her ear, sending delightful chills down her spine, she knew that in the morning, she would regret nothing.

She tilted her head back to give him better access to her neck. Each kiss he trailed down her skin made her heart race faster. A small wanting sound escaped her, which seemed to tell him he was doing something right. He nipped at her breast, and she gripped the feather-down blanket beneath her. When his mouth met her hips, she arched her back, reveling in the excitement of what was to come.

To her dismay, he paused and looked up at her before venturing any farther. The pupils in his eyes were dilated, making them appear fierce in the moonlit night. Adalina wished they had lit the fire before starting as the crisp air wafted through the balcony doors. She shivered, but she wasn't sure if it was from the cool breeze or from the promise of the pleasure she was about to experience.

His voice was heavy with desire as he asked, "Are you sure this is what you want?"

Was he out of his mind? Of course, this was what she wanted. Why else would she have let things go this far? Unable to wait any longer, she slipped from under him and pushed him onto his back. He seemed more than happy to oblige. Shock flickered across his face, but a smile crept across it as she straddled him.

Warmly, she answered, "This is exactly what *I* want." She didn't want to think about her failure as a dragon rider descendent, or about the men in the palace waiting for her answer. All she wanted was to lose herself to this stranger. To be free for at least one more night.

"How about you? Are you certain this is what *you* want?"

"Surer than a sailor with his trusty compass." He gripped her thighs firmly.

When she lowered herself onto him, he let out an animalistic growl. It both delighted and terrified her. He was a stranger to her, yet their bodies were a perfect fit. And he was following her lead. Judging by the way his fingers clung to her thighs, he delighted in it.

The buzz from the ale was wearing off, giving her clarity. But she didn't stop. If anything, having a clear mind only deepened her desire. It fueled her like a fire being fanned. He kissed her deeply, and she moaned at the taste of him. It didn't take long for them to find a steady rhythm against one another. Tingles raced through Adalina, and she reared her head back as her ecstasy built. It was like reaching the top of a mountain only to plunge off into the open air. Her voice echoed into the night as she cried out to the darkness.

The man flipped her onto her back without pulling out of her and smoothed her wild hair from her face. The spark in his eyes told her she was in for a long night. And in all honesty, she wished it would never end.

Adalina's legs were tangled in the sheets as her new friend—if she could call him that, as she still had not bothered to ask him his name—traced his fingers along her lower back. Perhaps it was better that they hadn't exchanged those pleasantries and had instead skipped to the fun. If he had known who she was, he certainly wouldn't have engaged in her little rebellion.

She only hoped that he would have the good sense not to tell anyone that he had bedded the prince's possible betrothed when he *did* find out who she was. It was unlikely that the heir to the Astarfallen throne would take a slight like that very well. If he was anything like Adalina remembered, that is.

Part of her wanted to ask the man what he thought of Prince Callum. Although citizens weren't typically well acquainted with their royalty on a personal level, there was a certain understanding amongst the masses. Especially in a place like Astarfall, where gossip seemed to spread like wildfire. Did the people here adore their prince, or did they find him as insufferable as she did? In his defense, it had been a long time since they had seen each other. Over a decade to be more accurate.

Besides, for the time being, she was content to laze about on the comfortable bed, watching the sun peek over the horizon with this stranger. A stranger who had spent the night pleasuring her in ways she hadn't even begun to imagine.

It had been nothing like sex with Harold back in Solaris. This man moved with expertise and ease. And he welcomed the moments when taking charge suited her fancy. Even if he *did* enjoy getting under her skin, that hadn't mattered much throughout the night. There hadn't been much room for conversation.

He leaned close to her and pointed beyond the balcony. "See that?"

Adalina rolled onto her stomach and shoved her massive bedhead out of her face. "See what?"

There was a wistfulness in his voice as he said, "The ships rolling out. When I was young, it always amazed me when I'd watch them go over the horizon like that. Like they might fall from the world."

Adalina smiled at the child-like wonder he was describing. She, too, had experienced it when she watched the birds fly toward the clouds—wondering if flying beyond them would take her to the heavens. Instantly, her mind went to Elettra and the reality of the morning set in.

Maybe it was the hangover she had, or maybe it was that he had shared something deep and personal with her and she felt the need to return the gesture.

"Last night, you asked me if I wished I had a dragon. The truth is, I've dreamed of it all my life. Just once I would love to feel the wind in my face and to see the world far below me."

"For our prince's sake, I hope his bride is just as passionate about it as you are."

Adalina teased, "I'm Solarian. He's not *my* prince."

He stared so intently at her that she felt a fiery blush creep across her face. Something like curiosity flickered in his eyes. Adalina resisted the impulse to wiggle under the sudden attention. Perhaps what she said was offensive. She would need to speak and act with more tact when she reached the palace.

"Have you ever—" he started, but trumpets bellowed outside. He sat up abruptly.

"What is that?"

"The palace bells," he said as he leapt out of bed and started getting dressed.

Adalina's heart sank. She didn't know what the sound meant. What if her family was panicked about her absence? It would be mortifying to have palace guards out searching for her on her first official day in the seaside city.

"I should be going." She jumped from the bed and tugged her dress on.

"Oh." There was a slight crease in his brow. Once again, there was something searching in the way he watched her. As quick as it came, it was gone. He promptly pulled his shoes on, but his shirt had met an unfortunate end when she'd ripped it off of him. It didn't seem to bother him, however, as he nodded. "Yes, of course. I should as well. Work to be done and what not."

They got to the door at the same time, and both reached for the handle. Adalina blushed and stepped back with a strangled laugh. She let him open the door for her and slipped out in front of him. They walked down the hall together in silence. She had never had such a blatant one-night stand before and wasn't quite sure how to send him off. When they reached the lobby, she tried to think of something charming or witty to say.

Instead, she faltered and shot a hand out between them. "That was, uh, very pleasant."

The man gave a deep, gravelly laugh and shook her hand firmly. "*Very.*"

Alfie waved excitedly at her companion. He had all his buttons this morning and was looking remarkably put together, unlike the last time she'd seen him. After offering her a warm smile, his eyes widened, and he gestured to the man to join him.

"Looks like I'm in high demand this morning." He winked. "This was—"

Adalina didn't wait for him to finish that sentence, too afraid he might ask if there could be a repeat of their night together. Or worse, if he could spend some actual time with her. She dipped out the door of the inn and onto the bustling street.

The people she passed offered cheerful, carefree smiles. This was not the appearance of a kingdom in great peril. Her companion and his friends had made no mention of the dangers posed to them or their neighbors. Instead, they kissed pretty waitresses, flirted with out of towners, and spoke of the ships leaving port as if it was the most wonderful thing they'd ever seen.

Why did they need Elettra so badly? And why should Adalina bow to their will when she could see no sign of a threat? She wasn't callous enough to wish ill on people, even ones she didn't know. But perhaps it had been a bit selfish and childish to indulge in sex with a man who was under the rule of the prince who was asking for her hand in marriage...

In the morning light, she wasn't so sure she'd made the right decision to sleep with the stranger. If anyone found out, it would embarrass the council and mortify her father. But it had been her choice to make. Just as she hoped, any impending offer of marriage was hers to accept or deny. All she could do was pray to the fates that this little escapade wouldn't come back to bite her in the ass before she had a chance to try to turn King Alistair's offer down. With a clear head, a determined heart, and a rumbling stomach, she marched toward the palace.

Seven

The pit in Adalina's stomach grew with each step she took through the city. She desperately wished she had eaten dinner the night before. The ale had done a fine job filling her belly, but she was paying for it now. By the time she reached the palace, breakfast had come and gone. Her mother scolded her, saying that if she hadn't stayed out all night, then she would have had the chance to indulge in the enormous buttery croissants and fresh melon that had been brought to them.

Little did her mother know, she'd been busy indulging in a handsome stranger instead. Adalina smiled to herself as she poured a lukewarm cup of coffee. Her grandmother sat on the terrace and watched her with knowing eyes.

"Let the girl be. Today will not be easy for her. There's no reason she didn't deserve to go out and enjoy the city."

Yes, the city... Memories of the man gripping her waist lingered like a phantom touch. She joined her grandmother and was grateful that there was an awning overhead to offer shade from the beating sun. A fleet of ships caught her eye. Men bustled about on the docks carrying large wooden crates, and she wondered if her new friend was somewhere amongst them, already hard at work for the day. And whether he was replaying their night together in his head, too.

Her father joined them next. His spirits were higher than she expected. With a pleasant look on his face, he inquired, "Did you enjoy your time in town?"

"Very much so." Adalina sipped at her coffee to hide the smirk on her face. Any joy began to fade as her family flitted around the room, preparing themselves for their presentation to King Alistair.

With a more serious tone, she asked, "What am I to expect when we get down there?"

"You'll be presented to King Alistair and Queen Gwendolyn," her mother said matter-of-factly as she attempted to press wrinkles out of her father's shirt using heat from a teapot.

"Yes, but what then? From the sound of it, the King makes it seem as if I have already said yes to the proposal to his son. What happens if I tell him no?"

Silence settled over them. Her grandmother tapped a finger on the arm of her chair. "I assume by the sour look on your face that you are still against the idea of marrying the prince?"

"*Callum*," Adalina grumbled bitterly. The reality of her situation was creeping back in, replacing the good mood she'd found in the Dew Drop Inn.

She tried to recall more about her encounter with Callum, but like most childhood memories, it was hard to grasp on to the hazy details. The prince had made quite an impact with his snotty attitude and beyond that she didn't remember much about him. She never expected she would be in a position where she would need to. Aside from flinging her into the water and showing off in front of the other kids with his mocking of her, she only remembered him being kind to his baby sister. A tiny little thing with a button nose and rosy cheeks.

"Some women would swoon over an eligible prince in line for the throne," her grandfather said slowly. "Perhaps it won't be as bad as you've built up in your head."

Adalina's grandmother added, "It might not be ideal, but it's the hand that's been dealt. I'll bet they thought you'd consider it a great honor that their prince is offering his hand to you in marriage."

Adalina wrinkled her nose. "It's so *transactional.* Like he's the coin and I'm the goods they wish to purchase. Actually, not even *me*. It is Elettra's power they want to have close to the throne."

Before anyone could respond, Adalina sniped, "No matter, I'm sure once the prince remembers who I am, he'll want nothing to do with me and we can all go home."

A knock at the door had everyone turning their heads. When her grandfather opened it, Uthred and Heely strolled in, side by side. They didn't even wait for an invitation. Adalina slumped into her seat and groaned as their cheery voices filled the room.

Heely said, "Now, I want everything to go as smooth as possible today."

Uthred agreed, "Yes, that is why we have had new clothing befitting the southern court commissioned for each of you. So that you will be more comfortable."

More comfortable, or more agreeable? Adalina didn't need anyone to dress her. Though it was a nice gesture, there was still something in the way he looked at her that made her fidget. Like he was trying to decide if what was beneath the clothes was worthy enough for his prince.

Her family remained silent. They were likely stewing on the fact that she still wanted to find a way out of this arrangement. Tension wove around each of them.

Heely stopped abruptly, his gaze falling on the dour faces in the room. His brow furrowed in concern. "Is something wrong?"

With great tact, Adalina's mother said, "My daughter is simply wondering how much of a say she really has here. When we agreed to come, she was assured that she would have the upper hand in this decision. But I believe her nerves are growing the closer we get to meeting with His Majesty. We would not wish to offend him, of course."

Shadows seemed to cast themselves into Heely's eyes as he said carefully, "No one is holding a sword to your back, but you need to consider the risks. Saying no might not only affect our relationship with this bountiful kingdom but might also result in the raiders coming north into our lands."

Adalina tilted her chin slightly as she said, "Are you saying that I, in fact, do not have a choice?"

Heely side eyed Uthred, who was listening with brows raised in amusement. Then swiftly, the Solarian Councilman said, "Our people have come all this way to see you do the right thing."

The right thing for others. Not for herself, he meant. Heat crept up her neck. They'd brought her there under the pretense that she could turn the prince's offer down. But in reality, they never dreamed she would actually say no.

"Now. If that's settled," Heely drawled with a note of condescension, "We are going to escort you all to brunch. Stick with Uthred or I and we will talk you through everything, make introductions, and—"

Adalina's grandfather's face had flushed a deep red during Heely's little *pep talk*. He held a silencing hand up and interjected, "I grew up in this court, or has everyone forgotten? My family will manage just fine on their own."

Heely's doubtful eyes slid to Adalina. Apparently, he was skeptical. And with good reason. First, she ran off the night before and now she had made it clear that she wasn't going to be as malleable as they'd hoped. He really should have known better after knowing her all these years. She feigned a dazzling smile. The same one she would use on the king as she tried to talk her way out of the arrangement.

Her grandmother shooed the men from the room and tossed the boxes to Adalina and her mother. "Get dressed, you two. Despite how we may be feeling about these circumstances, it is best not to keep royalty waiting."

Fates forbid, Adalina thought sarcastically. But despite her stubbornness, she gasped when she saw what was inside the box. A stunning sea green gown made of the silkiest fabric she ever felt flowed down into a skirt. It was similar to tulle, but it was far lighter than the fabrics they used in her mother's dress shop. It was almost like the sea foam found when the tide came in.

Her mother sighed dreamily as she held up her own gown. "By the heavens." She hugged the dress to her face. "I would love to visit the seamstresses while we're here."

Adalina's mouth widened into a smile. "We could go now. No time like the present."

The more she thought about standing in front of Astarfall's nobility and denying the king's request to his face, the less confident she felt. She didn't know the man, which meant having no idea how he might react to such a blatant refusal. Would he punish her family? Or Solaris? Her people *did* rely on Astarfall for their trade ports... And what if the raiders did move north? It wouldn't be the first time trouble in the south set its sights on Solaris instead.

"Nice try." Her mother tried to scowl at her, but Adalina caught the faint smile beneath.

The women dressed hastily. The sleeves on Adalina's dress were nearly translucent and met at the top in a thin strap that tied together. Her grandmother helped her adjust them and whispered into her ear, "I am sorry you are in this position."

Adalina considered the people down below on the streets, going about their day as if they didn't have a care in the world. "Do you believe the threat is so great that this is really necessary?"

"I suppose that is what I hope to find out today," her grandmother mused.

"I've seen the way everyone is carrying on out there. I do not see any sign of despair or fear."

Her grandmother finished with the ties and turned Adalina to face her. "Astarfall is a proud kingdom. They are blessed to hold the magic that they do and for many years they have lived comfortably knowing that none other compares to their power. They may not show it, but if King Alistair has called us here, then things are worse than they appear. Fear sometimes hides far beneath the surface."

If her grandmother thought there was the slightest chance of real danger, then maybe Adalina had misjudged. Her grandmother was considerably more experienced than she was. Perhaps she was looking past any signs of terror amongst the people. Seeing only what she wanted to. What if she was merely grasping for a reason to say no? If she denied the proposal, it meant going back to trying to wake Elettra on her own each month with the possibility of it never working. Even if marriage, in this case, was a gamble, so was choosing not to go through with it.

It felt like her mouth was full of cotton. She tried to swallow and fought the urge to choke. Suddenly, her palms were sweaty. Silently, she followed her mother and grandmother out of their rooms and into the wide hallway.

It was bright with a long skylight above. Adalina couldn't pull her gaze away from the clear blue sky as they made their way to the brunch the royal family had planned for them. It was hard not to feel like a caged dragon with the skylight's glass standing between her and the open air. Nerves turned into a fiery heat in her chest as they made their way downstairs and stepped through a set of wide doors.

All eyes fell on them as they entered. Most courtiers smiled pleasantly, but it was challenging not to notice the few furrowed brows and down turned mouths. Was it because they did not think this entire situation was necessary? Or was it because she wasn't one of them? Maybe they viewed her as nothing but a naïve country girl from the provincial kingdom in the north.

It had been a long time since a Solarian and Astarfallen performed the binding rites. And she wouldn't blame the courtiers for not wanting their crown prince to marry an outsider. Perhaps they had intended to place their own daughters before him. If Adalina agreed to the marriage, she might very well be shattering their dreams. Just as she might be shattering her own.

Uthred motioned for them to join him. There was a small group beside him; two women and a tall man with dark golden streaked hair. Her grandparents bowed, and Adalina's heart gave a jolt with the realization that this was King Alistair.

She and her parents followed suit as Uthred said, "May I present to you, Lady Adalina of Solaris? Granddaughter of the Dragon Warrior, Calida."

King Alistair's eyes shone gold in the sunlight. "It is an honor to have you in our home."

Adalina knew she should return the gesture of kind words, but nothing came to her. It was as if her voice had been swept away entirely.

Her grandmother spoke instead. "The honor is ours."

The grin he gave her grandmother made him appear boyish. "Warrior Calida. I feared I might never again stand in your grand presence. And you, Sir Bellamy. It warms my heart to see you both looking so well."

Adalina regarded her grandfather's response carefully. It was a curious thing to see him in the coastal court when she had only ever seen him at ease in Solaris. It was easy to forget that this was once his home.

Bellamy looked the king up and down appraisingly and his words were laced with the tiniest hint of disapproval as he said, "You're the spitting image of your old man."

King Alistair chuckled goodheartedly. "It's been too long since you've visited."

"Last we saw you, your son was but a pup at your side. I hear he's quite the wielder."

"That he is." King Alistair's face glowed with pride.

"It seems you have done right by your father's legacy, and your kingdom."

King Alistair's mood turned grave, and it was as if dark clouds had passed over his face. "I have tried my best, but I'm afraid there are some things even my father could not prepare me for."

"How bad?" Calida asked cooly.

"Bad," he answered, seemingly unbothered by her forwardness. "The attacks have moved beyond the western border and into the outlying villages. They're inching closer to the heart of our kingdom—to the city itself. I sent a small force to assess the danger and three did not return. They have been named dead. Though the bodies have not been recovered."

Adalina's hands began to tremble. This was far from what she hoped to hear. A few courtiers were watching them with open curiosity, so she tried to calm her hands by clasping them tightly.

As if also noticing the attention, the dark-haired woman beside King Alistair put her hand lovingly on his arm and spoke. "I do not know that this is the place to discuss these matters. This brunch is so that our families can get reacquainted. There will be time for this after."

King Alistair pinched the bridge of his nose. "You're right, my love. Let us share a meal first. Afterward we can retire to my study so that I may show you the first-hand accounts."

The queen placed a gentle hand on Adalina's back and led her away from the rest of the group. She was soft-spoken and had incredibly kind eyes. She was exactly as Adalina would have pictured the queen of a magic-gifted kingdom. She, like the waitress from the Dew Drop, seemed to glide through the room at Adalina's side.

"I imagine this is all terribly overwhelming for you. But I do hope that you will keep an open mind in the coming days." The tone she used calmed Adalina down to her bones, washing away any sort of anxiety she'd had moments ago.

"Days?"

"I understand the pressure you and your family must be under. With your man, Heely, in your ear, I am sure it is all deeply overwhelming. I would not expect you to make such a big decision without first knowing what is on the line. Without getting to know the people of this land."

Giving her time to make her choice was a generous offer. But it was one Adalina suspected was meant to persuade her into giving them the answer they wanted. As of now, she was far removed from the kingdom of Astarfall. A stranger in their streets. Although she wasn't a callous person—willing to let innocent people suffer—her priority was her own home. Her own freedom.

More than that, it would be easy to say no after witnessing how at ease the people in the city were. But after hearing the king's brief account, she was already more uncertain than she had been earlier that morning. The effort he was putting toward keeping his people at ease made it seem like the danger must be incredibly great. Otherwise, why bother? Why not just be open with them and explain it was a few rogue raiders?

They walked over to a buffet lined with food of every variety. Thinly sliced salmon, dishes of herb crusted roast, an array of cheese, and so much more were arranged for easy picking. The queen handed Adalina a silver plate, but before they could access the food, a familiar face turned toward them.

It was the waitress from the Dew Drop Inn. She still had that same air of grace about her, only now she was dressed to match it. Like nobility. Adalina never would have guessed that she'd been serving drinks in a tavern the night before.

Seraphine's jaw dropped and her eyes widened into large, round saucers. "Oh!" she gasped, dropping the full plate she was holding.

The queen flicked her fingers toward it and a wind picked up out of nowhere, setting it back into Seraphine's hands. The girl squeaked, "Aunt Gwendolyn, hi."

"Hello, dear." Then, warily, Queen Gwendolyn asked, "Have you seen my son? I was hoping to introduce him to Lady Adalina."

"I-Uh," Seraphine sputtered, unable to peel her eyes away from Adalina. Then she craned her neck and practically squealed behind her, "Alfie!"

The man from the Dew Drop Inn popped his head over her shoulder. He, too, was dressed as a guest and not as someone in service to the household. Adalina's curiosity piqued, despite her horror. His eyes nearly leapt out of his face as he took in the sight of her. "Holy *shit.*"

This was not happening. Adalina had regretted very few things in her life up until this point. Out of all the people in the vast kingdom of Astarfall, what were the chances that she had run into the queen's niece? And that it would be her and the man beside her that witnessed her little indiscretion the night before.

Queen Gwendolyn narrowed her eyes at them. "Alfie, have *you* seen my son? If the two of you are trying to cover for him again, I will be highly cross with you."

"Nope," Alfie's voice cracked, "haven't seen him since...."

Seraphine shot him a glare. Queen Gwendolyn tapped her foot impatiently and a few of the people standing outside yelped. A strong breeze had picked up, blowing branches into a few of the tables. Adalina would have been impressed by the queen's show of power if she hadn't been so busy worrying that her actions had finally come back to bite her like a feral dog.

Alfie's eyes darted around the room and fell suddenly on someone standing behind Adalina.

The queen turned first and clasped her hands together. "There you are. May I present Lady Adalina of Solaris?" She sounded exasperated.

Adalina took a deep breath, praying to the fates that Seraphine and Alfie would keep what they knew to themselves. Bracing herself, she turned. She didn't think she could be more horrified than she already was until she came face to face with a familiar dimpled smirk. It shouldn't have been possible for her to keep standing upright when her stomach plummeted as fast as it did.

Eight

The man from the inn—the one who only hours ago had her moaning on her back—was standing before Adalina with a silver crown resting on his head. When recognition dawned on him, his mouth popped open in shock, but he promptly shut it. Although his brows were still raised in surprise, an amused smile spread across his face. Like there was a jest only they were in on. And she supposed that was true, considering the queen had no idea what they'd been up to the night before.

Queen Gwendolyn's tone was formal as she said, "Lady Adalina, this is my son, Callum. You may remember each other from when you were younger. You met once before if I remember correctly?"

"Yes," Adalina managed to squeak.

She narrowed her eyes at Prince Callum's ability to mask his shock. Adalina wasn't as practiced at hiding her feelings. And right now, the embarrassment was overwhelming. This man had seen her naked. She could still feel the ghost of his lips trailing down her skin.

To her dismay, her face flushed, and a fire built in her belly. It rose, rivaling that of the flame she experienced each month with the call to wake Elettra. But this wasn't the magic of her people. No. This was white hot mortification.

The dimple in Prince Callum's cheek deepened as he grinned and bowed to her. "A pleasure to meet you." When he righted himself, he took her hand and raised it to his lips for a kiss, but she snatched it away quickly.

Queen Gwendolyn's eyebrows rose in what appeared to be amusement. With a disarming laugh, she said, "It seems the pleasure is yours alone, dear son."

"I didn't mean offense," Adalina hurried to say. "I-I... Would you excuse me?"

She fled from the room, leaving behind the stunning landscape of food and a very confused crowd of people. Once in the hall, she pressed her forehead to the wall and cursed at herself. *Stupid, stupid, stupid.* She shook her head against the bright wallpaper, wishing she could transfer the embarrassment to it.

Callum's gravelly voice was full of laughter as it filled the hallway. "I must say, I've never had a lover flee from me so fast before. And *twice* in one day. I'm afraid I may be losing my touch."

Adalina craned her neck to peer around him, then she glanced back to make sure there was no one within earshot to overhear the implication. She was met with an ounce of relief when she realized they were utterly alone.

"I am not your lover," she seethed without looking at him. Humiliation slowly turned to outrage at herself. How could she have been so clueless? So reckless? She recalled the way everyone in the tavern had been staring at them. It was no wonder. They hadn't envied her for capturing the attention of the most handsome man there. They'd been envious that she'd caught the eye of their prince.

He sidled up to her. His breath was hot on her cheek as he said playfully, "It sure seemed that way last night."

Did he think this was a joke? If anyone found out, she would be a laughingstock. Everyone would know she'd given herself to him freely without realizing who he was. What if they decided that was as good as saying yes to the proposal? Fire roared in her chest. In an instant, the anger with herself channeled into resentment for him. He was a rake. No one in that inn had seemed the least bit surprised that he'd set his sights on a woman for the night. Had they all known that he would take her to bed with him before she herself had decided? She'd thought it was all her idea and that had given her a sense of liberation. But had she simply been one of many who had fallen for those infuriatingly charming dimples?

His hand found her waist, sending pleasant shivers up her spine. A betrayal of her own body. She spun on him with a hand raised to shove him away, but he caught her arm. Gripping her wrist tightly, he pressed into her until she was pinned between him and the wall. Her pulse quickened and heat bloomed between her legs. She cursed herself for reacting to him this way. But perhaps her body hadn't yet caught up to her head and didn't know that they were furious with him.

She stopped struggling against his hold, and asked through gritted teeth, "Did you know who I was when you sat down with me at that tavern?"

"No." An infuriating smirk was still plastered on his face. "But I'll admit, this morning something you said caught my attention."

Asshole. She clenched her fists. "And yet you didn't say anything? Instead, you wanted to see my discomfort when I found out here?"

His grip loosened around her wrist, but he didn't release her. "I meant no harm in it. Truly. There is no trickery here. No joke at your expense. I honestly couldn't be sure..." He looped his fingers through one of her curls and mused, "Did your hair used to be lighter?"

Adalina slapped his hand away. He was *impossible*. Nothing he could say would stop her from seething with frustration and embarrassment. Still, she asked, "What was it this morning that made you guess who I might be?"

His dimple deepened, as if recalling a fond memory. "You told me you are Solarian, and I am not *your* prince. When we met as children, you said something similar with that same resolution."

Adalina's mind drifted to the past. With an urge to take her feelings out on him, she hissed, "You mean right before you threw me off the dock?"

His smile faltered slightly. Defensively, he said, "We were just kids. And it was one simple nickname I wanted you to use."

Pompous Prince. Adalina scowled. "If you had the slightest inkling of who I was this morning, you should have said something."

"The bells chimed, and you were rushing to leave. Besides, what would it have changed? We'd already slept together."

"But I wouldn't have been caught off guard in there in front of everyone. In front of your *mother*. Fates, if they all find out what happened..." She huffed heavily and shook her head as if she might rid herself of the mortification that way. "I never would have slept with you if I had known. Last night was supposed to be no strings attached."

His eyes darkened and his lips parted as if ruminating on their night together. "You're right, but does it really matter now? If the council has it their way, we'll be doing a lot more of that in the near future." He winked.

"Like hell!"

He shrugged. "Have it your way."

How did he not see that they had made a boneheaded decision by sleeping together? He didn't seem to care an inkling about how humiliated she was. Instead, he was acting like he didn't have a care in the world. There was no sign of empathy on his smug face. Rather, he was wielding this annoying optimism like a sword.

She opened her mouth to give him a piece of her mind, but Seraphine popped into the hallway. With a hand on her hip, her sharp eyes darted between Callum and Adalina, who was straight-backed with fists still clenched.

Seraphine spoke slowly. "Is everything alright, you two?"

Callum shrugged. "Someone's having morning after regrets, that's all."

Adalina crossed her arms.

Seraphine blew a sharp breath out of her mouth. The air shimmered with the faint sign of magic, and a gust of wind pushed him away from Adalina. Filled with satisfaction, she slipped from the wall and joined Seraphine at her side.

The wind-wielder snapped at Callum. "Your mother is requesting that the two of you return for the king's speech."

Adalina sniffed. "I am *not* going anywhere until he admits that last night was a mistake."

She glared at Callum, who had regained his composure by now. It only made her more determined to make him say it. There was no end to his flippant disregard for how a person's actions affect those around them. Even a prince's actions. And although she was not innocent—in fact, she could argue she was the instigator—she could at least admit the mistake they had made.

Unaffected by the slight blow he'd just taken from Seraphine, he held his hands up in mock defense. "I admit sleeping with a stranger the night before meeting our fiancés wasn't our most charming moment. But I don't understand why either of us should be embarrassed. It rather worked out in our favor, didn't it? I think *you* should admit that you had fun and enjoyed my company."

Adalina rolled her eyes. The fact was, she should have been more careful. Should have known last night would blow up in her face. And more than that, she shouldn't have been surprised that he didn't share the sentiment, but rather looked at the whole thing as if it were a grand jest the fates had played on them.

A frown tugged at the corner of his mouth as he explained, "If I had realized who you were when I sat down, I would have said something." The frown shifted into a sneer as he continued. "I mean, when I last saw you, you were a snotty little know-it-all. We can't be blamed for not recognizing one another sooner. I don't see why you should let this ruin anything," he paused and raised an accusatory eyebrow, "and in my defense, it was your idea to not exchange names."

"Not helping," Seraphine snapped at him.

Callum raised his hands defensively. "I just mean, there was no harm done. For the last few weeks, the council and my parents have been telling me that I'm meant to marry you for the good of our country." His brow furrowed thoughtfully. "An arranged marriage didn't surprise me, but I see a rare opportunity in what happened between us last night."

Adalina was so stunned that he was still trying to diminish her embarrassment that she couldn't form words.

He continued to dig his hole as he said, "Would you please lose the anger and look at all this in a different light? Think about it, I met and talked with you as a normal man, *not* as the prince who is being pushed upon you. I saw you for who you really are. We got to know one another without all the pomp and circumstance." He gestured to the closed doors leading to the brunch.

All true, except she wasn't so sure the man she'd been with last night *was* the real him. Not when he was being so annoyingly nonchalant, despite her obvious embarrassment. How could she marry someone who couldn't take her seriously?

He took a tentative step closer. "What's done is done. Just admit you genuinely had a good time with me and that maybe all of this isn't so bad after all."

Adalina crackled with annoyance. It was just like a pampered prince to think she should be thanking him for a good romp in the sheets. If Heely found out about them, he would say sleeping together as good as sealed the deal. She and Callum practically consummated the engagement without even realizing it.

He shook his head with a roll of his eyes. "I do wish you would relax."

That did it. Adalina's mouth popped open. "You have some nerve—" She shoved him away from her, but he stepped into her path to stop her from leaving.

Seraphine scolded him. "Callum, that's quite enough. You've said your piece. Now allow her to feel the way she needs to."

Callum ignored her and attempted to place a hand on Adalina's shoulder as he said, "Don't let something like this get you so worked up."

Seraphine rolled her eyes. "Want me to hit him with a gust for you?"

A little humbling never hurt anyone. Not even a prince. Unable to ignore the fire in her veins, Adalina raised her chin in the air. "Yes, actually."

Seraphine snapped her fingers, and a blizzard worthy wind knocked him into the wall. He grunted, but Adalina didn't wait to see if he was alright. She spun on her heel and returned to the brunch.

Nine

Adalina returned to the gathering with Seraphine by her side. The beautiful wind-wielder wore a proud smirk on her face. Adalina had to admit it had been satisfying to see Prince Callum flung through the hall as if he were no more than a feather. But she wondered why his cousin had been so quick to take her side.

"I appreciate your support back there. But can I ask why?"

"Callum has a bad habit of being infuriatingly upbeat in situations that make him uncomfortable. And he tends to try to get others to react the same way to make him feel more at ease. Sometimes he needs a little reminder that not everyone wants to pretend things aren't a big deal."

Adalina wasn't sure what to make of that. Nothing in Callum's offhanded reaction indicated that he felt the slightest bit of humiliation that Adalina did. Even if he did and was simply good at hiding it, then that was just as frustrating. Her grandparents' marriage was built on mutual trust and understanding. They didn't hide anything from each other and certainly never invalidated each other's feelings.

Would Callum be the sort of husband to keep his thoughts and emotions closed off to any wife he may take? Guarded or not, he was clearly not the man for her.

After a moment of silence, Seraphine said, "I only tell you this, because it's clear the two of you have gotten off on the wrong foot."

For the second time, Adalina thought with annoyance. As children, their encounter had been brief, but it had been enough to leave a foul taste in her mouth. She hadn't forgotten the sting of that embarrassing moment or the laughter of the other children as she'd begrudgingly dragged herself out of the water soaked down to her undergarments. And now this.

Silently, the women found a spot near the food table. The king was already making his speech, and all attention was on him. He appeared to be in higher spirits than when her family had spoken to him earlier. That, or he was just an expert at putting on a confident front.

Trying her best not to draw attention, Adalina leaned close to Seraphine and whispered, "And should I believe him when he says he didn't realize who I was right away?"

He had seemed sincere as far as that went. She didn't want to believe he'd deceived her. But if he was hiding his embarrassment as Seraphine suggested, could he be hiding more from her?

Seraphine had to bend down a bit as she was slightly taller than Adalina. She answered with sincerity, "I know Callum better than most. He would have come clean if he'd known. Of that, I am absolutely certain."

"So it really was an unfortunate coincidence," Adalina mused. "And does he... go in search of company like that often?"

"He's not as much of a rake as the rumors make him out to be. Alfie owns the inn. He and Callum have been best friends most of their lives. The prince spends much of his time there. When I saw the two of you together, I just assumed he was having his last hurrah before getting engaged."

The door beside them opened and Callum walked in indignantly. His hair was adorably disheveled. It really wasn't fair that he could pull off the windblown look like that. He glanced at the women and wisely chose a spot to stand on the other side of the room. A brooding scowl muddied his good looks as he leaned against a large marble column and crossed his arms. Adalina didn't have an ounce of sympathy for him.

Instead, she rolled her eyes and said, "I'm inclined to believe he's a scoundrel and a philanderer."

Seraphine chuckled, drawing a few stares from people nearest to them. "I mean, he's not exactly known for being pious. But," she paused, and gave Adalina a pinned look, "it appears you might not be either."

There was nothing in her tone to indicate that she thought it was a bad thing. Simply that it was something Adalina should take responsibility for as well.

"You have a point." Adalina tapped her foot on the floor in mild frustration. "He just really gets under my skin."

"Understandable." Seraphine shrugged, "But I'd say, judging by that scowl, we made him pay plenty in the hall. Maybe it's time to start fresh."

Adalina fought the stubborn urge to argue. She could try to be civil for the remainder of her time in Astarfall. Everything would be resolved in a few days. Perhaps her grandparents could find a way to council the king on his troubles. Maybe there was another way to protect Astarfall and Solaris without uniting the two of them in matrimony.

Which would mean *without waking Elettra.* Her chest constricted at the thought, and she had to remind herself that King Alistair's plan would not ultimately give her what she wanted. The dragon would not be solely hers to command. And she would be married to a man she could never love.

Prince Callum might have been good in bed... really good, and strikingly handsome, but he wasn't the sort of man she envisioned for herself. She needed someone who took her seriously and didn't dismiss her. She'd had enough of that with the other men in her life. Apparently, he had not changed much from the boy she'd known. If bound to him in marriage, it was likely one of them wouldn't make it out alive.

Eager to stave off the emotions that were stirring in her like a hurricane, she asked Seraphine, "The queen is your aunt?"

She hummed in response. "My father's sister."

"So, if you don't mind me prying, why do you work at the inn?"

"I don't *really* work there. I just like to help Alfie out when I can. Besides, I am the result of a torrid affair." She snickered and lowered her voice as if delighting in the gossip despite it being about her own circumstances. "Even though his first wife had already learned of the affair and run off with her coachman in revenge, the court disapproved of my father's choice to marry my mother. My aunt, however, has always accepted me with open arms, but honestly, I enjoy helping out at the Dew Drop. I love the people and being on my own. It's nice to know that I don't *need* anything from anyone."

Adalina tried to mask her surprise at how boldly Seraphine shared the scandal of her parentage. Once again, she was reminded that life at court... and in Astarfall would be much different from what she was used to in Solaris, where people whispered quietly about one another. It was a refreshing change of pace even if it was a bit daunting.

As for Seraphine's eagerness to make her own way... Adalina appreciated that. There had been times when she'd considered leaving her small village and venturing off on her own simply to put distance between her and all the unwanted opinions on how she should live her life. But the draw of the dragon had always stopped her. Until the day came where she lost all hope in waking Elettra, she was tied to Solaris.

Adalina continued to listen intently as Seraphine talked, but Callum kept drawing her gaze. Each time his eyes shifted to meet hers, she turned away and hoped he hadn't noticed her staring. Seraphine continued to explain her father's holdings as one of the lords in western Astarfall and her childhood home, which was called Windshire.

The longer they talked, the more Adalina admired how kind and friendly the woman was. It felt as if a seed of friendship had been planted between the two of them. She hadn't experienced much ease in that aspect before. She'd been too busy with her mother's shop or feeling a bit out of place amongst the women in Solaris, who had already found marriage and started their families.

Seraphine, however, was a kindred spirit. Someone who wasn't afraid to live the way she wished and was ready to fight anyone who tried to tell her to do otherwise. It helped lessen the pressure in Adalina's chest, knowing she might already have a friend so far from home. Even if said friend *was* Prince Callum's cousin.

As King Alistair finished his speech and stepped into the crowd to join his son, she realized how grateful she was to have Seraphine at her side. Prince Callum didn't rejoin them until King Alistair and Queen Gwendolyn led him over. Despite being a few years older than Adalina, he still reminded her of the young boy she had met all those years ago when flanked by his parents. It was a wonder she hadn't realized who he was sooner. Though his baby fat had been replaced with a more sculpted frame, he had the same smile and troublemaking glint in his eyes. Just one more thing to remind her of how foolish she was.

King Alistair offered a warm smile as he said, "I am glad the two of you have had a chance to get reacquainted."

Prince Callum's golden cheeks turned a deep red.

Enjoying the first hint of real discomfort from him, Adalina said, "Oh, yes, we certainly did."

Oblivious, his father mused, "You two were quite young when you last visited."

Yes, and even then, he was a spoiled, entitled—

Queen Gwendolyn clasped her hands together loudly and measured Adalina with a studious gaze. "Yes, well, let us all retire to the study. Your family is already waiting there for us, dear."

The king and queen linked arms and walked ahead, leaving Adalina and Seraphine with Prince Callum. The blush had gone from his cheeks, replaced once again with a smooth mask of indifference. Except for his eyes, which darted to Seraphine cautiously as he held his arm out for Adalina to take.

Seraphine scolded him, "Behave yourself. Or next time, I may just string you up like a flag on one of those ships out there." She winked at Adalina before turning on her heel to meet Alfie, who was snickering in their direction a few paces away.

Adalina suppressed a smile and looped her arm through Prince Callum's. Some of the irritation with him had begun to wear off, and she was eager to get this next bit of business over with so she could go back to her room for a hot cup of tea and a bath. Surely, she could handle a few hours by his side.

They strode silently past whispering courtiers and wide-eyed palace staff. Their stares were like a weight on Adalina's shoulders, but she was determined not to let it show. She straightened her posture and walked confidently down the sunlit hall. When they came to a curve, the walls opened up on one side. Rather than closing the palace off from the view of the sea, it was lined with a white stone railing that shimmered like a fish's scales. It allowed a clear look at the harbor, and she could even spot the Dew Drop Inn.

The people below bustled this way and that, busy with their day of work and shopping. Adalina wished she could ask them if they knew about the threat at their borders. And if they did, were they frightened, but simply good at putting on a show?

To the brooding prince at her side, she asked, "Have you seen it? What they say is happening in the west?"

His mood darkened, and for a moment it was as if the clouds had blocked out the sun. But he quickly replaced it with an easy smile. "I have not. But I was present for the reports."

"Is it as bad as they seem to think?"

A muscle ticked in Prince Callum's jaw. "I'm not sure how much my father told you and your council."

They came to a double door and muffled voices sounded from within. Prince Callum reached for the handle, but Adalina pushed his hand away lightly. With the most commanding voice she could muster, she demanded, "From here on out, I want you to promise me your honesty. Swear that you won't keep things to yourself."

As if he couldn't be bothered, he scoffed and said, "I don't—"

"You don't owe me anything. But if I am expected to take this whole thing seriously, I need to know that there will be no more games on your part. We had our fun last night, but this isn't one night we're facing anymore. Marriage is for a lifetime. I will not lie; I am inclined to deny your father's request. But if I am to march into this room and hear him out, I need to know I can trust you."

"You *can* trust me." There was raw honesty in his tone, so at odds with the lighthearted man she'd been fighting with earlier. Despite his sincerity now, Adalina couldn't help remembering the boy who shoved her into the water for not doing as she was told.

Callum was a prince of Astarfall. Used to getting his way. Accustomed to people bowing to him and his whims. But he would not find that in her. If he thought she was that sort of woman, then he was going to be sorely disappointed.

And even if he was being honest now, things could change as fast as the winds at sea. It was best to keep her guard up. For now, his words brought her enough comfort to at least reach down and open the door.

They stepped into an airy study. Two floor-to-ceiling windows overlooking the water were opened wide. The scent of old parchment was faint, and she took a moment to marvel at the bookcases. They were plump, crammed with books. Some didn't even fit on the shelf and instead were stacked on top of one another in little towers on the floor. Her fingers itched at the prospect of digging into them. They must have contained every folktale, history, and story ever written. She wondered about Astarfall's history, curious if any of the books held their own account of the war her grandmother had fought. The one that they had set into motion but had not finished.

Everyone in the room quieted. How much had she and Prince Callum missed? Her parents were in the corner, looking pale and nervous. Her mother's eyes shifted between the king and Adalina's grandmother anxiously.

To Adalina's surprise, it was her father who broke the silence. "Why not send a large force, Your Majesty? An army? With their abilities, they should have no trouble—"

"I am afraid our magic isn't enough. The reports..." King Alistair sucked in a sharp breath and Queen Gwendolyn touched his hand gingerly. It seemed to give him the strength to continue as he said, "The reports claim that there is a creature of great size and power. That it rose from the shadows."

In all Adalina's readings, she had never heard of a creature that crept out of the shadows. She pinned her gaze on her grandmother. She had gone as still as stone. Their circle seemed to be at a loss for words.

"It rose?" her grandmother asked.

King Alistair elaborated, "With *wings*." He glanced nervously out the window. "I have tried to maintain a strong front for my people. Only those in my innermost circle know of the beast. I did not dare risk including that in my correspondence with your council for fear that the information might get leaked and spread mass panic throughout our countries."

Adalina locked eyes with Prince Callum. He held her gaze and pushed a pleasant smile to the surface. And although fear wasn't reflected in his eyes, it was clear in the tension in his jaw and shoulders. Why was he hiding what he was feeling with fake smiles? She fidgeted with her skirt. The hope she'd been holding that perhaps King Alistair might not need Solaris' help after all began to dim.

The king's voice grew hoarse as he said, "I do not know what it is or where it came from. But if the reports are true, then combating it with a creature of the same size and magnitude could mean defeating it and sparing many lives."

Elettra. That was why they needed a dragon. Adalina's mind spun.

Her grandfather shook his head. "Soldiers' minds can play tricks on them in battle. Until you can be certain—"

The King's face turned red, but calmly, he said, "I would rather be safe than sorry. I do not know exactly what we are up against. And I will not send more men out there to scout if we do not have a way of protecting them. My armies are vast and capable. But I cannot in good conscience risk the casualties if there is another way."

Adalina's grandmother prodded at the reports stacked on the king's desk. Quietly, she asked, "Do you suspect who is behind the attacks? Who could have the ability to summon and control such a dangerous beast?"

Adalina waited eagerly for an answer. The rebellious group must have been small or skilled enough to maneuver undetected for this long. What sort of men or women could be a match for Astarfall's strength?

With a slight quake, King Alistair said, "There isn't enough evidence to give us a solid suspect. But tensions have been higher than usual with the Festiri King due to difficult trade agreements."

Uthred interjected, "If I may." He placed a letter on the table. "Our spies in their court have told us of a man hired by the Festiri King. He comes from across the sea and is a rumored alchemist. If my intelligence is correct, this man harnesses power through enchanted objects."

Adalina wrinkled her nose. Festiri—the kingdom to the west of Astarfall—kept to themselves. They were isolated by a mountain range and a vast forest that separated them from their neighbor. They were hardened people and easily offended, but would they go through all this trouble over a trade agreement that could be negotiated through diplomacy?

The king continued, "If your spies are correct, then it's possible that he is using alchemy to control the great beast that has been spotted during the attacks. But I do not wish to speculate. I do not have enough information to determine who might be coming after us."

To Adalina's wonder, Prince Callum stepped forward. The very action commanded the attention of everyone in the room. "May I share my theory?" He arched an eyebrow and waited for his father's nod. "It's not the first time there's been a rebellion in Astarfall. And the perpetrators certainly weren't a bunch of hairy imbeciles from Festiri."

Couldn't he just come out and say what he needed to say? Adalina tapped her foot impatiently, but everyone else listened intently.

He continued, "Isn't there a possibility that our enemies have been lying in wait for half a century? That the peace we thought existed since Calida's war was really just a ruse meant to lure us into a false sense of security until they were strong enough to strike again?"

Adalina wanted to believe that what he was saying was ridiculous. That multiple generations later, hatred wouldn't still run that deep. But despite the practiced ease with which he moved, his words were laced with an undercurrent of seriousness. Enough so that the silence in the room weighed heavily.

Adalina's grandmother met him standing. "You mean you believe it could be the frost breathers?"

The corner of Uthred's mouth tipped up as if he found the prospect laughable. Even the king pressed his lips into a thin line. They might have found Callum's theory absurd, but Adalina's throat tightened.

"Who else?" Prince Callum asked with a careless shrug that didn't match the tension rolling off everyone else in the room. "You drove them into the western mountains, did you not?"

"What was left of them," huffed her grandfather with a hint of satisfaction.

Prince Callum nodded in acknowledgment. "True, you decimated their forces all those years ago. But that does not mean they didn't rebuild. That they weren't able to scrounge up a beast from the depths of whatever hell they went searching in."

He paused and sat on top of his father's desk, knocking a few pieces of paper to the floor. "They were once Astarfallen. They're familiar with the land. Aware of which villages would be easiest to target first if they wanted to test our defenses."

Adalina found she'd been holding her breath. The frost breathers were a thing of nightmares. Stories of boogeymen told in the dark. Men capable of manipulating water into something cold and sinister. Callum's grandfather had banished them to protect his kingdom.

Even though frost breathers were Astarfall born, their magic was a twisted version of the sort that Callum and the others held. They were born with the ability to summon a bone chilling freeze uncommon in a land that was never intended to grow cold with the changing seasons. It was something that threatened the prosperity of Astarfall and, on more than one occasion, nearly starved them all. They had once been outcasts amongst their people because their magic wasn't useful.

And because of their superior and extremist way of thinking, they were convinced that the people of Astarfall should rule beyond their borders. It made them bold and dangerous. They had believed that their magic—gifted to them by the heavens—should have them reigning over all. And when they were expelled from their home, they had set their sights on the rest of the world. Starting with Solaris. But their leader, Rothin, had been no match for Adalina's grandmother's fury... or her dragon.

Adalina hadn't lived through their reign of terror. She only knew the stories. But that *alone* was enough to make terror induced goosebumps prickle on the back of her neck.

King Alistair attempted to reassure them as he said, "My son's theory is just that. A theory. There is nothing to substantiate it. But it would be unwise to rule anything out yet."

Prince Callum picked at his nails. "If it's true, I don't see a reason to believe we can't rid ourselves of them again. My grandfather expelled them once before, and Warrior Calida battered them into nothing. We can do it again. And if it's the Festiri," he snorted, "well, we can handle a few brutish westerners."

Adalina narrowed her eyes at Prince Callum, and a chilling sense of dread washed over her.

She couldn't hold her tongue any longer. Facing the prince, she said, "The frost breathers were a ruthless and relentless faction. They wrought destruction without sparing a second thought for the innocents they hurt. Their sole purpose was to wreak havoc on our home because they believed power was *owed* to them. If they are behind these raids, then it seems they were not so easy to get rid of before."

Surprise flickered in Prince Callum's eyes, and he countered, "Then we will have to do a better job this time."

Adalina stepped up to him. With him sitting, they were nearly nose to nose. "If they've been harboring resentment and a need for revenge for half a century, then it will not be so simple. We'd be dealing with *generational* hatred. And they'd be coming for you. The grandson of the man who exiled their fathers and grandfathers. They'd come for me. The granddaughter of the woman who burned their people alive."

The muscle in his jaw ticked. Maybe she'd gotten through to him. Nothing was more dangerous than a leader who believed himself to be untouchable. But with a deep breath, Prince Callum squared his shoulders and tilted his chin up. He looked like the stubborn, freckle-faced boy who had dubbed himself *Callum the Courageous*.

King Alistair stepped in and gingerly said, "Let's not get ahead of ourselves. Perhaps we should take a moment. Tensions are high."

Adalina's face flushed with embarrassment. She'd lost her temper and scolded the prince in front of everyone. What was it about him that made her lose her senses?

"Apologies, Your Majesty," she said to the king as she took a step back and rejoined her family.

Her head throbbed. She should have eaten something. The last thing she wanted was to faint in front of all these men. The room spun as if she'd had too much ale. All eyes were on her now and the silence was nearly crushing. All she wanted to do was slink into the shadowy corner of the room. What she wouldn't give to be home in Solaris with the chill biting at her cheeks and the birds dipping in and out of the dreary winter clouds.

Her mouth was too dry to speak, and, to her relief, it was her grandmother who stepped forward in her stead. "Now that we've established the severity of the situation and the possibility of who is behind it all, my concern is for my granddaughter's role. What if the ceremony between Lina and your son does not work?"

A vein stuck out on King Alistair's forehead, but he calmly said, "Whether or not it works, Adalina will be an honored member of this family. She will stand to become Queen of Astarfall when I am gone, and our two countries will be stronger with this alliance."

"But in said circumstance, you would not have the dragon." Her grandmother raised a slender eyebrow. "How will you stop these attacks, then?"

Adalina glanced at Callum and tried to read what he might be thinking. He had moved from his father's desk and was leaning against a bookcase. He met her look with a pinched mouth and more worry in his eyes than before. But when he noticed his mother watching him, he quickly began to pick at his nails again. Acting like he had better things to do.

She couldn't stop staring, despite the conversation happening around her. Prince Callum was such a contradiction. He was clearly competent enough to have theorized who their enemy was. But he was also quick to slip on the facade of a relaxed prince the moment anyone looked at him too closely.

King Alistair spoke with authority. "If the rites are not enough to wake the dragon, then my men will step up and do what needs to be done. We will fight. I will have no choice. But I pray to the heavens it does not come to that. In my heart of hearts, I believe this will work. I know the stories. Of kings and queens in the days of old. The Great Binding was once a time-honored tradition of our two peoples. It can be so again." He sucked in a sharp breath and glanced at Adalina with anticipation.

She needed to say something. Anything. But the words would not come. She couldn't marry Prince Callum. He was so wishy-washy and dismissive. And it was clear from their argument at brunch that they couldn't work harmoniously together. They navigated the world too differently.

But how could she tell them that when they were all counting on her? Her gaze fell to the papers scattered on the king's desk. A messy charcoal sketch sat on top of everything else. It depicted a beast like she had never seen before. All brittle bone, spikes and claws. Nothing like the dragons she'd read about. And certainly nothing like Elettra, as she had been described to her.

She thought of the smooth earth covering Elettra's sleeping body in the cave and the gentle curve of her tail. Beneath it all were glittering scales. A beautiful dragon who had lived with honor. In comparison, the creature in the drawing felt... wrong. Unnatural and not of their world.

Adalina was startled as her mother spoke. "Naturally, my daughter must be allowed time to process all of this before making her decision." She stepped from the corner and lifted her chin. "Because ultimately, it *is* her decision."

Adalina almost couldn't believe her ears. It was very rare that her mother spoke to anyone in such an authoritative tone. Yet here she was, standing up to the king for Adalina.

King Alistair gulped. "Of course."

Prince Callum walked to Adalina and placed a hand on her elbow. "I'll see you out."

Before she could object, he was steering her out of the room and away from all the expectant faces. She didn't know whether she should be grateful that he was helping her escape, or if she should be irritated that he had taken it upon himself to usher her out as if she were a damsel in need of saving.

Once in the hall, she pulled from his grasp. "I can find my way from here, thank you."

After several hurried strides away from him, he called after her. "Adalina!"

She turned to find that he had followed her.

His eyes shined like water when the sunlight hit it just right as he said, "Please don't let my foolishness earlier in the hall sway your decision."

She bit her lip. "We are simply two very different people."

Recalling Seraphine's suggestion that they attempt to start fresh, she added with a sigh, "I will not hold it against you, but that doesn't mean my answer will be yes."

"Understood." Ease slinked back into his body.

He was close enough to her that she could feel the heat of his body. He smelled like clean linen and the salty breeze, and she couldn't tell if she was smelling it on him or if his scent was still on her from their night together. It was enough to make her desire for him return. She really needed to get that under control if she was going to make her decision with a clear head.

She narrowed her eyes. "Why are you so willing to go through with this? You could have your pick of princesses or ladies of the court. Why tie yourself to me on a gamble?"

His face became unreadable as he said, "My father believes we need your dragon."

"But you do not? I recall you saying yesterday that you do not see the appeal."

Emotions seemed to be at war within him. He frowned but shrugged as he said with surety, "I believe that with our numbers and our magic, we could dispose of this problem. But I am not yet the king, so my opinion does not matter. I am bound by my duty to take his lead."

Adalina studied him. Callum was confident to the point of arrogance. But it seemed he was also loyal to his father. Willing to sacrifice his freedom for duty. Still, he didn't seem to like dragons. And that was something she couldn't understand. Without another word, she turned and headed back to her rooms. This time, he did not follow.

Ten

Adalina's family gave her the space she craved for the rest of the afternoon. And when she declined to join them in the grand hall for dinner, they did not press. They trickled out the door one by one, chatting amongst themselves about the seafood they were looking forward to, but her grandmother lingered.

She took Adalina's hands and squeezed them tight. "Don't be too hard on the boy. Remember that he is in the same position that you are."

"It's not just about him."

He certainly played a large role in the decision, but when it came down to it, Adalina needed to determine if the threat was worth the sacrifice. Not only for herself, but for her family's dragon as well.

Her grandmother's face softened, but a few worried lines remained, and she offered a meek smile. "If you are concerned about Elettra not waking—"

"Part of me is worried about what happens if she *does*. I might feel better if there was a way to prevent Callum from invoking his rights to the dragon bond, to make sure only I could ride her..."

Aside from selfish reasons, Adalina simply did not trust Callum enough to give him that sort of control. She was the granddaughter of a dragon warrior. The bond was always intended to be between her and the dragon. In her wildest dreams, it never included a third party in the mix.

"It is not so simple as that." Her grandmother gritted her teeth, then explained, "Through the rites, you and Callum will be bound. Both in matrimony and in magic. I have not witnessed these rites myself, but I have an understanding of the history recorded. If you wake Elettra by using Callum's power to fuel the fire in your veins, then your magic will be pieced together like thread in a shirt."

Adalina bit the inside of her cheek. "There will be no undoing it?"

"Only in death. There is no way around it. With the connection to you, it will be possible for him to bond with the dragon as if he were Solarian himself."

"How would he do it? Call on his rights for the bonding, I mean." Adalina needed to know if there was a way to sabotage it should the need arise. If she married him, she wanted assurances.

"Through offerings. Same as you've done each time you have tried to wake her. He would offer his blood and a gift dear to him."

Adalina was utterly deflated by the answers she was getting. "So, short of physically standing in front of him to stop him, there would be no way."

Her grandmother tilted her head sadly and gripped Adalina's shoulders lovingly. "No one can take away what is rightfully yours, Lina." And with that, she slipped into the hallway and out of sight.

Adalina stood there dumbly, unsure of what to do with herself. She wanted to believe her grandmother's parting words but couldn't. Not when she was still navigating the new court and the royals who oversaw it. King Alistair seemed desperate enough to do whatever it took to keep his people safe. And Callum didn't strike her as someone who would listen to his wife's wishes if there was something he really wanted to do.

She sat down to a plate of dinner that had been brought up for her. The delicious citrusy vegetables were nearly enough to make her worries melt away, if only for a moment. She was finishing up her last bite of golden fried fish and dreaming of crawling into bed when there was a soft rapt at the door.

Reluctantly, she abandoned the dessert she was about to start on and went to the door. She opened it, expecting to find Councilman Heely eager to lecture her on the role she was meant to play while at court. But instead, Prince Callum stood there grinning.

Instinctually, she began to close the door, but he stopped it with his foot. Annoyed, she allowed him to open it and step into the room.

She drawled, "Aren't you supposed to be giving me space in order to make my decision?"

He plucked a piece of lint—which apparently only he could see—from his shoulder and said, "The council thought it best not to let you dwell on reasons why you should say no."

Her temper reared its head slightly. "That's really not necessary. Rather, I might think of more reasons to say no *in* your presence."

He chuckled. "I'm sure you can. But before you throw me out or shout for Seraphine to come blow me off the balcony, hear me out."

He was once again dressed down in a linen shirt, unbuttoned at the top carelessly. It was as he had been the night before when she mistook him for a common man. She tried to ignore the fluttering in her stomach as she recalled what was beneath that shirt.

Adalina crossed her arms and nodded for him to go on.

He brushed a hand through his hair and said, "You wanted honesty, right? The council thought if I could show you one of the outlying villages, you might be more inclined to sympathize with the people who are at risk."

"The council wants you to take me to the border. Where a great beast supposedly lurks," she said flatly.

"No," he said through a light chuckle. "They want me to take you to a village outside of the city. The skirmishes have not come that close to the heart of Astarfall, so there is no risk. It is simply a chance for you to see more of the country and to spend some time with me."

"Do they know that we already spent time together?" She placed a hand on her hip and jutted it out.

His eyes followed, and he licked his lips. "Are they aware I bedded you last night? No. I don't think they would appreciate our night together as much as I did."

Heat crept across her chest. Suddenly, she became vastly aware that they were alone in her family's private chambers. Just beyond the sitting room was her bedroom. And a large empty bed practically begging for a good romping. As he closed the gap between them, her heart sped at an alarming pace.

As if reading her indecent thoughts, Callum said, "Or we could stay in." He reached up to touch her hair, but she swatted him away.

"Let's go," Adalina managed to say as she slipped away, placing as much space between her and the dangerously handsome prince as she could. "Will Seraphine and Alfie be joining us?"

"Yes but..."

"Perfect," she said briskly as she swung open the door to the hall. At least with a buffer there, she might be more likely to stay focused on the matters at hand and not where she would like to *put* her hands.

The sun had already begun to set over the ocean's horizon. The way it cast a warm glow onto the water was mesmerizing. Though the sunset in Solaris was just as beautiful—ducking behind the rolling hills in the countryside—the one she witnessed now gave her delightful goosebumps. Or perhaps it was the man who held her hand to avoid losing her in the crowd.

The streets were bustling, but as they ventured into the outskirts of the city, a quiet calm settled in the atmosphere. They approached two pillars flanking the wall surrounding the city where a handful of guards were lazing around. Three were caught up in a game of dice, crouched in the dirt and hooting at one another playfully.

Callum cleared his throat, drawing their attention. It took only a split second for recognition to flicker in their eyes and two of the guards went tumbling onto the ground with a start. Adalina suppressed a snicker and wasn't at all surprised to see a smirk on Callum's face. As a child, he had enjoyed getting a rise out of people—startling the cooks in the kitchens when they were carrying plump sacks of flour or leaping out of trees to scare the little girls when they were playing behind the palace.

The more time she spent around him, the more she could spot glimpses of the boy she had met all those years ago. Even the small dimple on the left side of his face was still there. The fact that she'd slept with him without recognizing him first still embarrassed her. Maybe she should blame all the ale she'd had. It would make her feel slightly less oblivious if she did.

"Your Highness." The brawniest of the group stepped forward and saluted Callum by placing two fingers over his heart.

"At ease," Callum said through a chuckle, "I'm not here to spoil the fun. We're headed just over there."

He pointed to a cluster of buildings less than a mile out that were lit by the warm glow of the setting sun and tiny dots of light from what she presumed were lanterns in the streets. All the ease in the guards was gone now. The big one shifted on his feet and twisted his gloved hands together.

"Without a guard?" From the hesitation in his voice, Adalina guessed it was likely the first time he'd ever questioned someone from the royal family.

Callum shrugged. "We won't be venturing further than Bellonna." He clapped the man on the shoulder. "Besides, I think I can manage to stay out of trouble for one night."

The guard forced a laugh. Something told Adalina that Callum's past actions indicated otherwise. But nonetheless, the guards moved aside, allowing her and the prince to pass without further argument.

Once they were a few paces away, Adalina asked, "How can they be so relaxed if the situation is as grave as your father makes it out to be? If there was a threat tiptoeing on Solaris' border, I highly doubt you'd see our sentries gambling or lounging about."

"Do you even have sentries up there?" he drawled rudely.

"That's beside the point." She huffed. In truth, they hadn't needed them. They had a signal in place to call any man capable of fighting to the great hall in case of emergency. But it had been so long since they faced any threat that the council had put more stock into making Solaris thrive; teaching boys to farm, build, and hunt rather than training them to be soldiers and guards.

Callum finally answered, "It's one thing to hear about danger and another to experience it. Those men haven't seen battle or witnessed what's happening on the border. And I think it's easier to distract themselves than to sit there staring into the dark, wondering what great monster might be hiding in the shadows."

Adalina glanced back at the guards. She could see that they were straight-backed and alert now. Two had stepped outside of the city walls to peer around the perimeter. Were they worried for their Crown Prince or were they embarrassed they had been caught slacking on their duties?

"Is that what you do? Distract yourself so the danger doesn't seem as real?" She attempted to keep her tone light and upbeat so Callum wouldn't clam up on her or take offense.

"I know the danger is real. I simply choose to confront it with a more confident disposition."

Adalina muttered, "Comes across as a tad arrogant, if you ask me."

He raised an eyebrow and mumbled back, "Better than being a skittish little mouse."

She didn't have time to retort as they reached the village called Bellonna. It was a quaint seaside town. And though the rising moon and peeping stars graced the streets with plenty of light, lanterns twinkled above on tall posts, as well. The houses and shops were painted in bright hues of pink, purple, blue, and yellow. It wasn't a practical choice, as it had likely taken the builders longer to finish than it would have if they had left the wood bare. But it was charming and Adalina found herself considering what color she would have chosen. Perhaps a sea green or a pastel orange like the color of coral in the sea.

When they came to a lively tavern, Callum's smile widened. Alfie and Seraphine were standing at the door chatting with some villagers with drinks in hand. Alfie greeted Adalina in a friendly way, but Seraphine hugged her tightly. She truly was one of those people that made you feel like you'd known them forever.

When she pulled away, she adjusted the seashell necklace dangling at her chest and clapped her hands together. "Shall we?"

"Heavens yes," said Alfie. "I need a refill."

Callum gestured to Adalina to enter the tavern first. She stepped into the bustling room where Astarfallen danced and drank merrily. Some eyes were glazed over from a bit too much ale, but everyone was in good cheer. Again, Adalina couldn't ignore the twinge of annoyance.

After the meeting in the king's study, she could no longer deny that there was something nefarious happening on Astarfall soil. Even if the information had come from secondhand accounts. In that room earlier, there had been genuine fear and concern. So why couldn't King Alistair just tell his people the truth? Didn't they deserve to know?

She studied Callum. Downplaying things seemed to be a trait inherited from father to son. How truly involved was he with his father's council? Did he think he and his people were invincible or, deep down, was he as worried as he should be? Now would be the perfect time to pry information out of him. He already had a drink in his hand and was drinking it like water. When he handed a glass to her, she sipped it slowly.

They sat at a table in the corner that gave a clear view of the tavern. A few children came running out of the back room in a blur of energy. The smallest—a little girl no more than five with blonde curls that seemed to refuse to be tamed by the pigtails they were pulled into—bee lined straight for Callum. He embraced her with the familiarity of family and ruffled her hair.

Her voice was high-pitched and sweet as she said, "Did you bring me anything?"

"I wouldn't dare visit without treats in hand," he said in mock offense. Then, presenting a crumpled paper bag, he handed it to the girl.

She squealed in delight as she tore it open to reveal several rainbow-colored sweets and began shoving them in her mouth; which earned Callum a stern scowl from the waitress approaching with another round of drinks.

She kissed the girl on the top of her head and scolded gently, "Slow down. And let the prince be."

"She's fine, Delilah." He turned back to the little girl and winked. "As a matter of fact, I wanted to introduce you to a new friend of mine."

The little girl peeked around him at Adalina and blushed shyly.

Adalina waved at her. "Hi, there."

"Hello," the little girl said with the friendliness of youth.

Callum leaned back in his seat. "This is Talia."

Talia reached up to grab a piece of Adalina's fiery red hair. "I like your hair. It's kind of like mine."

"It is," Adalina agreed, letting the child twist her finger in one of the curls.

"Alright now," said Talia's mother, Delilah. "Off with you."

Talia skipped off to rejoin her friends, who had taken to a rambunctious game of tag. They ducked and dodged between the adults. Adalina laughed as one of them slipped under an elderly man's legs, earning a loud grumble about how they should be in bed by now.

Alfie and Seraphine were huddled close together, lost in their own little world, so Adalina leaned into Callum and nudged his arm. "You're good with her."

A soft smile touched his lips. "She reminds me of Ivy."

"Ivy?" Adalina tried to place the name but couldn't.

Callum cleared his throat uncomfortably, as if he hadn't meant to bring her up. He nursed his drink and said, "My sister."

"Oh, the little princess. I remember her as a baby when we were here that summer." Her throat tightened at the sudden sadness that befell Callum's face.

"There was an accident some years ago. She uh," his voice trembled, and he poured himself another drink. "She didn't survive the injuries."

Adalina's heart dropped. "I'm sorry, I didn't realize," she whispered, feeling foolish for not knowing. She'd been so busy drowning in her troubles, and only concerning herself with what she wanted. So much so that she hadn't even noticed the princess' absence. Her face flushed, and she bit her lip. He must have thought she was either selfish or oblivious.

"Thank you for sharing that with me." The words fell flat as she said them out loud. But opening up like this to her, even in a tavern with their bellies heavy with ale, gave her a small glimmer of hope that there might be something more to him.

"I don't talk about it often. You'll find paintings of her in the palace, and we celebrate her birthday every year. But it's difficult to talk about her without recalling our last days together."

Adalina had never lost anyone close to her. She couldn't fathom losing a sibling so young. Or the pain King Alistair and Queen Gwendolyn must have felt. Something like that left agonizing scars behind.

She opened her mouth to say more, but he threw back his drink and flashed a dazzling smile at a few village women who waved as they passed by. Just like that, his tides turned. Her hope deflated slightly, and she slinked back in her chair.

A few moments passed and Alfie took to singing a lively song about a man who followed a siren out to sea, only to realize the beautiful woman was, in fact, a manatee. Everyone laughed and joined in as he began the next tune. Seraphine danced around the tables with boundless energy.

Callum's eyes lit up as he watched his friends, but he was quieter than he had been before. Hoping to fill the silence between them, Adalina softly joked. "So, is this your idea of wooing me? Plying me with more of that fruity ale I love, introducing me to the adorable children of Astarfall, and making me listen to slightly bawdy songs?"

The playful jab caught his attention, and he chuckled. "Do you really think so little of me?"

"I think it'll take a lot more than this to sway my decision."

Callum leaned an elbow on the table and studied her carefully. "You find me arrogant and pompous." He raised an eyebrow. "I'm not a fool. I remember that summer you came to the wedding when we were kids. And while it's true that I might not have been the kindest to you, I never meant any actual harm."

"So?" Adalina turned toward him with a leveled gaze.

"So, you're not the only one with preconceived notions about who the other is. From what I've seen, you're still a bit of a self-righteous know it all."

The flippant way he said it kept the words from truly stinging. But it also didn't deter her from trying to figure him out.

She scoffed. "Why do you want to marry me, then? If I'm so unbearable."

Now a lutist was playing alongside Alfie. The barkeep joined in, too. They clapped and their voices boomed merrily through the room in a messy duet.

"Who says I do?" Callum snorted into his drink. "Marriage means having yet another person to be responsible for. I really don't see the appeal."

"You could say no." It was what she wanted, wasn't it? But why then did the bitter taste of disappointment rest on her tongue, replacing the sweet taste of the ale she sipped?

He laughed deeply and shook his head as he said in a mocking kingly tone, "Because it is the duty of the heir to pledge themselves to alliances that benefit the good of many." Back to his normal voice, he added briskly, "At least that's what my father says."

"So what is this, then? Why bring me down here?"

He shrugged. "Maybe I'm just trying to show you that there are people worth protecting in Astarfall."

"My hesitance doesn't come from not wanting to protect these people or my own. If you're right and it is the frost breathers... If they're back for vengeance, then we all need to be afraid."

His body grew taut as he leaned toward her. "Then why not say yes? Let's get the ceremony over with and see if this dragon is up for another battle."

"That's just it." Adalina leaned her head against the wall. "I never expected to have to share Elettra. When I've imagined what my perfect life might be like, it was just her and I. And it most definitely did not include a transactional marriage."

Callum laughed and stood so fast his chair fell back. Her heart skipped a beat as he held his hand out to her. "Come now. You make it sound as if we're trading goods."

She stared down at it, debating whether to take it. "Aren't we, though? A crown for a dragon?"

Callum wiggled his fingers until she slipped her hand into his. Drawing her up and into his chest, he said, "It doesn't *have* to be that way. We can make our marriage into whatever we wish it to be. You want it to be in title only? Fine. But if you want to give it a chance... give *me* a chance, then I will make an effort."

Adalina's thoughts were like a tangled ball of yarn. Was he offering her a partnership? Love? Surely, he wasn't thinking that through. He couldn't promise any of those things to her. Not yet. Not when they were little more than strangers in a tavern again.

But as he began to move to the music, guiding her body with his through the crowd of people, she felt just a tiny sliver of wonder. She tried to picture what their marriage might look like if she said yes. But before she could think any further about it, a scream tore through the night outside.

Eleven

Magic rippled through the room like a wave. It crackled and popped amongst the people inside. It took a moment for Adalina to realize it was coming from the Astarfallen. Light blazed from several hands, a storm of wind circled around Seraphine, and Callum's eyes had turned a blazing fiery gold color. She had only glimpsed his magic briefly before at the Dew Drop Inn when he lit the man's pipe. This was different. More intense. It was her first time witnessing the full power he held.

"What's happening?" she asked, thrown by the sudden change in demeanor of everyone in the room. It was shocking how quickly they had gone from bright and cheerful to alert and fierce. Like their joy was a candle that had been snuffed out.

"Stay here," Callum commanded in the same tone he'd used when they were children and he bossed her around.

He led the way for the other people in the tavern. They trickled out the door behind him. Even Alfie and Seraphine. Adalina wasn't about to sit there like an obedient pup and wait for them, so she followed. The crowd was thick, and she couldn't quite find her way out the door itself. She settled for standing at the threshold on her tippy toes to get a better look at what was going on outside.

Someone whimpered in pain, but she couldn't see them or how severe their injury was. There were a few shouts of confusion and then more screams coming from all directions in the village. But this time, one of them also came from inside the tavern. When Adalina turned around, she found several strange men scattered throughout the room. They wore black tattered robes and had veiled masks on their faces, giving them an eerie identical appearance. It also made it impossible to tell who they were or where they came from.

The sounds of a fight came from outside the tavern. The men—whoever they were—must have had the place surrounded, knowing so many of the villagers would be there on such a nice night.

Adalina's heart thudded in her chest and deep down she sensed the heat of her dragon magic. It was a small flame, begging to grow bigger, but unable to since Elettra was still sleeping in the cave. This was the first time she felt the spark when it wasn't a new moon. It distracted her and destroyed all her instincts.

It was unfortunate since one of the masked men took the opportunity to lunge and grab her. She yelped, drawing the attention of the few people still standing in the doorway. Their shouts were drowned out by the chaos outside. Adalina reared back, slamming her forehead into the man's skull. He howled and released her long enough for her to put distance between them.

Her head throbbed and white light danced in her vision.

The Astarfallen who heard her cry for help were already fending off the other strangers in the tavern. One woman raised her hands, summoning a wave of water from the sink behind the bar. It slammed into an attacker with such force that he was thrown into one of his comrades. The other Astarfallen utilized their magic with proficiency and grace, taking out each trespasser with ease.

Adalina inched into the corner. She was useless with no magic to fight with and little experience in hand-to-hand combat. She bumped into a chair and a tiny whimper came from under the table. A little girl with wild curly blonde hair was huddled beneath with tear-streaked cheeks.

"Talia," Adalina knelt and whispered to her, "stay there. Don't make a sound."

The back room was too far for her to get the girl into a safer space. It was best to keep her hidden where she was. Adalina stood but didn't move. She might not be any use in the fight, but she would be the only thing standing in the way of any attackers and the defenseless child.

The veiled assailants were fighting back the people of Astarfall now with their own magic. Fates be damned. Was Adalina the only one there without any of her own? They used strange silvery whips, slashing at the elements wielded by the Astarfallen and cutting through it like butter.

For the life of her, Adalina couldn't place the type of power or where it came from. She'd never seen anything like it. The tip of a whip cracked into a villager's shoulder, slicing through muscle and bone. Adalina shivered violently as the Astarfallen fell to the ground, screaming in agony.

The man who grabbed her before came into her line of sight. He rushed toward her with blood dripping from under his mask. She hoped she'd broken his nose. His head whipped between Adalina and the cowering child. He murmured something, sounding pleased. Fear lurched through Adalina at the prospect of what he would do to the helpless little girl. She clenched her hand into a fist, stepped forward, and swung hard. The man dodged it easily, but her fist still connected with someone's face.

She gasped as Callum rubbed at his nose, which had a bit of blood dripping from it.

He shouted indignantly, "Hey! We're on the same side."

"Shit," she yelped. "Sorry!"

The man—who had hit the ground when he ducked out of her strike—scurried away from them. Talia screamed as he grabbed her leg and pulled her into him. He held her with her arms pinned at her sides as she thrashed and wiggled, trying to escape his grasp.

Callum cooed at the man, "Now, don't you do anything stupid. You didn't come for the girl. You came for me, isn't that right?" A grin spread across his face and Adalina fought the impulse to slap it off. They should have been negotiating with the man, not goading him.

The man's eyes were barely visible through the dark veil, but the snicker he gave sent chills down Adalina's spine. She looked around desperately for some sort of weapon. Anything she could wield against him while his attention was on Callum.

The prince took a step to the side, causing the man to turn his back to Adalina. Even though the fight was still raging around them, everything seemed to slow. She grabbed the leg of a chair that had been broken in the scuffle.

Callum continued with a playful hint to his words, as if inviting the man to play a game, "Come on, admit it. That's why you came here. Someone let it slip that the Crown Prince of Astarfall would be in the village tonight. Who was it? A bribed guard? An ambitious Lord or Lady? Maybe a frightened citizen?"

The man holding Talia—who was still fighting with all her little might—gave nothing away. They wouldn't get any answers from him willingly. And every second he had the girl in his clutches put her at risk. So Adalina, gripping the splintered chair leg, swung... and missed.

But as she faltered and fell forward, she tumbled into the man. The impact knocked Talia from his arms. The man hit the corner of the table with a crack. But Adalina's concern was for the girl.

She cried out, but a gust of wind had already swept the girl up before she could hit the ground and sent her sailing into Callum's arms. Seraphine's hands glistened with the power she'd just used, and she nodded to him then turned to grab hold of a man who had Alfie by the throat.

Adalina scrambled to her feet, afraid of the man's retribution, but he wasn't moving. Blood seeped onto the floor, dripping into the rough wood's cracks. She inched closer, looking for any sign of breath. When she found none, she reached for his veil.

"Stop," Callum commanded, "let me."

He handed Talia to Delilah, who disappeared promptly through the back room with her sobbing daughter wrapped tightly in her arms. He joined Adalina on the floor. The room had quieted as most of the attackers had either been taken down or had fled by now; perhaps too tired from the fight that the Astarfallen had put up.

With bated breath, Callum lifted the veil from the man's face to reveal rough jagged scars and a mean mouth.

Adalina gulped, then asked, "Is he dead?"

"Yes. Looks like he hit his head in the fall."

"I killed him." Adalina braced herself for a rush of guilt, but none came. "I've never killed anyone before."

"I think it's safe to say you can keep a clear conscience as it was more your clumsiness that did him in." He offered her a smile, but it didn't reach his eyes, which were back to their beautiful deep blue color. They no longer shined like before. If anything, he looked exhausted, like he might collapse at any moment.

"Who were those men?" she asked.

"I don't know. But I have a feeling we'll soon find out."

He gestured to the three men on their knees outside. Their hands were bound in front of them with rope that shined like starlight. The villagers were gathered around them with slightly slouched shoulders. They were tired, too. Perhaps it was the strenuous use of their magic. Or the shock of being attacked so close to the city. Some were being tended to by the village healers. Others lay on the ground, as unmoving and limp as Talia's attacker.

Callum stood and held out his hand to help Adalina up. She took it and he pulled her close to him. So close she had to place a hand on his chest to keep any sort of distance between them. His heart pounded fiercely.

"Thank you for protecting Talia," he whispered.

"You don't owe me any thanks, Callum."

"The threat to my people—"

"Is closer and worse than I wanted to believe," she finished for him. She saw that now. And so did the people closest to the heart of Astarfall. She had a feeling that tomorrow they would all awake with a grave sense of dread. The kind that settled over a person like a wet blanket. Suffocating and stifling. King Alistair would have a hell of a time keeping them in the dark now.

"I can't say I truly believe that your dragon is the answer to all our problems. But I do know that we only survived tonight because we all stood together. And even then, our magic could only do so much. Look at them. They're drained."

Adalina glanced back at the villagers. Their pale, sullen faces etched themselves in her mind. Callum confirmed her suspicions. They were drained from using their magic to fight. Like using muscles for harder work than they were used to.

Callum, too, sounded fatigued as he said, "If this was but a *taste* of the fight to come... If our foe truly does have a monster under their control, then I am willing to do anything I can to keep my people safe."

"Even if that means marrying a self-righteous know-it-all," she tried to joke, but it fell flat.

"Yes, even that," he said huskily.

Adalina wrapped her arms around her stomach. What sort of men were these to fight the way they did? And more than that, how had they summoned a beast that could only be rivaled by a dragon? There was so much they still didn't know. It was like swatting at shadows in the dark.

She understood the king's desperation now. And she couldn't forget the frustration at being helpless in the face of danger. It was by the luck of the fates that she had stopped that man from hurting Talia. She never wanted to feel that way again.

"I will marry you, Prince Callum, but I will not give up my control or freedom in exchange. *If* the ceremony works and Elettra wakes up, I want to be the one to ride her. I will not sit helplessly on the sidelines. I want to fight, too."

"My father and his council might have a bit of a problem with that."

Looking into the frightened faces of the villagers, her resolve hardened. She and Elettra were a package deal. To sit idly by while everyone else fought to protect their homes wasn't an option. She might not be a trained warrior, but that flame in her chest had begged to be released tonight. That magic was hers and hers alone.

Meeting the prince's eyes, she said, "I don't give a shit."

Callum smiled genuinely now. "No, I didn't expect that you would."

Twelve

This time Callum did not lead Adalina to the king's study. Instead, they ventured up a winding tower that led into a spacious stone room. Its balcony gave a fuller view of the kingdom. Little clusters of villages could be seen far and wide. Even Bellonna, where the villagers were now placing fortifications around the perimeter using large pieces of lumber with barbed ends sticking out at anyone who might try to approach.

She wondered how sweet little Talia was doing. Perhaps Callum could have a gift of some sort sent down to her. Something to comfort her when the night grew dark. Part of her wanted to ask him to bring the girl and her mother to the palace. To protect them in the heart of Astarfall. But what of the other children? What they truly needed was a plan to keep them safe in their own beds.

The council was already gathered, sitting at a large round table that took up nearly the entire room. Her family sat amongst them watching her with worry plainly written on their faces. Everyone stood and bowed to Callum, and Adalina fought the urge to shrink away from the attention.

The tension Callum had been carrying since the attack melted away the moment everyone's eyes settled on them. He coolly replaced his frown once again with a relaxed half smile. One she noted didn't quite meet his eyes. Before he parted from her, he reached over and brushed his fingers against the inside of her wrist. There was a bit of reluctance in his step as he made room for Adalina's family.

Her grandmother was the first to rush to her, followed closely by her mother. The women fawned over her, checking her over for injury. She assured them, "I'm fine, truly. I'm unharmed."

Queen Gwendolyn tugged Callum by the hand. "And you, my son. Are you alright?"

Callum smiled fully now as he looked down at his mother. "I fared better than any foe I faced tonight."

Adalina gritted her teeth. They had barely gotten out of there unscathed and the same couldn't be said for several of the villagers. She knew she should keep her thoughts to herself, but she couldn't hold her tongue.

She turned to the queen and said, "Our *foe* did not come unprepared tonight. They knew what they were doing. And they wielded magic, I think."

King Alistair rose from his seat. "Astarfallen magic?"

Callum shook his head. "None that I've ever seen before."

Her grandmother took a startled step back and asked, "Did they wield ice?"

Adalina thought about the silvery whips they'd seemed to summon from nowhere. It hadn't looked like ice, though it shimmered the same as freshly fallen snow when the sun hit it just right in the early hours of the morning. If you paid enough attention, it was easy to spot a faint glimmer when the Astarfallen used their powers. However, according to her books back home, it was common amongst magic found in other parts of the world, too. Because of that, what she'd witnessed in the tavern did little to indicate what their attackers were using.

Adalina bit the inside of her cheek, wishing she could give them the answers they needed. "I don't know what it was, exactly. But they looked like whips."

Callum added with a hint of curiosity dripping in his tone. "It's possible that they were made of ice. But it was hard to tell in the chaos."

King Alistair gritted his teeth and muttered more to himself than to them, "Enchanted objects." As he met his son's eye, he asked, "Could it be that the Festiri alchemist sent them?"

Callum shrugged. "There's nothing to indicate that either of our suspicions are wrong."

Uthred spoke loudly, grabbing the room's attention. "Regardless, eight are injured. Three dead. And that is after only a small sample of what these rebels have coming our way. If they had sent more men. Or if rumors of the beast are true and they decide to bring it next time, then those numbers could be catastrophic."

King Alistair nodded. "Yes, we are aware of that." His face was drawn. But it was the only sign of exhaustion.

Adalina marveled at the extraordinary amount of effort it must take for these men to remain so calm and collected.

Callum interjected. "We will not be caught unawares again. Three have been brought in for questioning, so it won't be long before one of them spills." His mouth tugged up at the corner as he added, "Besides, after the wedding, with Elettra awakened, I doubt they will be so bold as to try something like that again."

Adalina's stomach dropped. Had he just announced their engagement? Sure, she knew it had to come out at some point, but he said it as if announcing he was going off to bake a cake. Heat prickled at her fingertips. It was similar to the sensation when her limbs fell asleep, and the feeling began to return. With a hiss, she shook them out and marched up to the table.

King Alistair's eyes lit up with elation. "That is wonderful news. We can start the preparations immediately. The sooner we act, the sooner—"

"There is one condition," Adalina interjected. "I will be the dragon's rider, not Callum."

The prince had announced their engagement but said nothing of their agreement. In her panic, the words tore from her before she thought better of it. She could tell from the indignant stares coming from the councilmen that she'd spoken out of turn.

Uthred sputtered, "In keeping with tradition, it is the husband who rides."

Calida snorted. "Is that so?"

Adalina smiled ruefully. It was no shock that her grandmother would stick up for her. She, after all, had continued to ride Elettra even after she had wed Adalina's grandfather.

Uthred turned scarlet red. "I just meant... when Astarfall and Solaris have performed the ceremony in the past, the Solarian queen has always conceded the dragon to the king."

Callum plopped into an empty chair and propped his feet carelessly on the table. He reached for Adalina's hand, and after a split second of hesitation, took it. Then he said, "The last time a Solarian became queen and bound her dragon to an Astarfallen king was many centuries ago. That was then. This is now. These are our terms."

He was standing up for her. In his own way, anyway. But that was enough.

Her stomach fluttered. Whether it was from gratitude for his words or the fact that his thumb was stroking the back of her hand, she wasn't sure. And she didn't care to dwell on it at the moment.

The rest of the council remained silent, but Uthred didn't seem satisfied yet as he said, "Lady Adalina, though I'm sure is very capable, is not trained in our ways of battle. Or any battle, for that matter. She is not a warrior."

Heely nodded eagerly. "He's right. Allowing her to join the fight would put her in danger. She's a seamstress for Heaven's sake!"

As right as they were, Adalina argued, "I'm not helpless. I simply haven't learned to fight yet."

Besides, it wasn't her fault. It was the council who had encouraged her to join as her mother's apprentice to "give her a sense of direction." And aside from her grandmother, the dragon warriors were gone. There was no need to train the women in her village in the arts of defense and war. There had never been a need for her to fight. But after tonight, she realized everything had shifted. That she no longer lived in a world of safety and comfort. Instead, they were all living in one in which young girls were in danger. Where shrouded men lurked in the darkness.

Again, she spoke, despite the heavy gaze of the council. "My grandmother can train me to battle on dragon-back. With her guidance I can—"

"And what if the dragon does not wake?" a young man with a freckle on his lip asked. "Or if she does wake and you find yourself without her nearby. Tonight, you had no dragon and look at the danger that put you in."

King Alistair ran his hand over his face, drawing it into a deeper frown. "He is right. We cannot risk it. Once married, you will be Princess of Astarfall. In line to take the throne beside my son. If anything were to happen to you, it would be a blow to us all. Our enemies will see you as a target. An easy way to strike terror at the heart of this kingdom."

His words, though said without any animosity, stung. It reminded her that as Callum's wife, she would be nothing more than a possession of the crown. Like an expensive vase they intended to safeguard and pull out, only to show off to the people when it suited them.

To her surprise, it was Alfie who raised his hand to speak. "If it weren't for Lady Adalina, a village girl would be dead, or worse."

Callum rubbed his nose and said under his breath, "And my face wouldn't still be throbbing."

Adalina squeezed his hand as tight as she could, making him squirm and drop his feet back down to the floor. He released his hold on her and stood, smoothing out his shirt as everyone's attention snapped to him.

"I will teach her how to defend herself on the ground. If we want the chance at having a dragon in our ranks, then there is simply no other choice. Those are her terms and I have already accepted," he ended with a shrug.

The council murmured in discord. One elderly man stood. He wavered a bit and the younger man beside him reached out to help, but the man shouted, "Get off me, you dolt!"

The young man shrank back in his seat, looking like a scolded child.

With more strength than Adalina expected from the frail older man, he said, "The attack tonight was too close to home. These men grow bolder with each passing day. We do not have much time to argue about the girl if we hope to meet this challenge head on. That is why I motion the prince readies the future princess for ground battle. And should the dragon wake, Warrior Calida will train her on dragon-back. But this needs to come with the caveat that if at any time it becomes clear the girl is not up to the task, the dragon will default to her husband."

It was a fair offer, but she couldn't help feeling like they were setting her up to fail. One wrong misstep and Callum could take the dragon from her. What was supposed to be a victory for her had turned into a noose hanging just above her head.

It felt as if a fever was coming on. She wiped her clammy hands on the skirt of her airy gown, which was still torn and dirty from the altercation in the tavern. King Alistair called it to a vote. With each "aye" in favor of the proposition, her heart sank lower.

She desperately wanted to believe that she could become a warrior both in the air and on the ground. But when she glanced at Callum's bruised nose, the prospect seemed about as likely as her waking Elettra on her own.

Thirteen

A porcelain plate floated in midair gently past Adalina's head. Actually, an entire dish set was currently meandering through the ballroom at the moment. She did her best to slip out of the way of the palace staff as they prepared for the post marital celebrations that would take place later that night. It was fairly easy to do since the ballroom opened up to the courtyard. It was an extravagant space with enough room to fit all the higher-ranking citizens of Solaris. Many of whom were coming in for the main event.

Heely fluttered around like an energetic hummingbird greeting them merrily and introducing them to all his new friends in the Astarfall court. Adalina passed by him and rolled her eyes at his exaggerated claims to have helped make the marriage happen. He'd done nothing but kiss any courtier's butt who would let him get close enough. She did have to give him credit, though. He had certainly made himself quite at home in the palace.

She, however, still struggled with that concept. She stepped outside and welcomed the sunshine on her face. It was easier to breathe out there where the walls didn't feel as if they were closing in on her.

Distracted with apprehension, she nearly crashed right into a woman arranging rosebuds in a floating vase. The beautiful piece plummeted to the ground, but a wind-wielder swept it back up just before it could crash to the floor.

"I'm so sorry!" Adalina exclaimed to both the woman and the wind-wielder.

They assured her that there was no harm done, but the heat of embarrassment was already blooming. Adalina hurried out of their way and steered close to the edge of the courtyard. A twinge of jealousy made her frown as she watched the Astarfall workers use their birth-given magic to do the most mundane of tasks. Water-wielders spun drinks in massive serving bowls, adding in a dash of mint and rosemary each time they tested a sip. Behind them, Astarfallen who were blessed with the ability to manipulate land and rock, worked together on a statue.

Adalina squinted to get a better view of the image they were manipulating out of the smooth, glittering white stone. It didn't take more than a glance to make out Callum's handsome smile. They'd included every detail, even the way the taut muscles showed in his arms when he was clenching his fists or holding tight to something.

She sucked in a sharp breath, realizing what this statue version of him was holding on to. They'd accomplished the soft curves of her body's shape just right. Statue Callum's hand clung to her waist while the other reached under her chin, tilting her smiling face up to him. Statue Adalina looked very much in love with the man whose eyes she was staring into.

The real Adalina scoffed. It seemed the sculptors had taken creative control to show anyone who stared upon their masterpiece just how in love the couple was. Was this a vision of what her life would become? Or was it a mirage? A dream just out of reach. Because at the end of the day she would not be marrying for starry-eyed love.

Callum may have offered to give their union a genuine chance, but that didn't mean she was ready to take him up on it. After the council meeting—where they had openly voiced their doubt about her—it was clear she needed to protect herself. Her position at court wasn't strong. She would soon be a foreign princess with few allies. Even Seraphine, who had become fast friends with her, was Callum's cousin—his flesh and blood.

It was hitting her that this was her new home. She'd hardly had the time to get used to the idea of being married to a man she barely knew, but now she realized that this palace would be hers one day. That as the Crown Princess, she wouldn't be returning to Solaris with the rest of her family after the ceremony. She hadn't even had the chance to say goodbye to the rolling hills or the sparkling creek where she spent most of her time reading. Or to the cave she so often visited.

Adalina's grandfather caught her eye from the other side of the courtyard. He waved at her with a broad smile. She offered one back, but the sight of him only drew her into further melancholy. She couldn't imagine that her grandmother had felt this way on her own wedding day. What would it have been like to be a bride without doubts? To know with her whole heart that she was going to share a happy life with a man she loved.

Her impending marriage to Callum was nothing more than a treaty between their kingdoms. Astarfall's magic and sizable army, combined with Solaris' dragon and endurance all tied together in two ceremonial ribbons. Ribbons that would be placed around Adalina and Callum's hands in just a few short hours. Her shackles.

"There you are!" Seraphine waltzed on air in a dress that, at first glance, Adalina could have sworn was made from sea bubbles. Behind her, several young women shuffled and giggled. Each of them wore some variation of the dress Seraphine had on.

Adalina gave the women an awkward wave. "I've been here the whole time."

Breathlessly, Seraphine said, "We expected you down at the picnic an hour ago."

"Picnic?" Adalina palmed her head. She'd forgotten all about the bridal brunch the queen had planned for her. Typically, royal weddings in Astarfall consisted of a few *weeks'* worth of festivities. Adalina's, however, was being expedited due to the circumstances. The villagers from Bellonna were still recovering from the attack. Two more had succumbed to their injuries in the night.

It made the entire day seem frivolous, though Adalina suspected King Alistair was putting on a show for his people's morale. After all, who didn't love a wedding? Adalina being the exception, of course.

"Never mind that." Seraphine clasped her hands together. "We're here to see to it that the bride has everything her heart desires today."

What Adalina desired was a cave to hide in. But she supposed she'd take the next best thing. "How about a glass of that fruity summer ale?" She smiled widely.

"Yes!" squealed Seraphine. She turned to one of the women and whispered commands before turning back to Adalina. "Now, let's get you inside."

The women flanked Adalina as they led her back into the palace and into a sunny room on the first floor near the ballroom. It was adorned with bouquets of coastal flowers. The perfume of pink sea thrift, purple hydrangeas, and bright roses tickled her nose. By the window, a gorgeous vanity awaited her with a mirror that rivaled the size of the one in her mother's shop back home.

As she sat, fire pricked at her fingertips. It had been happening since she woke up that morning. Actually, since the attack. But her dragon gifted magic had never presented itself this time of the month. Part of her wondered if far north, deep in her slumber, Elettra sensed what was to come that night. If some deep-seated connection told the dragon that soon Adalina and the magic of Astarfall would be calling on her. Demanding that she leave the comforts of her cave for yet another battle.

Seraphine began poking and prodding at Adalina, but she didn't mind. It kept her grounded in the present and soon there was a cool summer ale resting in her hand. The women fluttered to and fro, fixing each other's hair or rearranging their dresses. Finger sandwiches were brought to them, along with silver trays of fruit. Despite the nerves twisting like a pit of snakes in her stomach, Adalina forced herself to eat a few things off the plate someone brought her. If she didn't, she risked stumbling down the aisle drunk.

"Did you see Uthred?" One of the girls hiccupped, nearly spilling her drink on the marble floor.

"Marianne! He's old enough to be your father," another one chided.

Adalina perked up, emboldened by the ale and the promise of gossip. She'd grown up in a quiet village and hadn't cared much for whispers about who had cheated the other on their price of grain or who the farmer's daughter was bedding. But what *those* people did never had much effect on her. However, as a newcomer in Astarfall, secrets and idle talk might help her navigate her way through her new life at court. The lack of allies was something she *could* change. But first, she needed to know more about the people she was surrounding herself with.

Seraphine pinned Adalina's hair back and placed a hair piece on her head. It was made of tiny pearls and dried starfish the color of the sky at sunset. It was beautiful but gave her a sinking feeling as she imagined the crown that would soon sit in its place.

The tipsy girl, Marianne, swatted in the air. "He is not. He's not even forty yet. I ran into him this morning in that cream suit of his and let me just tell you the things I would do—"

"Please," drawled the other woman, "no need to tell us the sordid details. Besides, he's married. And not only is she brilliantly clever, she's also stunning." The woman turned to Adalina with wide eyes. "Wait until you see her."

Marianne chuckled and pointed her drink in Adalina's direction. "Actually, that Councilman Heely of yours isn't hard on the eyes either."

Adalina cringed. Heely was a petite man who tried to make up for his size in political stature. Not that he was a bad man. Just not Adalina's cup of tea.

The women broke out into laughter, even Adalina. They spent the better part of the hour gossiping about eligible men at court and which of the groom's friends they planned on dancing with that night. Each woman was lovely in her own way. None of them stuck their noses up at Adalina as she listened silently to them. Being new to court, each woman vowed to help her get comfortable there. She wasn't sure she could call them allies or friends yet, but it was a start.

The youngest girl in the group batted dark lashes at her and said, "You are so lucky. What a dream to marry and love a prince! The two of you will be so happy together."

The women erupted into excited chatter.

Adalina lost track of what they were saying. Love? She didn't have the heart to ruin their fun by telling them that she wasn't sure love was in the cards for her and her husband to be. Her stomach knotted itself tightly, like the end of a thread. She clenched her hands together, trying to hide the slight tremble that was creeping in.

The doubt must have been obvious on her face because Seraphine leaned in close to whisper. "Are you alright?"

"Yes," she answered quickly. "I was just—"

The door swung open, revealing her mother and grandmother. The two women rushed to her, kissing her cheeks, and spouting out greetings and well wishes. Seraphine and the others stood, dipping into slight curtsies, and excused themselves from the room.

Alone with the women who had raised her, tears filled Adalina's eyes.

Her mother beamed as she held out a garment bag. "My love, this is yours."

Adalina tugged at the blue satin ribbon, and the bag opened to reveal a stunning white dress. It was scalloped at the top, angling down into a v on the bodice. There were slits at the side that would reveal a bit of her skin, but in a way that wasn't wholly immodest. The skirt flowed down, littered with tiny seashells and pearls. It looked like something Adalina imagined a mermaid would wear if she had come to land to marry her true love. Like something from the storybooks that she loved to read so much.

But this dress belonged to *her*. This was no fairytale. It was her life. Her fate. To trade a life of passion and fulfillment for the slightest chance at a dragon. One that she may never get to ride herself if the council had it their way. She stepped away from the dress, unable to touch it. "It's so..."

"Astarfallen," her grandmother said flatly. "I agree. That is why your mother stayed up late, making you this."

She gestured to another garment bag in her mother's arms. When they opened it, Adalina gasped. It was a wrap for her shoulders. Sheer fabric held it together so it could be easily attached to Adalina's wedding dress. The sleeves would leave her arms bare—a good thing considering the warmth—and flowed down to the hem of the dress. And embroidered on it was fire. Delicate flames licked down the fabric in an elegant design.

"I know you're afraid," her mother said, "but we are here, and we will not let you forget where you came from. I know your father and I haven't always been supportive of your dreams of waking Elettra, but we are here with you now and we stand by you until the end."

The tears began flowing now like an unstoppable flood. Adalina embraced her mother and soon her grandmother joined them. When they pulled away from each other, her grandmother stared at her intently.

"What's wrong, Lina? Talk to us."

It was like a flood gate opened with the question. Words spilled out of Adalina quickly. "I'm afraid." A sob threatened to escape, and she stifled it with the back of her hand.

Her grandmother stroked her hair gently, like she had when Adalina was a young girl.

Adalina took her time before explaining, "When Callum and I agreed to the engagement, he said that he would try to have a relationship if I wanted it. But even if I want to give Callum a chance, it isn't a wise choice. The way he approaches things is far too different from me. And he might have stood up for me last night, but that doesn't mean he will do it again. Especially if he comes to believe that taking Elettra will benefit him and his people."

Her mother handed her a tissue and Adalina wiped the tears away before continuing, "I'm handing him so much power already. I have to protect myself. I have to keep him at arm's length. I don't have the luxury of developing anything more with him."

"When all of this is over, you may feel differently about that." Her grandmother's voice was hopeful, but Adalina couldn't cling to that sort of hope. She needed to be realistic.

"And if he decides I'm not ready to fight? If he takes Elettra?"

"These are things we cannot control at this moment. No matter how hard you try. All you can do is face the challenge in front of you."

Adalina nodded softly. The tears had stopped flowing, and she spotted people taking their seats outside in the courtyard.

Taking on her familiar stern tone, her grandmother said, "Time to get you into this gown. Or else Heely and Uthred will come looking for us and I'd hate to have to give them both a walloping on such a sacred occasion."

It didn't take long to get the gown on. The fabric was thin; in line with typical Astarfall fashion and soon Adalina looked every bit the bride that she was. With teary eyes, her mother and grandmother led the way out of the room and down the corridor. The women chatted in front of her, lost in their own little world.

Suddenly, someone reached from a doorway and pulled her in. Her yelp was cut short when she realized it was Callum. He was shirtless and his pants clung low on his hips. Adalina's pulse raced as her gaze trailed down to his navel.

"I didn't mean to frighten you." The mischievous glint in his eyes said otherwise. Before she could get a word in, he added, "I heard your family in the hall and thought you might be with them. And, well, I couldn't resist getting a look at you." His voice was free of tension, which was a bit on the irritating side since her tears had barely dried and she'd spent so much of the day worrying.

At her silence, the mischief in his eyes faded, and they became wide and searching. They flitted from her hair and down to the dress. His mouth hung open as if to say more, but for the first time since meeting him, it appeared he was speechless.

She shook off the butterflies fluttering around in her stomach and said, "Well, you've gotten your look at me. Now, is there a more pressing reason you accosted me when I was on my way to walk down the aisle?"

"I just wanted to make sure you were..."

"Coming? Not abandoning you at the altar. I had half a mind to, but I already had a dress, so..." She smirked, but he didn't return the gesture. For the first time, she noted soft worry lines on his forehead. So, more seriously, she said, "I'm fine, Callum. I'm willing to do this if it will help our people. And I'm choosing to put my faith in you."

"I meant what I said. I will help you train like the council wants." He gestured to his nose. "I think our first order of business will be working on that aim."

Adalina blushed. "Sorry for punching you."

"I do think you made it a bit crooked." This time, he offered a goofy, lopsided smile. "I suppose it was a bit too perfect, anyway. It has more character now."

Despite the turmoil still resting on the surface of her thoughts, she snorted. "It's not crooked."

"So, you *do* think it's perfect." He grinned.

But this time it didn't get under her skin. Instead, it sent goosebumps along her arms and neck. Fates be damned. There was just something about him that made her ignore all sense.

"I think we're going to be late to our own wedding if we don't get out there soon." She needed to put space between them before her wanting body made her do something she shouldn't.

She ducked out of the room, unsure how to feel. It was kind of him to consider how she might be feeling, but maybe he'd simply been worried she would back out of their deal. It was difficult to tell with him, considering they were still, by all accounts, strangers to one another. And he didn't truly owe her anything.

Fourteen

Adalina's father and grandfather lingered at the edge of the ballroom, where it opened to the courtyard. Beyond the finished statue of her and Callum stood the entrance to the garden path that would lead her to the marriage altar. Both men smiled warmly at her in greeting.

Her grandfather whistled. "I always hoped I'd live to see you in your wedding dress. Granted, I thought we would be spending this moment on the hills of Solaris, but you look so..." He choked up and paused, then cleared his throat before continuing, "You look like you were always meant to be here."

Her father offered an arm to her, and she took it. When he whispered to her, his voice was rough. "I know I've been hard on you, Lina. But I only ever wanted the best for you. You say the word and we can head straight back to that carriage."

It was such a heartwarming thing for him to say that she glanced up at him in surprise. His opening up like that was the best wedding gift he could give her. Perhaps she'd spent so long fighting the grip he had on her life that she had often failed to see the tender love he had for her. It also made her wonder if she should be careful of misjudging others, too… like the man she was about to face.

Her grandfather took her free hand and looped it through his arm. "Give me a signal and I'll push that little snot right off this cliff."

Adalina chuckled. "I appreciate the sentiment, but I do believe King Alistair would arrest us if we murdered his son right before his very eyes. And I wouldn't want to ruin my dress in the dungeons."

Both men nodded, but there was no more laughter as they came to the path's opening. Ahead, hundreds of people sat in neat little rows. Some who hadn't gotten there in time stood on the outskirts, craning their necks to get a good look at the soon to be Princess of Astarfall.

The women from earlier waited at the side of the altar with modest bouquets of flowers. Seraphine slipped Adalina a small wave, causing a few of the petals on her bouquet to fall to the ground.

Callum stood at the head of them all. His hair was windblown, and the setting sun made his eyes sparkle darkly like the sea behind him. With his hands folded in front of him, he appeared strong, confident, and regal. At this moment, Adalina was able to look past the boy he once was. She was awestruck by the sight of him. He looked like a king already; born and bred for this. For commanding armies… For marrying a stranger in order to save his people.

It should have added to her nerves, but it did the opposite. It settled the storm in the pit of her stomach to find him waiting for her, stoic, and patient. Love between them might have been absent from the day. But seeing this side of him gave her the courage to continue.

Adalina drew in a deep breath. When Callum laid eyes on her, his lips parted slightly. She squared her shoulders and took strength from her family walking beside her. Under the canopy, her husband to be adjusted his shirt and tugged at the collar. She held his steady gaze, placing one foot in front of the other as she braved her walk down the aisle. By the time she reached him, he had fidgeted so much with his collar that two of the buttons had popped off.

She leaned in and whispered jokingly, "Don't worry, I know how to fix that."

Waves crashed below the cliff relentlessly and for a moment she thought perhaps he hadn't heard her. The laugh he gave in response came out as more of a choke. This was a different Callum than she'd become familiar with. One who didn't wear a practiced mask of good humor. Now that they were at the altar, it appeared he couldn't hide his nerves any better than she could.

He was more akin to the man he'd been the morning after their night together at the Dew Drop Inn. When he hadn't put on his facade and instead had told her of his dreams while they were tangled in the sheets. If only they could go back to pretending that she was a mere wedding guest, and he was a dockworker. Then maybe there would be a chance for love. And maybe she wouldn't feel like the very earth beneath their feet was about to shift, plunging them into the unforgiving sea below.

A hush fell over the crowd. The only sound was the sea beating the rocks like a drummer keeping rhythm. King Alistair stepped forward to preside over them, as was his right as Astarfall's monarch. But it was Callum who lit the torches on either side of them.

With hands raised to the sky, he mumbled something. Adalina leaned closer to listen. At first, it sounded more like a plea than a command. In response, stars glittered so brightly in the sky that they outshined the setting sun. And with a flick of Callum's wrists, the torches blazed to life in a dance, reaching up for the evening sky.

Adalina's mother and grandmother approached. They knelt in front of each torch, setting trinkets on the ground around them. Offerings from home. A locket forged by a Solaris jeweler. Stones from the river at the bottom of the hill. Gems that had been found littered in the rich soil of their home. They set each offering down with reverence.

Adalina watched in fascination. Callum, too, seemed enthralled by the ceremonial gesture. This was the first wedding of its kind that anyone there had witnessed. A magical binding and marital ceremony which were being performed as one and the same.

When they finished, her grandmother joined King Alistair and said, "With these gifts, we honor the Great Bonding between man and dragon. A gift for a gift."

While each step brought Adalina closer to the possibility of waking Elettra, she couldn't help thinking about how Callum would be able to use this same ritual one day to claim the dragon for himself. She winced, drawing a concerned furrow from Callum. She tried to relax her face so he wouldn't see her doubt about him rise to the surface when they were in the middle of what was meant to be one of the greatest days of their lives.

Adalina's breath caught in her throat as the sky darkened so suddenly it felt like a blanket had been thrown over them. Even the crowd gasped at the sudden shift that could only be a result of the vast power that was colliding.

Calida gestured to the torches. "Light to replace the darkness."

The fire blazed brighter in response to her words. Even though Adalina had said the words herself many times, something buzzed in her chest. Excitement, nerves, or something more, she wasn't sure.

It was King Alistair's turn to speak. "We gather here for the great binding. To bring together Prince Callum of Astarfall and Lady Adalina of Solaris. In their union, we ask that the heavens bestow upon them the gifts of our ancestors. We beseech the fates to join the power of the dragon to the magic of the heavens."

He drew a blade from his belt and reached for his son's hand. Adalina held her breath, expecting him to cut into the flesh, but instead he handed the steel to him. Callum, who seemed to already know what to expect, held his other hand out to Adalina.

With a quick glance at her grandmother, who gave her a subtle nod, she placed her hand in his. He pressed the sharpened blade into her palm, and she hissed as blood rose to the surface. Then he handed the knife to her and held his hand out so she could do the same to him.

Her grandmother gestured to the two of them, sending them in opposite directions so they could hold their hands over the torches.

As their blood fed the fire, Calida proclaimed, "Blood for blood. May these offerings honor the strength and connection we share."

The fire roared and Adalina leapt back with her arms over her face to shield her from the flame's wrath. Callum caught her from behind. When she turned toward him, he took her hands in his and clung to them. King Alistair took two ribbons from a small table and began to wrap them around their hands and wrists. The final binding. The one that would declare their hearts and souls to one another.

Callum's fingers found the soft spot on her wrists and caressed. Adalina focused on that touch to keep her rising panic at bay. This was it. After this, they would be husband and wife. Because of the ritual, they would be more than that. Which was even scarier. Already, the cool rush of Callum's power was wrapping around her hands and arms. It seeped into her skin, making her veins glow for a brief moment before settling into her own magic.

The only thing keeping her from running far away from all of them was knowing that in this exact moment, he was simply *lending* his power to hers. Tending to the flame of her magic. This did not bind him to Elettra. Not unless he decided to perform the ritual himself. But this act opened that doorway to him, whether she liked it or not. She took a trembling breath.

King Alistair boasted, "Even in death, you shall not be separated, for a piece of your soul will always belong to the other. Today, Solaris and Astarfall come together in a most ancient tradition. Let what is bound never be broken."

Adalina swore every single person there—Solarian and Astarfallen alike—held their breath. Even she didn't dare move as she waited for a sign that it had worked. She'd prepared herself to feel the heat of her magic flood her chest. Or for the feeling of lightning in her veins that might let her know that Elettra had awoken.

But in truth, all they could do was wait. If the ceremony worked, it would take time for Elettra to follow the pull to Adalina. The one that told the dragon where her bonded was waiting. Since the attack in the tavern, Adalina's power had been erratic; coming in random spurts in the form of tingling. At that moment, she could sense the familiar warm ebb of the magic inherited from her grandmother. But it was difficult to tell if it was because of Elettra's awakening or if it was from Callum's power which had caressed her own.

He cleared his throat and leaned in with wicked amusement. "I believe now we seal it with a kiss."

"Oh," Adalina said lamely. She'd been frozen, too consumed with thoughts of Elettra to realize they still needed to end the marital portion of the ceremony. A fresh wave of embarrassment washed over her.

With their hands still bound by the ribbons, she stood on her tippy toes to meet Callum's lips. The moment they joined in the kiss, the ground beneath their feet gave a fierce rumble. It shook the foundation of the cliff, earning frightened gasps from the people closest to the edge. Adalina's heart leapt into her throat and then, as quickly as it began, everything went still again.

Adalina had to hand it to King Alistair; he could throw one hell of a party. Although the quake had shaken the wedding guests' nerves as much as it had shaken the chairs beneath their butts, they didn't show it now. They danced, ate, drank, and celebrated as if it was their last chance to do so. In truth, no one was sure yet if there was anything to celebrate. Only time would tell if it all had been for nothing. And it seemed they were all content to do so with glasses brimming with stronger stuff than ale.

Adalina, however, couldn't lose herself to the same distractions. Instead, she wandered the courtyard, desperately feeling for any sort of indication that Elettra was on her way. The hope that had filled her as the ground quaked with the end of their ceremony had deflated by now. But her grandmother assured her that if it *had* indeed been a success, then the dragon would be drawn to Adalina, just as Adalina had been drawn to the caves each month.

She trailed her fingers along the table that was piled high with cakes, tarts, and trickling fountains of seaside punch. A dozen golden candelabras held sky blue candlesticks. She hovered a finger over one of the flickering flames. It licked at her skin—hot, but not unbearable. The sensation was similar to what she'd experienced earlier that day. It was like her magic, which was just out of reach.

Each time someone looked in her direction, she took a page out of Callum's book and offered them a confident smile. There was no need to let them see how uncertain she was. Not until they knew for certain if the rites had worked.

Several performers wove their way through the crowd. One balanced orbs of water in their hands, turning and spinning them around their wrists only for them to settle into their palms once more. Another took a flaming sword and plunged it expertly into his mouth and down his throat. People watched awestruck and cheered wildly when he removed the flame without injury.

A few guests near the table filled their drinks and said cheers, but when their eyes flitted to Adalina, she caught the uncertainty and fear in them. Despite her best efforts to exude confidence, wherever she went, a fog of foreboding seemed to follow, making those nearest to her seem uneasy.

Uthred stepped into her path. He actually was a handsome man now that she was seeing him a bit more disheveled. There was no gorgeous woman attached to his arm, though, and she wondered where his fabled wife was.

A bit too casually, he said, "A shame it didn't work."

"Oh?" Adalina furrowed her brow. After the ceremony, everyone seemed to be avoiding saying anything to her about Elettra's absence. She supposed they didn't want to approach the subject and make her uncomfortable. If Elettra didn't wake, then the wedding had been in vain.

Uthred nodded. "Perhaps it's for the best. We could not hope that one dragon could protect a kingdom as large as this one." His breath was heavy with hops. It seemed he'd been enjoying himself quite a bit. Which was surprising for a man as composed as him. He winked. "Though it would have been a sight to see."

Fiery prickles ran up Adalina's spine. Who was he to say Elettra wouldn't be up to the task? Or that the ceremony hadn't worked. She sniffed. "The night isn't over yet. There's still hope."

They were a long way from Solaris. Maybe the quake had been a sign and Elettra was just taking a while to get there. She had been sleeping for a long time... Maybe she needed to stretch her wings first. Or maybe, Adalina was kidding herself. Ignoring whatever response Uthred was giving her, she turned and stared up at the sky.

"Enjoying the view?" Callum had replaced Uthred beside her. He was squinting upward.

"Enjoying the festivities?" she countered with an amused smile, and nodded to the flute in his hand which was filled to the brim with something bubbly and pink.

Callum chuckled. His golden skin was ruddy from drinking and there was a slight sway in his step. "We're celebrating."

Adalina crossed her arms. "There is nothing to celebrate yet."

He put a hand over his heart as if she'd broken it. "Is our union not cause enough?"

She narrowed her eyes. "How will you feel if it turns out that my hand comes without a dowry?"

"I will take comfort in the fact that my *wife* is quite impressive in bed," he purred.

With a shake of her head, she turned to search the crowd for Seraphine. If she was going to be forced to spend the night waiting anxiously, then she'd much rather spend it with the only real friend she seemed to have at court so far.

Callum grabbed her arm and pulled her into him. Her body responded immediately to his with heat blossoming between her legs.

His breath was hot against her ear as he whispered, "Do not despair, dear wife. I believe your dowry is not lost to us, after all."

"Wha—"

Callum pointed north just as cries of joy and surprise rang out in the crowd. The clear night sky allowed a vivid view of a massive, winged creature flying gracefully in their direction. As she neared, Adalina glimpsed glistening scales the color of gemstones native to Solaris. Deep reddish-purple like amethysts and sapphire blue. They shined like shooting stars. Her wings seemed to blot out the moon, leaving only the floating lanterns and stars to give them light.

Elation had Adalina feeling like she might float away. Elettra was there. It had worked. Tears welled in her eyes, and she nearly forgot to breathe. Her knees buckled, and she was grateful for Callum's firm hold on her. She leaned into him, and warm tears streamed down her face. Normally, she wouldn't have wanted him to see her in such a state—afraid he might view it as weakness—but nothing else mattered at this moment. The fire in her heart grew, spreading through her body all the way to the tips of her toes. Callum hissed and withdrew his hands from her as if he'd touched fire. Adalina stared down at her skin, which showed no sign of burn or injury, then back up at the approaching dragon. Elettra was awake. And so was Adalina's magic.

Fifteen

The crowd melted away from Adalina's thoughts like steel armor in a ravenous fire. All that existed in her world was the dragon hovering before her eyes. Wisps of her hair whipped her in the face with the final beats of Elettra's wings as she landed on solid ground with a thud.

Elettra was grand in size. The top of Adalina's head reached the lowest part of her shoulder. She sucked in a sharp breath when the dragon met her eye. They were emerald, bright and alert, and there was a flicker of recognition in them. The scaly creature tilted her head to the side as if assessing Adalina and her worthiness. Elettra's face was lean, her neck and torso all muscle, and covered in shimmering scales. The horns on the top of her head were as long as Adalina's forearms, and twisted gracefully upward.

It was daunting to stand before her now, and Adalina tried to square her shoulders. Anything to look more competent in the face of such greatness. What would Elettra think of her when she realized her rider was an inexperienced klutz of a woman?

There wasn't a murmur to be heard in the crowd. The wedding party was too awestruck and terrified of the creature whom they had only ever heard tales about. A beast long lost to their world, save for a few of the elders, like her grandmother, who had lived through their glory.

Adalina gasped. Her grandmother. She whipped her head around in search of her. But the older woman was already there, standing a few feet to the side with tear-filled eyes. Elettra, as if following Adalina's movements, turned to her as well. Her grandmother bowed to the dragon and placed a hand over her heart. In turn, Elettra lowered her massive frame to the ground, bowing deeply in a show of respect.

Her grandmother's voice rang strong as she said, "Hello, old friend. Good of you to come."

Something like laughter danced in the dragon's gaze before she returned it to Adalina. Elettra took a step forward, rocking the silverware and dining sets on the tables. When she paused, Adalina lost her nerve. She'd waited her entire life for this moment, but now that it was here, she couldn't bring herself to move. What if she wasn't worthy of Elettra and her loyalty? What if she was in over her head, just as the council suspected?

Her grandmother gingerly pushed her forward. "It's okay, dear. This is your moment."

Adalina took a shaky step forward and mimicked the bow she had just seen her grandmother give the dragon. Her mouth was dry, and her lips cracked as she offered the ancient creature a small smile.

"I am honored that you answered our call."

When she was young, there had been many nights under the waning moon when her grandmother would speak of the first Great Bonding between man and dragon.

Her grandmother would whisper in reverence, *"The first encounter was by chance when he stumbled upon the injured beast. For many weeks, the man tended to the dragon's wounds. Before leaving the sleeping beast, he would leave an offering—a sign that he had been there should the dragon wake when he was gone. And then, on the night of the new moon, the dragon woke. He breathed magic into the man—a gift to repay his kindness and the offerings shared. No one could have imagined what that act could have meant. In that moment, the honored dragon had solidified the bond that had grown between them in those weeks."*

"No longer were the people of Solaris powerless," Adalina whispered the end of that story now as she pulled the shawl her mother made off her shoulders. "For the Great Bonding had granted man and dragon a connection that would extend through generations."

Taking another step forward, this time more sure of herself, she placed it at the dragon's feet.

Without hesitation, Elettra eagerly swiped the delicate fabric into her clawed hand. Clinging to it, she bowed deeply and released a low rumble. It resembled a cat purring and caught Adalina off guard with the gentleness of it.

Simultaneously, the crowd finally seemed to take a full breath. There were a few whispers, and the tension dissipated. Still, Elettra's attention never left her. Although the dragon's face was smooth and nearly unmoving, Adalina could sense something like curiosity there.

The moment was everything she had dreamed of and more. But something in Elettra's mood shifted, and she swatted once at the ground, leaving claw marks behind in the earth. Adalina gasped as angry heat bloomed in her chest. She furrowed her brow, confused, because there was nothing for her to be upset about. Elettra had come. And she recognized Adalina for who she was—for the bond they shared. So why was Adalina breaking out in a sweat and getting the urge to knock something over?

Callum came into her peripheral at that moment. He carried himself like the royalty he was. If there was any carnal fear in the presence of the dragon, he didn't show it. Elettra snorted and a puff of steam formed in the air. The prince had the good sense to stop in his tracks.

Sensing she needed to intervene, Adalina said, "Elettra, this is Prince Callum of Astarfall. My... husband," she hesitated, the word tasting strange on her tongue. "It was through our binding that my call was strong enough to wake you."

Elettra narrowed her eyes at Adalina as if to say, *I already know that, silly girl.*

Even so, the dragon dipped her head in a quick, shallow bow. Adalina had the faintest sense of irritation—an emotion she guessed by now, belonged to the dragon—at having to do so. Getting hints of what Elettra was feeling was an interesting development, to say the least. Summoning the fiery magic at will rather than waiting for it to ravage her once a month was to be expected. But to share the very nerves of the ancient beast was a shock. Something she couldn't have prepared herself for.

Right now, the more pressing matter was making sure Elettra didn't roast Callum like a pig on a spit. He had paled exponentially in the few moments that had passed and the king's guard gripped the hilts of their swords a little too tightly for Adalina's liking. If they dared to draw on Elettra, Adalina wouldn't hesitate to stand in their way.

It was Callum who said with the most commanding tone she'd ever heard him use, "Hands off those weapons. Now."

Adalina smirked as they immediately followed his order. But Elettra appeared to still be sizing him up, her head bobbing ever so slightly from side to side like a cobra preparing to pounce.

"Callum," Adalina said softly, "maybe we should give her some space."

She nodded to the crowd. It had to be overwhelming for Elettra to have spent so long slumbering in her isolated cave, only to awake and find an entire kingdom waiting for her. Not to mention the burden they were about to place on her...

"Perhaps you're right." He smiled stiffly and adjusted the jacket he'd put on when she wasn't looking. He waved a hand at the guards. "See the wedding guests out."

With a click of their heels, they did as he bid. Aside from Callum, only King Alistair and Adalina's grandmother remained. They watched carefully, as if they were chaperones. Elettra looked the king up and down thoughtfully. Then, seeming to decide he, like his son, was no threat, she turned her attention back to the shawl in her clawed grip. She sniffed at it and rumbled happily again. Pride swelled in Adalina's chest. It appeared she liked the gift.

"Perhaps a ride?" King Alistair suggested.

Callum shot a concerned look at Adalina and gulped. "I-I don't know about that. She did just travel all the way here, after all. Perhaps it would be best if we fetched her some dinner and—"

Elettra flopped onto her belly and extended a wing towards Adalina. It was an invitation. And judging by the glare the dragon was giving Callum, it was one that was not meant for him. Again, Adalina found herself delighted. The binding granted power to her husband, but it seemed the dragon still had a say. Even if Callum backed out of their deal, or if they didn't complete Adalina's training to the council's liking, then maybe Elettra would choose to give her loyalty to Adalina alone. It was a small hope she clung to tightly, determined not to let anything ruin this for her.

"I, er..." Callum scratched at his collar and Adalina had to suppress a grin. It was amusing to see him rattled. "I'll see to the food. You go ride."

Now *that* surprised Adalina nearly as much as Elettra's appearance. It was their wedding night. And although these were a special set of circumstances, they would still be expected by the council and the whole of the kingdom to consummate the marriage. A dragon did not negate the fact that Astarfall would eventually need an heir.

That thought sparked a blush in her cheeks. Memories of the other night—tangled in the sheets with Callum claiming her as his own—made her clench her legs to stop the heat from spreading. She wasn't sure she was ready to repeat that night just yet. It would come with strings attached, now. They weren't two people playing at being like everyone else. They were married. They were royalty. The idea would take some time to get used to. Besides, she had dreamed of this moment for so long. There was nothing in the world she wanted to do more than to climb onto that dragon's back.

Her grandmother chuckled. "Well, go on. What are you waiting for, girl?"

"Don't you want more time with her?" Adalina couldn't imagine what her grandmother must be feeling seeing Elettra after all these years.

"This is your moment, Lina. It is time for you to take the torch from me." Her grandmother steered her toward Elettra and kissed Adalina firmly on the cheek. "Go on, my love."

Wordlessly, Adalina sidled up to the dragon. Elettra rolled to the side slightly, letting her access the softly curved spikes on her neck. They were spaced wide and evenly, but when Adalina attempted to grab them, her grip slipped, and she yelped as she began to fall. Her butt slammed into something hard, and she looked down to find that Elettra had caught her with her tail. The dragon lifted her up to her back as if she was as light as a feather.

Adalina shifted from Elettra's tail and onto a soft curve in her spine which allowed her to sit comfortably. It wouldn't mean much in the way of security when they were in the air, but it felt as if she and Elettra were two pieces of a puzzle coming together.

With tears stinging her eyes, Adalina leaned forward and whispered, hoping only the dragon could hear her. "What took you so long, old girl?"

Years. *Years* of trying to wake her and the moment had finally come. She allowed the first tear to fall as Elettra rumbled gently, as if in apology.

"You're here now," Adalina responded. "That's what matters."

She inhaled slowly, reveling in the moment. The scales were as smooth as she imagined. Like the soft skipping stones that she used to find at the bottom of the river in Solaris. Already, she felt like she was on top of the world. Astarfall rested far below, ready for a peaceful slumber. But Adalina would not sleep tonight. Instead, she would take flight.

Words couldn't describe the feeling of soaring through the night sky. Adalina clung to Elettra's long neck. It took several minutes for her to be brave enough to sit up straight rather than hug close to the dragon's body. Her stomach somersaulted with each bob and weave Elettra made. But only once did she nearly lose her seat when the wind caught on her dress. Her heart plummeted at the thought of falling to her death, but Elettra shifted expertly, lurching Adalina back into place.

After that, Adalina hiked the dress up to her thighs and tucked it safely under her legs. Below, the landscape changed from views of the city to farmland. And soon they were coasting over the sea. The water was pitch black and foreboding, except for where bits of starlight reflected on its surface. Adalina didn't dare close her eyes for even a second for fear of missing any of the view.

Elettra flapped her wings in a steady rhythm, matching Adalina's own beating heart. A proud rumble from the dragon shook her and she laughed. It seemed her friend was enjoying herself as well.

Adalina tipped back to embrace the breeze on her face. But the wind caught her hair, releasing it from the pins and hindering her balance. She quickly adjusted and pressed herself closer to the dragon. Elettra's long neck and massive head helped lessen the danger of a sudden breeze knocking Adalina off.

She shouted over the wind and beating of wings, "Thank you, Elettra. Truly!"

The dragon roared. It shocked Adalina, and she almost slipped. Elettra once again shook, plopping her back in place before she could fall to the dark beach below.

She wasn't sure how far they'd flown in the few short hours they had been out there, but they had come back to land now. Fields of crops came into view, but there was something... not quite right about them.

"Elettra, do you think you could go a little lower for a moment?" She wasn't sure what cue to give the dragon, so she assumed asking was the next best thing.

Elettra dipped slightly, allowing Adalina to get a better look at the way the crops withered. What should have been a field lush with grain was a dead and sad thing. It was odd, considering Astarfall enjoyed weather that allowed their fields to prosper year-round.

If crops were dying, then it needed to be addressed sooner rather than later. Blights were a greater danger than pillagers on the border. Without enough grain, people would starve. She made note of it so she could bring it up to Callum later and then told Elettra she could rise again.

Adalina shoved the tiny thread of worry to the back of her mind and focused on the moment. More than a dozen little lights winked in the shadows like the fireflies she used to catch when she was a girl. She still wasn't familiar with Astarfall outside of the city walls. Therefore, she didn't know how many outlying villages were on this side of the kingdom. And while she expected that there were more like the one that Callum had taken her to, she was interested to see one so large and vast.

"Elettra, can you get us any closer to those lights over there?"

The dragon reared back in response, and a sense of dread washed over Adalina. For some reason, Elettra didn't want to get any closer.

"What is it? What do you see?" Adalina asked fruitlessly, knowing the dragon couldn't answer her.

Suddenly, her vision darkened around the edges. She gasped as her sense of sight sharpened, narrowing in on the lights. It was like looking through a sailor's spyglass, giving her a clear view without needing to get closer.

Her heart skipped a beat. There were no lanterns lighting up a sleepy little village. There were no sturdy-built homes or taverns. Instead, there were countless tattered canvas tents shaking in the crisp night breeze. And the lights... they were fires. More than she first realized. There had to be roughly more than two dozen. This was no village. It was a camp. And Adalina had a sneaking suspicion it didn't belong to any of the Astarfallen.

"Back to the palace, Elettra! Quickly."

With a sharp change in direction, Elettra soared silently back the way they had come. Adalina's vision had returned to normal, but she soaked in every landmark she could. A vast forest, two villages, a mountain range, and a cove on the coast. Based on the position of the stars, the camp had been set up west of the city. The location of the reported attacks.

There was no doubt in her mind that she and Elettra had stumbled upon an enemy camp. Now she just needed to find out what the king would do with that information. Or what her new husband would do?

As the palace came into view, towering in their path, Adalina fought back frustrated tears. She had known there was a chance they would have to fight. But that was for a few rogues. Not an *entire* army. She clung to Elettra's spikes, taking comfort in the power beneath her. Tonight, she had gotten what she wanted. Her dreams had come true, carrying her high into the sky. Only for it all to come crashing down. Because in all her years, one thing her dreams never included was a *war*.

Sixteen

Leaving Elettra was as difficult as Adalina expected. The dragon, however, seemed perfectly at ease in her new quarters. The moment they landed, Uthred and Councilman Heely had been there to greet them. Heely was all grins, while Uthred's ever amiable smile faltered each time Elettra breathed too heavily for his comfort.

It was then that they presented Adalina with her father-in-law's wedding gift to her. King Alistair had apparently been as confident as he'd said about the ritual working. He had commanded his builders to create an elegant cave-like structure attached to the palace. It overlooked the sea but was deep and dark enough to provide Elettra with safety and comfort.

The earth crafters' magic did wonders in such a short time. They had even fashioned a mound for Elettra to sleep on. Adalina's shawl was at the center of it. The dragon climbed up sleepily and snuggled on top of the sheer fabric, which was beginning to brown from the dirt. With a soft smile, Adalina said her good nights.

But as soon as she was outside the cave, sadness settled over her. If she'd had things go her way, they never would have stumbled across the encampment. It wouldn't have existed at all. But there was no changing the circumstances. So, she gave her detailed account to the men waiting eagerly at the mouth of the cave. Uthred paled in the moonlight and swayed slightly on his feet, mirroring what Adalina was feeling inside.

Heely was harder to read. His face, though stoic, showed no sign of panic. She envied his ability to keep his composure as he muttered, "I will get word to Solaris so they can mount their defenses."

Uthred shook his head, and his eyes sharpened. "Yes, and I should call the king to his study." Then he pinned Adalina with an expectant look.

She sighed. She supposed as the princess, it would fall upon her to go wake her husband. "I'll get Callum."

They parted quickly. Adalina took the stairs two at a time, dodging a few straggling wedding guests who were wandering drunk in the halls. When she reached the double doors to Callum's royal chambers, she froze. She had yet to see the rooms she would now be expected to call her own and didn't quite know what she was about to walk into.

When she stepped inside, she took one quick glance around. With the urgency of what she'd seen, there was no time to explore. It was cozy but put together. There was evidence of Callum here and there. Boots were carelessly tossed on the floor. There were random heaps of books scattered around on tables and chairs. It was simplistic in its elegance, with neatly arranged furniture, a breakfast table, and several doors leading to various private rooms. Most breathtaking, though, was the balcony. It overlooked the docks and was large enough that she wondered if Elettra might fit if she attempted to land on it.

Unsure which room was his, she tried the door nearest to her. It opened to an enormous washroom with a tub that sat beside another set of terrace doors. She wrinkled her nose. The last thing she wanted was for some nosy sailor to look up and see her washing.

Shutting the door promptly, she tried another. This time, she instantly spotted the four poster bed and Callum slumbering peacefully in the middle. *Completely nude.* A little presumptuous, wasn't it? She rolled her eyes at him, naked and sprawled out in the bed. With a huff, she grabbed one of the fluffy pillows and hit him with it.

With a silky, mocking tone, she said, "Wake up, Your Highness."

He shot up, startled with his hair a tousled mess. Most women would likely swoon and giggle at how adorably panicked he looked, but Adalina didn't have the time or the patience. She crossed her arms and glared at him.

He yawned as he stretched his arms high above his head. "Finally decided to join me? Why don't you slip out of that dress—"

"There's been a... development."

"Judging by that scowl, I'm guessing it means you're not here to crawl into bed with me."

"No, I most certainly am not."

"Pity." He feigned a pout but didn't hesitate to get out of the bed and pull on a pair of pants. "Are you hurt?" Although his words came out as casual as ever, there was an urgency in the way he moved. Like he didn't want to let on that he was worried.

"I'm fine," she reassured him. "Elettra and I found a camp. To the west."

There was a tick in his jaw. "Tell me everything. Leave no detail out."

"I've already told Heely and Uthred everything I know."

"I want to hear it from *you*." His frown deepened as he waited.

She softened. The fact that he wanted to hear it straight from her mouth almost made her forget that he'd assumed he'd be bedding her when she came back from her flight. She cleared her throat. Then she told him everything. Her estimation of how far she and Elettra had flown, the landmarks she noted on the way back, and the rough count she had made of the tents and fires.

When she finished, Callum gave her a simple, curt nod.

She bit her lip. "Only someone with access to the border could move a force of that size over without notice."

"You think it's the Festiri," he guessed.

She ran her hands over her arms. No matter who it was, it gave her a chill. "I think it's worth looking into. At the very least, the Festiri could be aiding them."

Callum's nostrils flared. He was thoughtful before saying, "There is a vast forest between us and Festiri territory."

Adalina waited for him to elaborate, but he didn't. Instead, he headed for the door, and she followed at a jog to keep up with him. But before reaching for the handle, he turned to her abruptly with a puzzled look on his face.

"What are you doing?" he asked.

Adalina returned the quizzical expression. "Coming with you."

"No. You need to stay here. Lock the doors and open them for no one but me."

Angry goosebumps prickled her arms as any warmth she'd felt toward him moments ago disappeared. "That sounds an awful lot like a command, *dear husband*," she spat the title out, hoping it would sting more that way.

"It is a request, *dear wife*." Callum smiled sweetly, but stood his ground, towering over her with his full height.

"In that case, I'm coming." Why shouldn't she? She was Princess of Astarfall. A dragon rider. And the one who gave the account in the first place. She had every right to sit in on the king's council meeting.

"They will not allow it," he said matter-of-factly. There was no indication that he said it to hurt her, but that didn't stop her from wanting to lash out.

"You are their prince. *Make them allow it*." Adalina crossed her arms, suddenly feeling very small and unimportant.

"I will stand up for you in every way that I can. But this is something you need to accept. Women do not sit on the council. Not even my mother is permitted to attend."

Adalina dug her nails into the palms of her hands. "That's a ridiculous rule. I'm the one bonded with the dragon. This concerns me and Elettra just as much as it does you."

Callum opened his mouth to speak, but Adalina raised a silencing hand. Surprise registered on his face and then his mouth tipped up into a smile that leaned more toward admiration than amusement.

Ignoring the satisfaction that brought her, she finished, "I will not be a decoration on your arm, Callum. I am capable of far more than that."

He tilted his head to the side and said, "Of that I have no doubt, dear wife. But you asked me to be honest with you and that is what I'm doing. If you come waltzing into that meeting with me, you will be removed."

Adalina shook her head. "This is bullshit."

"What a vicious mouth my pretty little wife has," he mused, twisting a lock of her hair around his finger.

He leaned down, letting his mouth linger just over hers. It sent her heart into an unwelcome pitter patter. Then he said, "I will talk to them about letting you into the council meetings. Remember, I am the prince, not the king. And you don't want to alienate the council so soon after being Crown Princess."

It hardly satisfied her, but it was a start. Still, she didn't want him to think she could be easily placated every time there was an issue between them. So, she sneered at him. "You should get going before I show you just how vicious I can truly be."

With a chuckle, he pulled away from her and slipped out the door. She caught sight of two men standing guard with swords and, had it not been for them, she might have still tried to follow. The door clicked behind Callum and Adalina stared at the lock. Deciding he wasn't going to dictate every little thing she did, she left it unlocked. He and his council could screw themselves.

The bed was as luxurious and comfortable as it looked. Between the nerves leading up to the wedding and the elation at Elettra answering their call, sleep claimed her almost immediately. Waves crashing on the shore lulled her into a deep slumber, but it was the out-of-place sound of feet padding on the floor outside of her bedroom that stirred her.

Sharing a bed with someone else was going to take some getting used to, and she was glad to have the ankle length nightgown on. She didn't want Callum to get any roguish ideas. Just because they had slept together already, didn't mean he'd be getting a round two any time soon.

She squeezed her eyes shut tight, holding back laughter at how ridiculous any other woman would find her. What sort of woman was more comfortable sleeping with a stranger than with her own husband? But Callum was a strange mixture of both, and she hadn't quite worked out what that meant to her yet.

The door to their room creaked as it opened, making her draw in an anticipatory breath. When the footsteps reached Callum's side of the bed, she decided to keep her back turned. It was easier if he thought she was still asleep. Then she wouldn't have to explain her reasoning for not wanting to consummate the marriage yet. A chill filled the room, but Adalina knew for a fact that she'd shut the windows. Had she forgotten to latch them? She shivered violently and huffed out a breath. Maybe she should ask him to use those powers of his to light a fire. She would never fall back asleep with it so cold.

Resigned to letting Callum know she was awake just so she could make sure she didn't freeze to death, she threw the covers off of her and sat up. A jolt of confusion bolted through her when she realized the windows were all still closed. Yet it was so cold she could see her breath. Something wasn't right. Before she could stand, a hand came around her, ripping her back onto the bed roughly.

"What the—" her words and her breath were cut off as a gloved hand covered her mouth and nose. All she could manage was a muffled, strangled cry. She lashed out aimlessly, but the hands only gripped her tighter.

An unfamiliar voice hissed at her, "Don't move, bitch."

Like hell. She struggled against the man pinning her down, but he was unbelievably strong and unmoving, like a pile of stones. Angry tears filled her eyes and, using the bounce of the mattress, she propelled her leg up. The man's grip loosened as her foot hit its mark. By the grace of the fates, she had heeled him in the head. She never knew she could be so flexible.

The man grunted. One hand went to his head while the other attempted to keep her down. With adrenaline granting her more speed than she'd ever had before, she scrambled out of his grip. They both got to their feet swiftly, with the bed being the only thing separating them.

She wasn't sure who this man was or what he wanted, but she wasn't about to waste time inquiring. She called for the guard, summoning a howl that rivaled even the fenrir that stalked the Solarian forests. Fear threatened to choke her at the realization that no one was coming. This man wouldn't have gotten into her chambers without first taking out the men standing at her door.

She reached for the only thing near her—a metal lantern—and poised to swing. Her voice shook as she warned, "My husband is nearby. And trust me when I say he is much scarier than I am."

The man stepped around the bed into the moonlight that trickled through the windows. He was swathed in all black and donned a silver veiled mask like the men in the tavern. He chuckled, sending the hairs on her arms standing on end.

"I do hope he'll join us soon," he cooed.

Adalina, trying to show a modicum of courage in the face of the intruder, jested, "You know, we're really not into that sort of thing." She inched sideways and gauged how quickly she could make it to the door before he caught up to her. Trying to keep him distracted, she added, "Although, it is a very new relationship, so I suppose I don't know *exactly* what he's into..."

The man tilted his head, as if confused. That would have to suffice. Adalina threw the lantern at his head and bolted for the door like a crooked arrow on the loose. There was some stumbling and scrambling, but the head start gave her just enough time to reach for the handle. It slipped out of her sweat slicked hand and before she could try again, searing pain tore through her scalp.

The force he used to pull her back by the hair sent her sailing across the floor. She slid across the rug and cried out from the burning sensation along the side of her thigh. Steel glinted in the moonlight as the man raised a blade in the air, ready to strike her.

Instinctually, Adalina kicked out with no particular aim. It landed against the man's knee, and he belted out in pain with a stumble. His angry cry was accompanied by an ear-piercing scream outside. Stunned, both Adalina and the man whipped their heads in the direction of it. Beyond the glass doors and the stone balcony railing, wings beat relentlessly.

Elettra screeched again as she hovered in place just outside. This time it was joined by the shouts of guards below. Adalina's heart soared. If she could just get to the balcony, then she could jump on her savior's back and leave this mad man behind.

He snarled, "Memories kept in the cold depths of hell will not be forgotten. The chosen will rise again and the world will bow before them."

She didn't have time to linger on his strange ramblings. The intruder grabbed her ankle, tearing her back as she clawed her way to the dragon. Adalina's determination turned to fury. Fire blazed under her skin like a fever and the man screamed in agony, but still did not let go. In her panic, all sound became muffled. It took her a moment to register that another man had joined them in the room.

Her attacker gave a loud grunt, and the grip on her slackened. She didn't bother looking back as she found her footing and ran for the balcony doors. She swung them open and a gust of wind blew into the room. It was warm and inviting. A relief from the bitter chill in the room.

Just as she was about to leap for Elettra, Callum called out from behind breathlessly, "Adalina, it's done."

Hair was matted to her face and warm beads of sweat coated her body. She hugged herself as the heat slowly crept from her. She shivered as shock set in. That bastard had sought to *kill* her. Or take her? She tried to make sense of it all. His words. How he'd gotten into her chambers...

When she turned back to the room, there were several guards with lanterns in their hands. Callum stood at the center of them. Blood coated his hands and arms, steaming where it met his cool skin. His gaze softened when it met hers, but every other part of him was tense. The lantern light cast a glow on him making him look like a vengeful God from one of her storybooks. There was an equally bloody sword in one hand. And at his feet, the intruder was laying lifeless with a gash through his back and burns on the palms of his hands.

Had she done that? Burned the man where he touched her feverish skin?

The gruesome scene stole her breath along with the adrenaline from the attack. Her shaking legs gave out, and she reached for something, anything, that she could cling to. Callum was there in an instant. He murmured reassurances into her hair as he sank to the ground with her in his arms, holding on to her as if both their lives depended on it.

Seventeen

It turned out Elettra could, in fact, fit comfortably on the oversized terrace outside of Adalina's bedroom. Although the threat had been swiftly dealt with at her husband's hand, the dragon lingered. She'd landed as gently as her massive frame would allow, sending a few loose stones tumbling three stories down.

The head of the palace staff tried to shoo her away at one point but was met with an indignant huff of steam. Callum had dismissed them and allowed Elettra to linger until she was confident that there would be no further issue on that night.

It was a brand-new day now and Adalina desperately wanted to go down to the cave. It was a strange adjustment, having to distinguish between her own emotions and the dragon's. From the moment she woke up, Adalina had been battling with an odd sense of vigilance. Like a threat lurked behind every footstep or flutter of wind. If Elettra was worried, she wanted to reassure her.

She smoothed out her dress, pleased with the simple yet elegant Astarfall fashion which didn't require any help from lady's maids. Having people constantly underfoot to see to her every need was something she would have to get used to. But after the night she'd had, she was glad people weren't fluttering around her first thing when she woke.

Callum was already at the breakfast table when she walked out of their room. A room that had been scrubbed clean, leaving no sign of the execution that had taken place the night before. She shivered at the memory of such a violation; for a man to have come into her bed without her having the faintest idea that it wasn't Callum... To think of the things he could have done. And that it very well could have been *her* blood staining the crystal blue and silver rug.

She grabbed a buttery pastry and a handful of berries from a bowl beside Callum. "I'm going to go check on Elettra."

She was met with silence. He glowered into the bowl of oats sitting in front of him. Then she noted how tightly he gripped the silver spoon and the way his shoulders slumped. Something was clearly weighing on him. It was a rare thing to witness this side of him. Although she didn't like the idea of him being troubled, she appreciated that he wasn't wearing his cheerful facade around her.

When he spoke, his words were sharper than she expected. "How are your wounds?"

"I'd hardly call rug burn a wound," she said flatly, but winced at the reminder of the angry red mark on the side of her leg.

"And your ankle?" He nodded to the bruising where the man had grabbed her.

"It's fine," she lied. The healers had wrapped it tightly, but there was still a dull ache. Like a ghost there to remind her of what happened.

Callum gestured to the seat beside him. "I'll re-wrap it."

"I don't think—"

"Sit down," he said curtly. "We need to talk about last night."

Heat prickled at her fingertips. Instinctually, she wanted to snap back at him. To retort that he could ask her politely. But his demeanor gave her pause. His face was sullen. The normally ever-present smile was drawn down. None of the ease he constantly presented to the world was there. Instead, he looked as if he was teetering on the brink of defeat. Like he might crumble at any moment. So, she sat.

He took herbs from a basket left by the healers and sprinkled them into her tea. It was meant to alleviate pain and swelling. She grasped the cup; glad he'd remembered or else she would have been uncomfortable later.

Gently, he reached for her calf and lifted her leg. With tenderness, he set it on his lap so he could access her ankle. When he removed the bandages, his fingers brushed against her skin. She shivered, and he froze.

Searching her face with an intensity that caught her off guard, he asked, "Did I hurt you?"

Very much the opposite, she wanted to say. She bit her lip. How was it that a man could be so heartbreakingly handsome and more so when his eyes filled with worry?

"I assure you, I'm fine. But are you?"

His shoulders tensed, but he shrugged it away. He withdrew the fresh bandages and began to wrap her ankle. His touch was so gentle—like he was handling a butterfly and feared he might break its wings.

When he didn't answer her question, she said, "You could have been a healer, you know. You're good at this."

Once the bandage was secured, he ran his thumb over it. The longer he stared at her ankle, the deeper his frown became.

She had to strain to hear him as he whispered, "I had practice with my sister. After the accident, the healers showed me how to tend to her wounds so I could help. It wasn't enough, though. I still lost her."

When he released her leg, he turned away from her and sighed. Adalina's heart broke for the young boy who had to sit by and watch his little sister succumb to her injuries.

"I'm so sorry, Callum. It must be hard for you."

There was a tick in his jaw and his voice was strained as he said, "This is exactly why you need to be able to protect yourself."

Slightly taken aback, she said, "I understand that. But I did fend him off. And Elettra—"

"Might not be there to save you in time if something like this happens again." His next words came out softer. "*I* might not be there to save you in time."

"We were all caught off guard last night."

Through clenched teeth, Callum growled, "I told you to *lock the door.*"

The door? He was mad that she hadn't listened to him? Even if she had, the man could have found a way in. He'd nearly beaten the guards to death. They'd been found in a crumpled heap. The healers thought they were dead at first. A mere locked door certainly wasn't going to stop the man from getting in.

"I don't see how that matters."

Callum placed his hands firmly on the table. "It matters because he was able to get past your guard. If the door had been locked like I told you, then he wouldn't have gotten in."

Adalina furrowed her brow. "There's no way to know that. He could have used magic. Or broken it down."

"It would have been one more thing to stand in his way." He met her gaze now. His eyes were dark like storm clouds. But his tone didn't match the ire. There was a note of desperation in it and his voice broke as he said, "When I give you a command, you *must* listen."

Was that a plea? Or an order? When Adalina hoped to witness the more serious side of Callum, this was not what she meant.

Her voice dripped with a warning as she said, "You are my husband. Not my keeper."

"I am your husband and your *prince* now." He leaned forward, appearing as menacing as the intruder had last night. It shocked her to see him this way. The prince who gave out smiles like they were candy was replaced with a man who teetered on agony and anger. It made her draw in a sharp breath.

As if noticing her sudden discomfort, he leaned back and tugged at his tousled hair. "I can't keep you safe if you don't listen."

"I couldn't have known something like that would happen."

"Now you do. We all do." He pushed his untouched breakfast aside. "They were in the palace, Adalina. In our bedroom. He could have..." His face reddened as he looked her up and down. "You just need to do as I say from here on out."

She shook her head. "You are not my master, Callum."

Still flushed red, he stood abruptly. The chair tipped backward and crashed onto its side. "Why must you be so hard-headed in this?"

Adalina stood as well. Anger spread like wildfire reaching down to the tips of her toes. Standing stiff-backed, she said, "Because I have just given up enough without having to kneel at your feet, too."

After blowing out a frustrated breath, he said, "You need to stay here until I can be sure the guards haven't found any signs of the intruder's friends. We can't be sure that he was acting alone last night."

"I will most certainly not stay here. I am going to see Elettra."

"*Impossible woman*," he snapped and strode across the room.

"*Irritable man*!" she hissed back. It was she who was attacked, not him. If anyone should be upset, it was her. He had every right to be rattled, but it didn't give him the right to lock her up like a caged bird.

"Fine. Go." He pointed to the door.

She stayed where she was and crossed her arms. "I'll go when I'm good and ready."

"Have it your way. I'm going to meet with my father and the guard."

"I suppose I'm not allowed to come with you to that, either." She hadn't forgotten the sting of being excluded from the council meeting the night before. A meeting that, had she attended, would have meant she wasn't there alone when the attacker came into their chambers.

Callum grumbled to himself and rooted around in a desk drawer. He tossed something to her and said, "Here. I intended to give this to you this morning under better circumstances. I know it's not as exciting as meeting your dragon and doesn't compare to her beauty, but I thought it would suit you."

Adalina turned the object over in her hands. It was a large pink seashell. Something clinked inside, so she turned it over, letting a delicate ring fall through the opening and into her hand. It was silver with a large square cut stone raised in the center. It was clear and sparkled where the sun hit it like the diamonds she had seen ladies of the court wearing. It was flanked by two smaller stones to match.

Callum mumbled, "Moonglass. It shines brighter in the moonlight and turns a faint blue."

Adalina's heart thudded at the gesture as she recalled him inviting her to walk along the beach in search of moonglass on that night in the Dew Drop. The ring was the most beautiful thing she had ever laid eyes on, aside from Elettra. She slipped it onto her ring finger. It was a perfect fit.

With a lick of her dry lips, she said lamely, "Thank you, it's lovely."

Callum nodded curtly. "If it pleases you, meet me in the guard's yard in an hour. That should give you ample time with Elettra."

"The guard's yard?" She forced herself to tear her gaze from the jewels on her finger.

"We need to start your training."

Then, without another word, he left.

Elettra walked beside Adalina to a large squared off area well away from the palace. The dragon's footsteps were surprisingly stealthy, considering her size. The guards who were training on the hard dirt-packed land froze as they approached. Their jaws dropped, openly gawking at their new princess and her fearsome beast.

To her surprise, Seraphine and Alfie were there waiting for her. Adalina—eager to see her new friend—jogged over to them. Seraphine greeted her with a low curtsy. Mischief glinted in her eye as she said, "Your Highness."

"Oh, please don't." Adalina blushed deeply.

Alfie dipped into a shallow bow. "Protocol. You understand?"

Adalina smirked at them. "Something I'll have to get used to, I guess."

Elettra waltzed up to Alfie, and he shrank back. The dragon, unphased by his hesitation at letting her get too close, sniffed at his head. His hair rose up to her nostrils and when she pulled back, it continued to stick up wildly in several directions.

He squeaked. "Good dragon?"

Adalina laughed as the faintest prickle of amusement hit her. Perhaps it wouldn't take as long as she expected to tell the difference between Elettra's emotions and her own. It was like smelling perfume from far away. Or an aftertaste. Lighter and a bit more out of reach than her own emotions were.

She smirked at Alfie. "I think she finds you cute. Like a puppy."

"Great. Just what every man wants to be viewed as."

Seraphine smoothed his hair down and kissed him on the cheek. "Could be worse. She could view you as a snack, instead."

His face paled, and he mumbled, "I'll just wait over there." He pointed toward a group of guards and bounded over to them.

The women laughed, and even Elettra released a few soft rumbles from her throat. When the laughter died down, Adalina fiddled with the ring on her finger. It would take some time to get used to the weight of it, but the way light sparkled off the stones like tiny dancing stars was mesmerizing. Seraphine, who must have noticed her fidgeting, grabbed Adalina's hand and held it up for a better look. Her eyes turned wide as saucers as she tipped Adalina's hand this way and that, watching the moonglass sparkle in the sun.

"He gave it to you!" she exclaimed. "I was worried he would chicken out."

Remnants of frustration with him lingered from their fight, but Adalina forced a light tone as she said, "He practically hurled it at me on his way out this morning."

Seraphine frowned. "He wasn't rude to you, was he? I imagine he's in one of his sour moods after what happened."

"He blames *me* since I didn't obey him and lock the door." Adalina averted her gaze from the beautiful ring.

Seraphine dropped her hand gently and tilted her head thoughtfully. "More likely, he blames himself for leaving you alone and not being able to keep you safe."

Adalina bit the inside of her cheek. Her instinct was to argue, still annoyed that he was trying to command her. But Seraphine knew him much better than she did. Was it possible that he was just lashing out because of the frustration he was feeling toward himself? Either way, he was out of line.

Seraphine sighed sadly. "Losing his sister was probably the darkest moment of his life. You'll find that he still carries that weight and maybe even a bit of guilt for not being able to keep her safe."

"Wasn't Ivy's death an accident?" Adalina still didn't know much about the incident. And she wasn't comfortable pressing Callum to talk about it.

"It was. But he'd been with her. They snuck away from the guards to go riding on their own. They were so young it had seemed harmless at the time. But after the fall..." Seraphine gave a tightlipped smile. "Well, there was nothing to be done."

"I see."

There was an ache in her chest as she once again thought about Callum as a boy. It was impossible for him to anticipate that something like that would happen. And holding on to that guilt, then wielding it against anyone who disappointed him would only ever complicate things. But it made sense now why he was so shaken by last night.

Seraphine nudged her in the side as they turned toward the training yard. "You should have seen him trying to pick out a ring for you. He was like a nervous child trying to decide what kind of candy he wanted at the store."

"Is that so?" Adalina almost smiled at the image.

"In the end, he marched down to the beach in the middle of the night and searched for the moonglass himself. Then asked the jeweler to have it ready by your wedding night."

Adalina fidgeted with the ring resting on her finger. Suddenly, it felt slightly heavier with meaning. It wasn't a trinket he had picked out of a dozen others. He'd been more thoughtful... more intentional with it. Now she wished she would have thanked him properly. And that he would have waited to give it to her when they weren't in a heated argument.

Day one as husband and wife, and they were already making a mess of it. What did that say about their future? Over the years she'd witnessed—on more than one occasion—her grandparents griping at one another, but never in the way she and Callum did. It wasn't exactly the sort of passion she had in mind for marriage. Nor did she want a man who lorded over her. She needed a *partner*. To be equal.

As a sort of melancholy came over her, Elettra padded closer. The dragon pressed her head against Adalina's arm. It threw her slightly off balance and right into Callum's chest. She hit it with a grunt.

He turned her toward him tenderly. His touch was steady and familiar. Goosebumps sprouted across her skin, and she realized she was frozen with her hands still pressed against his chest. The faintest feeling of amusement broke her concentration, and she peeked over to find Elettra watching them with quiet fascination.

"Sorry," she uttered.

"Glad to see you decided to come." The hint of boasting in Callum's voice stirred up her annoyance with him once again.

"You did *ask*."

"Right, then.," he said more formally, then stepped away from her. He walked to the center of the training field, which had cleared out of the practicing guards. "Let's get to it."

Part of her wanted to ask about the meeting he'd gone to, but another part of her wanted to see if he would give her an update unbidden. Would he expect her to just go along with her day aimlessly, not knowing if more intruders had been found or if she should keep one eye open when she went to bed later that night? The kingdom of Astarfall might be fine putting their faith in their king, but Adalina was not.

Regardless of her opinions on the matter, she joined Callum. After last night, it was clear that she desperately needed to learn how to defend herself. Since coming to Astarfall, she had been in two attacks. That was two more than she'd been in, in her entire life.

"Our goal isn't to turn you into a soldier." Callum regarded her with an appraising gaze. "Rather, I need you to be able to save yourself when no one else can."

Adalina nodded. "That's something we can agree on."

His mouth tipped up in a half smirk. The dimple in his cheek made butterflies stir in her stomach. But it was short-lived as the lesson began. Callum didn't waste any time delving into the basics. He started by showing her defensive stances and ways to block the most vulnerable parts of her body.

This time, she didn't question him or argue when he gave her commands. This was more important than her pride and between the two of them, he was the professional in this matter. As the Crown Prince, he had been trained in the art of battle.

After an hour of footwork, Adalina was already exhausted. And hopeless. She continuously tripped over her own two feet, fumbled with what to do with her hands—more often than not, forgetting to guard her face—and had embarrassed herself with a rather simple kick that ended with her face down in the dirt.

Each time she made a fool of herself, Seraphine would smile encouragingly from the sidelines and tell her she was doing great. Elettra, who had taken to bathing in the sun, stirred each time Adalina grunted from a tumble. Callum, however, only spoke when correcting her. The formality of it was driving her mad.

"Let's take a break," he finally said after an hour and a half.

Adalina wandered over to Elettra as Callum called for the palace staff to bring them water. The dragon looked up at them with disinterest when they approached her and rolled to her side lazily. Long lashes touched the tops of her scaly cheeks when she closed her eyes, acting as if she hadn't had enough rest over the last fifty years.

Adalina sat down, resting her back against the dragon's warm belly. Seraphine and Alfie were still across the yard, laughing together cheerfully. Callum plopped down on the ground in front of Adalina and handed her a flask of water.

"Drink."

Adalina glared at him.

"If it pleases you," he added mockingly.

With a roll of her eyes, she tipped the flask back, instantly satisfied by the cool rush on her tongue. This was exhausting. Between her mixed emotions when it came to Callum and the exertion of training, she desperately wanted the day to end.

"This is never going to work, is it?" she asked absentmindedly, unsure if she was referring to learning to fight on the ground or their marriage.

Callum bit his lip and leaned forward, resting his arm on his knee. "I think it's just going to take some time to... learn."

Learn to defend herself? Or learn to navigate each other? Either way, his words didn't inspire much confidence. If only she had the abilities that he and his people had. Not that wielding the elements would be any easier than wielding a sword or her fists.

Callum was quiet as he pulled a pouch out of his bag. He tore at a piece of dried salmon and handed the larger piece to her. "This will help with the soreness."

Wishing she had eaten a hardier breakfast; she took it gratefully. It settled heavily in the pit of her stomach as she said, "I think I may have burned that man last night. One minute I was thrashing my way to Elettra and the next it was like I'd been overcome with a fever. It sounded like I'd hurt him and then after everything, his hands had burns on them..."

Callum's mood lightened a bit as he said, "It's possible. Your dragon magic gives you a connection to Elettra, who is essentially fire incarnate. And considering your grandfather is Astarfallen, it's possible that some sliver of his power has been lying dormant in you." For the first time all day, he offered her a full smile and added, "Regardless, we need to focus on you knowing how to defend yourself in hand-to-hand combat."

She threw her head back in joking despair. "I was afraid you would say that."

Callum stood and offered a hand to help her up. "One more round and then I'll take you to the Dew Drop for a proper meal. Deal?"

A full meal and a pint of fruity ale sounded divine. And he was asking, not telling. Elettra grumbled as Adalina took Callum's hand, stirring her from her slumber. He was still smiling and this time she wanted to soak it up like the sun on a dragon's back.

Feeling the weight of their fight lifting off her shoulders, she said, "Deal."

Eighteen

The next morning, Adalina's muscles were so tight she could barely drag herself out of bed. There was a note on the breakfast table and, beside it, a package.

Dearest wife, I am off to the docks. Good luck with training today. I imagine Calida is a more grueling instructor than I am. Take this as a token of my faith in you. Calida helped a bit, but I will accept your thanks in the form of a kiss.

Sincerely yours,

Your irresistible husband.

Adalina snorted as she set the letter down. The package on the table beckoned her with its air of mystery. She tore it open, and her mouth fell agape as she lifted fine leathers from the tissue paper they were nestled on. There were two pieces. Tailored pants made of hardy but supple leather and a vest to match. Adalina ran her finger over the embroidery on the left side of the vest. One small, delicate flame and a snapdragon that would rest over her heart when she put it on. The flowers were made from a pink thread that turned peach at the bottoms of the petals. It contrasted beautifully with the red and orange flame.

It was gorgeous, and she eagerly stripped out of her nightgown. The pants fit her like a glove. But the vest was the crowning jewel. She slipped on a fitted cotton shirt made for horseback riding and then pulled the vest on over it.

When she caught sight of herself in the mirror, her stomach flipped. She looked every bit the warrior that her grandmother had been. Like the dragon riders in her history books back in Solaris. Now all she had to do was learn to ride as they did.

Elettra was spinning in circles when Adalina arrived in the courtyard. Her grandmother had a hand on her hip and was grumbling. "If you hold still, I can help."

Adalina's eyebrow lifted. "What is going on here?"

A rush of despair coupled with irritation hit her suddenly. Apparently, Elettra was incredibly bothered. The dragon reached back toward her butt and snapped her teeth.

"She has an itch she can't scratch," her grandmother explained dryly.

A laugh bubbled up from Adalina's throat. Elettra stopped spinning and glared at her as if to say, *I'm glad you find my discomfort amusing.*

"Can I help?" Adalina asked.

Elettra gave a resigned sigh and plopped onto the ground. Adalina scrambled behind her and began scratching.

"Here?" she asked.

The dragon shook her head.

"How about here?"

Elettra stretched her neck and leaned her rear end into Adalina's scratching. The frustration she'd been sensing from the dragon a moment ago was replaced with absolute delight.

Adalina's grandmother chuckled. "Now if we're quite done with the dramatics, shall we get on with Lina's lesson?" Her question was pointed at Elettra, who sighed in response.

Adalina and the dragon both stood at attention while her grandmother paced in front of them like a general preparing to give a speech to his men.

"Now, riding for fun and riding into battle are two incredibly different things," she began, but paused. With a wink, she said, "Those leathers look good on you."

"Thank you," said Adalina, chest bursting with pride.

Then, back to business, her grandmother continued, "As I'm sure you've already realized, your bond gives you more than the ability to ride the dragon. In the dark times, our people struggled. While our southern neighbors were blessed with power from the heavens and prospered, we faced many hardships."

Adalina knew this by heart. She cut in to recite, "*So one day, a man ventured near the forest. He was the only one brave enough for such a task; for the last seven nights, a new child had been stolen at the edge of the woods by a hungry serpent. But tonight, none would be taken, because a great winged beast had triumphed against it.*"

"Precisely," her grandmother said with a pride-filled smile. "And so, in honor of the dragon's help, the man left offerings. For without the noble creature, more children would have been lost. One day, he ventured a bit further and noticed blood on the ground. He followed the trail until he came to the magnificent creature. The dragon had been injured in the fight, so the man tended to his wounds for weeks."

Adalina glanced between Elettra, who was listening intently, and her grandmother. "I know all of this. I don't see how this is going to help prepare me for what's coming."

"Because everything you need in order to understand and fully appreciate your bond can be found in this history. Once strong enough—on the night of the new moon—the grateful dragon breathed magic into the man, solidifying the bond that had grown between them in those weeks. No longer were the people of Solaris powerless. For the Great Bonding had granted man and dragon a connection that would extend through the ages."

"Yes..." Adalina said, hungry to see where this was going.

"And because of the strength of that bond, you are able to access Elettra's emotions. Interpret her thoughts and needs. It will allow you to fight as one. Just as a soldier's sword is an extension of him, so is the tether between you and Elettra."

Elettra nudged Adalina on the shoulder. The warm sensation of affection and love filled her, and she hoped that the dragon could sense that she returned the sentiment.

Her grandmother continued, "And in that same thread, your senses will be sharpened. Vision, sense of smell... if you are open to Elettra, then she can share these things with you. The key is to relax and embrace it. This will give you an advantage your enemy does not have."

Adalina recalled how she had wanted to get a better look at the tiny lights and how, thanks to Elettra, she'd been able to see the enemy camp from afar.

"It happened on our first flight together. Elettra shared her sight with me."

"The stronger your bond grows, the stronger that ability will become. Not only will she be able to lend you the ability to see as a dragon would, but she will also be able to share what *she* sees even if you aren't with her."

"Why didn't you tell me about that before?" she asked her grandmother.

"Because of the pain on your face each time you tried to wake her, to no avail. I didn't want to tell you just how much you were missing out on. I couldn't bring myself to add to your loss."

Those years had been hard on her, but she'd never considered that it might have been equally difficult for her grandmother to witness. She fought back the swell of emotion. All was as it should be, finally.

Her grandmother gave her a mischievous smile. "It's time to mount."

Adalina's heart sped as Elettra offered her tail as a lift. Once she was settled on the dragon's back, she waited for her grandmother's instruction.

"You cannot fight on a dragon's back if you cannot balance on it."

Adalina's thighs screamed in discomfort as she tightened her grip. Damn Callum and his training. The change from strolling leisurely in the countryside of Solaris to fighting and riding was taking its toll on her. But she found solace in knowing that her muscles were building.

That one day, she wouldn't need a long soak in the tub every time she trained.

Her grandmother's voice carried up to her as she said, "Trust your instincts. Don't fight Elettra's movements but embrace them. Think of yourself as being one."

She recalled how she'd thought of them as two pieces of a puzzle coming together on that first night. When Elettra began to strut around the courtyard, Adalina allowed her hips to move in sync with her. It wasn't unlike riding a horse, which she'd been doing since she learned to walk.

Her grandmother watched them thoughtfully. "If you need to, use the spikes. They're intimidating, but they can also be your lifeline. And your thighs are going to burn like hell, but your muscle memory will be your greatest asset. Staying on her back, no matter the speed, will soon become as natural to you as walking."

Adalina knew this would be something she could do. It was the fighting that worried her.

"And what of battle?" she asked, hating how uncertain she sounded.

Her grandmother clasped her hands together. "Rely on Elettra. She has been to war before and knows her way around a battlefield. That is an advantage you'll have over me. Neither of us knew what we were doing back then." Her eyes became unfocused, as if recalling a terrible memory.

Elettra, too, tensed beneath Adalina.

Her grandmother's attention returned to them, and she said, "It's best to rely on verbal commands. Elettra's hearing is impeccable and she will hear you over the wind and battle cries. But there are a few swift signals you can give in urgent situations."

Adalina sat forward, eager to learn them.

"A pat and a click of your tongue to take to the sky will suffice."

Adalina tucked the information away, hoping she could remember everything. If she didn't, it might result in some serious mistakes. And on a dragon's back, that was something she couldn't afford.

Her grandmother continued, "A sharp hiss through your teeth will call for quickfire."

Elettra pawed at the ground, leaving slashes in it. It seemed she was eager as well.

"Two taps on her neck to go low. One to go high."

Adalina tapped Elettra once, and the dragon beat her wings, lifting them off the ground. They hovered slightly above Adalina's grandmother. She gave another tap. Paused. Then another. Elettra followed the command, lifting them just out of earshot. Human earshot, that is. Adalina's hearing sharpened.

There was no need for her grandmother to raise her voice, as she said, "If ever there is a time that you need to send Elettra off on her own, she will heed your verbal commands. This gives an advantage if you want her to scout or stand guard without you." Her smile broadened as she finished, "And most importantly, reward her with lots of treats when you return home."

Adalina caressed Elettra's smooth scales and chuckled. "Naturally."

Then, with two taps on her neck, Adalina commanded Elettra to land back on the ground.

Adalina asked, "What happens if we come across the beast in the king's reports?"

Her grandmother pursed her lips. "During the Great War, dragons fought on the same side, never against one another. Although they have been used to hunt larger prey, they have never faced anything that matched them in size or strength in battle. It is something the two of you will need to learn to do if the time comes." She softened as she said, "Trust each other and you can face any threat that comes your way."

Adalina couldn't shake the dread that twisted her stomach into knots.

Her grandmother asked, "Now that all of that is out of the way, would you like to give it a try?"

"Give what a try?"

A rueful grin spread across her grandmother's face as she said, "Firing."

Adalina's pulse jumped. Was she seriously about to witness a dragon breathing fire? It was so surreal that she had half a mind to pinch herself to be sure she wasn't dreaming.

To Elettra, she said, "Let's go to the water. Steer clear of the harbor, though. We don't want to burn the place down."

The dragon obeyed, flying away from the palace and out to the sea. Adalina gripped one of the spikes on the base of her neck. Becoming fluid with Elettra would take some practice and, for now, it felt good to have something to hold on to.

Once they were well away from the shore, Adalina scanned the area for any ships. They weren't close enough to the harbor to hit any accidentally, but she spotted a crowd gathering on the pier. A few were using spy glasses for a clearer view of their princess and her dragon.

An audience wasn't ideal, but who could blame them for their curiosity? Adalina squared her shoulders and said, "Only aim down at the water. Please." She didn't know what to expect when it came to quickfire and preferred not to risk any of it going too far or astray.

With a deep, steadying breath, Adalina pressed her tongue against her teeth and made a sharp hiss. The fire in Elettra's belly crackled and popped as she summoned the flame. Her scales went hot, and Adalina was grateful for the leathers protecting her legs.

Then, in a flash, a storm of fire crashed into the ocean in little bursts. It was like watching deadly falling stars. One after another, Elettra spat them like venom.

The crowd on the dock erupted into applause and unabashed whoops of cheer. Emboldened, Adalina tapped Elettra's neck once, and they soared higher. She wanted to see how far the quickfire could carry. It would give her a boost of confidence, knowing that they could engage in a battle from afar. As long as she could stay seated on her dragon, she might not have to use the skills Callum was teaching her.

With another hiss from Adalina, Elettra shot fire at the rolling waves below. Steam bellowed from the water as it washed the fire out. Elettra, who seemed to be enjoying herself as much as Adalina, stopped flying in lazy circles and dove toward the water.

She gasped as they plummeted to the sea. Just before they plunged into it, Elettra swept up and flew so close to a massive wave that sea spray coated Adalina's face. The scent of salt and... something more. What was it? She inhaled more deeply. Earthy and fresh. Like driftwood and a walk on the beach... Callum.

She craned her neck to follow the direction the scent was coming from. They were too far from the palace to see the courtyard clearly. But thanks to the sharpened sight Elettra lent her, everything came into focus. And sure enough, Callum was there, standing beside both of her grandparents. His grin was ear to ear, and he cupped his hands around his mouth to let out a loud whoop. Then he put an arm around her grandmother, and the no nonsense woman beamed with delight at something he said. That was an impressive feat on Callum's part. It stirred something in Adalina's chest.

"Back to the palace, please!" she said over the crashing waves.

When they returned, Adalina's grandfather whistled wildly between two fingers. His face glowed with pride as he said, "You are the spitting image of your grandmother!"

She blushed at the compliment, which meant more to her than he could know. Once they landed, Elettra snuffed through her nose and laid down with a dramatic thud. Adalina laughed as she got a sense of sleepiness.

"I think Elettra wants to take a break," she said as she slid off her back.

The dragon rolled so the sun could shine on her belly and her eyes fluttered shut.

Callum met Adalina at Elettra's side. His lips were parted in silent awe, making the blush from earlier take a turn from her face and delve down to her chest.

He shook his head and said, "That was... You were..."

Her grandmother placed a hand on his shoulder. "I believe what the princeling is trying to say is that you were incredible up there. How do you feel?"

Adalina continued to stare into Callum's eyes as she answered, "It was invigorating. I could actually *feel* the fire building inside of her. Words can't describe how amazing it was."

Callum handed her a flask. "You appear to be a natural."

"Did you doubt it?" she teased, taking a big swig of water.

"Doubt that you'd be able to do whatever it is you were determined to do? I haven't doubted that since the moment you stood up to me on that dock."

Adalina laughed at the confusion crossing her grandparents' faces. To Callum, she rolled her eyes. "I was a child."

"You'd made up your mind, then. And you're doing it again." His sincerity threw her off-kilter.

Their fingers brushed as she handed the flask back to him. "Then I suppose I should be grateful that I didn't end up tossed into that water like I was back then."

He made a clucking sound with his tongue. "I admit, it would be a pity to see that brilliant outfit of yours ruined by the sea."

His gaze raked over her and for a moment it felt as if she was standing before him stark naked.

Her grandmother chuckled and took Adalina's grandfather by the arm. "Come Bellamy, you can buy me a drink at that charming little inn."

They took their leave and Adalina caught excited whispers between them. She couldn't decipher them, though. Not with Elettra snoring just a few feet away—the abilities lying dormant with her.

Callum's voice dripped with something close to desire as he said, "It truly does fit beautifully in all the right places."

Adalina crossed her arms over her chest and shot him with an indignant look. The outfit truly was tailored to perfection. Pants hugging each of her soft curves so as not to wear with chafing. Though her thighs and abs burned from the effort to keep her seat, the clothes had made it exponentially easier to ride.

Callum offered his arm to her, and she took it. They walked up the pebbled path toward the palace.

"Your grandmother said that at higher speeds, loose clothing could catch on the wind like a sail. And despite what my past actions may indicate, I really would hate to see you be blown out to sea."

"I appreciate that." Adalina wrapped her fingers around his forearm and smiled at courtiers they passed on their way to the dining room.

A few councilmen they came across looked away when she met their eye.

"What's gotten into them?" she asked, feeling like they were avoiding her.

Callum swatted at the air with his free hand. "They're just out of sorts. They'll get over it."

"Over what?"

"Over you sitting in on the council meetings."

He said it so matter-of-factly that it took a moment for the weight of it to sink in. Her heart sputtered in her chest.

She halted and turned to face him. "You convinced them?" her pitch came out louder than she intended, earning a sneer from one of the pouting men.

"Did you ever doubt me?" Callum flashed a dazzling smile.

She had. But maybe she'd been wrong about doing so. Standing on her tippy toes, she planted a kiss on his cheek. When she pulled away, there was a soft blush along the bridge of his nose.

Wholeheartedly, she said, "Thank you, Callum."

Nineteen

The next few days went by without incident. Adalina finally felt as if she was falling into a routine. Each night she and Callum found themselves staying up at all hours of the night talking. It was getting easier to be around him. More comfortable. When it was just the two of them sitting on the terrace overlooking the harbor, it felt like they were back in that room at the Dew Drop Inn.

They still hadn't been intimate since that night. But they were exploring each other in other ways. Simple things at first like their favorite colors. Blue for Callum. Their favorite foods. Cake which he claimed he would eat for every meal given the chance.

Under normal circumstances these were things most people would know about one another before getting married. But each night, they delved a little deeper. She'd still only skimmed the surface, but it was a start. One that made facing the days as his wife just a little easier.

Then each day when she woke, they had breakfast together. He was no longer looking at her like a porcelain vase that needed to be placed on the highest shelf. Since her show on Elettra, everyone had been staring at her with newfound reverence. And she was eating up every second of it.

After breakfast, the rest of her mornings were spent with Elettra, flying in circles around the city under the sharp watch of the guards. They still didn't know how the intruder had gotten in and King Alistair was being vigilant with all the women in the royal family. Queen Gwendolyn and Seraphine included.

Training with her grandmother was her favorite part of the day. But of course, time had to be split between that and hand-to-hand training with Callum. When all was said and done, Adalina was going to be in the best shape of her life. Already, she was feeling stronger. Her legs no longer shook like a gelatine dessert by the end of the day.

She found herself in the training yard now, dodging blows from her husband. Something she never thought she'd be doing when she was young and imagined being married one day. It certainly was a marriage full of surprises. But if Callum was difficult to figure out before, it paled in comparison to their time in the yard. The man was like night and day when it came to her training. All smiles and effortless movements when giving her instruction. And then stern and direct the moment she failed at a new maneuver he tried to teach.

Although she was far from the warrior her grandmother was, she had finally gotten the hang of blocking Callum when he came at her directly. However, it was day four of her training and she still couldn't escape when he snuck up on her.

Elettra snorted loudly with humor as Callum swept up from behind, pinning Adalina's hands so they were tightly crossed over her chest.

He sounded energetic and not the least bit winded as he said, "Imagine I'm holding a dagger to you. Remember the arm twist I showed you to disarm your opponent."

She groaned in frustration. With their height difference, she really despised this move.

"Okay, forget about disarming me. Just get out of my hold, Adalina." Now he just sounded bored.

She wiggled fruitlessly. Her first instinct was to try to kick him, but with his lean muscular body pressed firmly against her backside, that would have been pointless.

His lips grazed her neck, sending delightful shivers down her spine as he leaned down and whispered, "You need to drop your weight."

Normally his corrections were laced with a natural sense of irritation—making her feel like a child in a school lesson—but this time his words had come out with a hint of a purr. Heat shot down to her core. Her body tensed in anticipation and longing. And without thinking she leaned into him.

"I knew that." She huffed with less sass than she intended. In a halfhearted attempted to get free, she pressed herself against him.

His words were laced with uncontained lust. "Hell, Adalina. Not like that. Not unless you've changed your mind about letting me under those riding leathers."

He grew hard against her lower back. Her desire spread and there was a wanting throb between her legs. Despite sharing a bed night after night without consummating their marriage, the memory of his attentive skills at the Dew Drop replayed in her mind.

Quickly, she shook away the thoughts. Between the attack on their wedding night, and their argument the following morning, her choice had been made. Not that Callum hadn't hinted at his desire. Still, he respected the decision to try to figure each other out before getting physical again. Their wants, their needs. It was best to take things slow. Now if only her damned body would remember that.

If she didn't slip from his grasp soon, she'd find herself quite uncomfortable with lust-soaked undergarments. She dropped her weight, going limp and earning a shocked gasp from him as his hold on her faltered. Like a flash of heat lightning, she slipped out of his arms and settled quickly into the defensive stance he had engrained in her.

Elettra chortled from her sunny spot on the grass.

"Well done," he boasted.

She swept her arms out and bowed. "Why thank you."

A round of applause sounded from the side of the yard. Heely, Uthred, and a few men from the king's council were watching her with semi-impressed expressions. Her face flushed and suddenly her attraction to Callum was the least of her worries. If she didn't learn how to fight well enough for the council's approval, they could challenge her for Elettra. Having them there made both her and the dragon nervous. Which meant her body got to experience twice the gut-wrenching anxiety.

The lounging dragon rose to her full height, causing fear to flash across several of the men's faces. Satisfaction filled Adalina at the sight.

She might not be a fierce warrior yet, but she did share a connection with a dragon. Which, in her not so humble opinion, was a far more fearsome feat.

"Sorry to interrupt," Uthred said merrily. "But we were hoping to have a word with the two of you."

Adalina and Callum exchanged questioning glances before joining the council at the edge of the field. Heely looked utterly at home, donning typical Astarfallen clothing. Even though the remaining Solarian guests from the wedding had chosen to return home, Heely remained. He'd decided that it would be beneficial for him to stay and act as Adalina's personal counsel. Which was pointless, considering she had her grandparents. Besides, he spent most of his time flitting through the court like a friendly butterfly, socializing with anyone who would give him the time.

"Go ahead, Uthred," said Callum.

"The scouting party we sent out to confirm Princess Adalina's account of the encampment should have returned today, but there has been no word from them."

To her surprise, Callum grabbed her hand and squeezed. But his voice was even as he addressed the council. "I'll ride out."

"No need," Heely interjected. "A rescue group has already been dispatched."

Uthred side-eyed him. Maybe the Solarian councilman was finally overstaying his welcome.

Clearing his throat, Uthred said, "And you are needed for another task. An invitation has come from Windshire. Your father is in the city today but asked that I give you this."

He handed Callum a note filled with scribbled handwriting. Adalina peered over his arm to read it. King Alistair may have been calm and collected when facing his people, but if his writing was any indication, he was in turmoil.

Callum finished reading before her and handed her the note.

"He wants us to speak to the lords on his behalf?" he asked with a hint of hesitation.

According to the note, he wanted them to do a lot more than that. He wanted them to raise an army. Bile rose in Adalina's throat. Windshire—the home of an esteemed member of nobility she knew next to nothing about—would be hosting an annual dinner. One that each lord within riding distance would be attending. Lords who had money and men. Men who could fight.

"The king expects war," Adalina said warily. She saw where things were headed but saying it out loud made it real. Fear settled deep into her bones, weighing her down.

A few of the men looked down at her over their haughty, stuck-up noses. Their disdain made it clear they didn't appreciate having to include her in their goings on. But what did the buffoons expect? They had practically begged her to marry Callum. They wanted her dragon? Fine. But she and Elettra were a package deal. These men would have to get over it.

Uthred looked down at his boots as he spoke. "Considering the rate at which things are moving, we need to plan for all worst-case scenarios. Should Prince Callum have to take up the mantle and call on the dragon bond—"

"You mean, should I be a complete failure?" Adalina crossed her arms. Elettra snorted and the air grew hotter.

Uthred wrinkled his nose at the slight scent of sulfur. "We just mean, if you *decide* that you do not want to fight after all, or if—fate's forbid—something was to happen to you, leaving the dragon riderless..."

Adalina tried not to dwell on the possibility of what might happen if she were to fall in battle or to an assassin's blade. But of course, she knew those things were a threat. There had already been one attempt on her life. What if things didn't work out in her favor next time?

She gnawed at her cheek and checked for Callum's reaction. His face was pale and his grip on her hand tightened ever so slightly. He was still hesitant around Elettra and had said himself that the dragon was Adalina's to ride. Would the council's concern make him change his mind?

She relaxed when she spotted her grandmother coming up the path. Her presence alone made her feel more at ease. Like a piece of home was always within reach. Her grandmother, however, had a hard and determined look plastered across her face.

"Gentlemen," she greeted them curtly.

Uthred's composure faltered slightly in the face of Adalina's grandmother. "Hello. We... we were just suggesting to your granddaughter that—"

She waved him off. "King Alistair has already told me."

Heely's shoulders slumped at that—like he was disappointed that the king was speaking to her without him—but he said nothing.

Her grandmother sneered at the men like they were mud on her boot. "I am simply here to get my granddaughter for her riding lesson."

Uthred didn't shy away from her like the others. "We wouldn't want to keep you. But this is of the utmost importance. We should be prepared for all possibilities. We must see him ride."

Adalina's jaw dropped. "But they're not bonded."

"We are not asking him to call on his rites. It is a simple matter of him getting experience before an emergency arises."

Callum grabbed Adalina by the elbow and said, "Excuse us. I'd like to speak to my wife in private."

Elettra followed them, nearly taking the group of men out with her long, muscular tail in the process. There were a few shouts and then a lot of indignant glares in the dragon's direction. Adalina snorted, trying to keep from laughing, but Callum ignored them, turning her to face him.

He kept his voice low as he said, "I know this isn't something you want to do, but—"

"You think they're right?" Adalina narrowed her eyes. "You agreed. When I promised to marry you, you promised Elettra would not fall to your command."

"I'm not backing out on that agreement."

Adalina tugged away from him, but he grasped on tighter.

"I'm not," he insisted more urgently. "But these types of things are done all the time. There is a plan in place for every scenario. If my father dies, there's a protocol that I'm supposed to follow to take his place. If *I* die, then there is a detailed plan for ways to protect you. It's simply what is done for royals."

Adalina bit her lip. It might be selfish to want to keep Elettra all to herself. She was aware of that. But up to this point, she hadn't cared. Soaring on the dragon's back with only the two of them high above the rest of the world was the most alive she'd ever felt. She wasn't ready to share that with anyone else. Not even the man who was by all rights her husband.

Her eyes darted to her grandmother. She was surrounded by the council. They were speaking in hushed whispers to one another. Some looked put out by Adalina's hesitation. She wished she could tell them to fuck off, but that wouldn't have been very princess-like of her, would it?

Callum caressed her arm affectionately. The gesture would have had her swooning after that moment on the training field, but her body apparently agreed with her head for once. She tore her gaze away from him and back to the people waiting for her answer. When her grandmother noticed her staring, the corner of her mouth perked up and she gave a subtle nod.

Callum took Adalina's hand and ran his thumb over her knuckles. "Don't be mad, please. Not after how well things have been going between us."

"I don't know what you mean," she said stubbornly.

He gave her a knowing look, likely recalling the way her body had curved into his during their training.

With a deep breath, Adalina relented. She peeled his hand off hers and stepped back. With a wave toward Elettra, she said, "Have it your way, husband. By all means, see if she will let you mount her. Because you sure as hell will not be mounting *me* anytime soon after this." She spat the words at him but crossed her arms with a vicious smile.

Callum pursed his lips like he had more to say. But Adalina suspected he didn't want to argue in front of the council. With a cautious gait, he approached the dragon. Despite her size, Elettra didn't seem to tower over him like she did with everyone else. Maybe it was the air of confidence he carried himself with; always seeming so sure of himself and what he intended to do.

Adalina controlled her breath as she watched him raise a hand to pat Elettra on the side of her neck. There was no reason why he couldn't give riding a try if Elettra was willing to let him. Logically, it made sense in case one day Adalina wasn't there to do it. She was the last heir in her grandmother's direct bloodline. Her grandparents never had any other children, nor did Adalina's mother and father.

Her mind betrayed her, allowing unwanted thoughts to creep in. If she and Callum failed to produce a child, then Elettra's connection to her family would end with her. *Or with my husband*, she corrected herself. By the rules of their magic, he *did* have a claim. Even if she liked to pretend otherwise. Sweat beaded on her chest, nearest to her heart. This wasn't at all how she envisioned her life going.

As if sensing a shift in Adalina's mood, Elettra side-stepped just as Callum was getting ready to mount her. She hissed and slammed her tail on the ground in a tantrum. He stumbled back a few steps just as Elettra bared her teeth. It was the first time Adalina had seen the dragon's fire power from this angle. Beyond the steam, deep in the dragon's throat, a small flame grew. The scent of sulfur filled the air and Adalina panicked.

Putting herself in Elettra's path to Callum, she held her hands up. "Stand down."

Adalina had secretly hoped Callum would be unsuccessful, but she didn't want to see him burned to a crisp.

Obediently, the dragon shut her mouth and sat indignantly on her hindquarters with a plop.

Callum's voice had a slight quake to it. "I do believe your beast was about to roast me."

She forced a laugh. "Maybe she's just grumpy. Or hungry?"

He dusted his pants off and shrugged. "I'll let the council know that today will not be the day that they get to see me astride a dragon."

"Good idea." She studied Elettra while her husband strode off toward the group of men.

"You can't set fire to people around here. Especially not *him*." She gestured wildly to Callum. "What's gotten into you?"

Her grandmother sounded amused as she said, "I believe *you* have."

"What is that supposed to mean?"

Elettra lowered her head when Adalina's grandmother settled beside her. The dragon rumbled gratefully as the woman reached up to scratch the base of her horns.

Her grandmother spoke softly. "It means that she values your connection. Enough so that she's opened her mind to you, and it seems you've returned the favor."

Adalina thought about the phantom-like emotions that mirrored Elettra's body language and moods. She knew all about the connection from her lessons and the time she'd spent exploring it over the last few days. But she hadn't put much thought into how much her own emotions could affect Elettra.

She shook her head and said, "I might have been annoyed with Callum and what was happening, but I didn't want her to hurt him."

Her grandmother released a full-hearted laugh. "That, my girl, was just a warning. If Elettra had wanted to hurt him, then there was nothing that could have stopped her. Maybe not even you."

Either way, Adalina would have to control her emotions and find a way to communicate with Elettra when it was time for her to step in to assist.

To the dragon, she said, "It was just one ride. We could have at least let him try."

Elettra blinked sleepily in response. It seemed she was done with the conversation. Adalina took the hint and linked arms with her grandmother.

She steered Adalina back toward the palace as she said, "Best to let sleeping dragons lie for now. We can resume your lessons tomorrow."

"How mad is the council?"

"Don't worry about them." Her grandmother swatted at the air as if she could brush the overbearing men off so easily.

"I don't know what to do. It's hard not to be annoyed that they want him to ride so bad. It feels like they've already declared me a lost cause. Like they think I'm sure to die the moment I engage in any sort of battle."

"You're doing fine, Lina."

Adalina shoved her tangled hair from her face. "It's not like I hate Callum. He's honestly not half bad when he's not barking orders at me. My annoyance can't be strong enough to make Elettra shun him like that."

Her grandmother stopped walking and faced her. "Did you consider that Elettra acted the way she did because you don't trust him yet? Frustration, annoyance, even pure anger... these are all things that any marriage will face. I believe the issue here may be that you have not yet let Callum in here." She poked Adalina's chest over her heart. "If you let that boy in, then so will Elettra. Until then, maybe keep him out of her line of fire."

Her grandmother pulled away and marched up to the palace, leaving Adalina alone with her words lingering in the air. She kicked at the dirt. They'd been married for four days. Despite their long nights talking, they still barely knew each other. How could she be expected to change that in such a short amount of time?

Things were moving quickly with Alistair's obvious intention to raise an army. The faction's threat was a dark storm cloud rolling in. No one knew if or when another attack would come. And now she had to add getting Elettra to let Callum ride her to the list of responsibilities that rested solely on her. She'd done this to herself, really. All those years of wishing for an adventure as grand as her grandmother's and it had finally caught up to her. What was it Solarians always said about fate? Oh, that's right, *don't tempt it.*

Twenty

The palace was filled to the brim with bustling staff and courtiers the next day. Adalina hadn't seen Callum since that morning's training session. Even then, they hardly spoke. The comfortable routine they'd fallen into seemed to have been fractured by the council's pressure for him to ride Elettra. To top it off, word that his father had all but declared they were going to war had been something they weren't prepared for. Tension wove tightly around them.

Callum hadn't mentioned Elettra's threat against him the day before, and he'd spent half their training time joking with the guards on duty. In front of them, he was all broad grins and jokes. But whenever Adalina failed to block a blow or fumbled with an offensive move, his eyes would darken with worry.

After that, she'd gone to the dining hall for a late breakfast. She sat back in her seat, ignoring the staff and socializing courtiers, and crossed her arms. Maybe he wouldn't channel his concern into their training if he stopped using all his energy constantly playing the happy prince. Even now, it chafed to recall how hard he had been pushing her. *"You have no idea what's coming and you need to be ready,"* he had snapped when she complained about having to do the same maneuver nine times in a row until she mastered it.

The thing that bothered her the most was that he was right. She didn't know what was coming. Sitting in on the council meeting before dinner the prior day hadn't been any help. They seemed to be scrambling to grasp on to any solid information they could.

She looked down at her plate with a scowl. The breakfast in front of her was growing cold. She crossed her arms tighter and glared at the dining room entrance. Across the hall was the king's study. The doors were shut tight with two armed guards standing watch. Callum hadn't joined her to eat, and she suspected it was because he was sequestered away in there with his father.

She began to fidget with the lace tablecloth. Everyone seemed on edge, tiptoeing around her while they prepared for the Solstice celebration. Winter was coming, and although Astarfall enjoyed mild weather during those months, they still held a grand ball to welcome the change in season.

Throwing a party with trouble on the horizon was frivolous. But by now, she'd come to expect the lengths King Alistair would go to in order to keep his people happy. To shield them from the ugly truth. And, if the gathering lured out any more would be assassins, then all the better.

She would, of course, be expected to attend at her husband's side. But Elettra would have to remain in her cave. She would take up far too much space at the party. That didn't stop Adalina from requesting that the kitchens send her a feast of her own, though. Mountains of braised lamb, an entire roasted pig, and even some older silver plates to lay out as a present for her to add to her collection of treasures.

The door across the hall clicked open and Adalina perked up. To her surprise, Heely filtered out first. He was spending an awful lot of time at the king's side. When he met her eye, he ducked his head and scurried off. No doubt trying to avoid her relentless questioning. What was the point of him being there if he wasn't going to pass information along to her? Especially when he was the one who had proclaimed himself her personal counselor; stating that he needed to remain in Astarfall for her own benefit.

King Alistair exited next, with Uthred whispering excessively into his ear. The king looked exhausted, with dark rings around his eyes.

Whatever business they were attending to was tiring him out and turning the optimistic man who had welcomed her to their kingdom into something sadder.

What she couldn't figure out, though, was why Uthred and Heely had been invited into the study, but she had not. When Callum strode into the hall, she pressed her lips into a hard, thin line. He, unlike Heely, had the balls to face her. Palace staff appeared at his side, asking if there was anything he needed.

"Food. Some cake if you have it." As they scurried off to fetch it, he shouted after them, "And ale!"

Adalina sat forward, leaning over her plate, and raised an eyebrow at him. "Isn't it a little early for that?"

"It's never too early for cake." He sat down across from her and brushed his hair back with a stretch of his arms.

"The ale, I mean."

He shrugged. Soon, there were several plates in front of him. Three of which held various cakes. Apparently, since he didn't specify what kind he would like, they'd brought him one of each. *Pampered Prince*, she thought sarcastically. Witnessing the way people treated royals was still taking some getting used to.

He thanked the staff with a dazzling smile.

Adalina didn't want to dote. Or shower him with any more attention than he deserved. She wanted answers. So, she pried, "What was that about? Has something happened in the city?"

She knew the king had been walking the streets the day before to assess any danger. And routinely, they were sending guards out to search for any other masked men. The trouble was, they were likely keen to hide in plain sight. If they were, in fact, within the city walls, then they weren't waltzing around in the uniform the rebels had taken a liking to.

"The city appears to be secure for now," he answered vaguely.

"Then what? Has there been any word from the rescue party or the scouts they were after?" she asked, eager for any tiny bit of news and praying it would be good.

Callum took a bite of yellow cake with candied lemons on top and made a sour face. With a shake of his head, he dipped his fork into a red velvety one. It seemed to suit his fancy more, and he took another bite.

Adalina cleared her throat impatiently.

With a sigh, he set the fork down. "They returned empty-handed. There has been no trace of the scouts."

Her stomach sank. It was far from what she hoped to hear. "Did the rescue party see the encampment? What if the men are being held there?"

"The men they sent weren't equipped for that sort of mission. If the missing scouts are in the camp, then getting them out will take a hell of a lot more than a handful of trackers." His words were clipped, drawing the attention of a few courtiers. He waved at them and then lowered his voice. "The council wants to move before the gathering at Windshire—so we can give the lords a detailed account of how many men are at the encampment before asking them to take up arms. My father is sending another scouting party out to gather that intel." He shifted uncomfortably. "They want Elettra to go."

Elettra, but not Adalina. She swallowed her irritation and said, "I can be ready, Callum. You have to admit I'm improving. If I push myself, I can—"

"They don't want to wait. The scouts leave tomorrow."

Her mouth tugged into a frown. "Without me."

"Yes."

"They want you to try to ride Elettra again?"

"Yes," he said more tightly.

"No," Adalina said simply.

No. There wouldn't be a chance to convince the dragon to even allow it. Even if she did, with the ball tonight, there would be no time to prepare him for the ride itself. True, he was in far better shape than she was, considering the years he'd spent building muscle and learning to fight. But what if Elettra changed her mind about him mid-flight? As amusing as it was to see Seraphine use her wind manipulation on him, Adalina's stomach twisted into knots thinking of him slipping from the dragon's back and plummeting to the ground.

Finished with his cake, Callum wiped his mouth with a napkin and placed his hands on the table with a decisive thud. "I'm going to take a nap."

"Seriously?" Adalina rolled her eyes. He and Elettra did have one thing in common: lazing about while in the midst of chaos.

"It's going to be a long night. We take our Solstice ball *very* seriously." He winked.

"Seraphine already filled me in," Adalina replied. It would be a late night of drinking, dancing, and gift giving.

Her stomach dipped. Gifts... she hadn't gotten anything for Callum. Their relationship was already strained by external forces. Perhaps getting him the perfect gift would remind him that she was trying to give him a chance. But she wasn't even sure what he would want. Embarrassment pricked at her. He waved goodbye, and she jumped up from her seat, startling a few of the ladies behind her.

"Sorry," she blushed and headed for the doors that led to the courtyard. If she left now, she'd have just enough time to go down to the shops and make it back in time for drinks before the feast.

She twisted the ring around her finger, a nervous habit she'd picked up as of late. What did one get a man they barely knew but shared a bed with? What sort of gift said, *I like you, but you drive me a bit mad sometimes? I tolerate you, but I'm not quite ready to open my heart to you?* By the time she made it to the market, she was at more of a loss than she'd been at when she started.

The afternoon flew by. Adalina made it back to her chambers just in time to find Seraphine leaning against the door. She was already dressed in a striking silk gown that had a slit down one side of the leg. As always, she was stunning.

Perking up when she spotted Adalina, she said, "You're late!"

"Drinks don't start for another half hour." Adalina clutched the package under her arm tightly, afraid that Seraphine might see it and tell her that it was an awful gift idea for Callum.

"We'll be lucky if we can get you ready in that amount of time." Seraphine corralled her into the room and over to the vanity beside her bed.

Though Adalina had planned to wear one of the many gowns that now hung in her closet—made by the finest tailors in all of Astarfall—she paused when she spotted a dress laid out on the bed.

It was a brilliant silver with delicate green beads woven in. They snaked along the skirt and bodice and reminded her a bit of seaweed. Awestruck, she trailed her fingers along the masterpiece.

"Seems Callum is starting the gift giving early," Seraphine guessed.

"It's breathtaking." Adalina was afraid to even pick it up. It looked so expensive.

Seraphine didn't waste any time, however. She gestured for Adalina to get out of her clothes and had the dress ready for her to step into. The fabric was lighter than it appeared, and the skirt swished with each movement she made like ripples in water.

Her friend had been right about one thing. It took a lot longer than Adalina expected to get the dress laced and her hair done. Seraphine pinned the unruly curls up as best she could. Using her wind manipulation, she attempted to smooth down any strands that dared try to escape her grasp.

"Finished!" Seraphine blew out an exasperated breath. "Now the real fun can begin."

With Adalina's hand in hers, she dragged her down the hall to the large open staircase that led to the grand ballroom. Both courtiers and citizens of the city moved around the room, talking and laughing with drinks in hand. There was a band on a small stage preparing for hours of playing.

Seraphine practically vibrated with excitement beside Adalina and soon she found that she was giddy, too. Guards were spread out through the crowd and lined the walkway outside. Security was at a high alert. For one night, they might actually enjoy themselves.

There hadn't been any more reports of the mysterious shadow beast. No more assassination attempts. And tomorrow, yet another scouting party would leave to assess the threat in close range. What if they, too, didn't come back? Adalina shoved the unwelcomed thoughts away quickly. War might be coming and for just one night, she wanted to feel normal. This could be their last chance to relax and enjoy time in her new home, having fun.

With Seraphine at her side, they wandered through the crowd. Once in a while, a courtier would stop her in order to make idle chit chat.

But there was no sign of Callum. She scanned the crowd, only half listening to a man muttering eagerly about a siren they had spotted off the eastern coast.

Adalina laughed politely at a joke he made about what he would have done when the siren waved at him had his wife not been standing right beside him, but her laugh faltered when she located a tall handsome man with a head of dark hair and piercing dark blue eyes. Callum's dimple was present as he smiled at something a woman beside him said.

Her hand rested on his shoulder, and her body was pressed against his side. She was draping herself over him in a way only lovers were bold enough to do. Callum peeled away from the woman, but she caught him by the jacket. Adalina's vision went white with rage. That might have surprised her more than the offense she was actually witnessing.

Seraphine let out a low, "Uh, oh." And then catching sight of Adalina's face, she said, "Wait, Adalina, that's…"

But she wasn't paying attention. She darted for her husband and the woman. Callum was in the middle of plucking her arm off of him when he spotted Adalina. His brows rose when she reached them, and he dropped the woman's arm like it was a piece of lint he'd found on his jacket.

Controlling her temper and her tone, Adalina greeted him, "Husband."

"Wife." His gaze raked over her, and his eyes darkened in that lustful way they had when she first stood naked in front of him. "You are stunning."

Not you *look* stunning. Or that dress is stunning. *You* are stunning. Maybe he hadn't meant it to flatter her, but it did. At least until she felt the woman's eyes on her. Adalina didn't want to give her the attention she clearly craved, so she kept her gaze trained on Callum.

As if picking up on things, he said, "I didn't mean to be rude. This is—"

"Lady Erabelle," the woman finished for him. She dipped into a low curtsey. "Councilman Uthred's wife."

Adalina allowed herself to take a better look at the woman. From across the room, she had appeared younger. But now Adalina caught the sight of delicate laugh lines around her green eyes as if she'd spent her entire life with a smile plastered on her thin face. She wasn't old by any means. Likely somewhere between Callum and Uthred's ages. And she was gorgeous.

"Pleasure to meet you," Adalina forced a tight smile.

"The pleasure is mine, entirely, Princess." Erabelle's voice had a chime to it and reminded her of birds chirping in the morning. Her midnight black hair flowed freely down her back and her gaze was sharp. Despite her easy smiles, there was an alertness to her. Like a hawk on the hunt. In her presence, Adalina felt like the commoner and Erabelle the royal.

As if sensing her discomfort, Callum offered a hand to Adalina and asked, "Care for a dance?"

In her surprising fit of jealousy, she hadn't realized the band had started playing, and that couples had already taken to the dance floor. It wasn't the urge to dance that made her take his hand, but the simple fact that she wanted to leave this woman behind, along with the bitterness she'd felt before realizing she was Uthred's wife.

Callum drew her gracefully onto the dance floor and placed a steadying hand on her waist. As he took her other hand, holding it up, he asked, "Is everything alright?"

"Fine," she said too quickly. "I mean, I'm fine. I just thought that..."

"That I was flirting with another woman for all the court to see?" He said it as if it was absurd, but lines furrowed between his brows as if the thought of her thinking it hurt him.

"I suppose for a moment I wondered."

He spun her in a circle and then pulled her in close to him. He smelled like the salty sea air and her heartbeat sped despite the slow tempo of the music.

With a low rumble, he said, "I wouldn't do that. Not in front of the court and not behind closed doors. I take our marriage seriously and I would never do that to you."

"Well, you can't blame me for letting my mind wander there. She was all over you and it's not like you and I have... have been together since that night at the Dew Drop."

"That night was more than enough to tide me over until the next," he teased.

She huffed. "Be serious."

"I am. We'll consummate soon enough."

Adalina rolled her eyes at the certainty in his words. She retorted, "The only time you're serious is when you're bossing me on that training field or slipping to and from your father's study." She hated the pout in her voice.

To her relief, he didn't seem to notice or simply didn't care. With youthful arrogance, he said, "Admit it. You were jealous when you saw Erabelle and I talking."

Heat prickled at Adalina's fingertips, and he hissed slightly. She raised her chin to him and said, "Even if I was jealous—and I'm not saying I was—I'd have every right, considering she was draped over you like a winter scarf."

Dancers spun around them in synchrony to a dance she wasn't familiar with. At some point, the song had changed, but Callum continued to lead her in their own dance.

He smiled ruefully as he said, "She was using her wiles to get me to agree to Heely and her husband's proposition."

Her attention perked up at that. "What is it that they're proposing?"

She had to admit it was interesting that Uthred would use his own wife to further his agenda. He and Heely were two sides of the same coin. Each one was a politician through and through; using their charms to get ahead in court. How else could they have gotten so close to the king? But Uthred didn't strike her as a man who would shamelessly ask his wife to flirt in order to get what he wanted.

Callum seemed uninterested in the whole matter because he ignored her question and asked, "So, were you? Jealous, I mean."

He tried to lead her to the left, but Adalina jerked him in the opposite direction as she said, "If I say yes, will you tell me what it is that they want you to agree to so badly?"

He recovered quickly from the stumble and attempted to turn her in the same fanciful move the others on the ballroom floor were doing. She resisted, nearly making him trip over her satin slippered foot.

He shook his head and chuckled. "They want to leave Elettra behind tomorrow. They say a dragon will draw too much attention from the encampment. They don't think it's worth the risk to show our hand so soon without first knowing what we're up against."

Adalina gasped as he dipped her low. When he righted her, his mouth grazed her neck, sending delightful shivers down her spine.

Ignoring the sensation, she mused, "It's not a bad idea. There's been no sign of the beast they're said to control. Why risk them calling on it before we're ready? I don't even know if Elettra is up to fighting shape yet and—"

"That is what I told them." Callum circled her, trailing his hand along her lower back.

"Well, then. There is nothing more to discuss."

She sidestepped him, moving away from his touch. If he agreed, then she didn't see what the issue was.

"My father doesn't want me going into the field unprotected." He snatched her by the waist and pulled her in firmly.

She squirmed. "Then don't go. Let the scouts go on their own."

Truthfully, she didn't like the idea of him risking his wellbeing. She groaned internally. If she couldn't handle seeing him off on a simple scouting mission, what would happen when they were facing an entire army?

"And miss all the fun?" He gave her a dazzling smile, his dimple deepening in his cheek.

Adalina continued to try to slip from his hold. She wasn't interested in dancing any more. Her feet were beginning to grow sore and the turn in conversation made her crave another ale. Seraphine and Alfie caught her eye, and she tried to steer Callum closer to them. He might give up on the dance if he saw his best friend and cousin.

After a few steps toward the edge of the dance floor, Callum gripped her wrist and forced it back onto his shoulder. He pressed her body against his and said, "Are you worried something will happen to me if I go?"

"No," she lied. Although she wished it was the answer, she found that she couldn't get the image of him falling from Elettra's back to his death or being cut down by the silver whips used by the masked men out of her mind. "I just think I should go with you."

"You're not ready," he said simply.

She growled and placed her foot strategically behind him. The element of surprise was on her side. He stumbled backward, just barely finding his balance, and saving them both from being dragged to the floor. With his grip still locked firmly on her, he turned them both in beat to the music once again. The room and crowd around them spun.

"I do love when you play hard to get, *dear wife*."

The way he purred the pet name sent a bolt of heat between her legs. His sly smile told her he knew it, too. Desperate not to lose at their little game, she attempted to pinch the sensitive spot by his neck. The one he'd shown her the day prior during their training that was sure to send a shock shooting through any man's nerves, no matter how big or how strong.

He caught her hand, though, with a rueful smile. "You *are* getting better."

She ignored the hint of pride she felt at his praise and spun away from him.

He caught her, and she snarled, "Perhaps I should show the council just how good of a teacher you are." She tipped her head toward the men gathered at the side of the room.

Callum grinned at the challenge. A few of the dancers nearby stopped what they were doing to watch as their princess and prince faced off in a rather unusual dance. Move after move, Adalina attempted to make him misstep while he blocked each one elegantly.

They stumbled off the dance floor slightly. Seraphine leapt out of their way just in time and Adalina caught her saying, "If that's not flirting, then I don't know what is."

Alfie scoffed. "She clearly can't stand him."

Seraphine patted him gently on the arm and shook her head solemnly. "Perhaps it's time we sat down so that I might explain women to you."

Twenty-One

Adalina woke to an unsettled feeling in the pit of her stomach. Which was strange considering she'd had pleasant dreams of flying with Elettra. Wind, freedom, and endless possibilities. Most of all, no one was there to smother her or watch her with judgment. When she opened her eyes, she found nothing out of the ordinary to bring on such nerves first thing in the morning. It was the same as each one she'd spent in Astarfall. There was shouting down at the docks, songbirds sang somewhere nearby, and the room was filled with a soft light.

When she attempted to turn and stretch, she realized she was pinned down by Callum's leg. It was laid across her own thanks to his incessant need to sprawl out on the bed each night. She had to admit, though, she was getting used to it. Each night that passed with him in her bed made it harder to imagine sleeping alone. And especially after the attack on her first night there, his presence made her feel more secure. So much so that she didn't really mind when his limbs wandered to her side of the bed.

Carefully, she tried to wiggle out from under him. There was a small groan of protest from him, and she had to stifle a laugh in an effort not to wake him. It had been a long night. The ball extended well into the early hours of the morning for some. When they left Alfie and Seraphine, the two of them were finishing a bottle of very expensive bubbly. Others had lost shoes... even dresses and shirts during a competitive game of cards. When she and Callum had retired to their room, the sounds of debauchery and celebration echoed faintly up to them, despite the thick stone walls.

With a grunt, she attempted to move once again, but Callum yawned groggily and rolled over. His arm found her, wrapping around her stomach. Butterflies fluttered at the intimacy of the touch. It was so familiar. Like something a blissful husband would do to his wife. If only their circumstances had been different, then she wouldn't be laying there stiff as a board, unsure of what to do.

She cleared her throat. "Callum. It's morning."

He hummed in response.

"Shouldn't you be preparing to leave?"

She supposed if the scouting party was ready to go, then someone would have sent word to him. But considering how unphased the Astarfallen seemed when it came to most serious matters, it wouldn't surprise her if they were taking their time to recover from the ball before setting out for the western border.

Callum's eyes popped open. "Oh, shit." Before sitting up, his gaze dropped to the arm he had wrapped tenderly around her. "Sorry," he muttered as he drew away and got out of the bed.

The absence of his touch was felt more strongly than she expected. But rather than admit it out loud—that she would be fine with staying in bed and eating breakfast together—she rose as well and began dressing for the day.

When the reality of the day and their lives set in, an argument rested on the tip of her tongue, but she tried to hold back. She wanted to go with the scouting party. But Callum had made it clear that the council and their preconception of her would stand in her way. Would they make a scene if she strutted down there and mounted the dragon wordlessly? Going against their wishes wouldn't win her any of their good grace. But wasn't this bigger than their opinions? Today, Callum and his men would creep dangerously close to the enemy.

As stated before, she agreed that perhaps it was too soon to show Elettra to the enemy. If they did have a beast to rival a dragon, then Elettra was Astarfall's secret weapon. That didn't stop her from wanting to tag along, though. She and Elettra could stay out of sight. Land before getting too close to the camp. To be near just in case anything went wrong.

Callum's birth-gifted power was strong. Enough so that the council was fine with sending their prince to the mountains which would place him close to enemy territory. But would he be a match for the faceless men and their silver whips? What if Astarfall's magic wasn't enough to stand against their foe?

She shivered as she recalled the terrible masks that veiled them to take away any individuality of the man underneath. That was likely the most dangerous thing about them. It was horrible not knowing who your enemy was. Instead, always wondering if the man they're passing on the street or even in the palace was working against them in secret.

And there was still the matter of who had told the rebels that Callum would be in the village the night they'd gone for drinks with Alfie and Seraphine. Or how the assassin had so easily gotten through the palace defenses without drawing attention.

The men who had been captured in the village attack still weren't talking, according to Callum. It was fruitless. Whoever was leading them seemed to either inspire enough fear or loyalty that they weren't willing to turn on him or her.

Callum grabbed the sword and scabbard that was sitting against the wall by Adalina's vanity. Funny how she'd gotten used to weaponry laying around. Like swords and daggers were nothing more than strange decorating choices her husband had made.

He paused and picked up a neatly wrapped package. Her stomach twisted with tiny knots as he turned it over and examined it curiously.

"What's this?" he asked with a note of amusement.

She licked her lips. After the tension between them on the dance floor, she'd drank heavily. It had lifted her spirits and made her forget about her irritation toward him, but it had also made her forget about the gift she'd gotten him for Winter Solstice.

"It's for you."

He spun to face her with his eyebrows raised. "Me? You got me a gift?"

"Well, isn't that the tradition?" She took a few steps closer to him and twisted her hands together nervously. What if he didn't like it? It wasn't quite as elaborate as the dress he'd gifted her. As a prince, he had everything he ever needed. It was what had made shopping for him so agonizing.

"Can I open it?" His eyes sparkled with anticipation.

"Sure," she answered, hugging herself.

Efficiently, he tore the wrapping off and opened the box. The smirk on his face dropped when he did, replaced with something softer. He pulled the trinket out and turned it over gently in his hands.

Adalina bit her lip. "I wasn't sure what to get you. But then I stumbled onto a sailor's shop near the docks. I remembered what you said about watching the ships when you were younger..."

The compass was made of the finest brass. It had cost nearly every coin she'd had on hand. In truth, she wondered if the shopkeeper had taken pity on her and undercharged her, noticing how uncomfortable and uncertain she was when she picked it up.

Callum said nothing as he rubbed his thumb over the smooth pieces of moonglass, which were inlaid in the compass housing. They had caught her eye the moment she walked into the shop. Mirroring the stones on her wedding ring.

"You probably don't have much use for it, but I thought you might fancy the craftsmanship and—"

"It's perfect," he whispered in awe. His eyes were misty. "Thank you."

She gulped with relief. "I'm glad you like it."

His gaze flitted to her gown, and he pursed his lips. "You can't possibly wear that."

She furrowed her brow and crossed her arms defensively at the sudden shift in conversation. "What's wrong with this dress?"

"It'll never do for the journey." He shook his head and placed the compass safely in his pocket.

Hope swelled in her chest. "You mean..."

"If you're to scout with us, then you'll need something more durable than that. Your riding leathers, to be more specific." He gestured to the drawers at the base of the armoire. "I'll wait in the sitting room for you."

Adalina sucked in a sharp breath. She called after him before he closed the bedroom door. "What made you change your mind?"

His hand rested on the pocket where the compass now sat. "Let's just say your compass reminded me of what direction I should be taking."

"But the council..."

Callum scrunched his nose. "If the council has a problem with how I run my missions, then they can go out there themselves. You were right last night. You're more capable than they or anyone else have been giving you credit for."

She pulled the riding leathers from her wardrobe and gripped them tight. "Thank you. That means a lot."

He took a step toward her and for a moment, she wondered if he might reach for her.

Instead, he looked her in the eyes and said, "I made a commitment to honor you and promised not to hold my power over you. It's easy to forget sometimes where our loyalties should lie. If you wish me to stand with you against the council, then that is what I will do."

When he left the room, tears pricked her eyes. His was a small declaration, but it filled her heart with more hope than she'd had since coming to Astarfall. For the first time since their binding ceremony, she felt as if he was truly on her side. Maybe there was a chance of working together comfortably in this marriage after all. A wide grin spread across her face as she pulled the fitted riding pants on.

***

The team was assembled and ready to go by midmorning. A few of the scouts had a sickly green pallor to them, but their eyes were bright and alert, nonetheless. It turned out that Alfie was joining them as well. Aside from tousled hair, he seemed more put together and energetic than the rest. He offered her an erratic wave and a lopsided smile.

"He's spry, that one," said Callum with the warmth of friendship. He and Alfie had grown up together and remained best friends even as they grew and took on the respective responsibilities of adulthood.

According to Callum, the three of them—Seraphine being the third—had always been inseparable. And although Alfie had taken over the Dew Drop Inn after his father's passing, Callum often invited him on his travels, trusting him, more than anyone, with his life.

Elettra—who would have preferred to lounge in the sun—was also wide eyed and focused on the task at hand. She knelt to allow Adalina an easy mount, swiping her up in that familiar way by using her tail.

The councilmen stood to the side with Uthred and Heely; all with skeptical scowls on their faces. There had been some argument as to her inclusion, but in the end, Callum stood his ground and won the battle. Adalina made a point of ignoring the lot of them entirely.

Callum and the other scouts were mounted on their horses and, with a nod from their prince, they set off. Adalina patted Elettra on the neck and clicked her tongue, signaling for her to take to the sky.

The heavy beat of her wings sent wind flying at the councilmen. There were a few indignant shouts, but soon she and the dragon were too far to hear anything other than the breeze blowing by them.

Elettra's stomach contracted as she took a deep breath, making Adalina's legs rise and fall. Pleasure tickled her senses, and she wasn't sure if it was Elettra's or her own. Soon, Callum and his group were mere dots below them. Like buttons scattered on her mother's shop floor. But the dragon followed their path closely, careful not to go too far ahead. It was the one thing Callum had asked of them.

With a slight nervous tremble in his voice, he had said, "Don't go off on your own. If anyone in the encampment spots you, then we'll be in for a fight."

When she asked if it would be better to go at night, he simply told her that it would hinder their chances of finding signs of the original scouting party that had been lost to them. At any moment, this could turn into a rescue mission.

In the meantime, their goal was to observe. Elettra's presence was merely a precaution. A way to keep them safe if the rumors about a hellish beast were true. The men rode fast, unhindered by the smooth terrain leading along the coast.

It was hours before they reached the rougher landscape near the western mountains. Adalina ran her fingers over Elettra's glittering scales, appreciating how they shined in the light like iridescent shells. Something delicate and white fluttered on top of them, and Adalina reared back to look at the sky.

Flurries? They were nearly unnoticeable. The clouds were clear but for a few angry tendrils of gray snaking through it. It was odd, to say the least. Snow would be falling by now in Solaris, but everyone—even a foreign princess—knew that Astarfall was spared from winter weather. She shivered and tapped Elettra twice on the neck.

Taking her cue, the dragon dipped lower until Callum and his crew came into focus. From there, Adalina couldn't see the encampment—it was blocked by the mountain's peak. If she rose higher, she should have been able to get eyes on it. But the instructions had been clear. Elettra was not there to scout. She was there for protection. Callum and Alfie insisted they would be capable of getting close enough to the camp on foot using a pass between the mountains without being spotted.

Using the jagged range for cover, Elettra landed heavily. The horses stamped their hooves in an open grievance about having the beast deign to come so close to them. The men, however, shrank back. All except Callum, who kept a respectable distance, but stood his ground.

The prince was all business, offering no smiles or warm welcomes. Adalina supposed that around the handful of men he'd put together himself, he didn't see a need to hide behind his optimistic facade. Were only those he found worthy able to witness the mask drop?

If so, what did it say about her? There were moments where the squeeze of her hand or the unabashed frown thrown her way made her think that maybe he was beginning to put her into that category. But then there were others where he gave her a carefree shrug or where he plied her with easy smiles.

He cut through her thoughts with a firm tone as he said, "I was just instructing everyone on the signal. If we end up in a situation we can't see our way out of—fates forbid—then we are to send up a flare, calling Elettra to our aid."

Adalina peered around. None of the men had packs on them. Added baggage would only be a burden. "Where are the flares?"

Alfie held his hands up and winked as a few tiny bursts of light shot out of his fingertips. Adalina raised a skeptical eyebrow.

Quickly, Alfie shrugged and said, "I assure you I can produce much larger ones. That was just for demonstration."

"Right..." Adalina smirked. Then to Callum asked, "And what will I be doing?"

He stacked driftwood and lit a fire as he said, "Waiting with Elettra."

"Of course," she mumbled under her breath and kicked at the dirt.

He didn't seem to hear her as he began barking orders at the men. It was just as well because she wasn't actually annoyed at being left behind this time. She belonged with Elettra. It was why she had come.

The reason she'd put herself in this position to begin with. And she truly was grateful that he had helped her stand up to the council so she could be there at all.

While the men set off on foot, Callum lingered a moment. He shifted uncomfortably on his feet, bouncing a bit with nervous energy.

Finally, he said, "If anything happens... If, for any reason, Elettra can't do anything to help, I want you two to fly back to the palace. Don't take any unnecessary risks."

"Aren't we here for just that purpose?" Her throat tightened.

As much as she had criticized his easy-going ways, *worried* Callum was turning out to be much worse. It reminded her how out of her element she was. How inexperienced she was in these matters, as much as she hated to admit it.

She placed a hand on his arm and kissed him on the cheek. It seemed like something a good wife would do, after all. A gesture to bring her husband comfort before embarking into enemy territory.

"Everything will be fine," she forced herself to say, not too sure whether she believed it. "I'll be here waiting for you when you get back."

A soft smile spread across his face. Wordlessly, he turned and broke into a jog to catch up to the others. She sighed and spun to Elettra, who was watching Callum with what she could have sworn was a frown.

"Looks like it's just us," Adalina chirped as she clasped her hands together.

Elettra gave a small shake of her head and some of the concern Adalina was feeling from her faded. After a while, the two of them settled in as comfortably as they could, considering they were in the middle of nowhere on their own. Her nerves were kept at bay with Elettra beside her. The dragon might not have been much of a conversationalist, but she was an excellent listener.

"I just can't figure him out," Adalina said as she handed Elettra the largest piece of dried venison in their pack.

They were sitting face to face on the hard dirt and her butt was beginning to fall asleep. Taking a smaller piece for herself and tearing into it, she continued with a mouthful, "One minute he's all smiles and treating the world like his own personal playground, but then the next I catch the faintest glimpse of an edge underneath the surface. Like he's bottling up all his fears and worries until it begins to spill out drop by drop."

Elettra huffed in response.

Adalina waved away the small puff of steam that drifted from the dragon's nose and exclaimed, "You see it too, right?"

A faint sensation of agreement warmed Adalina's chest.

"What he did for us today *was* kind. He could have just as easily refused to help."

Elettra gave a curt nod, and Adalina's heartbeat slowed to a steady rhythm. She tried to put an emotion to the sudden ease she was experiencing... Appreciation. That's what she was picking up from the dragon.

She glanced over at the mountain range. The sun was sinking below the rocky peaks. It was getting late. Though it was difficult to tell how long it would take the men to make it to the camp on foot—if it was even still there—her stomach twisted into knots. Something didn't feel right. It was too quiet. Like everything around them had gone still. Her heartbeat thudded in her ears and Elettra's large tail twitched, making the horses dance in place irritably.

Adalina didn't dare take her eyes off the sky beyond the rocky ridges. If a flare went up, she wanted to be ready. Perhaps she and Elettra had gotten too comfortable waiting around. She might not be an experienced warrior, but she should have known better than to let her guard down for even a moment. No matter how far removed from the mission she might have felt in staying behind.

What if they had been captured? What if they'd spotted the missing scouts and tried to sneak in on their own to retrieve them? She didn't know Callum well enough to anticipate what he might risk in order to save his people. Would he do something foolish? Like trying to take on an army without a dragon present to give them the upper hand?

Every muscle in her body went rigid. With a thudding heart, she got to her feet. If she and Elettra took the pass through the mountains, they could get close enough to the camp without the risk of being spotted in the sky.

Elettra, as if anticipating her decision, stood as well. The dragon was buzzing with excitement. But not the good kind. It was the sort of nervous energy one got when they were about to do something dangerous and possibly stupid.

It didn't get more dangerous than sneaking up to an enemy camp on foot. But Adalina couldn't wait around any longer. She would never forgive herself if something happened to Callum and the other men. Especially when she could have done something to help them.

When they got to the opening of the pass, she spoke low to Elettra, "When we get to the other end, we must remain out of sight. Stay close to the ridge. We only reveal ourselves if we meet trouble on the other side. Got it?"

A low rumble came from Elettra's throat in agreement. That was all Adalina needed to find the courage to take the first step.

Twenty-Two

The pass was wide. Adalina guessed it was manmade so that Astarfallen villagers on the other side of the range could pass through easily when bringing supplies to and from the city or other villages. As far as she knew, this territory mostly consisted of farmers and a few secluded villages. Many of which had become deserted with the recent pillages made by the faceless men.

Leaving Solaris had been hard on her. But she couldn't imagine being forced away from everything you knew due to violence. It wasn't fair to them. But if these rogues were using those raids to weaken the border, it was working.

When they came to the end of the pass, tents rose in the distance. The only thing separating them, and the mountain range was a field of ice. So slick that the setting sun reflected off of it, casting lights like the ones that lit up the winter sky at night in Solaris. But it was the number of canvas tents that made her skin crawl. Had she not already witnessed the vast camp from above, she'd have thought she was looking at a mirage now.

Then she heard it. The heart stopping sound of men crying out in battle. She signaled for Elettra to back up. The dragon did as she bid, pressing her massive body into the side of the mountain. Adalina peered around one of the large stones to get a safe view of the field. Arrows blotted the sky, imbedding themselves into the frozen ground around Callum and the others.

He and his men launched their power at the archers and dodged arrows with an ease she envied. But no matter how skilled they might be, there were too many of the faceless men to fend off. And the icy landscape separating them gave the archers an advantage Callum and his men did not have.

Adalina's heart lurched into her throat. She had to get them out of there. If she could avoid the arrows, she and Elettra could fly the men to safety. But even a dragon was not immune to arrows if they aimed at the right spot. She couldn't risk it.

If the men were closer, they could use the pass for cover and fly from there. She took a bold step, but Elettra's tail swept her backward. The dragon hissed, filling the air with putrid steam.

"We need to get their attention," Adalina explained. "There are too many archers for you to risk going out there. If we were already in the sky..."

Her thoughts raced. Even if they had flown instead of taking the pass, Elettra would have had to land in the line of arrow fire to let the men mount her.

"This is the only way," she pleaded as she tried to climb over the dragon's tail.

With a resigned sigh, Elettra put her tail down. Adalina slipped from the pass, remaining close to the rocks, and whistled through two fingers. Collectively, the men whipped their heads around. When Callum met her eye, his face flushed a deep red and his nostrils flared.

"Get out of here!" he shouted furiously.

"Get to the pass. Elettra can get *all* of us out of here!" she shouted back, equally furious that he would waste time trying to get her to leave without them. Couldn't he see she was saving their asses?

Before Callum could respond, an arrow met his shoulder. The sound of it puncturing leather, skin, and muscle was sickening. For the first time, Adalina didn't appreciate the enhanced hearing that Elettra was sharing with her. Bile rose in her throat, accompanied by unadulterated fear.

Alfie grabbed Callum by the uninjured arm and pulled him toward the pass. The others followed, still shooting their magic—which came in the form of water, earth, and wind—back at the arrows to block any from hitting their mark. Adalina backed up a step, ready to mount Elettra and give them all a hand up. But Alfie's eyes widened into saucers.

"Behind you!" the shout tore from his throat in desperation.

She spun around, tripping over her own feet and hitting the ground just before a veiled man could strike her. He stumbled a few steps away from her, giving her enough distance and time to regain her footing.

Fire rumbled from Elettra's belly, and a hiss escaped through her nose, but she remained hidden inside the pass just as she had been ordered to do. Adalina could deal with this bastard all on her own. She balled her hands into fists and when the man advanced on her again, she kicked him in the shin. There was a crack, and he hit the ground, shouting profanities at her.

Deep satisfaction flooded her chest, and she reared back to kick him again. This time, her foot connected with his chin. The man stopped moving. Had she killed him?

She jumped when Callum reached her side. His eyes were stormy, and she could tell he was frustrated with her, but pride filled his voice as he said, "Knocked him out cold. Well done."

"And this time, it was on purpose," she said, unable to hide the puff in her chest.

"Well, you do have a magnificent teacher." He winked, but groaned as he held his injured arm close to his stomach.

"We need to get you out of here," Adalina said, ushering him into the pass and glancing behind to be sure they weren't followed.

There was no sign of more faceless men, but arrows continued to rain down near them. She tensed, even though it appeared they were out of range.

Two of their men stepped forward as if to pick the unconscious man up, but Callum shook his head. "Leave this one. Bringing him will be a risk. And getting information from him isn't worth the fight if he wakes. Besides, if he's anything like the others taken during the tavern attack, he won't speak a word of their plan."

They nodded in agreement and walked to Elettra, looking like someone was asking them to jump off a cliff at freefall. But the dragon simply offered her tail to help them up. One by one, they climbed onto her back, leaving enough room at the front for Adalina and Callum.

Once mounted, Callum said with pain laced in his voice, "We can't leave the horses behind."

"What if the rogues follow us?" Adalina asked with a furrowed brow.

It felt good to have him sitting securely behind her, but she feared the injury he'd endured. What if he fell off? She nestled between his legs and gripped his thighs tightly.

His breath was warm on her neck as he said, "It would take them time to cross that icy terrain of theirs. If we hurry, we'll be fine. They have safety where they are right now. I doubt they'd risk that by leaving and making themselves vulnerable just for a few scouts."

Adalina nodded and signaled for Elettra to take off. With two taps, the dragon kept low, not wanting to rise any higher than necessary. She was still Astarfall's secret, assuming the man Adalina had knocked out hadn't spotted her in her hiding place.

They landed by the frantic horses and the men slipped off the dragon on shaky feet. One had turned green, and she worried he might be sick from the flight. Alfie wasted no time scrambling across the pebbled path to the horses. He gestured for the others to hurry. They were running so fast they were almost a blur in the dim light of the evening.

Adalina dismounted before Callum and reached out a hand to help him down. He grunted in pain and Elettra freely offered her tail to help him. Blood was soaking through his clothes and Adalina gasped at how much there seemed to be. His handsome face had taken on an eerily pale shade, and he stumbled a few steps. She threw his uninjured arm around her shoulders and helped him to a flat stone. He shuffled his feet and collapsed with a huff when they reached it.

Her panic rose, filling every crevice of her body, when he slumped over slightly. His head rolled as if he was trying to hold on to consciousness. She dropped to her knees in front of him. She'd never seen him like this. So... fragile.

She couldn't figure out what had gone wrong. How had the archers caught sight of them? Why did they risk going out in the open like that?

"What happened out there?" she breathed.

Alfie joined her and answered, "They had the entire field surrounding the camp encased in that ice. We wanted to get a better count of the tents. To see just how many men they had with them, so we tried to get closer. But it was like walking on a frozen lake."

With a weak bite, Callum said, "They knew we were coming. They waited until we were far enough on the ice that it would be difficult to run back. And then the arrows came."

She swore as her gaze fell to his wound. She pulled the torn shirt away to get a better look. There should have been an arrow there. She'd seen it hit him with her own eyes. No one had pulled it out. Yet there was no longer anything there. Still, it was clear something had sliced through his shoulder.

One of the other scouts stuttered, "I-ice. The arrows. They were..."

"Ice," Alfie finished. "Magic crafted."

Not an enchanted object. Otherwise, there would have been a physical item still in its place. They hadn't come from an alchemist. The men weren't Festiri. Her head spun. That left only one possibility. Only one type of person could wield frost and ice with their bare hands. It was the confirmation they needed. Knowing that her grandmother had defeated them once before should have brought her a sense of comfort. But defeat had come at a cost. If the frost breathers really were back, then so many lives could be lost.

Callum reached for her with concern clouding his eyes. "You're alright?"

"Yes," she answered, confused. "Of course, I am."

Relief passed over his face, then he growled as Alfie pulled the shirt off him completely.

Adalina grabbed the shirt from Alfie and tossed it on the ground. Guilt gnawed at her as she took in the sight of Callum. She hadn't meant to distract him. To make him let his guard down.

Her voice cracked as she said, "I didn't mean for you to get hurt. I was trying to save you."

"I'm just glad *you* are safe," he said with a smile. He sat up straighter with a grunt and added, "Besides, I've been in worse scrapes than this." He attempted to shrug but hissed in pain.

Well, at least he was the same old Callum. And despite the blood loss, the color was returning to his face.

Alfie snorted to himself, then handed Adalina a needle. "You can sew, right? Callum said you learned in your mother's shop."

"Y-yes, but..." Nausea rolled in her stomach as she looked at the torn flesh and the blood running from the wound. "I'm not a healer."

"We need to stop the blood loss. Even with as fast as Elettra can fly, it's not a risk we should take. And if we hope to get him to a healer before an infection sets in, then it needs to be sewn up."

She shook her head vehemently. "I can't."

Alfie handed her something that looked like a thick black thread. "I believe in you." Then he joined the others who were facing the mountain pass. They were poised for a fight on their horses' backs.

Callum took a flask and poured its contents onto his wound with a hiss. "Come on, we both know you've been itching to stab me with something since we met."

She chuckled uncomfortably. "Interesting that nearly getting yourselves killed hasn't impeded your ability to make a joke out of any situation."

He scoffed, but quieted down as she threaded the needle with trembling hands. It took her a few tries to get it, but once she did, she poured the alcohol in the flask over it. *Just pretend you're mending his shirt,* she said to herself. If she tried hard enough, maybe she could convince herself that this was no worse than pushing a needle into really thick fabric.

There was a sickening pop as the needle punctured his skin. Her stomach lurched, and she gagged loudly. "Oh shit, I think I'm going to be sick."

"*You're* going to be sick?" Callum said incredulously.

She pushed it through the other side of his skin and drew the thread away in an effort to close the wound. But the resistance of getting the thread to pull through brought bile to her throat. Her eyes burned and began to water.

"Callum," she croaked.

Hoping to quell the lightheadedness, she let go of the needle and pressed her head between her legs. Small white dots clouded her vision and Elettra grumbled behind her.

"I think I'm going to—"

The world turned bright white before fading from her view as darkness claimed her.

Twenty-Three

When Adalina came to, she was flying. With a jolt, she scrambled to grab hold of Elettra, but the steady arms wrapped around her gave her pause. It took a moment to regain her bearings before realizing she wasn't alone on the dragon.

Callum was mounted behind her with his arms bracing her on either side. The tension in her shoulders melted away, and she leaned back, into his warmth. The mountains were gone, replaced by the smooth terrain surrounding the palace.

His breath tickled her ear as he said, "Welcome back, dear wife."

"What happened?" she asked, reaching for her head, which was throbbing.

"You fainted," there was laughter in his voice. "Seems we can rule out healer as your life calling."

"I told you I wasn't up to the task." She crossed her arms, confident in her seat on Elettra's back and Callum's hold on her. But then guilt crept in. "Are you okay? Who finished dressing your wound?"

"I did," he said proudly. "Did a fine job, too, if I do say so myself."

She wanted to roll her eyes. A small laugh bubbled up in her throat. "I suppose you're never going to let me live this one down."

"Ah, who would have guessed you know me so well?"

She shook her head, then her gaze fell to the dragon's graceful, spiraling horns. "Elettra's been following your commands?"

Callum's laugh vibrated against Adalina's back and he said, "I think she was less worried about arguing with me and more concerned about getting you out of there as quickly as possible."

She caressed Elettra's neck, embarrassed by how relieved she was to hear that. The loyal dragon hadn't heeded Callum's authority as Adalina's husband, but rather relented in order to keep her safe.

Elettra chortled in response as if to say, *Of course, silly girl.*

Once the palace was within view, Adalina realized how desperately she wanted to put her feet on solid ground. As much as she loved being in the air with Elettra, after passing out and waking up in the sky, she was weak and disoriented.

Callum's hands flew to her thighs, and he gripped them firmly as Elettra descended. The dip tickled Adalina's stomach, but his touch sent an electrifying feeling elsewhere. They hadn't been this close to one another in a while, unless you counted their bed in which he spent most of the night tossing and turning, throwing his limbs around carelessly. This was somehow much more intimate.

When they landed, Heely and Uthred were there to greet them. Uthred was stone faced, waiting properly to the side while she and Callum dismounted. But Heely was in a frenzy. He waved his arms wildly at the palace staff.

"Get them some warm blankets! And ale. Lots of ale."

They scurried off to do as he commanded.

Then he turned on her. "What happened out there? Tell me everything. Leave no detail out."

Taken aback, Adalina narrowed her eyes. "I will report to my father-in-law. You may hear our account then."

Who was he to demand anything from her? Especially information, when he had spent the last week shadowing the king like he was a courtier of Astarfall. Fear from earlier turned to indignation as she added, "Remember, Heely. You are a Solarian councilman meant to serve *me.*"

He smoothed out his shirt and, more calmly, said, "Of course."

He and Uthred exchanged a look of confusion. Perhaps because they had yet to hear her speak with such unharnessed ire. Clear from the distressing sight of Callum's blood, the weight of what they'd witnessed settled over her. Ice, frost, and magic that was unhindered, untied to any sort of enchantment process but was instead called upon by sheer will. Who else could do such a thing but the exiled Astarfallen? The men her grandmother had valiantly fought against in defense of Solaris so long ago.

Heat flared through her, and she felt as if she might combust. This was personal. These men were spoken of in hushed tones. Stories of their malevolence and the lives lost because of it had stuck with her throughout her life.

She glanced at Callum, who was taking a tonic from the healer. He winced when he moved. She hated seeing him this way. Hated what those bastards had done to him. And a new fire burned in her belly. One that she would tuck away and use to keep her people safe. To make her grandmother proud.

King Alistair and Queen Gwendolyn strode out to them. They gave Elettra a respectful nod, which she seemed to appreciate judging by the happy rumble she made in return. Adalina's fury from the day lessened when her grandmother appeared next. She stood beside Elettra, placing a hand on her head like the old friends they were. Then Alistair implored Callum and Adalina to spill everything.

Callum did most of the talking, considering he had been the one to reach the thick of it first. With each detail he gave indicating that they'd been correct in their theory about the frost breathers having something to do with the attacks, his father grew pale and sickly.

When Callum finished, Alistair said, "Frost like that found so close to the sea... there is no disputing what sort of magic is responsible."

Adalina recalled the painful icy sensation she'd gotten from the would-be assassin that had broken into her room. "During the attack in our chambers, the intruder said something about the chosen rising again. Do you think they're here to finish what they started? To conquer land for themselves."

Her grandmother shook her head vehemently. "They're certainly here for the land, but this feels more personal than that. Otherwise, why not target a smaller, more defenseless kingdom like they did before? Instead, they're choosing to risk a fight with people who wield powerful magic that rivals their own."

"That's why they broke into our room." Adalina inched closer to Callum. "Maybe they expected to find you there, too."

Her grandmother nodded. "What better way to get their revenge than by killing the grandson of the king who banished them and the granddaughter of the woman who defeated them?"

Through clenched teeth, King Alistair added, "And in the process, getting rid of the heirs to the throne."

Things were seeming bleaker by the minute. Adalina dug her nails into her palm, but Callum put his hand in hers and held it firmly. She welcomed the touch, but it didn't stop the anger and helplessness. Hatred was a powerful motivator. And these men had little to lose. They'd already lost their homes and the lives of many of their people in the Great War.

Elettra's tail twitched as Adalina said, "Whoever is leading them has instilled loyalty, fear, or both. Until we know who he or she is, stopping them will be difficult."

King Alistair's gaze was filled with respect as he agreed. "My daughter-in-law is right. If we find the leader, then we stand a much better chance of ending this without risking any Astarfallen lives."

Finally, something she and the king agreed on.

Heely caught her eye as he ducked his head and slipped through the crowd back into the palace. She wished she could do the same. Go and hide in her room while she grappled with revelations of the horrid day. The whole situation was too much for anyone to handle alone. But she was glad she didn't have to. She looked up at Callum with a half-smile.

Adalina was tense and her muscles protested when she moved with the crowd back toward the palace doors. She had desperately hoped Callum had been wrong about the frost breathers being the culprits. Her people had a horrible history with them, but she was curious now to know more about his family's part in it.

King Alistair called Callum to his side and leaned in close to talk to him.

Her grandmother fell into step with her and furrowed her brow. "Are you sure you're alright, Lina?"

Adalina's doubts tumbled out of her mouth, "I understand why they would have wanted revenge after losing to you in the Great War. But why would their descendants go through this much trouble? Why would they risk going to war for something that happened so long ago?"

Her grandmother gulped. "The old Astarfallen King wronged them in the worst way imaginable. You've heard the stories about horrible frostbitten magic coming for our lands. But the men who I fought weren't born bad. Their leader, Rothin, and his inner circle were the real problem. When they were in Astarfall, they did everything they could to find prosperity despite their king's resistance."

Adalina sighed. "Wanting to prosper doesn't make you a bad person."

Her grandmother clucked her teeth. "Not unless you're willing to hurt others in the process. Their propaganda got others who shared the same power into trouble. The king feared that with their rise in power, their magic would be catastrophic to Astarfall's climate and lifestyle. The king thought he needed to keep things the way they were in order to preserve his kingdom's way of life. To keep the fields free of blight, to maintain weather that would attract travelers from all over the world. He claimed the frost wielders were unnatural. A danger to Astarfall. The king simply didn't want their kind around. He made the people fear that they would use their abilities to plunge Astarfall into an eternal winter. The people turned on any frost wielder they came across. Fear turned to violence. When the king exiled them, it wasn't with a kind hand. Women and children born with the ability to wield frost died."

A lump formed in Adalina's throat. "But they were innocent. They didn't deserve to be punished with the same severity as the radicals."

"Still, they all paid the price. After that, everyone was afraid. Those coined *frost breathers* were exiled. They had nowhere to go and nobody but Rothin to turn to and trust. That's when he decided to make a new home in Solaris. It was his inner circle that believed they could rule beyond Astarfall. They intended to take the world by icy storm, starting with Solaris. Those who were innocent before became soldiers out of necessity. What other choice did they have when they were watching their children and babies starve to death in exile?" Tears filled her grandmother's eyes as she finished, "I have to live with the choices I made back then to protect Solaris at the cost of those men's lives. It grieves me to know that you may have to face similar choices."

"Do you think this can be resolved without bloodshed? If we can plead with them, or make things right after what happened to them? There has to be a way to fix this without it costing lives in Astarfall."

Her grandmother pursed her lips and wiped away her tears. "Maybe at one time there was the possibility of that. But I'm afraid these men have been raised on stories of how they were wronged. It may be too late."

The frost breathers were before Adalina's time, but the stories were enough to set her teeth on edge. Worst of all was the look on her grandmother's face. Adalina saw through her hardened expression. And she swore she caught fire glinting in her eyes.

This was unfinished business for her grandmother. And for Elettra, who was watching them all with sharp alertness. At one time, it might have frightened Adalina. But after the attack in the village, the attempt on her life in her room, and Callum's wound, it was starting to feel personal to her, too. If these faceless men refused to see reason, then they were cowards. Hiding behind their masks and their icy fortress. If it came down to it, she had to keep her people safe, right?

One thing she was certain of was that ice and frost had a weakness. Fire. And that was exactly what Adalina had.

Despite Callum's protests, the palace healers tended to his wound. They fawned over his handiwork at sewing himself back together and he soaked up the praise with sly glances in Adalina's direction. She rolled her eyes in joking exasperation. He really was never going to let her live this down.

He seemed happy to lounge lazily as one person after another came to pamper him with food, gifts, or words of encouragement. Once the parade of his adoring fans cleared out, she flopped on the sofa beside him. He moved his feet quickly before she squished them and propped himself up on his elbows.

"How are you doing?" he asked with sincerity.

"Fine," she said, though she was still trying to process everything.

Knowing it really could be the frost breathers should have either comforted her or terrified her. They had been defeated once before and that gave her hope that they could be again. But really, the moment she and Callum had gotten back to their chambers, she'd felt rather numb. Unsure of what to do with herself while they waited for King Alistair to make a plan.

All he seemed to have so far was to send Callum to Windshire. She and her husband would go and request that the ruling nobility ready their men in the event of a fight. But it would take time and effort to convince the nobles to give up enough gold to pay and feed an army. Especially when King Alistair had gone through so much trouble keeping the severity of the situation from them. Only telling his innermost circle might very well be his downfall. If the lords didn't believe Callum when he presented the threat to them, then they would never secure their support.

Her chest ached at the thought.

To her surprise, Callum sat up and scooted closer to her. "I'm hesitant to admit it to you, but I was afraid out there."

"Who could blame you? Anyone who says getting shot doesn't frighten them is lying."

"No," he shook his head, and a few strands of his hair fell over his eyes. She fought the urge to push it back and run her fingers through it as he said, "I was afraid for *you*. When I saw you on that field, it was like someone plunged a knife into my heart."

"Nope," she teased, "just an arrow in your shoulder."

His laughter didn't reach his eyes. "I was worried I wouldn't be able to..."

He bit his bottom lip, and for a moment she longed to taste it again. To lose herself in his kiss if only to make them both forget how horrible things could have gone that day. But she held back. They were home safe and now they knew what they were up against.

When he didn't finish his sentence, she asked, "Afraid you wouldn't be able to protect me?" She shifted, pulling her feet crisscross onto the sofa to face him. "You do recall that I had a dragon sitting behind me, right?"

He paled, and she wondered if he might be sick. With a heavy gulp, he said, "I need to tell you something."

She placed her hand on his thigh and leaned in. "What is it?"

His hand found hers and she noted the slight tremble in it.

"There was a cavernous hole in the ground. Something was stirring inside of it. Even from across the field I could hear it clawing, desperate to get out."

Her breath hitched in her throat. If the rumors were true that the frost breathers did have an enormous beast under their control, then Elettra would be at as much risk as they were.

He grabbed both her hands and held them tight. "All I felt was dread. Like the whole world had turned sour."

"Why didn't you mention this when we landed?"

He lowered his voice. "Because someone had to have warned the frost breathers that we were coming. And no one knew except my father, the council, and your man Heely."

"You think there's a rat in the palace?" She couldn't believe she was saying the words out loud. Court politics were nothing new. Scandal, lies, and scheming were common themes within any society like this. But to be on the short end of it. To be the one betrayed… It was sickening.

Callum reached up and rested his hand on her cheek. The urge to pull away didn't come and instead she leaned into the touch, taking comfort in him being there.

As if trying to sound like his carefree self again, he said lightly, "Aside from the whole passing out on me in my time of need, you didn't do half bad out there."

Adalina laughed. "I didn't do anything at all out there."

"You showed up. You protected yourself and you saved us. You could have stayed behind like I asked. It would have been the safer choice. No one would have blamed you."

"The council would have cheered," she countered.

"Sure, but despite what everyone said, you were willing to do the hard thing. And you did it beautifully." His eyes sparkled as if recalling the moment. "When you kicked that asshole the second time, I wanted to take you then and there."

Warmth spread from her fingertips to her chest. It was comfortable and inviting, similar to laying in the sun and looking up at the clouds. It was moments like these, where he was giving her his raw, authentic self, that she felt like they were back at the Dew Drop Inn. Like they could shed themselves from all the titles and expectations placed upon them.

She ran her fingers along his bandages, treating them as carefully as a butterfly's wing. The sickening sound of the arrow puncturing him echoed in her mind. All that blood on his coat and then on her hands as she tried to tend to his wound flashed before her. When she'd seen him out there on that icy field, she had been so afraid of losing him. It was something she wasn't prepared for.

And to find out that he had been just as afraid of losing her... How was it possible for her heart to ache with fear and be so full of affection at the same time? Maybe time would only bring them closer? Perhaps something more meaningful than a marriage of title could be forged in the hardships to come.

"Callum," she said, grabbing the hand still holding her cheek, and lowering it. "I think we can make this work. Beyond marrying for the convenience of our kingdoms. Maybe we can find a way to trust each other."

She'd been so concerned with him taking something from her that she hadn't considered maybe he would do the opposite. That marriage to him meant gaining a partner, not a keeper. He had stood up for her more than once and that had to count for something, right? And today, he had admired her for the decisions she made for herself.

A relieved grin spread across his face. He shifted to sit side by side with her and drew her into him. She allowed him to wrap his arm around her shoulder, tucking her into his side.

The warmth in her fingertips extended to her core as she thought about his admission, that he had lusted for her out on that field. She choked out a laugh, "Wait, you mean to tell me that while we were running for our lives, you were thinking about much you wanted to bed me?"

"I admit, it wasn't the most opportune time. But how could I not when you were wearing that scowl I love so much on your face?" He chuckled, sending shivers down her spine. "You do this thing with your nose. It scrunches so adorably when you're angry. Even more so when you're being violent."

She swatted at his chest, but kept her head pressed against him. "You're a scoundrel."

"And you, dear wife, are irresistible."

She chuckled lightly. Soon, sleep beckoned her as she closed her eyes in the safety of his embrace.

Twenty-Four

King Alistair's answer to all their problems came in the form of a party. Adalina supposed she shouldn't have been as shocked as she was. If she'd learned anything from her time in Astarfall so far, it was that they preferred to do things in style.

She peered through the carriage window, keeping a steady gaze on Elettra who glided above them. King Alistair was persistent in the importance of allowing the people to see the Crown Prince and his bride arrive together. A united and strong front. Unbreakable. Rather than waste energy on an argument, Adalina instructed the dragon to stay close.

The legendary stronghold called Windshire stood between the western mountains and the city. The ride passed in a blur of blue and green. The sea dazzled her on the left and vast lands owned by various nobles stretched along the right.

Seraphine sat across from her on the edge of her seat. Wistfully, she said, "I haven't been home in ages." Her cheeks flushed when she looked at Adalina. "The view of the sea is just as stunning as the one from the palace in the city. But Windshire is old. Ancient, really."

Alfie held his hands up and wiggled his fingers. "They say it's haunted by the lord who built it and his wife. They wander the halls, keeping a watchful eye over their descendants."

Seraphine snorted. "I can assure you there are no ghosts. Only dusty old cobwebs and a few stray cats."

The excitement buzzing from the pair was infectious. By the time the fortress came into view, Adalina couldn't wait to get out of the carriage. However, she hadn't minded the ride. Sitting beside Callum was becoming a comfort. Especially when his long legs shifted to touch hers.

The fortress sat on high ground with a steep hill rolling down to the beach where a small fleet of ships was anchored. When the carriage hit a bump, Callum grunted and rubbed his shoulder. It was healing nicely, but he would need more time before the bruising stopped bothering him.

Adalina frowned. Windshire was close enough to the mountains that she could see their brown peaks without using Elettra's shared sense of sight. Which meant the mountain pass and the faction's encampment was closer than she was comfortable with. Expectations were running high and as they pulled onto the large stone path leading to the gates of the estate, Callum grew tense beside her.

"Are you okay?" she asked under her breath, leaning close to him.

"I can't stop thinking about that pit we saw. About the archers..." He blew out a frustrated sigh. "If we can't convince the nobles to back this war, then—"

"We will." She grabbed his hand and squeezed it. "We'll make sure they understand there is no other option."

Callum smiled ruefully at her.

"What?" she asked, blushing, and tucking a strand of hair behind her ear.

"It's just nice to have you here. You're hard to say no to."

"Let's hope the nobles agree." There was an edge of uncertainty in her words that she couldn't conceal.

Especially since she and Callum would be ambushing them with the proposition. Seraphine's father, Lord Timber, had put together the feast under the guise of simply wanting the nobles together so they could meet their new princess. It was an opportunity for them to get to know the heirs to the throne without the king's distracting presence.

What would their reaction be when the two of them asked them to join them in a war?

The walls surrounding Windshire rivaled even the city where Callum's palace stood. They towered high above the carriage and even craning her neck to get a better look, Adalina couldn't see the tops where guards stood on the parapets. The only reason she knew there would be any guards was thanks to Seraphine's detailed description of her childhood home.

A large gate drew open, allowing their carriage and others to pass through. Inside the walls, people shuffled around, brimming with excitement. Adalina and the others exited the carriage one by one. She turned in awe, taking it all in. Ladies in the finest dresses she had ever seen and men who strutted around like proud peacocks filled the massive courtyard. Some filtered through the doors of the ancient estate, while others shouted orders to the staff that they'd brought with them for the feast.

Adalina pressed herself into Callum's horse, who had been led behind the carriage. Grazer nipped at her hand in search of treats. Callum sidled up to them and slipped a carrot under the warhorse's mouth. He gobbled it up happily.

"There are a lot of people here," Adalina said dumbly. She'd been warned that Lord Timber would pull out all the stops for the nobles they'd invited to the feast. There were several prominent families and a handful of generals whom they would need to charm into joining their cause.

She lowered her voice as she said to Callum, "I don't understand why your father can't just command them all to take up arms."

"The royal family may hold the power, but it is the nobles who have the people's ear. Even a king must ask before taking. Otherwise, he loses the faith of his people."

She wanted to retort that hiding the truth from his people was going to be what made them lose faith, but she held her tongue. The truth would come out tonight. Of that, there was no doubt.

Instead, she countered with, "Why not ask the people to fight directly for the crown? Why go through the nobles?"

Callum patiently answered, "Without their support, the subjects who live in their territories will not send their husbands, brothers, and sons to fight." He smirked. "Besides, they hold the purse strings. We simply don't have the budget to feed and pay an entire army. Not unless we want to reallocate resources from things like the guilds, repairs, upkeep, and such and put it into a war effort. The other option would be to raise taxes..."

"The people would suffer for it," Adalina mused. Solaris was a large territory, but they didn't have as many people. The villages were small and cared for themselves. But Astarfall relied on taxes to be contributed back into the community. A war would bleed their resources dry. Unless the nobles saw fit to shoulder some of the burden.

"And that is why, dear wife, we must be our most charming selves." He flashed a wide smile and left her side to greet a broad built older man. They hugged tightly, patting each other heavily on the backs.

"Ah my boy!" said the older gentleman, who was dressed in thin layers of finely made linen.

"Uncle Timber, you look well," said Callum cheerfully, as if he and Adalina hadn't just been talking about the importance of what they needed to do. He swept an arm out to her, and she reluctantly left his horse's sturdy side.

The man pulled at his long white beard as he studied her.

Callum took her hand and said, "Allow me to introduce you to my bride. Princess Adalina."

"It is so nice to finally meet you. I'm sorry I could not attend the wedding. I... My heavens, is that what I think it is?"

An enormous shadow was cast over them as Elettra flew lower, looking for a safe place to land. Men began shouting for carriages to be moved and women gasped loudly, exclaiming as the dragon's wings sent a wild wind beating down on them all.

The fire in Adalina's veins flared at finally having Elettra near again. To Lord Timber, she said, "That is Elettra. I hope you don't mind she came along."

"Not at all. Not at all, dear girl," he said, unable to take his eyes off the dragon. "I've been looking forward to this moment."

Elettra landed gracefully and curled her claws into the dirt as if happy for a break after the journey. She nuzzled her head into Adalina when they approached. A small crowd of noblemen inched closer, taking in the incredible sight of a dragon for the first time.

Both Heely and Uthred joined them, stepping closer to Elettra than they ever had. A few of the nobles shot them impressed looks. Adalina sensed amusement from the dragon. It seemed the councilmen were trying to show off to the others; acting as if they were held in such high esteem that there was nothing for them to fear where Elettra was concerned.

The dragon, however, with a playful glint in her eye, huffed out a puff of smoke that encircled Heely and Uthred, earning shocked whoops from them both. They promptly rejoined the nobles and their families, turning red in the face as laughter filled the courtyard.

"On that note," said Lord Timber with good humor, "let's get to the feasting!"

Callum grabbed hold of his sleeve. "My father's correspondence explained everything?"

"Yes, nephew. It did." Lord Timber looked around, making sure no one was listening in, then said, "You have my support and my men. Windshire is Astarfall's oldest stronghold. It has withstood centuries. And we stand between the heart of the kingdom and those who wish to wreak havoc on it."

"I'm glad to hear it. Your support alone makes us stronger. But what of the others?"

"I am aware of the stakes, but these nobles to the east and north... They have their doubts. And rightfully so. They have only received secondhand accounts of everything that has led to this moment. And your father's done a hell of a job easing their minds. They will be your greatest challenge."

Adalina furrowed her brow. "Then shouldn't we gather them all now? To get it over with and convince them of just how serious things have become?"

"Best to let them fill their bellies first. And a fine bit of ale wouldn't hurt before making your case." Lord Timber winked at her.

As she followed the men into the enormous stone manor, it felt like the stones were pressing down on her, stealing her breath away. One night. That was all they had to make these men believe that the frost breathers were back. And that this time, it would not be so easy to exile them from the lands. One night to make sure they had a chance at saving them all.

The halls of Windshire were eerie. It was the only way for Adalina to describe them. Where Callum's palace was all open doors, windows, and light; Windshire was dreary and confined. Like a coffin. It was the last place she ever envisioned Seraphine—who exuded sunshine—growing up.

She was on her way to the great hall where the feast was taking place. Callum had gone off with Alfie in search of their favorite vintage, which apparently could only be found in his uncle's wine cellar. Although it was her idea to meet him at the feast, she was coming to regret it now. She didn't enjoy being on her own in the unfamiliar estate.

Tapestries that hung on the ancient stone walls fluttered in a ghost-like breeze. Even though none of the windows were open. It was like a gale lived freely in the house, wandering back and forth on its own. The only explanation for it had to be the powers that Seraphine's family held. As wind-wielders, perhaps it was a normal occurrence.

Adalina sucked in a deep, steadying breath, still thinking of the ghosts Alfie had teased her about. But as she turned down the hall, it wasn't a ghost she crashed into. It was Heely.

"Apologies, Princess," he said hurriedly.

She smoothed out her hair. "Not to worry." Her heart was nearly pounding out of her chest. She was embarrassed to admit she was completely freaked out. Especially since Windshire was apparently one of the safest places in all of Astarfall.

Taking in his unruly appearance—which was quite strange for the always put together councilman—she asked, "Is everything alright? I would have guessed you'd be at the feast already. The nobles and generals should be gathered there by now." She gestured toward the staircase.

Heely sputtered, "O-of course, I was running just a bit late."

"Oh?"

It was all very unlike him. Especially after nearly a week of him following the important men of Astarfall around like a relentless shadow.

"Y-yes. I was having a drink with Uthred."

Adalina narrowed her eyes as her gaze darted between the stairwell and the doors lining the hall. There were several divots in the hallway and two other staircases leading to the second and third floor of the manor. She wished she'd seen which way he'd come from.

He bowed shallowly to her. "I best be off. Already late enough." Then he loped to the stairs leading down and took the steps two at a time before she could ask any more questions.

As she followed at a leisurely pace, she tried to shake the suspicious feelings off. She'd known Heely all her life. He was a social and political climber but had never struck her as a truly dangerous man. When he wasn't trying to involve himself in her life choices or fighting to keep her grandmother off the Solarian council, she hadn't really thought much of him at all.

Before she reached the top step, Uthred came jogging down the hallway. What was going on with these men today?

She put a hand on her hip. "You and Heely must have really been at it today, huh?" she half joked.

Confusion flashed across his face as he slowed to a stop in front of her. "What do you mean?"

She pointed to the stairs. "I just ran into Heely. He said your drinks together made him late for the feast."

Uthred furrowed his brow. "I admit I had a few too many and am running terribly behind, but I haven't seen Heely since we arrived."

Alarm bells went off in Adalina's head. "I must have been mistaken," she uttered and reached for the banister.

But Uthred blocked her way. He slid close to her, placing himself between her and the steps.

"Perhaps I could escort you down." His breath was hot with the sweet scent of brandy.

She leaned away from him. "I suppose that would be fine." She certainly didn't need an escort, but she was eager to get to Callum so they could begin their work.

"Thank you." Uthred bowed and stepped aside to take his place on the other side of her. "May I ask, how have you been enjoying your time at court, Princess?"

"It's been just fine."

"I'm sure it was a big adjustment for you. Heely says that you were very cross when Prince Callum first excluded you from the council meetings."

Irritation grated on her. "It was *your council* that tried to exclude me, not my husband."

Uthred hummed gently. "They certainly can be narrow minded. But you truly seem to be gaining their trust. Between your advancement in your trainings and the way you saved his royal highness and the others during that nasty tiff at the encampment..."

After what felt like an eternity, they reached the bottom of the stairs. Troves of people moved around the room, chatting idly with drinks in hand.

A tray floated by in the air and Uthred grabbed two drinks from it. He handed one to Adalina and said with a hint of sarcasm, "I'm glad to see things are starting to work out between you and Callum. A husband should be careful not to take his wife for granted."

"Prince Callum," she corrected him. He might be favored by the king, but men like him and Heely made her nervous. It was hard to tell where their loyalty ended, and their ambition began. The prospect of facing a dozen men like them throughout the night left a foul taste in her mouth.

In an effort to change the subject, she asked, "Where is *your* wife, councilman?"

Uthred maintained a relaxed composure, but his eyes sharpened as he said, "Erabelle has a mind of her own. *I* am not her master and keeper."

Was he implying that Callum was *her* keeper? Adalina sniffed indignantly and maneuvered around him when she spotted Seraphine. With a clipped farewell, she left Uthred behind.

Twenty-Five

S eraphine greeted Adalina with a hug. The great hall was cramped with neatly arranged tables. The only space left was a dance floor where jesters performed flips and tricks. Several ladies swarmed Adalina and Seraphine, fawning over their gowns and asking for palace gossip. Seraphine swiftly placated them with a little tea she'd picked up from the courtiers.

A young woman inched closer to Adalina. She had large doe eyes and cropped brown hair.

Sweetly, she said, "Princess, I do so hope you'll accept the invitation to my wedding in the spring."

"Oh," Adalina said, slightly caught off guard. "I'm sure we would love to attend."

She hadn't thought ahead to the spring. Not when their futures were so uncertain. But she couldn't bring herself to point it out to the girl. Not when she looked so hopeful.

The girl clapped in delight and said, "My fiancé hopes to join the court. Perhaps we could live in the palace one day." Then, with a gasp as if the most brilliant idea had just dawned on her, she said, "If you need any ladies-in-waiting, I'm quite skilled!"

"I will absolutely let you know."

She warmed instantly to the young woman who was so eager and full of life.

Once the girl was drawn back into the gossip, Seraphine winked and flicked her fingers at Adalina. A slight gust of wind swept her right into Callum's arms.

"Hello there, dear wife." His body was familiar against hers, and she had the urge to curl up into his arms. Maybe then he could shield her from all the stares they were receiving. Every head seemed to have turned in their direction the moment they touched.

"We have an audience," she said with a hint of laughter.

"Should we give them a show?" He placed his hand on the small of her back.

She laughed freely now. "I hardly see how that's going to convince them to take the threat seriously."

His easy smile faltered briefly. "First, they need to take *us* seriously. Seeing that this union is strong will mean that Astarfall truly does have a dragon on their side. And with a dragon... they just might be brave enough to fight."

She placed her hand over his heart. "This union *is* strong, Callum."

With all that was to come, she needed to believe that. It might not have been one held together by love, but they were bound to one another. She had made her choice and the longer she remained in Astarfall, the more she realized she'd made the right decision.

A smile returned to his face. It wasn't the practiced one he used on others. This one made his eyes crinkle in the outer corners. It was one she noticed was reserved for those closest to him. But it was short-lived. Lord Timber clinked a knife against his chalice, drawing attention to the head table.

Silence fell over the room as he stood and began, "Good lords and ladies of Astarfall. I invited you all here in good faith to celebrate the union of our prince and princess."

There were a few pleased murmurs in the crowd, and Adalina laughed as Alfie rose and clapped enthusiastically. Seraphine placed a hand on his shoulder, drawing him back down into the seat next to her.

Lord Timber cringed slightly in Alfie's direction, then cleared his throat. "We are here to witness the strength of this union and alliance with Solaris. To allow you to see firsthand that the dragon has awakened and stands ready to defend all of us."

There were a few agreeable whispers, but Adalina's heart skipped a beat when she noticed a few of the noblemen shaking their heads doubtfully.

Lord Timber, however, continued, "As you know, our land has recently been plagued with raids here in the west. Villages just beyond that mountain ridge out there have been affected, and the cost to them has been grave."

A nobleman with puckered lips—like he'd been sucking on a lemon he didn't enjoy—stuck his nose in the air. "King Alistair assured us those were raids for supplies. A few thieves eager to take advantage of the solitude near the border to make easy coin."

Callum turned toward the sour-faced man's table. "That's how it began. But we now know that those men were testing the borders to see if we had anyone defending it. To find out if there was anyone who would stop them from moving an army onto our territory."

A woman sitting a few seats down tilted her head. "And you've seen this army for yourself?"

"We have." Callum grabbed Adalina's hand and locked his fingers around hers. "The information my father has recently passed to all of you is true. The tavern attack near the city, the assassin sent to mine and my wife's chambers, and the encampment found on the other side of those mountains. It's all true. And if we don't act fast, then—"

"You want us to raise arms?" the woman asked.

Adalina already liked her. Even if the woman appeared as skeptical as the others, she was bold enough to ask questions. Questions which would undeniably lead them to the truth.

Emboldened by the woman, Adalina answered, "We do. With your support and your men, we can undoubtably rid Astarfall of the threat."

The sour-faced man stood now. "And the beast they are said to control? Have you seen that with your own eyes?"

Callum responded this time. "We have not seen that for ourselves. But there was a pit. It was large enough to house such a creature."

Adalina noticed the nobles growing more hesitant. Their postures went rigid, and fear drew their faces down. Quickly, she said, "That is where Elettra and I come in. We will protect your armies from any threat from above."

The woman gave her a sympathetic smile. "Forgive us, Princess. We are only just now learning how dire things are. It is an investment to feed an army, to offer them enough coin to risk their lives... and although there is a dragon to defend them, the rider is inexperienced. If I'm not mistaken, you have not seen battle before."

Callum gripped Adalina's hand tighter and said, "Elettra is a seasoned fighter. And Adalina's bond with her is strong. I have complete faith in my wife and ask that you do, too. I know it's a lot, but if we do not act, the consequences could be devastating." There was a slight clip in his voice, and she guessed he was trying to suppress any rising emotion while so many were looking to him for answers.

The great hall broke out in heated debates. Each lord and lady conversed amongst one another about what they should do. If they should wait until the attacks reached their doors or if they should risk fighting a war that they weren't sure they would win.

Lord Timber's voice bellowed over the noise. "Friends, please take the night before deciding. The prince and princess will be happy to answer any questions you may have but let us feast and enjoy each other's company in the meantime."

For the first time since the speech began, everyone in the room seemed to agree. Callum's shoulders finally relaxed and his grip on her hand loosened. He led her to the head table, and they took their seats beside Alfie and Seraphine.

Over his cup, Alfie snorted, "Well, that went well."

"About as well as could be expected," Callum chuckled and clinked his glass against Alfie's before taking a drink.

Adalina fiddled with her wedding ring. "Do you think they'll agree?"

Seraphine smiled wickedly at her. "I think you were both marvelous, and they'd be cowardly not to."

Adalina relaxed into her seat and filled her glass with the wine Callum and Alfie swiped from the cellar. Soon she lost herself in the incredible food on her plate. Piles of clams and oysters, crab mixed with breading and vegetables, and a magnificent salad made of seaweed soaked in a ginger dressing. By the time she finished, her head buzzed faintly from the wine and her belly was so full she thought she might burst.

Callum and Alfie excused themselves to go play cards at a table filled with eastern nobles—no doubt planning to work their charms on them—leaving Adalina and Seraphine alone at the table.

Uthred's wife strolled up to them. Her dress was made entirely of brilliant white pearls, and it contrasted beautifully with her long raven hair. Her smile was sweet as she dipped into an effortless curtsey.

"Princess, you look stunning, as always."

"As do you, Lady Erabelle."

Seraphine rested an elbow on the table and chimed in. "It's a pleasure to see you here. You came with your husband?"

"I did." Erabelle waved her hand carelessly. "He's taken to a round of dice with your father. Let us hope neither of them bets a small fortune this time."

Seraphine chuckled. "I wouldn't leave the two of them unattended for too long."

Erabelle sighed. "You're probably right. I should go check on them. I just wanted to pay my respects."

Adalina smiled as Erabelle curtseyed once again and set off to find the men.

Seraphine downed the rest of her drink and laughed into her empty cup. "Watch out for that one."

"What do you mean?" Adalina's ears perked up.

"She's high born, but Uthred had a different sort of upbringing in court. His father had to fight tooth and nail to get her father to agree to the match."

"Why?" Adalina was beginning to enjoy courtly gossip, though she'd never admit it out loud.

"It's actually a situation rather similar to mine. Nasty rumors of his mother having an affair, though it was never substantiated. Still, when people start talking, it's hard to get them to stop. Even if it's a load of horse shit."

Adalina scrunched her nose. Affairs weren't unheard of. And she wasn't judging anyone for following their heart. But it wasn't how she was raised. Her grandparents and her parents were faithful partners. She'd grown up witnessing their devotion, even at the hardest of times. That was the sort of love she longed for. Not a love that burned out like a short-wicked candle.

And although her marriage wasn't one born of love, the idea of Callum ever taking a lover made her want to vomit. What did that say about her feelings for him? Was it possible that she felt more than she was ready to admit? Or maybe she needed to lay off the expensive wine.

Her gaze wandered to him a few tables over where Alfie was collecting winnings from Lord Sour-face. Callum was deep in conversation with a burly man beside him. It seemed he'd decided to forgo his carefree facade. Instead, his face was made of stone, serious and intense.

Seraphine refilled their glasses and paused for a thoughtful moment. "I suppose that's why Uthred tries so hard around my uncle. If he has a place at the right hand of the king, then he can finally leave the distasteful rumors of his parentage behind."

Adalina trailed her gaze around the room. There was no sign of Uthred or his wife. Perhaps they'd gone to bed. She spotted Heely, who was drinking with one of the lords in a dark corner. It gave her a strange feeling in the pit of her stomach to see him conversing so intimately with influential Astarfallen men.

She tried to rid herself of the nagging nerves by taking a longer swig of wine and licked her lips. "Sometimes I wonder why men try so hard. It's not as if they don't already have power in this world. Yet still, they bow and scrape for more. More money, more power, more land. While us women have to fight like hell just to get the chance to *speak* on things that matter."

Seraphine tipped her glass toward Adalina's in cheers. "You're changing all of that, my friend. They listened to you tonight." Her drink spilled as she shifted quickly in her seat to face Adalina. "No. They didn't just listen. They *heard* you. Callum was right. He needed you tonight."

Adalina's drink caught in her throat, and she choked. Regaining her composure, she asked, "What do you mean?"

"The council was worried you might be too bold if you came. That you might speak out of turn and put the lords out. Callum cursed them all and said that he couldn't convince them without you. He fervently stated that it was your boldness and your courage that would sway the nobles in our favor."

Adalina's chest buzzed, and heat flushed her from head to toe. She pinned her sights on her husband a few tables away. When she caught his eye, she smiled brightly. When Seraphine pulled her to her feet to draw her onto the dance floor, he raised an amused eyebrow.

The women danced until their feet couldn't take it anymore. By the end of the night, Adalina had been approached by several lords and ladies of the court. They asked about Elettra, about the threat they had witnessed, and about the training she'd been undergoing.

She was more than happy to answer any and all of their questions, certain that it was leading them one step closer to their goal. When she and Callum returned to their room, the two of them were high on success.

Callum's words rushed from him. "Lord and Lady Grey said they will send fifty of their finest soldiers! Lord Brime—"

"Lord *Sour-face*," Adalina corrected with a giggle as she flopped onto the bed.

Callum laughed. "Lord Sour-face will send any grain he can spare to feed the men when they march to the city, and he has one of the largest forces of men in all of Astarfall."

He kicked off his shoes and joined her on the bed. They laid side by side staring up at the ceiling, which was painted with little winged babies.

With a relieved sigh, he said, "With Lord Sour-face's support, the rest will follow. I knew he'd be the hardest to convince. With his pledge, the others will find it in them to say yes."

"We'll have an army to defend Astarfall," Adalina said dreamily as she rested her head against Callum's shoulder.

"The frost breathers won't stand a chance against our numbers."

Adalina yawned as sleep came to claim her. But despite the victory of their night, her mind turned on her. She dreamed of Uthred and the condescending tone in which he talked about her marriage to Callum. And of the lie she'd caught Heely in.

When her eyes fluttered open, it took her a moment to remember they were in their room at Windshire. She groaned, wishing she could fall back asleep. But her restless mind wouldn't allow it. If Heely hadn't been with Uthred for drinks, then where was he? Nothing had ever seemed to keep him from a meeting with the king. And these circumstances should have been no different.

She rolled into Callum, snuggling in close to him, and squeezed her eyes shut. It was too awful to consider that the one person at court who was supposed to be loyal to her and only her could be hiding something. Especially when someone was betraying them to the enemy.

Try as she might, sleep wouldn't come back for her. And when footsteps grew louder in the hall, her heart leapt into her throat. She and Callum both jolted upright when someone came barreling through their door.

Elettra—who was sleeping in the courtyard just outside their window—screeched, mirroring the sudden intrusion.

Callum's body stiffened.

Adalina reached for his hand.

Seraphine stood in the doorway, her hair wild and her eyes filled with despair. "Windshire is under attack."

Twenty-Six

"How many?" Callum's words were clipped as he pulled his boots on roughly.

Adalina didn't waste any time shedding her gown and trading it for her riding leathers.

Seraphine trembled. "Thirty, maybe more. It's dark and they're shrouded in those damned black cloaks."

Adalina flinched as something hit the walls surrounding the estate. From outside the window, she could hear Elettra's warning rumble. She was ready for a fight and eager for Adalina to get out there.

Callum pulled on his jacket. His hair was messy and there was a shadow of stubble along his jawline. He looked like how she felt. Distraught. Tired.

He asked, "How many men does your father have here at Windshire?"

Seraphine moved aside as he stepped into the hall, then she answered, "Ten of his personal guards are here. The soldiers are all at home with their families or in the barracks a few miles out. We're surrounded. There's no way to get word to them in time."

Adalina followed closely behind Callum, but the hall was chaotic. People were rushing out of their rooms in a frenzy, unsure of where to go or what to do. Each time a blast hit the wall, screams echoed through the corridor in response.

Callum grumbled, "We've only brought nine guards from the palace. That makes eleven fighters, if you include me and Alfie."

Seraphine countered, "Twelve, including Adalina."

"Right." His gaze snapped to her.

She stepped aside to let a woman carrying a crying child pass. "How many men did the nobles bring?"

Seraphine shrugged. "Each has a personal guard. They're the best of the best. But it might not be enough for a battle. This was meant to be a simple feast. Taking up arms was supposed to come *after*."

"We were too late," Callum growled. "This place is filled with no-blemen who never see the front lines. Women and children who need defending..."

Adalina placed a calming hand on his shoulder. "Don't think like that. We have Elettra. That gives us the upper hand."

The woman who had spoken up during the feast met them at the stairs. She was bewildered and still in her nightgown. With a violent shiver, she asked, "Why now? Why have they come?"

Callum ran a hand over his face. "Gathering the nobles in one place... How could we have been this foolish?"

The woman gritted her teeth. "None of that matters now. The question is, how are we going to keep them from taking Windshire?"

He stiffened. "Taking Windshire would tip things in their favor."

Although Adalina didn't know much about military strategy, even *she* could see what a prize Windshire was. Taking it would mean getting one step closer to the king's palace. To the heart of Astarfall. And if a few nobles were killed in the process, then all the better for the faction.

She hated the fear in her voice as she said, "Windshire would give them the perfect position to launch an attack on the city. It would give them a safe place to recoup after battles. We can't let them take it. No matter what."

Callum gave a curt nod. His breath frosted in the air, much like hers did when she used to walk the hills of Solaris in the winter. Except,

Astarfall didn't grow cold enough for that to happen with the season. She shivered, eerily aware of the shift in the atmosphere.

People were gathering, rubbing their hands together and clutching blankets around them tightly. All at once, they were asking what they should do, where they should go. They might have been strangers to Adalina, but they were her people now. Astarfall was her kingdom. And she wasn't about to give up either without a fight.

After a brief pause, Callum said to Seraphine, "The ships. They could carry everyone?"

"Yes," Seraphine said with a growing smile. A plan already seemed to be formulating in her mind.

"Can you sail it?" Adalina asked. She wasn't sure if Seraphine had ever actually captained a ship, though she, Alfie, and Callum spent a lot of their free time down at the docks.

She scoffed conceitedly. "Of course." She turned and whistled, drawing everyone's attention. "Keep calm. My father and the other men are on the battlements now. They will not give up without a fight. As for the rest of you, there are tunnels leading out to the ships. Women, children, anyone who is unable to fight, follow me."

Adalina and Callum descended the stairs with Seraphine. They were met at the bottom by Lord Sour-face and Lord Timber. Seraphine and Alfie were already shuffling people toward the cellars where the tunnels would be.

When only Adalina and Callum were left, Lord Timber said, "You two should go with them."

Callum stared at him incredulously.

Lord Sour-face quickly stepped in. "Your Grace, you can't be here. If they breech the walls and find you, they will kill you or hold you for ransom."

Callum sneered at the men and tore his jacket off. He ripped the royal emblem from the jacket's breast and said, "Then let's make certain they do not see me. What sort of leader would I be if I sent those men out there to die alone?"

Lord Timber set his sights on Adalina next.

She tilted her chin up and said, "I'm coming too. With Elettra, I'll be out of reach. It's the whole reason I'm here, is it not?"

Lord Timber's lips pinched together. "Shouldn't His Grace be the one to ride her into battle?"

"No. My wife rides her dragon," Callum said with finality. He smiled at Adalina, but it didn't reach his eyes.

The men conceded defeat and led Adalina and Callum outside. Elettra was waiting in the courtyard. Her horns glinted in the moonlight and her gaze was set on the west, where smoke billowed in the sky. Adalina got a rush of adrenaline, and she wasn't sure if it belonged to her or the dragon. Likely both.

Astarfallen men were on the raised walkway built into the walls surrounding the stronghold. They ducked down on the battlements, dodging familiar icy arrows. Callum winced, and she knew he must be feeling the ghost-like pain of being hit with one so recently.

Her teeth chattered as she watched the men above wield their heaven granted magic. Sparks shot from their hands, drawing from small fires or starlight. Others were using buckets of water to hit their targets with impressive force. Some even raised loose stones from the wall to career them at the masked attackers below.

"What in heaven's name?" Lord Timber drew her attention.

"Is that snow?" Callum whispered in disbelief.

Flurries floated down to them. They were delicate and faint, just like they had been when she'd ridden to the mountain pass. But there was no denying the drop in temperature. No ignoring the panicked reactions from the men in the courtyard.

The walls were the worst. She was overcome with dread as she realized frost was seeping through the cracks of the ancient stone.

Lord Timber's voice quaked as he said, "They'll freeze us all to death."

Callum turned to him. "Is everyone out of the manor?"

"Yes. My head of house has made sure of it," Lord Timber said with an air of certainty. "My daughter will have everyone in the tunnels by now. And any man left is on the battlements as we speak."

Elettra snorted and held her tail out to Adalina.

Callum nodded, "Mount up. I'll join the men on the battlements."

"Are you sure?" Her stomach sank. She didn't want to leave him so close to the ground where the frost breathers could get to him.

He closed the gap between them and took her face in his hands with a gentleness that nearly broke her heart. They shook as the ground quaked from another strike at the wall. "I'll stand with my men. I'll be alright. In all the centuries that Windshire has stood, it has never been invaded."

"Yes, but have the *faceless* ever tried to take it?" Adalina was afraid to call the masked men what they were. To say frost breathers out loud was to speak her fear into existence.

He moved his hands to her waist and his grip tightened a fraction, as if he was frightened that she would slip from his grasp forever.

Her voice broke as she asked, "The traitor, do you think they're responsible for this? Did they send the faceless here to stop us from raising an army?"

The idea had already been considered, but now it seemed irrefutable. She would make their betrayer suffer when she got her hands on them. What sort of coward sent evil men after innocent families? Their own neighbors. Maybe even their friends.

Callum said lowly, "It's the only possible answer. They couldn't have known we would be gathered like this unless someone told them."

Fear flooded her chest. "Then do not trust anyone while you're up there."

Her eyes flitted to the battlements above them. Suddenly, she couldn't shake the vision of him being pushed by whoever had the gall to betray them like this.

She gritted her teeth. "What do you need me and Elettra to do?"

"Fire on them," he said simply.

"*Burn* the faceless men?" Her eyebrows shot up in surprise. "All of them?"

She thought of the tale her grandmother had told her. Of how *not all* the frost breathers started out evil. Many had been forced into it. She wasn't so naïve to think that she'd get out of this without taking a life. But to kill them all without giving them a chance to surrender first felt wrong. Burning your enemies alive in a mass execution was no way to keep a crown. She didn't want to make the same mistakes Callum's grandfather had made.

With a shake of her head, she pulled away from his embrace and said, "One day you will be king, and I will be queen. I don't want to be the sort of leader that people fear. We can't be rulers that breed the sort of hatred in the hearts of men that will last for generations."

An icy arrow cleared the wall and landed a few feet away. Its tip dug into the ground, sending a trickle of frost along the dirt and rocks.

"Lina," he sighed. "We need to do what we can at this moment. What's best for those men up there needs to come first."

Wasn't that how they'd gotten into this situation in the first place? His grandfather exiled the frost breathers because at the time, it was the easiest and most expedient way to solve his problems. Even her grandmother—whom Adalina worshiped—had fought with an iron fist. And now those choices were coming back to haunt her and Callum.

She took hold of his jacket, pleading with him. "Shouldn't we be the ones to break the cycle? Elettra and I can scare them off if we just—"

A man fell from the battlement with a crack. She gasped at the angle of his neck. Broken. Lord Timber ran to his side and his shoulders drooped.

Callum sighed as he answered, "At this rate, we won't be able to hold them off for long. Not when we're fighting against Astarfallen magic, no matter how twisted."

She bit her lip. "What if we distracted them with Elettra? If I buy us enough time to get everyone out of here. You and the other men could get to the ships..."

"An attack on this scale changes things, dear wife. We are no longer dealing with small skirmishes. They have officially declared war. This is what it's going to be like until there is one group left standing."

Her hesitation double in strength. She glanced up at Elettra. It seemed they were sharing the sentiment. The dragon didn't want to commit mass murder any more than she did.

There was nothing left to do but mount. With the aid of Elettra's tail, Adalina slipped onto her back. With one last look at Callum, she signaled for the dragon to take flight. Once in the air, her fingers flitted along Elettra's scales in hopes that the familiar feeling would calm her trembling hands.

The dragon rose high enough to stay out of the archers' range. From there, Adalina could see every inch of the massive granite estate. In the dark, it was more foreboding than before, towering high with the intimidating walls surrounding it. Outside of those walls, masked men had gathered around the perimeter nearest to the gate.

Something shimmered in the air around their hands. Adalina's heart plummeted. The magic that flowed from them crept up the walls of Windshire, leaving behind a glistening frost. The same frost she'd seen seeping through the cracks. The wall creaked and a few stones crashed to the ground, earning shouts of approval from the attackers.

Callum and the men, however, responded with fierce determination. They wielded every bit of power they could, striking any frost breather that dared to get too close to the wall and gate.

Adalina pressed her heel into Elettra's side to turn her. Giving the faceless men a wide berth would keep them from being caught in the crossfire. With sights set on a few men trying to climb the wall, Adalina hissed through her teeth. Fire shot in wild spurts from Elettra's mouth. Each one left angry black scorch marks on the stone where the men had once been. Bile rose in Adalina's throat. What if the council was right about her? Maybe she didn't have the stomach to kill in battle.

Twenty-Seven

Soaring on Elettra had been a dream come true so far. Knowing she had an all-powerful dragon on her side had brought her comfort. But Adalina had never commanded her to use her fire on people before. Nor did she ever consider what it would mean when the time came to do so.

Stone arrows sped through the air from the top of the fortress' walls. Adalina spotted the earth-wielders. They released another round. Each point of the arrow shimmered with what she knew to be Astar-fallen magic. The arrows shifted as the faceless men below tried to dodge them. An ordinary shot would have veered straight, missing the moving target. But these arrows followed them as if they had a mind of their own. As if the wind was on their side, guiding them to their bullseye.

Her gaze strayed to Lord Timber standing amongst his archers, hands outstretched, and a silver, steady wind flowing from them. But for every frost breather the men protecting Windshire beat down, two more stepped from the shadows in their stead. The walls groaned louder with each icy blast cast against them.

What if she could stop them without resorting to a massacre?

What her men needed was a distraction. Something to make the frost breathers lose their focus.

"Elettra, I need you to screech."

The dragon's horrifying bellow vibrated through Adalina. It shook her to the core. But it also did the trick. Every faceless man tipped their head to the sky. She tapped Elettra twice, signaling for her to get closer to the standoff. Gracefully, the dragon veered around the fortress, aimed for the heat of the battle.

Adalina gritted her teeth as the faceless men shouted to one another, pointing at her and Elettra. A handful of the frost archers abandoned the wall and aimed for her. There was a loud whistle as one narrowly missed her ear. But she couldn't retreat. Not yet. Not when the wall was weakening as much as it was. If it fell, Callum and the others would perish with it.

Elettra dipped and rose like waves in the sea, keeping them from getting pelted by the icy power. With so many of the frost breathers distracted by the dragon's arrival, it was buying Callum and the others time. They gathered their strength, pulling from the natural elements of Astarfall and began battering the frost breathers closest to the gate.

Callum yelled and cursed the frost archers who were focused on her and Elettra. He raised his hands, drawing starlight to him in beautiful streams. An alarming glow brightened his eyes and formed around his palms. Effortlessly, the power drawn from the sky plummeted from him and into the faceless men, relieving Elettra from having to focus on dodging the icy arrows.

But it hadn't stopped the men trying to take down the gate. The force they used was so great it rocked the ground. Adalina's heart leapt into her throat as Callum tumbled smoothly onto another part of the parapet. He was quickly joined by Alfie, who steadied him. Alfie's eyes were wild. His hair was more mussed than usual. With a flick of his wrist, he shook the earth beneath the frost breathers, tossing them back.

Adalina pressed her heels into Elettra's sides, steering her tightly around the stronghold. Alfie's move had helped, but the faceless men were already advancing on the gate once more. At this rate, it wouldn't hold much longer.

Adalina had hesitated for too long. She knew that. But her stomach turned as she desperately tried to think of another way to fend off the frost breathers.

"We need to separate those men from the fortress. Can you draw a line of fire between them and the gate?"

Elettra's response was heated. Quite literally. The dragon's fire grew in her belly, heating Adalina's thighs and calves. A great rumbling like wind on a stormy night built in the dragon's throat and, with precision, she released the flames. It set the ground on fire in a neat straight line and forced the faceless men back in a panic.

Someone on the ground shouted orders at them and together the men raised their hands to call on their powers. A shield of ice formed above them, blocking the blazing flames out. They pressed forward, taking great strides in unison.

Several of the faceless men slipped from under the shield. Adalina hissed through her teeth and Elettra released spit balls of fire. Two of them met their mark. The men caught like kindling. Their screams tore through the night making Adalina's skin crawl.

This was her last chance to spare any more bloodshed. Summoning the courage she imagined her grandmother must have had in battle, she shouted down to the rest of the faceless men, "I am Princess Adalina of Astarfall, granddaughter of Dragon Warrior Calida. I demand that you stand down now!"

Her vision sharpened with Elettra's help, allowing her to gauge their reactions. The man who had been shouting commands to the others froze. There was a patch on his black robe, silver embroidered with Rothin's insignia: a jagged mountain with claw marks through it. She remembered the detailed drawings of it in her history books. None of the other men bore that patch. Which meant this man was important. Perhaps the most important of them all. There was a good chance this was their leader.

He peered up at her with the veil masking any other distinguishing characteristics. He lifted it slightly to uncover his mouth and smiled. But he said nothing to her offer of surrender. Gave no response or retort. No demands of his own. He simply *smiled* at her. Fire burned in her own belly now and if she had the ability, she would have scorched him herself. Would have burned him where he stood leaving nothing but ash.

If she killed their leader, would the rest lose faith and surrender?

"Kill him," Adalina growled. Then, with a hiss through her teeth, she commanded Elettra to fire at him.

As if anticipating her decision, an icy shield formed around him. He was more powerful than she thought to block fire like that on his own. The man snapped his fingers, and something shrieked in the distance. Her stomach plummeted as she realized only one thing could make that sort of noise. A dragon. The rumors were true. These men controlled a beast that could rival Elettra.

The Astarfallen defending the stronghold paled. The momentary distraction cost them dearly.

There was an earth-shattering crack and she turned to find that the gate had given in. The stone was blasted, and frosty tendrils rose in bellows from its carcass.

Lord Timber shrieked at his men, "Abandon post!"

Frost breathers began to slip through the opening. A woman's scream came from inside the fortress walls. When Adalina's gaze found the source, she cried out. The young woman with cropped brown hair held onto a man who had fallen to one of the frosted whips. Blood soaked her hands as she cradled him with tears streaming down her face.

Fire burned in Adalina's veins. She roared as a frost breather's whip met the girl's neck and tore her from the man she loved. The man she'd planned to spend the rest of her life with.

Elettra fired on the man this time without command. Fire streamed in a line as thin as the whip. Flames licked up the frost breather's back, but it was too late. The young woman, who had been so full of life and hope, was gone. Her unmoving body was sprawled out lifelessly beside her fiancé.

No. This is all my fault. Her stomach twisted and rage filled her.

The men defending Windshire fled the parapet around the wall. It was utter chaos as they ran for the tunnels that would lead them down to the sea.

Frost breathers—what was left of them after the battle—filtered in through the gate. They'd done it. They had taken the stronghold. With it, the enemy would have a foothold in the heart of the kingdom. It would give them a place to rest their heads, to recoup, and grow stronger. It would truly change the tide of things.

With a tap from Adalina, Elettra rose until the dark sea came into view. There was one lone ship left. Seraphine must have smartly left it for them, just in case. Already, the men who had stayed behind to defend the stronghold were filtering out onto the beach. When the other ships came into view, she breathed a sigh of relief. They had already set off.

She squinted and her eyes focused, narrowing in like she was looking through a captain's glass. Seraphine stood at the wheel, the wind whipping her hair around her face. Women, children, and the elderly clung to each other on the deck. They were safe.

And with the remaining Astarfallen making their way onto the beach, the fortress was empty... but where was Callum?

Her pulse raced, and fear lanced through her. She scanned the battlements frantically, her heart stopping each time she spotted a lifeless body. Her breath didn't return until she found him. He was alive. He leaned over the wall and waved to her. Worry was replaced with a prickle of irritation. Why would he stay behind when their world as they knew it was crumbling around them? She glowered at him, but commanded Elettra to swoop toward him.

Another screech echoed in the night. It was closer this time.

Elettra's wings beat heavily with exhaustion as they hovered near the wall to retrieve Callum. He climbed on and settled behind Adalina, placing his hands on her waist. She fought the urge to shove his touch away and scold him for giving her such a scare, but there wasn't time. Elettra was sky bound again.

Adalina glared back down at the faceless men. Their frozen shield had doused out most of Elettra's fire, save for a few spots raging here and there. They filtered through the openings, charging through the space where the fortress' gate once stood. Once they claimed Windshire, it would put Astarfall in a vulnerable position, leaving the city more exposed than ever.

She couldn't let that happen. With one last look at the ship carrying their people to the safety of the city docks, her resolve hardened. This time not only did her eyes sharpen with Elettra's connection, but all her instincts did as well.

She'd been a fool to believe she could make these men surrender. To have faith that there might be some slice of humanity left within them. That they would abandon their need for vengeance in order to live.

They'd made their choice when they decided to ignore the chance that she'd given them. It was time to do what she should have done from the start. There was no option but to do as Callum asked the first time.

She shouted to him, "I should have listened to you. I'm so sorry!"

"There's no time for that now!" he roared back, pointing to a dark shadow moving their way in the sky.

Elettra hissed as the beast flew toward them. Its movements were rigid and awkward and as Adalina's vision focused in on it, she couldn't see any scales or flesh. Only jagged bone. Bile rose in her throat.

To Callum, she asked, "Do you trust me?"

He chuckled. "Do I have a choice?"

They would need more fire than what Elettra had released only moments ago. Her eyes roved over the fortress. For centuries it had withstood ambushes, storms, even the darkest of nights. She closed her eyes, embracing the fire burning in her veins. Sweat beaded on her forehead and Callum tore his hands from her waist, hissing in surprise behind her. But she ignored him. She blocked everything out. The only thing that existed was her, Elettra, and the flame building within them.

Her grandmother's advice to relax and trust in the bond and the instincts that came with it rang in her ears. For a moment, it felt as if she was inside of Elettra's mind, sharing her thoughts and emotions. She caught a glimpse of memory. Things that she had never experienced herself. Other dragons with swords plunged into their hearts. The screams of terror as men shrouded in black blew frost so cold and deadly from their own mouths that the innocents in their path instantly froze to death. And her grandmother saying that they would do what they must. No matter the cost.

Adalina had been utterly wrong to go into battle, relying on defenses only. The men had known it. Callum had known it. There was still time to right her mistake. But the more she leaned into that bond and those memories, the hotter she became. Rage and anguish danced in her. And the need for blood, for charred bone, and burned flesh grew so strong, her vision darkened.

It felt like she was fire incarnate. And for a moment she couldn't differentiate between her own emotion and Elettra's.

Lost to madness and fury, Adalina bared her teeth and commanded, "Burn them."

Twenty-Eight

The fire Elettra released was like nothing Adalina had ever witnessed before. It was an array of blue, purple, and a red so deep it resembled blood being spilt. It swept through the courtyard, incinerating any man in its path.

But there was nothing controlled about this fire. It was chaotic. Wild. A living, breathing thing that wanted more. Wanted to consume everything and then some. As it hit the manor, the stone rumbled. It would not burn, but the flame was so hot, so strong, that it was shocking its very foundation and weakening the integrity of the fortress. The ground shook, and the walls began to crumble.

The scent of scorched earth and flesh returned Adalina to her senses. Slack jawed, she stared in despair at the damage she and Elettra had done.

The few faceless men left, dropped their icy defenses. There was no sign of their leader among the living or the dead. But another man shouted at them as they turned to flee, demanding that they return to defeat Elettra. He roared at them to wait until the beast arrived.

Promising that they could still win. Despite that, the men pushed past him and fled out of the gate.

It was then that it occurred to Adalina that although they were dealing with frost breathers, these were not the same warriors her grandmother had faced. Generations later, the ideals, and radical thinking might have been the same, but the men were not. They moved with the quickness of youth. Of men who were in over their heads. Their leader may have inspired them to take up arms against Astarfall, but they had not been prepared for the wrath of a dragon.

Windshire was no longer visible through the hurricane of smoke and flame. Elettra rose, proud of herself for the strength she might not have thought she still had. For a moment Adalina wondered if they should go after the frost breathers. To get rid of their problem now, like she should have done from the start.

Fire and fury still burned in her very marrow. It was an intoxicating feeling. She could end them all as quickly as a match might light a candle. But Callum ran his fingers over her arm, drawing her away from the murderous thoughts.

He choked on the rising smoke. "It's not safe. We need to go."

He said something else in her ear, but a terrible screech drowned it out. Her blood turned cold, and an eerie chill crept up her spine. The scream that tore through the wind was pure agony. The beast had arrived.

Callum went rigid behind her. "We need to go, now."

With an erratic beat of her wings, Elettra turned toward the ships sailing back to the city. Adalina's heart raced, and she turned to keep her stare pinned on the sky above Windshire. The screech died down and nothing rose behind them. There was no sign of a fearsome beast to rival Elettra, but it didn't settle her nerves any. Not even when they reached the city. Just the cries of the monster and the brief glimpse she got had been enough. It confirmed the reports. The frost breathers had a dragon of their own. Or something that eerily resembled it. And even Elettra was spooked by it.

It didn't take them long to reach the city on dragon back. When they landed, Elettra collapsed on the ground in a sleepy haze. Adalina patted her affectionately on the head.

Trying to conceal the tremor in her voice, she said, "You did good tonight."

"You both did," said Callum from behind. He gestured to the palace attendants and asked that they fetch Elettra refreshments. "She'll need her strength if the beast dares to come this close to the city." He eyed the sky warily.

Adalina kissed the dragon on the cheek. "Rest now."

Elettra seemed happy to oblige, closing her eyes and laying her head on the crook of her thick, scaly arm.

It was nearing dawn now and Adalina longed to see the sun again after such a dark and terrible night.

She and Callum hurried to the dock to meet Seraphine and her father. It took the ships slightly longer to return to the city, but with the wind-wielder abilities, they were able to sail quickly enough.

As they walked hurriedly, Callum said, as if still processing, "I can't believe you burned down the fortress."

"I didn't necessarily burn it down..." With guilt building in her gut, she added, "I didn't mean for the fire to get so out of control. Elettra was just so angry. *I* was so angry. We just lost ourselves to it, I think."

There was no other way to describe how their fury had built like flames in a forest. Each one's rage encouraging the other.

When Seraphine stepped off the ship, guilt piled on heavier. Adalina might have kept the stronghold out of the enemy's hands, but she had also just destroyed her friend's childhood home. She wanted to shrink into herself but settled for pressing against Callum's side. He placed a steady arm around her and gave her shoulder a comforting squeeze.

Lord Timber was bewildered as he said, "What happened out there? The goal was to destroy the enemy, not Windshire!"

Callum argued pointedly, "Things got out of hand. But the frost breathers had taken it. What good is a fortress to the enemy if it's not left standing?"

Lord Timber turned on Adalina, spit flying from his mouth as he shouted, "You were meant to have burned the men from the start!"

"Uncle," Callum soothed, "It was not her intention—"

"Intention be damned," he growled. "This is war. Hesitation could get us killed. It can get *you* killed. And for what? To spare our enemies from death?"

Adalina took a step away from him and his wrath. He could beat her up about her mistake all he wanted. But she couldn't apologize for following her gut. For wanting to give them a chance to turn their back on revenge and a war that nobody in Astarfall wanted.

She raised her chin. "I was trying to prevent more loss of life. If they had surrendered, then Astarfall would not have to fight again."

"But they didn't surrender, did they?" Lord Timber asked, still seething.

Lord Sour-face stormed up to them. "You need to control your damned wife!" he snapped at Callum.

Callum bared his teeth. In a lethal tone, he said, "Careful. You overstep."

Even Adalina was inclined to quake in response to the warning in her husband's voice.

Lord Sour-face's eyes widened, and he shrank back. More calmly, he said, "Twelve. We lost twelve men tonight. And a girl. The council was right to want *you* to ride the dragon, Prince Callum. The princess didn't have the experience to be up there. To make decisions on her own."

For once, she was speechless. There was nothing she could say or do to prove to the men how sorry she was that Astarfallen lives had been lost. She bit the inside of her cheek until the metallic tang of blood touched her tongue.

Seraphine's eyes darted between Adalina and the men. Diplomatically, she said, "We are all recovering from the horror of the night. Our enemy is out there, not standing on this dock."

Lord Timber softened at his daughter's words. "Apologies, Your Highnesses. Tempers are running high. We have much to grieve tonight."

Seraphine turned to Callum, who continued to glare at Lord Sour-face with clenched fists.

Gently, she said, "We also have much to celebrate. If not for Adalina, more lives would have been lost. And our enemy could be making themselves at home in Windshire right now." Raising placating hands, she continued, "We need to organize the soldiers within the city walls and find a place for those who fled Windshire."

"Yes," Callum said, clearing his throat. "The beast we'd heard about was there. It didn't follow, but we'll need round-the-clock guards posted on the battlements. This time we'll be prepared if the frost breathers march on us or send their creature in their stead."

Seraphine and Alfie went to work getting the residents of Windshire settled into town—some being put up at the Dew Drop Inn, and others being housed by citizens in the city walls. Adalina bit back the bitter taste of failure. Wordlessly, she took her husband's hand when he offered it and walked with him to the palace.

King Alistair welcomed them back and gave Adalina a tight hug first. "I am so glad the two of you are home safe."

She tensed. "We are glad to be home." The word rolled off her tongue, and it occurred to her that she actually *was* glad. And looking forward to crawling into her bed. The tension left her shoulders, and she returned the hug briefly.

The king clasped his hands together. "Right, then. Callum, if you'll join us." He nodded toward the council chambers.

"We'll be right there." He shifted on his feet, facing Adalina, as the king and Seraphine's father left them in the hall.

Adalina bit her lip. She wasn't ready to face the council's sharp words and heated glares when they found out just how badly things had gone because of her. She shook her head at Callum. "You go."

"You're sure?" he asked with searching eyes.

"Yes. I'll be sure to lock the door." Exhaustion barely let her get the joking words out.

"You did what you believed was best," Callum started.

"My best cost Seraphine her home."

Callum brushed her hair back and his fingers lingered in her curls. "We don't know that. Windshire might still be salvageable."

Now that the fire in her bones had been released with Elettra's flame, her body sagged. As the adrenaline wore off, she recalled the moments leading up to burning so many of the faceless men alive. How was it possible that she was seeing the dragon's memories? That she felt the fire as if it was in her own belly begging to be released? She couldn't imagine what Callum thought of it all. And the way he was looking at her now with worry clouding his eyes made her nervous.

"Do you think I've gone mad?"

His face brightened. "No one without their right mind could do what you did out there. You ultimately won this battle for us."

"You stayed behind when you should have run." She recalled the fright he'd given her when she realized he wasn't fleeing for the ship with the others. But the more she thought about it, the more she appreciated his presence there. "You stayed behind with me when you didn't have to."

"Always," he said, raising her hand to his lips. With a quick and simple kiss, he bid her farewell and joined his father and the council.

Twenty-Nine

W hispers came from every corner of the palace the next day. Each time Adalina turned around, there seemed to be people speaking in hushed whispers behind their hands. Since word spread about the attack on Windshire and how close the frost breathers had come to the city, the atmosphere in the palace had shifted significantly.

Adalina—eager to see how Elettra was doing—rounded the hall leading to the courtyard. Heated voices stopped her in her tracks. She ducked behind the corner of the wall and listened.

"King Alistair is in over his head," hissed an angry man.

"He's lost control of the situation, but what can be done?" mused another.

"It's no fault of the princess that things went so awry. The council should have known better than to allow her to keep control of the dragon."

She stiffened at the mention of her and Elettra.

The second man spoke again. "One thing we should be thanking the fates for is that the nobles have agreed to raise their flags. Men are coming from the villages in troves to declare their allegiance to stand and fight for the crown."

Her stomach rolled with nausea. It wasn't how she and Callum had hoped to gain the nobles' support. None of it had gone how they intended. She tried to take solace in knowing that they would at least have the numbers to stand against the frost breathers, but the victory fell flat. Lives were lost in the process of claiming that victory. The girl with cropped brown hair wailing over her love flashed in Adalina's mind, nearly knocking the wind out of her.

One of the men huffed. "Let's just hope King Alistair knows what he's doing."

She balled her fists. She hadn't agreed with the way her father-in-law handled things, but now she knew the cost of making decisions in a situation where there weren't many good options. What were these men and their gossip doing to help? To be afraid was one thing, but to question the king was another. What more did they want from him? He had married his only son off for the good of his people. Had acquired them a dragon that offered protection. Since Adalina came to Astarfall, the council and the king had been spending sleepless nights trying to solve the crisis.

The men were still talking, so she pressed herself close to the wall.

"Something must be done soon. If he isn't up to the task, then perhaps another will be."

The other man scoffed. "What, you mean the prince? Please, until now he has done nothing but gallivant around town with that innkeeper. He's no more qualified than his father."

Adalina didn't want to hear another word. Nor did she want to tuck tail and run. With her head held high, she strolled around the corner toward the gossiping men.

"Good afternoon, gentleman."

They immediately broke into bows. "Princess," they said in unison. They exchanged nervous looks and then mumbled something about how they'd best be off to attend to their busy days. Adalina's first instinct was to say something that would make them second guess their wagging tongues. But knowing it was King Alistair's mistake to have kept the full extent of the threat from his people stopped her. She settled for glaring at their backs. Now that the truth had come out, it seemed the trust between the citizens and their royal family was fractured.

Callum met her near Elettra's cave. Adalina gestured for him to join her on the blanket she'd laid out. Meanwhile, a few of the braver children from Windshire kicked a ball around with the dragon. She used her tail to swat it gently back and forth with them, letting them score by kicking it into her cave, at which point she would retrieve it for them. A comforting warmth touched Adalina's chest as Elettra's happiness extended to her.

Adalina leaned against Callum, resting her head on his shoulder. He glanced down at her with a flicker of surprise, but didn't move away as she asked, "Have you heard the whispers?"

"Yes," he said neutrally. "Though I'd say they're turning rather loud for whispers."

"Everyone knows I hesitated last night." The events at Windshire played repeatedly in her mind. The sickening scent of burned flesh, the crunch of bone as men fell from the battlements...

Callum placed a finger under her chin, tilting her head up to him. His eyes were wide with wonder as he said, "Lina, *you're* the reason the other nobles agreed to mount their arms."

"What?" She inhaled sharply.

"How could they not after witnessing your power? There isn't a warrior out there who can say they haven't hesitated before. You did right by Astarfall last night."

Her head spun. Lord Timber and Sour-face had been so furious with her on the docks. She had just assumed that the others were as well.

Callum moved his hand from her chin to her cheek. His thumb was calloused, and it made goosebumps prickle on the back of her neck as he caressed her.

With a quiet fierceness, he said, "No one should ever fault you for trying to do the right thing, dear wife. You're better than the rest of us and I have to believe that in the end, that is what will save us all."

The honesty in his gaze was startling.

Tears stung her eyes. She blinked them away quickly and sucked in a sharp breath through her nose. "I'm relieved to hear that I was able to sway them. But people in the palace are not just talking about me. There's discontent surrounding your father. He needs to address it before the talk spreads like a wildfire that he can't put out."

"He's decided that we're to make the next move. He wants to attack the frost breathers before they have a chance to attack us first."

Even though she knew it was coming, hearing it out loud felt like a blow to the gut.

"When?" she asked as her heart stuttered.

"Tomorrow. I could tell he was afraid to say it in front of the council, but what choice did he have? They need to prepare. We all do."

"If they know, then the traitor might know, too." Fear stirred in her chest, constricting it until it was hard to breathe.

Callum's voice was hoarse as he said, "Until we know who the traitor is, we're in danger. It's killing my father, not knowing who he can trust."

"There's something I have to tell you." She looked up at him, meeting his eyes. They had dark rings around them. The only sign she'd get of the worry masked beneath his carefree facade.

"Go on."

Adalina gave him a full account of her run in with Heely and Uthred before the feast. Once the adrenaline from the attack had worn off, she hadn't been able to get the councilman out of her mind. The strange evasiveness and lie Heely had told. And Uthred's insistence that they hadn't been together.

Even though the weight of the night was still heavy on her heart, she didn't want to keep anything from Callum. Not when so much was happening so fast. If she had learned one thing from the night before, it was that she should trust his instincts more.

When she mentioned Uthred's snide remark—implying that Callum wasn't treating her like an equal in their marriage—he scoffed. "Uthred has some nerve. I'll give him that." His thumb grazed her jawline as he added, "Is that how you feel? Like I'm trying to be your keeper?"

"Maybe a little at first, but you've proven to me that you're on my side when it counts."

She shuddered in delight as he ran his thumb over her lips. The terror and thrill from the previous night swept through her mind once again. The council and noblemen were vocal about their disapproval of how she handled things. But Callum hadn't made her feel bad for even a moment. There was no "*I told you so.*" The significance of that made her tilt her chin up invitingly. He leaned down and pressed his lips against hers.

The kiss was brief, but it sent butterflies fluttering around wildly in her stomach.

With a soft laugh, he said, "Dear wife, I do believe I'm growing on you."

"You might be right, dear husband." Part of her wanted to lean against him again. To continue sitting with his steady presence by her side while they watched Elettra play with the children. But her nerves twisted. "About Heely..."

"He's been there for every council meeting. He was the one who proposed that we go into the village for drinks that night of the first attack—"

"You said it was the council." She bolted upright to face him.

He nodded. "Heely suggested it, but the council agreed and told me to go."

"So aside from your father's inner circle, he was the only other one who would have known. The only other person who could have told the frost breathers where we would be..."

Nausea churned in her stomach.

Callum's tone was solemn and almost apologetic as he continued, "And if he wasn't having drinks with Uthred last night, then where else could he have been? Why rush down the hall in a frenzy and lie to you?"

"I don't know. I can't imagine him betraying us." Despite their differences, Heely didn't strike her as a traitor. But wasn't that the point? If he was up to no good, then it's precisely what he would have intended. "What could the frost breathers possibly have to offer him?"

"Power, money... The usual things that blind people into betrayal." Callum chuckled and joked, "I forget how new you are to palace politics."

Adalina shook her head with a sarcastic smile. Then, more seriously, asked, "What do we do now?"

He glanced up at the palace. "We can't take this to my father on a whim. If we're wrong, it might spook the real traitor."

"And if we're right? If Heely is the rat?"

Callum's eyes glittered mischievously. "Then we need evidence." He stood, offering her his hand. "Come, dear wife. It's time to do some snooping."

Her husband really was a marvel. Only he could hear news of betrayal and sabotage and find a way to summon that boyish grin of his. She took his hand and leapt up. This was quite a way to spend their honeymoon period. Most young couples might be off traveling the countryside or basking on a beach. But they weren't like most young couples. Their beginning had been one of assassins and plans behind closed doors.

Adrenaline coursed through her veins as Callum looped his fingers around hers. It was nice to have something to distract her from the night before. She would make up for her hesitation and make them see that she could do what needed to be done.

There was urgency in Callum's step, but she spotted a bit of excitement. Like they were about to play a game of tag. One thing she could say for sure was that life with him would never be dull or predictable.

Heely's room was as put together as Adalina had always believed *he* was. Shirts were arranged neatly in the armoire, shoes shined and lined in a row. There wasn't much in the way of personal belongings. She suspected most of his things were still in Solaris, where he would eventually be expected to return.

But it also proved how little she really knew about him. Thinking back to life in Solaris, she only ever recalled him involving himself in other people's affairs. He had never married and had no kids or family to speak of. His parents had passed away some time ago from natural causes. Heely threw himself into his work as if it was his entire personality.

Callum sifted through a trunk at the end of the bed. Adalina hurried over to the desk, hoping for a letter with a seal representing the frost breathers. Of course, that would have been far too easy. But what better way to prove he was a traitor than with correspondence with the enemy?

Instead, there was another sort of note on the desk. It was unfinished, with ink blotted on the page as if Heely had been pressing the quill too hard.

Fellow Councilmen,

I find that it is imperative that I remain at court permanently. I ask that you grant me leave and allow me to take on the title of ambassador. In my time here, I have grown close to the king and his council and find that my particular gifts would be best used...

Adalina scrunched her nose. What sort of influence did he think he could have on the Astarfallen court?

A pile of papers beside the unfinished letter caught her eye. She shuffled through them, her nerves going wild. There were quite a few letters from the Solarian council wishing him well and asking how Adalina was adjusting to life at court. There was one from her father reminding Heely that his job was to advise her to the best of his ability. That one she scoffed at. He'd given her zero help or advice.

A bird cawed from the window, making her jump and drop the letters. She knelt, trying to gather them up and hoping he wouldn't notice they were out of order when he returned. One caught her attention as she reached for it under the chair. It looked as if it had been crumpled and then someone had tried to smooth it down again.

It wasn't addressed to anyone in particular and read:

The time has come. As the power of Rothin grows, so too, does the wretch who dwells beneath the great chasm. Let him reign terror over those who doubted. May he usher us into the new era. Revenge is ours.

Adalina gripped the parchment. It wasn't signed and read more like a speech than a letter to someone. She and Callum turned to each other at the same time. As she held the paper out to him, he too grasped something in his hand.

Exchanging the items, they both frowned. Adalina took the handful of coins from Callum and peered down at them. It was a small fortune.

One that would be enough to buy a nice estate. But they were old currency. The depiction on them wasn't King Alistair's likeness, but rather someone who looked like an older, gruffer version.

Callum glanced up from the parchment she'd found and nodded to the coins. "My grandfather. That currency hasn't been in circulation since..."

"The frost breather's first emergence," she guessed.

"Yes," he confirmed. Then, turning back to the paper in his hands with a whistle, he said, "Well, this is odd. And a bit over the top if you ask me. I prefer snappier speeches." He pursed his lips. "Why would he keep something like this in his room?"

"I don't—" Adalina gasped as the jingle of keys came from the hallway. "Someone's coming."

Callum shoved the letter into his pocket and took the coins to do the same. Then he placed a finger over his lips and herded her toward the window. Once he opened it carefully, he motioned for her to climb out. She shook her head. They were three stories up and there was no terrace.

But when the door handle began to turn, she saw no other way out. She scrambled out the window, using a small lip in the stone to stand on. Inching aside, she made enough room for Callum to join her. He shut the window behind them and held a hand up, signaling for her to be still and quiet.

Her heart pounded so hard it echoed in her ears. With sweat-slicked hands, she felt herself slipping. "Callum, I can't do this."

"I've got you," he said as he wrapped one arm around her, pinning her tightly to the wall with her face pressed against the cool stone.

With her eyes squeezed tight, she concentrated, trying to send every ounce of her fear toward Elettra and thought, *we could really use some assistance.*

Within seconds, beating wings came from below them. Braving a glance down, she saw glittering scales shining in the sunlight. Elettra was hovering below them at the second-story windows.

Callum's voice was filled with amusement. "Would you look at that? You know, I do think I'm starting to see how a dragon can come in handy."

Then, with a smirk, he dropped.

Adalina bit back a scream and was relieved when she found he'd landed swiftly on the dragon's back. Summoning every ounce of courage and trust she could, she too, let go. With a hard thud that jarred her tailbone, she landed on Elettra.

Haughtily, Adalina said, "Told you dragons were amazing."

Elettra gently lowered them onto the ground, and Adalina thanked her with a good scratching behind the horns. "You're my hero, you know that?"

Elettra stretched before padding back over to the children, who were shouting at her to finish their game. Adalina watched in quiet fascination as the fearsome beast wagged her enormous tail in glee when one of the children ran up and kissed her on the snout. All those years of dreaming about waking the dragon, and never once did she consider this is what it would be like.

Thirty

Heely's arrest was done swiftly and quietly. Only Adalina, Callum, the king, and his council knew of it. For now, King Alistair wanted it kept between them; insisting that the last thing they needed was a fight with Solaris, too, for arresting one of their beloved council members.

All that time Adalina had spent wanting to earn the council's acceptance, and now she'd finally got her wish. They congratulated her on a job well done. It seemed some of their ire about Windshire had faded. Maybe there was hope of making up for that mistake. But now the pressure was on. They could change their minds about her again at any moment. It occurred to her that perhaps she should stop making these wishes. Each time one was granted, it didn't go the way she envisioned it.

There was an unsettling chill in the dungeons. It was brighter than she imagined but felt as if the sunshine drifting through the high-set windows wasn't actually reaching anyone sitting inside. She hugged her arms around herself and watched Callum pace for the hundredth time that morning. His heated glare burrowed into Heely, who was huddled in the corner of the cell.

Callum demanded, "I will not ask again. If the coins and the letter don't belong to you, then explain how they came into your possession."

Heely raised his chin in a poor attempt at holding on to any semblance of control he had left. "I can't explain it. Someone must have put them there." He turned to Adalina in desperation. "Please, you know me. You know I would never do anything to jeopardize Solaris."

"That's the problem," she sighed, exhausted from hours of going in circles with him. "I do not know you. Not really. All these years, and I couldn't say who you spend time with when you're not working. Or who you turn to with your troubles. Nor can I say how far you are willing to go to rise in power."

Heely huffed a bitter breath. "This is ridiculous."

"Yes," growled Callum. "It is. You're wasting our time. Who is your contact with the frost breathers? Who is their leader? And what do they have planned next?"

A groan tore from Heely's throat before he exclaimed, "I don't know!"

They weren't getting anywhere with this line of questioning. Adalina stood pressed against the bars of his cage. "Listen to me carefully. This can all go away if you just come clean. Where were you during the attack on Windshire? You weren't on the battlements, and no one recalls seeing you on the ship." She shifted to a more pleading tone, hoping to soften him toward her. "Please, Heely, help me get us out of this mess."

His mouth twitched into a frown. "I'm a coward." Tears filled his eyes. "When the attack began, I hid in the stables until I could get a horse and slip away. I swear it's the truth." He sniffed. "I can't help you, Adalina. I swear to you I am innocent." His tone grew urgent as he begged, "Please, please believe me."

Adalina threw her hands up and spun on her heel. "Callum, this is pointless."

"Perhaps a few nights alone will help his memory."

Heely grew angry as he shouted, "I spoke up for you! I defended you and pled your case to the council. I demanded they give you a chance!"

All of that was news to her. As far as she knew, Heely had been rolling over for the Astarfall council, trailing behind them like a lost puppy. If he had spoken to them on her behalf, nothing had come of it. Callum seemed to be the only one able to sway their minds when it came to her. No. There was nothing to point to Heely's innocence at the moment. Nothing more she could do for him.

She and Callum turned their backs on him. As they ascended the stone steps, she tried to block out Heely's desperate cries for her not to leave him. Despite their efforts, they were walking away without any answers. In fact, they were leaving with more questions than they'd started with.

Once they reached the main hall, she whispered to Callum. "It doesn't make any sense. He is insistent on his innocence. Do you think those tears were genuine?"

"Fear can bring tears to a man's eyes, too. He knows his life is on the line."

"We need to find Uthred. He should know that Heely is still insisting they were together earlier that night."

"Then let's ask him," Callum shrugged. "They've spent a lot of time together. Let's see what Uthred has to say on the matter. See if he's noticed Heely doing anything suspicious like sending correspondence outside of the palace or going unaccounted for at all."

They tried finding Uthred in his rooms first. But his wife answered alone, saying he had gone out on the king's orders. She wasn't sure when he would be back and suggested they try again in the morning.

By now, Adalina's stomach was growling. She stomped down the hall, frustrated with the day. They'd wasted hours with Heely. It was time that could have been better spent with Elettra or scouting the perimeter of the palace for any sign of frost breathers. After their defeat the previous day, they would no doubt be nursing their hurt egos and coming up with a new plan. A better plan.

When she and Callum reached their chambers, she threw open the door and flopped down on the sofa. Pressing her fingers to her temples, she groaned. Strong hands took hold of her feet and began rubbing them.

She peeked at Callum, who had sat on the other end of the sofa. He pulled her legs onto his lap and expertly worked his fingers into the soles of her feet. It sent goosebumps along her arms, but instantly drained the tension from her body.

He chuckled. "Dinner will be here soon. You'll feel better after that."

"Will I?" She wasn't sure she'd feel better until the frost breathers were taken care of. Until she knew her people were all safe.

"You haven't eaten a proper meal since breakfast. An oversight on my part."

"My mood is not from a lack of food."

The dimple in his cheek grew more prominent as he smirked. "I'd beg to differ."

She sat up, drawing her feet away from him and sitting cross-legged. Studying her husband's bright expression and the way he lounged comfortably on the sofa, she asked, "How do you do that?"

"Do what?"

"Turn it off like that. One minute I catch glimpses of you where it seems the weight of the world is crushing you, then the next it's like you don't have a care in the world."

He shrugged, as if trying to brush off her question. "I just don't like to dwell on things I can't control."

She shifted on her knees, so she was right beside him. "Is that the truth? Because I think you do dwell. I think these things are constantly on your mind, but you don't want anyone to know."

After a moment, the carefree mask dropped. He looked at her with raw emotion. There was a touch of turmoil mixed with sadness. It drew his face down and darkened his eyes. In truth, it broke her heart.

His voice was a mere whisper. "That's why. The way you're looking at me right now."

She licked her lips, which had gone dry. "What way?"

"Like I'm a wounded bird in need of consolation. It's how people treated me after my sister's accident. As if I couldn't handle it and would shatter into a million pieces at any given moment." His gaze fell to his hands and Adalina grabbed them tightly. When he looked back up at her, some of the sadness had dissipated. "So, I stopped giving them a reason to think that. Started putting on a show so they wouldn't be afraid."

"That's not your responsibility. You shouldn't have to pretend," Adalina's voice broke. "Especially not with me."

"I want to take care of you. Keep you safe."

"The best way to do that is to be open with me. Look at what we've accomplished so far. You taught me how to defend myself. You support me when everyone else doubts me. Even when I doubt myself." With a soft smile, she added, "And sure, maybe you can't rely on me to tend to your wounds out here," she paused, gesturing to his shoulder, then said, "but maybe I'll have better luck at the ones in there." She placed her hand over his heart.

The grateful look he gave her chipped away at the wall she'd built around her heart. More and more lately, she'd sensed it breaking. But only now could she admit it. After everything they'd been through in such a short time, it was impossible to deny that her feelings had grown.

Something shifted in her and suddenly she wanted to share everything with him. Her hopes, her dreams, and maybe even her heart. And right now, in this quiet moment... her bed. Heat blossomed in her core. If this was to be her last chance to let him in—truly let him in and be vulnerable—then she needed to take it. She stood, offering her hand to him.

"What are you doing?" he asked with a genuine note of surprise.

"If we're to march into battle tomorrow, then I want to make this last night together count."

He took her hand and followed her to their room. Their bed beckoned them, warm and inviting. Her heart pounded in her chest as her desire for him built. Seeing him open and genuine with her and knowing she might be the first person he'd shown that to in years, made her pulse race.

She pulled away and slipped off her dress, letting it fall to her feet. She planned to get into bed and ask him to join her, but he moved faster than anticipated. Shedding his clothes, he pinned her lightly to the wall with his hands pressed against it on either side of her head. The laugh he gave in response to her shocked face was a low rumbling timber that made her knees weak.

There was a hunger in his eyes. Like he needed to devour her, to make her his.

His leg snaked between her thighs, and he ran his fingers through her hair, sending a wave of desire through her. He lifted his leg, pressing it into her wet undergarments. The thin veil of fabric was the only thing standing in his way.

Shivers wracked her body from head to toe. It had never been a question of whether she wanted this man. Circumstances beyond their control had been battering at them like a ram at a palace gate. They'd been forced together but letting him into her heart and deciding to trust him... that was *her* decision.

She stifled a cry of pleasure as he reached down and moved the lace aside. His fingers were warm as they dipped into her, finding her sweet spot. She moved her hips, urging him to explore deeper.

He leaned forward, panting into her hair, and whispered, "I'm yours, dear wife. Heart and soul. If you want me to reveal everything to you, then that is what I'll do."

He trailed kisses down her throat to her breasts while whispering in between each one, "I have been enamored with you since the moment I met you." A kiss landed on her stomach as he sank to his knees. "Since the moment you refused to be told what to do by the young prince who commanded you on that dock, I knew you would take the world by storm. That nothing would stand in your way."

A thrill shot through her, watching him—the future King of Astarfall—kneeling before her as if he was hers to command. As if he would do anything she asked of him.

There was a rasp in his voice as he said, "I knew you were the only match for me when you stood up to me in the hallway at that brunch." His fingers inched further inside of her, moving gently, and earning a small gasp from her as they met their mark.

"Callum," she whispered his name, savoring how sweet it felt on her tongue.

He kissed her lower abdomen and breathlessly said, "I have fallen more deeply for you each time I've witnessed you stand up for yourself, each moment you've spent trying to help our people..."

A moan escaped her lips as he pulled her lace undergarments down, leaving her completely exposed to him. She had no words. Nothing she could say to match his confession to her. No way to respond to the intensity of his mouth pressing against her arousal. Her hips moved into his touch. The wetness swept from her core, making her legs tremble with each flick of his tongue.

She sucked in a deep breath and tangled her fingers in his hair as a scream of ecstasy tore from her throat. Callum looked up at her with a sly smile on his face. The late evening light highlighting his blue irises was intense, like the night sky when the moon was at its fullest. It was nearly enough to send another shot of pleasure through her.

She drew him to the bed with shaking hands. He laid back as she climbed onto him with a pleasant gasp. Her hair cascaded around them as she leaned down and kissed him deeply. Her hips found a steady rhythm, and she said, "I'm sorry I didn't see it sooner, Callum. I'm sorry for not being brave enough."

She sat up straight, letting the length of him reach deep inside of her as she moved more urgently. Suddenly, she was desperate to show him just how grateful she was to know the truth now. To prove to him that she felt the same. It might have taken her some time to catch up to him, but they were there now, together. The possibility of becoming a true husband and wife was within reach.

His fingers dug into her hips and a growl rumbled from deep in his chest. It only fueled her deepening desire. Her mind grew foggy with pleasure, and she knew if she didn't say the words now, then she would lose them.

Staring into his eyes as she rocked against him, she nearly said, *I love you.* But they were caught in her throat. Was this love? Everything was moving so quickly, what if she was wrong? She bit her lip, holding back. Afraid that it might break the spell they were under. Instead, she kissed him more fiercely than ever before and willed him to understand that she would get there someday. Because someday *would* come for them. Their story wouldn't end tomorrow on that battlefield. They would make sure of it.

When she pulled back, a brilliant smile spread across his face, and he rolled her, pinning her beneath him. His words filled her with contentment as he whispered, "My dear wife."

Thirty-One

Callum traced lazy circles along Adalina's bare shoulder. Chills ran down her spine and she pressed her face into the soft pillow while she stared out the terrace doors, watching the fisherman taking their boats out for the day.

She and Callum had been up most of the night exploring each other's bodies and opening up about themselves. Breakfast had been brought to them earlier than usual, since they would soon be marching with the army. The sun hadn't even risen over the horizon. But it would be a long trek to reach the frost breather camp. And King Alistair was determined to keep the fighting as far away from the city walls and villages outlying it as possible. The sooner they eradicated the frost breathers, the sooner they could quell any discord festering amongst the people. It was only then that they could honestly tell them they were safe.

Callum was in the midst of telling her another story about his little sister and how fierce she could be. When he finished, he said, "After she was gone, I felt like I might shatter into a million pieces."

Adalina rolled onto her elbow, resting her head on her hand as she faced him.

It sounded like it pained him to say it out loud. But he continued regardless, "I used to dream about escaping to a world where I wasn't a prince. Where the lives of thousands didn't hang in the balance of every choice I made."

"You would have taken to the sea," Adalina said encouragingly. His love for that was one thing he had never kept to himself.

He sighed, laying back on the pillows and ruffling his already mussed hair. "Just me, a small crew, and the open sea."

She nudged him in his side. "I'll be part of your crew. And Elettra, of course."

His eyes sparkled with amusement. "I think she likes me, but she's just not ready to admit it yet."

Adalina snuggled into the crook of his arm. "I used to dream of running away on the back of a dragon. Each time she refused to wake up for me, I wondered why I wasn't good enough. It didn't help that half the village thought I should give up, while the other half whispered behind my back that I just wasn't strong enough."

"That sounds lonely." He ran his fingers through her hair, taking time to twirl each strand around his finger.

"It was," she admitted.

"Maybe what we've both been missing is a partner. Someone to share the quiet, lonely moments with." He kissed her gently on her forehead.

"Someone to lean on when things get to be too much," she added.

"I think my mistake has been trying too hard around you. I wanted you to think I was fearless. That I could take care of you. I should have been true with my feelings and trusted you more."

She leaned up to look him in the eyes and really drive the point home as she said, "You should trust others, too. Your people will have more faith in you if you don't pretend around them. They deserve to see the real you as much as I do."

His gaze dropped, lingering on her lips. Her heart fluttered, but as she leaned in to kiss him, there was a knock at their chamber door.

Callum shouted with a gruff voice, "We'll be right down!" Then to Adalina, he frowned. "I guess that's our signal."

Her breath hitched in her throat. War.

The last thing she wanted to do was leave the warmth and comfort of Callum's arms, but what other choice did they have? Shrugging off the blankets, she went to her wardrobe and pulled out the riding leathers he'd gifted her. She would ride Elettra into battle today, and she needed to be prepared to move quickly and efficiently.

Callum did the same, and she glimpsed the moonglass encrusted compass she'd given him as he slipped it into his pocket.

When he noticed her watching, he shrugged. "So my dear wife can guide me even when she's not directly by my side."

A warm smile teased her face, and she joined hands with him as they left the room.

The nobles were waiting for them at the gates with Elettra nearby. They were somber and fidgeting anxiously. It was contagious, because soon Adalina was spinning her wedding ring around her finger.

King Alistair marched out of the city to face his army. He was fully coated in armor and led a muscled warhorse. The men buzzed as he began to give them his speech about defending their land from those who wished to take it from them.

Adalina's grandparents came to bid them farewell. They would remain at the palace with Queen Gwendolyn.

Her grandmother's eyes darted between Adalina and Callum knowingly, as if she saw that something had changed between them. That in one night they had altered the course of their marriage. She blushed deeply.

Elettra's amusement prickled through Adalina, and she shot her a glare. Was nothing a secret in this family? As if in response, Elettra inched closer to Callum. She lowered her head so he could scratch behind her horns.

The gesture may have looked like a small one to most, but Adalina knew the significance. She sensed it, as a rush of affection flowed into her chest. Elettra was following Adalina's lead and opening her heart to Callum.

Her grandmother chuckled. "May the fates look kindly upon you."

"You aren't coming?" Callum raised a playful eyebrow.

Her grandmother shook her head. "I'm afraid our fighting days are over."

"Speak for yourself," huffed her grandfather. "I've still got some fight left in me."

When King Alistair finished, the army marched on foot. Adalina and Elettra joined them. There was no telling how long the battle might last. And if the dragon was expected to stay in the sky the entire time, then it was safer to rest her wings until the moment came for them to fight.

As they walked further from the city, fog shifted along the ground, snaking around their legs and obscuring the view ahead. Adalina couldn't wait for the sun to fully rise, eager for the brilliant light. In the meantime, she found comfort in the ballads of victory and bravery the men sang as they walked. Led, of course, by Alfie and his beautiful voice. She took solace in their presence, knowing that she and Callum would not be outnumbered this time.

It was her first time seeing such a vast force. And she couldn't stop her mind from wandering to thoughts of each man and the family they'd left behind. The nobles had called their men to arms at lightning speed and she was in awe of the power emanating from them. But there was a nagging sense of dread tugging on her at the same time.

They hadn't walked more than a couple of miles when a chill crept through the air.

She bit her cheek. "Something feels wrong."

"I agree." Callum ran a frustrated hand through his hair. "Remember the plan. Fire where you can, assuming our men aren't in the way. But if that *thing* comes, you and Elettra will focus on the threat in the sky. You can't worry about what's happening on the ground."

"I'll make sure the beast doesn't spill a drop of Astarfallen blood," Adalina confirmed.

"My father and I will be at the rear. The king can't risk being caught on the front lines."

She knew all of this already, but she had a feeling he was restating the plan in order to calm his nerves. She nodded, but heat flared in her chest. This time, she would be ready to do what needed to be done. She would take a page out of Callum's old book and control her emotions. It wouldn't be like Windshire. Protecting him and his men was her priority. No matter what it took.

His gaze was searching, and he pressed his lips into a thin line before saying, "The fog is growing thicker."

She sidestepped closer to him. The only warmth to be found was coming from his body.

Horses whinnied in a panic and the hair on her neck rose. Elettra leaned forward, peering into the thick, frigid mist. Adalina's vision sharpened with the dragon's, allowing her to narrow her gaze past the rows of soldiers. But even with the enhancement, all she could make out in the fog were countless shadowy figures. Unmistakenly human. Undoubtably frost breathers considering they shouldn't have been running into so many people this far from the villages. And they were creeping toward the army. Since she was using dragon sight and the men still appeared a decent distance away, they couldn't have been close enough to engage in battle yet.

"I think it's an ambush," she hissed angrily.

Callum halted and thrust a fist in the air to signal the others. Adalina prayed to the heavens that the alert would trickle up the line fast enough. The fog was too thick to allow every man out there to see him themselves.

Under his breath, he whispered back, "How close are they?"

"No less than one hundred yards from the front line," she guessed with deep uncertainty. It's not like her dragon bonded abilities came with a measuring stick.

Callum turned to the general at his side and whispered in his ear. The general tapped the soldier in front of him, passing along the message. If they wanted to maintain any sort of upper hand, they needed to keep quiet. Pretend as if nothing was amiss.

Adalina stood on her tippy toes to reach Callum's ear. "If Heely is in the dungeons, then who warned the frost breathers that we were attacking?"

Deep down, she knew this was no chance encounter. What were the chances that the frost breathers were advancing on the city at the very moment the Astarfallen army was marching on them?

Callum tensed. "I don't know." There was regret in his voice as he said, "We can't afford to spare any lives today. Do you understand?"

The young girl from Windshire, who had clung so tightly to her beloved that she lost her life because of it, flashed through Adalina's mind. She balled her hands into fists. "I understand."

Elettra was already waiting for her, poised and ready to take flight. Adalina grabbed Callum and pulled him into her. Clinging to him like her life depended on it, she planted a firm kiss on his mouth.

"No goodbyes, please," he said with a lopsided smile.

Adalina smiled back, then mounted the dragon. Her heart screamed at her to convince him to join her. To get him off the ground and keep him out of harm's way. But her head knew better. Callum wasn't going to leave his men.

"On my signal," he said lowly, holding two fingers in the air this time.

He lowered one finger. Adalina sucked in a breath. Elettra dug her claws into the ground anxiously, and the heat of a fire already rumbling through her belly made Adalina shift uncomfortably on her back. To think, this was the same beast that had been playing with children the day before. Today was different. She was ready for a fight. But was Adalina?

Callum lowered the last finger. She exhaled. The air shifted. It sparked with the army's unleashed magic. Power teetered on the edge, making sparks dance along Adalina's skin. Elettra leaned back on her haunches in preparation to take flight. Adalina's eyes were glued to Callum's hand. If only she could stop time, prevent what was about to come.

The men inched forward on light feet. It felt as if they had reached the end of the world and Adalina couldn't imagine teetering over the edge. And then Callum's arm dropped. Men disappeared into the fog, running bravely and blindly toward their enemy.

Nerves violently twisted every fiber of Adalina's being as she and Elettra took to the sky. It was only a matter of minutes before they rose high enough to see into the fog. It was unnatural in the way it snaked around the army. As if it hadn't come from the sky, but from some sort of magic. Once out of it, warmth returned to her body and light from the rising sun cast a warm glow around her.

If it hadn't been for the fog, she could have destroyed the frost breather's army before they ever reached the Astarfallen. But by now, the armies were upon each other. With her view obscured, showing her only shadow figures, it was impossible to tell who was who.

"Can you clear it?" she asked Elettra, desperate to destroy the frost breather's advantage before it was too late.

Elettra inhaled, her chest and belly expanded, and when she released her breath, the wind that tore from her was so warm it steamed in the sky. The fog sizzled as the dragon's breath reached it and the men of Astarfall whooped. Soon their cries of relief turned violent. Blood lust was apparent in every sound they made as they fully closed the gap between them and the frost breathers.

Adalina gripped Elettra's horns desperately as she peered down below. With sharpened vision, she could make out every detail.

The front lines held firm. Various forms of magic pulsed, pushing back the faceless men who whipped ice as if it was a blade. Hissing through her teeth, Adalina commanded Elettra to fire on any frost breather who wasn't directly engaged in close combat with one of Callum's men.

They lit up in a blaze and it wasn't long before the battlefield looked like it had little bonfires burning throughout it. When Elettra whipped her head and snarled toward the rear of the Astarfall army's formation, Adalina stiffened.

A group of frost breathers had broken through the front lines and, using their icy shields, had forced their way toward the king.

"Callum." His name was like ash on her tongue as she watched him leap in front of his father's horse and slash a man down using the rays of the sun.

King Alistair was already engaged in battle atop his horse. Guards worked tirelessly to keep the frost breathers at bay. And all around them, the Astarfallen dealt lethal blows to their opponents using their heaven gifted magic.

The trouble was the frost breathers were Astarfallen themselves. Born with a twisted version of the same magic in their veins. A much darker version that took the nature of the land and forced it into something troubling and cold. And it matched Callum's army in strength.

Adalina glanced around in desperation. There was still no sign of the creature made of wing and bone. Going to aid Callum wouldn't be going back on her word. She tapped Elettra twice, commanding her to get closer to them.

Shards of ice fired on King Alistair's guards, taking them out in troves. Both he and Callum were exposed.

Adalina shouted at Elettra, "Save them!"

Elettra swooped down, fire rumbling. With a heavy breath, she released her flames on the men surrounding Callum and his father. Adalina marveled at the control the dragon exercised this time and tried to ignore the fact that maybe it had been her own emotion alone that had made them lose control at Windshire.

Elettra expertly controlled the line of fire and hit only those she wanted to.

But they had drawn too much attention. The enemy shouted, pointing to the sky and aiming their frostbitten arrows at Elettra's heart. From below, Callum summoned the light of the sun to him and, in a bright blast, shot it at the hordes of frost breathers. Some collapsed from the direct impact. Others shielded their eyes, shouting from the temporary blindness the hot white light caused.

The sky darkened, as if also tired from the effort, and storm clouds began to blot out the sun. They were as dark and foreboding as Adalina's mood was becoming. Even after the horror at Windshire, this battle didn't compare. There was so much happening at once, as earth, wind, water, and ice collided. More than ever before, she felt incredibly ill-prepared.

Elettra circled around and Adalina sensed the fire building once again in both the dragon's stomach and in her own. The king's men gravitated to him and their prince in an attempt to create a shield with their bodies and their magic to keep them safe. Sweat beaded on Callum's forehead as he used what little power he could summon from the blocked out sun to hold off the frost breathers advancing on them.

Adalina hissed once again, telling Elettra to release the pent-up fire. But before she could claim her victory, a shrill screech froze everyone in place. Her heart plummeted. The great beast had come at last to defend its masters.

Thirty-Two

A dalina's muscles went taut with immediate fear. Every instinct screamed at her to run from the danger, despite the protection that Elettra offered her.

Callum's string of curses filled her ears as a ghastly beast resembling death incarnate dove out of the stormy clouds. Where Elettra was graceful and regal, this monster was twisted and wrong. Rotten, torn scales stretched in patches over its boney body like someone had tried to plaster its skin back together.

Black venom seeped from its mouth, falling on the men below. Frost breathers and king's men alike fell as it dropped onto them. There was a sizzle as the venom burned through their flesh and turned their skin a sickening black like frostbite.

No rider sat on the beast's back and she wondered if anyone had any control over it at all as it aimlessly snapped at the bodies below. Desperate cries tore through the air as the monster snatched up any man in its path and gnashed them in its creaking jaws. The dragon before her exuded evil down to its very being. Its broken, twisted wings struggled to keep it in the sky and several times, it dipped suddenly, only to fight to rise once again.

The way it dove made Adalina's breath catch in her throat. The movement was so fast and aimless that it nearly crashed into the ground headfirst. There was no indication that the beast had any sense of self preservation. She grasped tight to that bit of knowledge.

Her voice shook with rage as she said, "We need to get rid of it before it does any more damage. They won't stand a chance down there if we don't!"

The familiar blood thirsty fire rose in her chest. Her vision darkened at the edges, and she had to set her sights on Callum to stay grounded. If she lost control, then Elettra would, too. And there would be nothing to stand in the way of the mindless creature.

But Elettra must have had her own fury to deal with, because she unleashed an anguished roar and with it, more fire than they used at Windshire erupted from her mouth. It plowed into the frostbitten dragon, pummeling him toward the ground.

The sudden shift in direction only seemed to give the creature a new target. It shook its body out, seemingly impervious to the pain that should have come with the fiery blow. A scream tore from Adalina as it lunged for Callum. Elettra, as if reacting to Adalina's despair, soared toward them.

Adalina's heart was practically beating out of her chest and all she could do was close her eyes and pray to the fates that they would reach Callum before the beast. At the speed the creature was going, a collision between it and Callum would surely kill them both.

Elettra slammed into the frostbitten dragon, and it rolled several yards away on the icy ground. Men dodged the lethal bone before being crushed beneath it. But when the creature came to a stop, it stood and shook its head. It felt like every ounce of fire was sucked from Adalina's veins and a cold sense of dread washed over her. The beast was utterly unharmed.

King Alistair shouted for his men and her stomach sank when she saw that the guards who had been defending him lay lifelessly at his horse's feet. A veiled frost breather grabbed the king's cape and tore him from his horse.

It drew the frostbitten dragon's attention toward them. Its beady eyes were pinned on Callum, who started for his father, but froze under the watchful gaze of the beast.

Adalina shouted at it. Its attention was easily claimed, and it snapped its mangled teeth and took a few skittering steps in her direction.

Callum shouted to the men racing to his father's side. "Get the king out of here!"

It took two of the men to cut down the king's attacker. But that threat was now replaced with the skittering beast of death who was whipping its head between them and Elettra.

In dismay, Adalina chanced one last longing look at her husband. If death was coming for her today, she would gladly greet it, knowing that the people she loved were safe.

Callum desperately pleaded, "Let Elettra handle it! Dismount! Stay with me."

She wanted to go to him. To be wrapped in his warm embrace once more. But she couldn't leave Elettra on her own. Couldn't ask her to take on a threat that she wasn't willing to face herself.

Her eyes welled with tears, knowing he may never forgive her, as she said, "I'm sorry."

She did her best to ignore his pleas and the pained shouts coming from the king. Gripping Elettra's spikes, she homed in on the target in front of her. The dragon of death. It smelled of rotting flesh and deep earth. Whatever hellscape the frost breathers had pulled this thing out of had to be nothing of the likes she'd ever seen.

Her words came out in a snarl, nearly as unhuman as the dragon beneath her. "Destroy it."

Elettra bellowed at the beast, drawing its sole attention to them. Elettra's fire lanced through it, knocking it back to the ground. The frostbitten dragon struggled to stand. Parts of its skeletal body still burned with the flame. It was like a fire made in the middle of a snowstorm. Flickering in and out, but trying to stay lit.

Then the monstrous creature took to the sky once again. As if their instincts were one and the same, Adalina didn't need to use her taps to direct Elettra into the air. Rocks tumbled as Elettra's wings beat furiously, carrying them after the frost breather's dragon.

It was smaller than Elettra was and faster than Adalina anticipated. It veered straight up like an arrow. Adalina commanded with a string of shouts for Elettra to follow it. But Elettra hesitated. Adalina pushed aside the prickling worry coming from the dragon. She got the sense Elettra was concerned for her. But she was a dragon warrior, and she could handle this. If they were going to catch up to it, they needed to follow it directly.

"Keep on its trail," she demanded.

Elettra tilted, rearing further back, and forcing Adalina to grip her spikes tighter. The edges dug into her palms, leaving indents.

It still wasn't enough, though.

"More!" she shouted.

Elettra did as she bid, angling them further so they could ascend upward, staying on the frostbitten dragon's tail. It was a steeper angle than they'd ever taken and Adalina was ill prepared in her haze of angry determination.

All it took was one slip of the hand and she was falling. It felt as if her stomach was thrown into her throat as gravity claimed her. Callum shouted from below, but the whistle of wind and a horrifying screech drowned him out.

Fire tore through her arm as she was snatched up with razor-sharp teeth. Stars flashed in her vision from the pain, but she didn't cry out. She couldn't. Not when she needed to fight the frostbitten dragon who had stopped her from hitting the ground.

Its venom slipped through the torn sleeve of her riding leathers, and she screamed in agony. As she danced in and out of consciousness, she recalled the icy water she'd fallen into as a child. They'd skated on the lake countless times before. But that one winter had been different. The ice hadn't been thick enough, and she'd dipped into the icy depths for only a moment before her grandfather pulled her out. It had been horrible. Bone biting cold. But this was worse.

Something slammed into the frostbitten dragon, jarring Adalina so hard that she felt a bone in her arm snap. The pain overwhelmed her, making her head swim. But in her heart, she knew help had come. That there was only one thing in the sky who could rival her captor.

"Elettra," she said with a pained smile.

With another strike from Adalina's faithful dragon, the creature tumbled into a freefall. How long had they been up there? Between the pain of her wounds and the dips making her stomach flip in a panic, it was impossible to keep track of time.

Through heavy eyelids, she could see Elettra coming in for another blow. But before she reached them, the beast threw Adalina. Tossed her like she was nothing more than a treat it had tried to steal from the other dragon.

Suddenly, Adalina was grabbed once more. Elettra's grip was gentler than the creature's. She clasped onto Adalina and held her firmly, careful not to apply too much pressure on the injured wrist. The intense pain was turning numb, but Adalina wasn't sure if that was because the bone was broken or because of the venom.

The creature continued to shriek above, even as Elettra dove over the army and placed Adalina in Callum's arms. He was trembling all over and it was a wonder he didn't drop her. She was finding it hard to catch her breath, but he soothed her with calming words that were difficult to discern over the shouts of men around them.

Adalina stared up at the sky, where two massive, winged beasts clashed with one another. Elettra's scales, so familiar and stunning, tangled with the rotting flesh and protruding bone of the other dragon.

With Adalina out of the way, it seemed there was nothing to hold Elettra back. The battle experienced dragon beat the smaller frostbitten one with her powerful, muscular wings. Bone rattled, overpowering the sound of fighting on the ground.

Elettra took hold of the frostbitten dragon's neck and tore it. Bone and what little muscle held it together ripped apart, and the frostbitten dragon's head plummeted to the ground. Callum was startled when Adalina tried to sit up. He attempted to coax her into remaining in his arms, but she couldn't. She needed to see this.

The frostbitten dragon's wings stopped beating and twitched violently before following the head to the ground. Men scattered, but not all were fast enough. Their screams were cut off as the creature's lifeless body crushed them.

Carefully, Callum set Adalina on her feet. She swayed, but he caught her and wrapped her uninjured arm through his to steady her.

Concern was woven in his tone as he said, "I've got you."

She gripped him with every ounce of strength she had left and watched as Elettra turned her vicious sights on the battlefield. A wash of dizziness nearly knocked Adalina off her feet as she sensed her dragon's maddening fury.

The soft, light skin on her belly glowed brightly and the scent of sulfur filled Adalina's nose. Elettra was going to fire. And there were still Astarfallen on that field.

"Run!" The cry tore from her throat in desperation. There was no stopping Elettra. Not when all she sensed from the dragon was pure rage.

Every able-bodied man bolted from the field. Astarfallen leapt over their fallen friends as they returned to where Callum and their generals were standing. Frost breathers also took heed of Adalina's warning and retreated toward the mountains.

But that only made it easier for Elettra. With the Astarfallen out of the way, there was nothing to stand in her way now. Fire erupted from her in a massive stream. Its golden light was nearly blinding.

Callum tensed. And every man near them seemed to be holding their breath in collective anticipation. No one dared to move a muscle.

But before the fire reached its mark, a fresh shield of fog engulfed the frost breathers. This time, they were ready for the heat of Elettra's fire. The shield glistened like ice on a lake in the midafternoon. The fire licked across it like it was searching for a weak spot; for a place to slip through the veil and burn them all.

Adalina leaned into Callum. Her cheeks were warm and wet, and she hadn't realized she'd been crying. Whether it was from the pain or the prospect of victory, she couldn't tell.

With bated breath, they waited. It felt like an eternity. Elettra's belly swelled once more, and she rained down her fiery wrath on the men beneath the foggy shield. This time, it broke through. Adalina took a shaky step forward with her heart pounding so roughly in her chest she thought it might burst.

When the smoke cleared, she prepared herself for the mass of lifeless, charred bodies they were sure to find. But there were none. Her stomach sank. There, where the frost breathers had retreated... where they had stood grouped together, sure to meet their end, the field was clear. They were gone.

Thirty-Three

Adalina called out to her dragon. Her voice was weak, no more than a croak, but Elettra's attention snapped to her, regardless. In a flurry of beating wings, Elettra landed before her and Callum. Her head dropped to the ground and all the wrath Adalina had felt from her before dissipated. A soothing rush of relief flooded her instead, and she embraced the dragon's large head when presented with it.

A general nearby was shouting in outrage, "Where did they go? How could they escape?"

Callum's voice was filled with disbelief. "They used the cover of the fog to slip away."

The general rounded on them. "Send the dragon after them. Burn the cowards before they have a chance to regroup."

Regret pinched at Adalina, and she stepped away from Elettra to study her. The dragon was exhausted. Her face sagged and there was the slightest tremble in her wings that only Adalina could see with their shared senses.

"She needs to rest," she said with as much authority as she could muster.

"But—" the general started.

Callum held up a hand. "We all need to rest. My wife is in no condition to ride."

"Then *you* should ride," suggested the general. His eyes were wide with panic.

Adalina didn't blame him for pushing the matter, but even Callum drooped with exhaustion. His face was drained of color except for the bruises and cuts he'd gotten in the battle.

Adalina shook her head. "Callum's fought too hard today. He has little experience riding Elettra and with as tired as he is, he might not be able to stay on her back. And I will not send her out there alone. Not when she's used as much strength and energy as she just did."

Even dragons had their limits. Surely these soldiers—men who had just fought so fiercely—could understand that. She, like them, needed to rest.

The general stared intently at Elettra as if really seeing her for the first time. His eyes tracked her slow movements as she settled into a sitting position behind Adalina.

Diplomatically, Callum said, "Every warrior here—human and dragon alike—will come home with us. I count today's battle as a victory. Despite our losses, the frost breathers now know we will not bend so easily to their will. And they lost their beast." He gestured to the twisted remains of the frostbitten dragon.

The general nodded and a bit of light returned to his eyes. He turned to his men, spreading the command that they would be going home. Each soldier brightened. Their shoulders sank with relief that they had lived to fight another day. That they wouldn't have to march into the mountain pass to the frost breathers' encampment.

Callum's breath was warm and delightful on Adalina's neck as he asked, "Ready to go home?"

She sighed and slumped into his side. More than ever before.

When they made it back to the city, it was in mass chaos. Citizens were boarding up their homes. The streets were eerily silent, but in the palace, the council and courtiers shouted and demanded to know what had happened out there.

Adalina left Elettra to eat, drink, and nap. Once she was feeling up to it, Adalina asked her to fly around the perimeter of the city in shifts. The dragon needed to rest, but it was also vital that she be a consistent presence in the event that the frost breathers found the strength to advance on the city walls.

For the time being, Callum was right. Although Elettra's fire did not finish the war, it had given them a battle victory. With the frost breathers retreating to their camp, it gave the Astarfallen army time to formulate their next move. It also gave King Alistair's men the reprieve they needed to swiftly carry the wounded back to the city. To Adalina's relief, there were far fewer of them than she anticipated.

They would mourn the loss of their slain soldiers, but every-one—even the stubborn council—had to admit that the casualties could have been catastrophic had it not been for Elettra.

For now, the army would have an opportunity to tend to their wounded bodies and hearts. No one knew when there would be an-other chance with the frost breathers growing so bold. Her only hope was that without the sickly dragon, their enemy would lose some of their confidence. A blow to their faith and their ranks was a small win, but a win, nonetheless.

After a visit to the healers, Adalina found Callum near the king's chambers, and they embraced each other tightly. She buried her face in his chest, inhaling his familiar scent. He showered the top of her head with kisses, and neither could bring themselves to pull away for some time.

"Your wrist?" he asked.

"Broken," she answered.

The healers had cleaned out the lacerations from the frostbitten dragon's teeth and placed a poultice on it to stop the swelling. Then they had wrapped it tightly to prevent movement, but it still hurt like hell. Worse were the white lines that trailed along her forearm. Scars left behind from the venom that had dripped onto her skin.

Callum turned a sickly green when she lifted her arm to show him.

"The healers said the venom caused superficial frostbite. They soaked it and said I'm lucky my arm wasn't coated with it, or they might have had to amputate."

Callum's eyes glistened sadly. "There are others who weren't so lucky."

Her stomach turned, recalling several of the wounded whose entire arms and legs were doused with the sticky black venom.

Queen Gwendolyn stepped up to them hesitantly. "My dear," she called gently to Callum.

He cleared his throat and pulled away from Adalina's grasp but claimed her uninjured hand in his. "Yes, Mother?"

Seraphine and Alfie stood beside the queen with sorrow filling their faces.

"Come with me," she answered.

Adalina and Callum walked into the king's room hand in hand. Every bone, muscle, and fiber in her being ached, but she needed to be there for Callum. His father's head was wrapped in gauzy fabric and his skin had a gray pallor to it. The only thing that brought her any hope was the soft half smile on his lips as he slumbered.

Tears drifted down Gwendolyn's cheeks, but she remained tall and regal. "Your father's wounds are worse than we first thought. They say he took a powerful blow to the head, but the healers are certain that with time, he will make a full recovery."

Adalina took comfort in that. But Callum's knees buckled slightly and, try as he might, he could not hide the horror on his face. When he noticed everyone staring, he cleared his throat. But rather than hide his concern completely, his eyebrows knitted together, and his mouth pressed into a hard line. He gulped and Adalina sensed he was holding back tears.

She fought back nausea, imagining how eerily familiar this must have been for him. Was he recalling the way his sister had looked when she'd been brought back to the palace to heal after her fall?

Despite her advice to him that he shouldn't hide his feelings from those who cared about him, she knew he wasn't going to allow himself to break down in a room full of family and healers.

His hand was clammy, and she pressed her body against his side, hoping to give him strength. His voice cracked as he said, "Then I will meet with the council in his stead. Someone warned the frost breathers that we were coming. It seems we were wrong about Heely."

"It seems so," Gwendolyn said meekly.

When they left the room, Callum's steps were slow and deliberate.

Adalina's grandmother rounded the corner and flew to her with arms open wide. "Oh, my Lina." She searched her body as if looking for any sign of injury. "You're alright?"

"We're fine. Both me and Elettra." Adalina tried to smile, but it was closer to a grimace.

"I'll go see her now. I just wanted to make sure you were okay."

Callum interrupted, "Your granddaughter was brilliant out there. You would have been proud of them both."

Adalina wasn't sure *brilliant* was the word she would use to describe what she had done out there. If it hadn't been for Elettra, they would be preparing a burial shroud for her as they spoke. Still, her heart warmed at the compliment despite the icy chill lingering in her limbs with the fading adrenaline. Her grandmother and the others dispersed, leaving only her and Callum standing hand in hand.

Voices of the councilmen drifted up the stairs. They were gathering, which meant Callum would need to join them soon. Adalina started to release his hand, but he pulled her back to him. He kissed her once on the lips. A fleeting gesture, but one that gave her strength.

"You should go rest," he said.

Her heart skipped a beat. As much as she longed to lose herself in a tangle of blankets on their bed, she couldn't bring herself to make him do this alone. "I'm not leaving you."

"As long as you're sure. What happened to you out there..." his voice cracked. "It was unfathomable. That could have been you in that bed." He gestured to his father's door with more urgency in his movement than she expected.

"I want to be with you," she said with gentle finality.

With a nod, they walked down to the study. The men were crammed inside muttering amongst themselves. A few trembled openly, while others tried to hide their fear with bright red faces.

Callum shifted uncomfortably beside her, looking like a nervous boy about to be tested. And she supposed, in a way, he was.

He would be standing in his father's place. With King Alistair nursing his wounds, it fell to his son to carry out his wishes. To keep them all safe. Something she knew weighed on him enormously.

When they noticed Callum, their moods shifted slightly. Their eyes brightened with the hope that their prince would lead them out of this dark day and back into the light. Adalina followed him to his father's desk. He gestured for her to stand at his side, earning a few surprised looks from the men around them. Even after all this time, they were still adjusting to her presence in these meetings.

No one objected though, as Callum addressed them, "Esteemed members, I regret to inform you that my father—" he stopped, sucking in a sharp breath. Adalina placed an encouraging hand on his back, rubbing it gently. He continued, "My father is injured, but in excellent hands. I have no doubt that he will pull through stronger than ever."

To her astonishment, he summoned a charming smile. Though she'd asked him to drop the facade around her, she didn't blame him for still using it now. If he needed it in order to protect himself in this time of uncertainty, then she would not fault him for it.

"Our next steps are crucial—" Callum stopped abruptly as the door opened and Uthred slipped in.

A sheen of sweat coated his forehead, and he shrank into the crowd. Her stomach flipped when Heely followed. She supposed, now that his innocence had been proven, it made sense that he'd been released from the dungeons. But she wasn't sure he should be in the study.

Callum must have shared the sentiment as he said, "Heely, this is a closed meeting."

Heely flushed as all heads turned to him. "I beg your pardon, your Highness. I am simply here to represent Solaris' involvement." His eyes flitted to Adalina.

Under his breath, Callum asked, "Do you wish him to leave?"

She weighed her options. She was embarrassed she'd wielded accusations at him so harshly. But she also didn't trust that he cared for her best interests. His position had always come first.

With a sigh, she answered, "The frost breathers won't stop with Astarfall. Solaris stands to lose as much as we do here. Let him stay. For them."

"As you wish," Callum said with a warning glare in Heely's direction.

The rest of the meeting continued uninterrupted. The men offered opinions on what should be done next, and they ultimately agreed that the encampment should be the top priority. Without a foothold in Astarfall, the frost breathers would be pushed back over the border just as they had been when her grandmother had faced them. They would arrest as many of them as possible and make them stand trial for treason.

A few voiced concerns that finding the mole should be the primary focus instead. It stopped everyone in their tracks and every man in there threw suspicious glares in their neighbors' direction. The distrust in the room was stifling.

Callum gave an appeasing nod, and said, "It *is* a top priority. A trusted few will be tasked with rooting out the traitor in our midst. But do not allow the betrayer to make us turn on one another. We need to work together now more than ever."

Adalina smiled at him with pride as he spoke with reason and authority. But more than that, she admired the raw honesty in how he was approaching the councilmen.

The next order of business regarded the leader of the frost breather army. The decision was unanimous that he would need to be dealt with differently. His capture was vital to the crown's endeavors. To parade the son of a bitch in front of his men and force him to face a very public trial would show everyone that his power was limited. That even someone who could inspire such radical ideals and violence could fall from grace.

When the meeting was called to a close, Callum shouted, "Uthred, Heely, we would like a word."

A few councilmen shot them wary glances as they exited the room. But Uthred held his head high. Heely approached more meekly. They stood on the other side of the desk, facing Adalina and Callum.

She didn't know what Callum planned to confront them with, but judging by his stiff posture, she guessed it was a matter weighing heavily on his mind.

He started on them immediately. "Where have you been, Uthred?"

"Speaking with sources on the border. I rode out yesterday to meet with them and find out what they know."

"These sources, are they Astarfallen?" Callum narrowed his eyes.

"Yes, from the mountains. They are the closest in proximity to the encampment. Elderly men who haven't dwelled in the village for some time but rather travel the range."

"And what did they have to say?"

"That they had seen the pit. That the beast was real." His eyes darted to Adalina. "But as I've heard, you have already taken care of that problem."

"We have." Adalina raised her chin proudly, ignoring the sting of the marks left from its venom. Then she asked, "Did they say anything else?"

"There have been rumors." Uthred shifted uncomfortably. His shoulders sagged a bit, and he looked tired. "I didn't want to say anything in front of the council. I fear it would cause discourse at a time when we need to be united."

"Spill it," Callum drawled as if bored. His mood changed; his facade stronger than ever. Perhaps an attempt at trying to appear as if nothing would shake him. Adalina knew better. He was getting nervous.

Uthred gulped. "They say they've heard whispers of a summoning. That there are more dragons where the one Elettra killed came from."

"If that's true, then why only send the one?" Callum's throat sounded tight.

Uthred shook his head. "That is all I know." He shifted on his feet as if ready to be dismissed.

But Adalina still needed to know something. "Why lie and say that Heely wasn't having drinks with you?"

Uthred glanced uneasily at Heely, who looked like he was going to be sick. Then said, "I wasn't sure he could be trusted. I invited him to drink to make him think that I was willing to work with him—to gain his trust—in case my suspicions were correct. I knew someone was leaking information and couldn't fathom that it would be one of our *own* councilmen." To Heely, he said, "I am sorry, old friend. I didn't mean for the lie to *wrongly* add to the evidence against you."

Heely sniffed indignantly. "May I go, Your Highness?"

Callum nodded. "You are dismissed. Both of you."

Heely scrambled ahead of Uthred and soon they were both gone. Callum sank into his father's seat at the desk and pinched the bridge of his nose. The carefree facade melted away, revealing the worry underneath.

"So, there are more dragons," Adalina mused quietly. "He mentioned a summoning. Perhaps they haven't called them up from the depths of whatever cold hell they came from yet."

"I hope you're right. If we act fast enough, then maybe we won't have to worry about them succeeding. It would be one less thing on our plate."

He reached out for her, and she climbed into his lap. She curled against him and stroked the side of his face. Stubble pricked the pads of her fingers, and she wondered if he'd simply forgotten to shave or if he hadn't been taking care of himself in all the madness.

Tilting her head slightly to look into his eyes, she asked, "Are you hungry? I can call for some food."

His gaze darkened. "I'm ravenous. But not for food."

Heat spread between her legs, and she wrapped her arms around his neck. "I can help with that."

Shadows danced over his face. His voice was broken as he admitted, "I thought I was going to lose you today. When you fell..."

Adalina grazed her lips along his cheek. "I don't want to think about today. Please, just make me forget it."

Their lips met gently at first. Then they both grew hungrier. Giving in, she sank into his hold. When his tongue parted her lips, she moaned at the taste of him. It was like sunshine and the fresh sea air—invigorating and delicious.

There were a million other places they should be: talking with the army's generals or making sure the councilmen were sticking to their orders. But in this moment, she couldn't imagine belonging anywhere but in Callum's arms.

Things might have been bleak, but they had accomplished the impossible today. They had taken away the frost breathers' upper hand. And soon she believed they would find the faceless leader. They would show the rebels that Astarfall was not to be trifled with. That together, she and Callum were a force to be reckoned with.

And after that, maybe, she and her husband would get their honeymoon. The hills of Solaris in wintertime with snow blanketing the lush green grass sounded nice. She could show him the house she grew up in, visit her mother in the dress shop, have dinner at her grandparents' cottage, and sled down the icy slopes.

Callum's hands found her waist, and he maneuvered her until she straddled him. A flush washed over her chest as he planted kisses on the skin exposed by her low-cut blouse. Warm shivers ran through her, and she leaned her head back, looking up at the ceiling. The moonlight trickling in through the windows met her wedding ring. It cast brilliant sparkles across the dark room, dancing like starlight.

She sighed pleasantly. The moment when she first met Elettra face to face, and this one here in the quiet study with the man she adored holding her while moonglass twinkled above them... If she had to pick the moments in her life, she most wished to revisit years later. It would be those.

Thirty-Four

Adalina woke with the worst crick in her neck. She moaned as she stretched out and then yelped as she hit the ground with an ungracious thud. Callum shouted and peered down at her from the chair they'd fallen asleep on with exhaustion still heavy in his eyes.

Adalina rubbed her backside as she rose, using the desk as leverage. "I think we fell asleep," she said through a yawn.

He placed his hand on her butt and pulled her closer. "Maybe we should make up for that lost time."

The room grew warm, as if feeding off the heat of his words. If he was the flint, she was the kindling. She leaned down, pressing her lips fiercely to his. He groaned, as if ready to devour her. But he paused as she placed her hands on his shoulders.

"How's your wrist?" he asked, concern replacing lust.

It hurt like hell if she was being honest. She gave him a half smile. "I wouldn't object to some of that pain relieving tonic the healers have. Especially before I ride."

Callum blanched. "Ride?"

She tipped her head and raised an eyebrow at him. "Yes... I'm a dragon rider, remember?" she teased and brushed her fingers through his hair with a contented sigh. It was a brand-new day. That meant anything was possible. They could find the traitor; be sure the city was protected before marching on the enemy's camp again. All of it was daunting, but a night of sleep had given her a fresh boost of hope.

Her husband, however, didn't seem to share the sentiment. A flush ran from his cheeks and down his neck. With his eyes downcast, it looked as if he was battling a storm within his own mind.

They both startled as the door to the study flung open. It was Seraphine, though she was nearly unrecognizable with bags under her normally bright eyes and red splotches blotting her pristine complexion.

Callum stood at once. "What is it? What's happened?"

Seraphine sputtered, "W-we've been looking everywhere for you."

Adalina's uninjured hand flew to his. She wound her fingers tightly around his, her stomach dropping along with the temperature in the room.

Seraphine, seemingly unable to get the words out, turned and scurried down the hallway. Callum and Adalina followed close behind. She had to jog to keep up with their long strides, and by the time they reached King Alistair's room, she felt as if she might keel over.

The king's private chambers were eerily silent. It was like the moment before a terrible storm hit, bringing in a dangerous wave. Adalina's breath hitched in her throat when she spotted Queen Gwendolyn by the bedroom door. She was dressed in a floor length nightgown and pale velvet robe. Loose waves of hair flowed down to her waist in a tangled web. And her skin... paler than Adalina expected it could get. She was every bit the vision of a wraith. And like a wandering spirit, she made no sound.

Instead, it was Uthred who came out of the room and spoke. "It seems things have taken a turn for the worse. The healers..." he took a pained pause, "they claim they have done all they can. They say he might not make it through the day."

Callum narrowed his eyes. "I don't understand. They assured us he would make a full recovery."

Uthred's eyes darted to the room, and he shifted in apparent discomfort. "Perhaps it would be best if you spoke with them." Then, with a dip of his head, he rushed from the room.

Gwendolyn offered Callum and Adalina a faint smile as they approached and said, "My dear, it might be best to use this time to say your goodbyes."

Callum plowed through the teams of healers to his father's bed. Adalina drifted silently behind him, unsure of what to do to comfort him. When King Alistair came into view, her breath was stolen completely. The man, her father-in-law, who was so full of life and light, was now a shadow of his former self. She couldn't believe the frail man laying before them was the same strong, unmovable king she'd come to know.

The curtains were drawn to allow sunlight in, but it did nothing to cast a glow on the dying king. A coughing fit tore through his chest and he jerked violently in the bed. His son was at his side immediately, holding a glass of water up to his lips.

Adalina lingered at the end of the bed, feeling like an imposter. By all accounts, this was her family now, but she'd spent most of the time since her marriage ceremony conflicted about her feelings toward her new husband. There hadn't been much time to spend with her in-laws.

Her nerves buzzed suddenly with an irritation that bordered on downright anger. She shook her head to clear her mind of the strange sense. What was happening to King Alistair was horrible, but no one in the room deserved her ire. Unless it wasn't her own emotion at all, but instead belonged to the dragon she was bound to. She turned, trying to focus on something, anything, to make the feeling go away.

With a glance back at Gwendolyn, her heart sank. The woman, who had held herself with nothing but dignity, and kindness since the moment Adalina had met her, now looked as if she could barely hold herself upright.

Without hesitation, Adalina went to her, leaving Callum to speak with his father. She ushered her mother-in-law to a sofa in the sitting room. From there, she could see long, serpent-like fish with bright orange scales jumping out of the sea in the distance. The breeze coming through the balcony door was heavenly, but Gwendolyn shivered.

Adalina draped a blanket around her shoulders and the kind woman smiled gratefully at her. "Thank you, dear. I'm afraid the severity of everything is catching up with me."

"I would be surprised if it wasn't." Adalina scooted close to her on the sofa.

Gwendolyn took hold of her hands and said, "I've noticed the shift between you and my son, and it makes me happier than words can express."

Adalina's cheeks warmed. "I'm sorry it took me so long to give him a chance."

Gwendolyn's laugh was light and genuine as she said, "Darling, it was three whole months before I would even allow Alistair to sleep in the same room as me. I understand more than you know. Our hearts are one of the few things that truly belong to us in this world. It is terrifying to share it with someone else."

"Callum is quite persuasive."

"Isn't that the truth?" Gwendolyn sighed softly. "I know he does a good job of pretending that things aren't as bad as they are—something I fear he has inherited from his father—but I can tell he's different with you. And that is what's going to help him get through what comes next."

"What do you mean?" She didn't like the shift in the conversation and glanced back at the king's room, desperate for Callum to return.

Gwendolyn's grip tightened, bringing a tingling sensation to Adalina's fingers. But she didn't flinch as her mother-in-law spoke low. "If Alistair does not pull through, then it will fall to Callum to take up the mantle. In any circumstance, that would be a daunting task. But with the frost breathers still rampant in Astarfall, it will mean pressure like my baby boy has never experienced before. There will be opinions aimed at him from all different directions. Council members, citizens, courtiers... they will all want to sway the new king. Each will fight to be the one to win his favor by helping him defeat these horrid men."

"And you're worried he won't know who he can trust." Adalina bit her lip. It wasn't likely something she could help him with. She was still getting her bearings in the court. They hadn't even figured out who was passing information to the faceless leader of the frost breathers.

Gwendolyn drew a sharp breath and Adalina turned to find Callum standing in the doorway, face drawn and shoulders sagging. His voice was softer than usual as he said to his mother, "He's asking for you."

With a pat, Gwendolyn left Adalina on the sofa and disappeared into her bedroom. Callum offered a hand, and she took it, allowing him to pull her back into the hallway. An uncomfortable silence hung between them. Gone was the playfulness of the morning when they'd woken in the study.

But to her relief, there was also no facade. Callum was openly mournful as he said, "It's not good."

She didn't bother asking if he was okay. How could he be? Instead, she asked, "What can I do?"

The corner of his mouth tipped upward. "Just you being here is enough."

She wanted to tell him she could do more than that. If he named it, she would do it. Anything to help him through the trying time. But Seraphine interrupted once more. Alfie was with her, and they clung to one another.

This time, she addressed Adalina directly. "The council. They're with Elettra." Her voice trembled with raw fear as she said, "And she doesn't look happy."

The unwarranted anger she sensed earlier in the room made sense now. Elettra was *fuming*. The moment Adalina stepped foot into the gardens, she was hit with so much fury it practically knocked the wind out of her. The sudden urge to break something overtook her so fiercely that she didn't even hear Callum calling after her as she broke into a run.

Ignoring the frantic footsteps pounding behind her as Callum, Seraphine, and Alfie fought to keep up with her, Adalina stormed up to the crowd gathered around the dragon. Elettra stood so straight-backed on her hind legs that she appeared to be doubled in size. Adalina felt small and miniscule compared to her. As if she were nothing more than a speck of dust at the foot of a magnificent Goddess.

The council members were cowed back, looking stricken. Adalina wanted to snap at them and tell them that they *should* be frightened. That they deserved it for getting Elettra worked up into such a state. But she bit her tongue, thinking the last thing Astarfall needed was a council burnt to a crisp while their king lay dying upstairs.

With a deep breath, she stepped between the dragon and the men and raised her hands. Then, she cooed as if talking to a child, "Elettra, whatever has happened, let me sort it out."

Elettra's eyes widened as she looked down. Her scales seemed to have brightened, glowing iridescently with the fire inside of her. But regardless of whatever anger she was overcome with, she lowered back down on all fours and nuzzled her nose into Adalina.

Turning on the men, she snapped, "What did you do to her? Why are you down here without me? Explain yourselves."

The men remained silent, with noses sticking in the air. Adalina scoffed at them. It seemed it was easy for them to act bold now that she had calmed the dragon and saved them all from a crisp death.

Callum's voice was laced with anger as he said, "I think it would be wise to answer your princess when she asks you a question."

In his presence, they suddenly seemed very small. Like mice standing before a lion.

The eldest one stepped forward and said, "We simply came down to assess the situation."

Callum bared his teeth. "And what situation is that? Considering my father is lying upstairs, I cannot imagine why your business would bring you here." He gestured to Elettra, who was glaring at them and blowing smokey rings beside Adalina.

Uthred clasped his hands together. "We apologize if it seems we've overstepped our bounds, but in light of this morning's news from the healers, an emergency meeting could not be avoided."

The older man shoved Uthred out of the way and spat, "It was our grievous error for letting you have your way." His beady eyes landed on Adalina, and she glared back at him in challenge. It didn't seem to deter him as he continued, "If you, Prince Callum, had ridden the dragon as we wanted in the first place, then we would not be in this vulnerable state. *You*, a trained warrior and Crown Prince who knows the importance of setting your empathy aside, would have burned those bastards where they stood at Windshire. There wouldn't have even been a battle yesterday and your father wouldn't be lying in his death bed as we speak."

Callum flinched and heat flared to life in Adalina's chest. How dare they put that on him?

The councilmen were as fickle as boy crazed schoolgirls. Just recently, they were praising her name for turning the nobles to their favor through her acts at Windshire. And now they were holding that same incident against her?

She snapped, "What do *you* know of battle and empathy? Callum fought like hell to hold Windshire. I never hesitated to ride headfirst into danger and—"

"But you *did* hesitate to hit our enemy with one killing blow. It would have ended then and there." The elderly man sneered at her.

Incredulously, Adalina took a step toward them. She trembled from head to toe and Elettra snarled with a wild toothy grin.

Seething, Adalina said, "I didn't hesitate yesterday. I did precisely what needed to be done."

The man lifted his chin and countered, "Resulting in you *falling* from your dragon's back."

The words stung worse than the frostbitten dragon's venom. She stumbled back a step.

Callum strode up to the man. The usual pleasant mask he wore around the public had slipped entirely. He was almost nose to nose with the councilman as he growled, "Watch yourself. You sorry excuse for a—"

Seraphine glided forward. "Let's be done with this, gentlemen. What is it that you are here to discuss? This meeting most certainly cannot be to debate any shortcomings you believe the royal family has." Her words were icy and laced with a threat. As if daring them to admit that it was exactly what they'd been doing.

Uthred was quick to respond. "No, of course not. What's done is done. We simply believe that it may be time to take a different course of action. To have Prince Callum ride out on the dragon and do what needs to be done."

Elettra snorted, matching Adalina's inclination to do so. She scoffed, "That's absurd. Callum has promised me—"

Again, she was interrupted by another councilman. He stuck his skinny nose in the air and said with confidence, "Promises mean nothing in the face of certain death. We are here to make sure that decisions are made for the good of all Astarfall." He raised a judgmental eyebrow at Adalina and finished, "*Not* for the happiness of one girl."

"*Woman*," Callum corrected with his returned cocky facade. He raised an amused eyebrow in return. "My wife, she is a woman. And a capable one at that. She is also *your* princess, so I suggest you wipe that look off your face and show her the respect she is owed." If smiles could have killed, then this one would have sliced right through that councilman.

A rush of pleasure washed over Adalina. The councilman shrank back into the crowd. And for a moment, she thought the matter had been settled.

But Uthred once again spoke. "We have no intention of showing any disrespect. We understand that the bond between you and Elettra—"

Through clenched teeth, Adalina said, "You can't begin to comprehend the bond between us."

"Regardless," Uthred continued, undeterred, "yesterday's battle was but a taste of what's coming. My fellow councilmen, though out of line, spoke the truth. You nearly died yesterday. And it's been said that your dragon nearly burned our own men alive after she killed the frost breather's beast."

The younger councilman piped in, though his voice was low, as if hesitant to speak. "They're saying the dragon was out of her mind with wrath. That she put our men and herself at risk just to avenge you."

"She would never harm our men," Adalina barked, but there was a pit at the bottom of her stomach. If she hadn't shouted for the Astarfallen men to run, would they have been collateral damage in Elettra's efforts to burn the frost breathers?

Uthred took a deep breath and held out his hands as if asking for peace. "We simply cannot afford to have a rider and a dragon who act out of emotion on the field. If the frost breathers do indeed have more tricks up their sleeves, then perhaps sending Prince Callum in your stead will keep you safe and ensure that there are no more surprises. He has been training his entire life to protect this kingdom. And his magic gives him an advantage up there that you do not have."

Adalina shook her head. Were they implying that she was too weak to do what they needed to protect their people? She had ridden into battle without a second thought. And had gone headfirst into the danger beside Callum. They were a team, and now they wanted him to leave her behind. Why? Because he was a man, and he was physically *stronger*? Because wielding his magic from the air may or may not be an added benefit? Because they believed he could cook the enemy alive with that practiced smile on his face? He'd never even trained to ride or command Elettra. What they were suggesting was a risk.

She turned to Callum with disbelief and froze when she saw him. Though he said nothing, he'd gone stone still. Through the cracks of his carefree facade, she could see doubt festering. There was a tick in his jaw, and his eyes had darkened at least two shades.

With her stomach twisted in knots, she shot a look of daggers at the councilmen. And for the first time since becoming Princess of Astarfall, she spoke with all the authority granted to her with that title. "Leave us. *Now.* I need to speak to my husband."

Once they were gone, Callum chuckled uncomfortably with his hands raised defensively as he took a step back from Adalina and the dragon that had risen behind her. She could sense Elettra's interest, and although her ire wasn't what it had been when she'd first found her with the councilmen gathered around, it sat very close to the surface.

Adalina, on the other hand, was calm, but the knots in her stomach remained. There was no mistaking the doubt she'd glimpsed on Callum's face when the council spoke of doing what they believed was best for all of Astarfall.

She released a breath, hoping to let go of the anger bubbling in her and said, "I understand the position you're in, but please tell me you're not considering leaving me behind."

The sea breeze ruffled his hair and his charming smile faltered. "If my father doesn't pull through this, then I will be king. *You* will be queen. What we want will no longer come first."

"So, if they ask you, you will ride Elettra. Without me."

"I would never want to do anything to break your trust." He closed the gap between them and brushed her hair from her face. "Right now, I just need you to trust *me*. I need you, Adalina."

Elettra sighed softly behind them, warming the air and making sweat bead on Adalina's back. It seemed the dragon was inclined to trust him. So why couldn't Adalina quell the uneasy feeling in the pit of her stomach?

Thirty-Five

Water splashed against Adalina's ankles as a small wave came crashing into the dock. She was grateful to have Seraphine and Elettra with her for some time away from the palace. After the dispute with the council, she needed to clear her head. Suddenly, the enormity of the palace and all the responsibilities that called to her from inside was stifling.

After an uncomfortably silent breakfast with Callum, he had gone to meet with Astarfall's war council. But when Seraphine mentioned she wanted to get out of the palace for a while, Adalina had quickly asked to tag along.

The last time she'd been on this particular dock—the one meant for personal use by the royal family—she was a child. It was only accessible from the palace, resting below the cliff where the gardens and courtyard stood. She glanced at the stone stairs that led up to the palace gardens and then back down at the climbing tree with branches that reached out over the water.

Back then, Callum had been the only one brave enough to venture out to the farthest branch, bouncing on it and ignoring the danger of falling into the fierce waves below. At the time, it had looked much more frightening. Now it seemed smaller than she recalled. More mundane. Just a tree over shallow water.

He'd been so sure of himself then. And still was most of the time. Looking back, she supposed he truly *was* Callum the Courageous. Which was something she figured he'd tried to cling to as a man who had experienced the trials and loss that came with age.

She sighed, "This is where Callum pushed me in, you know."

Seraphine arched an eyebrow. "He was quite the little shit." She snorted, "Still is."

Adalina's smile twitched. "I'm afraid he's going to let the council sway him. And the worst part is, how can I fight him on it? Who would trust a dragon warrior who can't even stay on her dragon's back?"

Elettra fixed her with a look of disapproval as if to say, *It wasn't your fault*. But Adalina had been the one to let her grip slip. To have been unprepared for the ascent. She reached up and scratched Elettra under the chin. The dragon gave her a pleased rumble, then went back to watching the fish dart back and forth under the dock. Every so often, she would attempt to swat at them, trying to catch them in her clawed grasp with no luck.

Seraphine pursed her lips. "They can't expect you to be perfect. No one is. Not even Callum. He's made his fair share of mistakes, yet no one holds that against him or insinuates he can't handle himself. Don't for a second let the council make you feel any less worthy."

Adalina clucked her tongue against her teeth. "I did also destroy your childhood home."

Seraphine swatted in the air. "It was a stuffy old place, anyway. Besides, when we rebuild, I'll finally get to add that atrium I've always wanted." She shot Adalina a sly but genuine smile. "I'm serious, Lina. None of those things should be wielded against you like a weapon."

Maybe not. But that sure wasn't stopping the council from doing it, anyway. Adalina leaned back with her feet still dangling over the water and let the sunlight bathe her in warmth. With the change of season, she'd expected chillier days, but Astarfall was a place of eternal summer. Permanent heat to match the fire in her own veins. And she had to admit it had grown on her.

Seraphine softened as she said, "Whatever choices he makes, just know it isn't with ill intent. Like the rest of us, he's doing his best."

Adalina responded with a pained whisper, "But he promised."

It didn't seem fair that just when they found a balance and trust between them, it was slipping away. She liked the way things were moving forward, but this felt like they were sliding back into murky waters once again.

Lost in a haze of doubt, she didn't register Seraphine's shout of warning until it was too late. An icy tendril snaked around Adalina's ankle, tearing her from the safety of the dock. It plunged her into the water, dragging her into the depths with such a force that her head slammed into the bottom.

Though the water should have been mildly warm at worst, it was freezing. The cold was crippling, and she struggled to hold her breath. The frigid water seeped into her lungs as she fought for freedom from whatever had hold of her ankle.

Sand swept up in a dark cloud as she was dragged along the sea floor. Above the water, Elettra's massive body was a shadow dancing back and forth at the surface. But whatever had her was too fast. It pulled her alarmingly far away from the dock and whipped her onto shore. As she emerged from the water, she gasped violently. It burned as air returned to her lungs and she choked to get the remaining sea water out.

Elettra and Seraphine were still pacing the water's edge on the dock in search of her. Adalina tried to call to them, but her voice faltered, coming out at more of a croak. She attempted again, but something wove around her arms, binding her broken wrist to the other. White dots clouded her vision. In a silent scream, she kicked out, sliding along the ground and cradling her hands close to her chest.

Blinking the salt water from her eyes, a figure came into focus. It was the faceless man with the insignia embroidered on the breast of his midnight black coat. He slinked toward her; head tilted toward the rope holding her hands in place. It shimmered with ice magic and the cold bit into the skin that wasn't wrapped with bandages.

Adalina snarled through the pain, "*Coward.*"

He halted mid-step.

A fierce smile spread across her face. She'd struck a chord.

With each beat of silence, rage built in her chest. Silently, she called for Elettra. Beyond the man, she saw the dragon's head lift in answer.

With a sniff in the air, Elettra's gaze fell to where the man had dragged her.

Adalina's smile turned rueful. "No matter. My friends will be here soon."

In response, the man chuckled. It was a low and grating sound. Like rocks being rubbed together. And it was arrogant. He truly thought he had bested her. But in his presence, her anger burned brightly, building in her chest, then her arms and finally, in her wrists.

The icy ropes melted away. Steam rose around her hands and water dripped down her bare arms. She got to her feet, never taking her eyes off him. This man was the root of all their problems. And she couldn't let him leave.

Nor could she kill him. Callum and the council were insistent that they make an example of him. And if she was to hold on to any shred of trust and respect that the councilmen might still have in her, she needed to bring them the enemy's leader alive.

Elettra's wings beat loudly above, and the stormy sound of her building fire filled Adalina's ears. But she raised a hand to the dragon, stopping her before she could unleash her fiery fury on the man.

"We need him alive," Adalina called to her.

His head whipped from the dragon to her. If she could see his eyes clearly, she suspected she would have found panic. He knew what it would mean to be brought in. Callum would parade him before the entire kingdom. Make a show of his shame. A warning of what happens when you violently challenge the crown.

Seraphine—who sat on Elettra's back with shaky confidence—summoned two wisps of wind. She aimed at the man's hands, wrapping it around them like shackles. But just before they fully clasped around him, he dove away.

Adalina bolted for him, determined to do anything in her power to make sure he didn't escape. But he grabbed her broken wrist tightly, making her cry out in agony. Elettra wailed and spitballs of fire pounded into the ground. They narrowly missed the man each time as he shielded himself with thin but incredibly sturdy panes of ice.

At Elettra's panicked call, guards shouted from the tops of the stone steps. They descended in a break necking pace. If Adalina kept the man there just a little longer, then they could still bring him in. The guards would be able to match his strength.

As the faceless man began to run, she shot her foot out. He tripped over her and rolled on the ground a few times before finding his footing again. This time, an icy arrow formed out of thin air. Two narrow lines of magic shimmered as he pulled power from both the sea and the deep depths of the land. Was that where the intense cold they wielded came from?

Seraphine blew a gust of wind at him, but before it could strike him, he threw the frost arrow and it embedded itself in Adalina's thigh.

Elettra screeched as Adalina grabbed the arrow. It melted away at her burning touch, leaving nothing but a bloody tear in her flesh. Between the sight of the blood and the pain, Adalina's vision blurred. Now was not the time to pass out.

Urgency fueled her as she scrambled to her feet and threw herself into the man. They rolled in the dirt and an elbow met the corner of her brow. It jarred her, knocking her back and making vomit rise to her throat. With a deep breath to quell it, she reached for the man again, but he was gone.

When she looked up, he was already darting out of sight behind the precarious rocky cliff that ran along the shoreline. She screamed against closed lips, letting fury take control and pounded her fists into the ground. Searing, red hot pain tore through her wrist and thigh, making the nausea return.

Guards rushed past her, following the man's trail. But someone stopped to kneel beside her. Seraphine brushed a cool hand along Adalina's uninjured arm and spoke in a calm, soothing tone. Adalina couldn't register what she was saying. Instead, her eyes met Elettra's.

The dragon's gaze flitted from her to the cliffs. It was clear she knew she should be going after the man but was too afraid to leave Adalina in her injured state. She wanted to tell Elettra to forget about her and go, but no words would come. She couldn't talk or think through the icy pain left behind by the arrow. Her whole body protested as she tried to stand, only to crumple back to the ground.

She stayed like that, furious with herself for her failure until strong, familiar arms scooped her up. Callum's scent wafted in the air, and she relaxed her head on his shoulder as she whispered, "I lost him."

"How the fuck did this happen, Seraphine?" he shouted.

"It... the attack... it came from the water." Seraphine's words tumbled out in stammers.

"What were you doing so far from the palace in the first place?" Anger tore through him in waves that even Adalina sensed.

Seraphine snapped, "She wanted to get away to clear her head. And can you blame her after that ambush from the council?"

Adalina winced and said again, "I lost him."

"You did everything you could," Callum reassured her gently as he placed her on Elettra's back.

She grimaced as she slumped forward and was relieved when Callum climbed up behind her and drew her into him. He held her with a surprisingly gentle touch as Elettra ascended, taking them back to the palace.

The wind was a divine distraction from the throbbing ache in her wrist and her leg. But it was short-lived as it didn't take Elettra long to land in the courtyard where they were met with an array of healers, guards, and palace staff. Several courtiers gasped as Callum pulled her down from the dragon's back.

Queen Gwendolyn shouted commands loudly, demanding that everyone give them space as Callum carried her up to their room. Adalina's eyelids were so heavy she could hardly keep them open for more than a few seconds at a time. The healers were already waiting, and it wasn't long before Seraphine came in with a wild look in her eyes.

She and Callum began arguing, but the healers had already given Adalina something for the pain and she couldn't quite keep up with what was happening around her. Her mind became fuzzy, and she yearned to lose herself to sleep.

Seraphine's voice was a sharp echo as she said, "We couldn't have seen it coming. How could we have known someone would attack us there?"

"We've been too reckless," Callum snapped. "I should never have let her put herself in harm's way. There should have been a small army of guards around her at all times. She nearly died on the battlefield. How could I have been so thoughtless as to think she would be safe, even here in the city?"

A man's husky voice that didn't belong to Callum said roughly, "You are the ruler, and you must do what needs to be done."

Adalina fought to hold on to consciousness. She should be speaking up. But unable to keep her eyes open, she continued to flutter in and out.

"You can't do that!" Seraphine's voice turned pleading. "She has proven how capable she is. She is as much a warrior as Calida. Callum, if you do this, you will lose her."

With a haughty air, the man said, "Better to lose her heart than to lose her as you did your sister."

If Adalina had the strength, she'd have risen from the bed to slap the man across his face. How dare he use that trauma against Callum in his time of desperation? But no matter how much she willed her eyes to open or her limbs to move, they would not obey.

"Enough!" Callum roared, but the voices were growing distant as sleep began to claim her.

As she drifted off, the last thing she heard was another man's warning, "If you do *not* do this, then you *will* lose her."

Thirty-Six

Callum was nowhere to be seen when Adalina came out of her herb-induced sleep. Someone—likely her husband—had moved her to their bed and, as luxuriously comfortable as it was, her entire body ached. With agonizing effort, she pushed herself to her elbows and peered around the room.

Snores drifted through the terrace door, and she was surprised to find Elettra there. The dragon snoozed comfortably in the soft morning light, though she had to curl into herself like a cat in order to fit. The space was enormous to Adalina, but to a sleeping dragon, it was rather cramped.

A tray sat at the end of the bed filled with fresh fruit and fluffy pastries. At the sight of it, her stomach rumbled almost as loudly as Elettra's snores. It tasted as delicious as it looked, and she regretted eating so quickly by the time she finished. An overly full stomach coupled with memories of the day before, made for an unpleasant combination.

As she tried to get out of bed with shaky limbs, the door in the other room clicked open. Callum strode into the bedroom and stopped with a startle when he saw her awake. Once recovered, he rushed in and immediately went to her side, placing her arm around his shoulder for support. He wore thick leather armor, easy for agile movements but strong enough to protect him. It was similar to her riding leathers and made her stomach lurch. Vague memories of him arguing with Seraphine and a man she couldn't place came back to her. She shoved them aside forcefully. Callum said himself that he didn't want to break her trust. She needed to have faith in him, but the concern clouding his eyes made it difficult.

"You shouldn't be trying to get around on your own," he chided her.

"I'm fine, really." She grunted from the pain in her leg as she stood and glared at it for betraying her lie.

"You need rest."

"There's no time to rest. What did I miss? What's our next move?"

Maybe getting caught up on all that had happened while she was asleep would help give her mind some direction. Anything to distract it from the way she'd allowed herself to be ambushed. The dock was so close to the palace, she'd foolishly thought she was safe down there. Especially with Elettra by her side.

But the faceless man had been ready. He'd known exactly what to do to get her away from the safety of her dragon. And because of that, not only had Adalina been injured, but she'd let him escape.

Callum helped her get dressed. Gently, he tied the laces at the front of her gown, his fingers brushing against her skin as soft as a moth's touch. His mouth was twisted with worry, and he gnawed at his lip while he concentrated on the ribbons.

"Callum, what did they say? What's going on?"

His lashes cast dark shadows on his cheeks as he gave her a quick glance. Then, stepping back, he said, "My father succumbed to his injuries late last night. He..." his voice cracked and with it, she caught wind of his grief. "He's gone."

"Oh, by the fates. I am so sorry." She reached for him, but he stepped out of her grasp.

His face smoothed over, masking any hint of sadness, and his tone hardened as he said, "We will grieve him later. Right now, he would want us to stay focused."

Again, she reached for him, but stopped short when he flinched away. Softly, she said, "But you can't possibly—"

"I am king now. And you are queen. We have a responsibility to act as such."

There was something laced in his tone that set her on edge. She narrowed her eyes. "What is that supposed to mean?"

As far as she was concerned they *had* been taking their roles seriously. They had ridden into battle, and had done everything possible to flush out the traitor who walked their halls...

"It means I have a part to play, and you do, too." This time, his voice broke with a hint of regret.

Heat flared in her cheeks and Elettra stirred from the terrace with a low growl. Adalina squared her shoulders and tried not to wince when she moved her wrist as she said, "And what, exactly, are these *parts*? Spit it out, Callum."

"The frost breathers are still occupying the land near the western mountains. We cannot afford to allow them to slip over the Festiri border to regroup. Astarfall will never be safe from their wrath unless there are no more of them left."

"Callum," she hissed, "What are you saying?"

She hated to ask when she already suspected the answer. What else had happened while she slept? She had been injured and lying in their room while the council—and fates knew who else—had his ear.

"I'm riding out to battle. On Elettra." His eyes welled with tears, as if it pained him to say it.

Her mouth went dry and white spots of anger began to blot out her vision. He reached for her this time, but she tore away and limped to the terrace. Elettra was alert and focused on the two of them, watching intently with no indication of what she thought of the declaration.

Adalina snapped, "You made me a promise."

"You're still injured." His hands were shaking, and his chest heaved with quickening breath.

Adalina didn't let it deter her. It was a weak excuse. With some herbs to ease her pain, she could handle riding the dragon. She argued, "I can stay on Elettra. I won't set foot on the battlefield."

Callum shook his head fiercely. "Lina, please understand. You lost your seat in battle. We cannot risk that again. Especially with a broken wrist and a wounded leg. I will not put you in harm's way."

"Do you forget so easily that I am in harm's way, whether or not I'm in the palace? Twice I have been attacked in our own home. Demanding that I stay here will not make me any safer."

Callum took a deep breath and a tight smile spread across his face. "You will have more guards. Both inside and outside of our chambers."

She crossed her arms over her chest. "So I am to be a prisoner. Your first act as king is to put your queen under house arrest?"

He didn't so much as wince at her words. Instead, he chuckled bitterly, sending furious goosebumps up her arms. Then he said, "Don't you get it? You have been so focused on forging your own path, so concerned that listening to the advice of others will mean giving all of your power away, that you don't even notice when your actions backfire on you."

Her nostrils flared. "I am more than aware of the mistakes I've made. But this is *war*, Callum. Mistakes are bound to happen."

His posture sank. This time he seemed to plead as he said, "Please let me do this. Let me keep you safe."

"It's not your job to protect me."

Callum's teeth flashed, and he looked away.

Adalina closed the space between them, praying to the fates that he would see reason. Her words came out rushed and unfiltered. "Is this really worth destroying what we've built? You would throw away my trust just like that." She snapped her fingers below his chin. "And for what? All because you're *afraid*?"

"Because if you fall, I can't catch you!" The words tore from him, raw and painful.

She took a shocked step back. The man's warning to Callum when she was losing consciousness echoed in her mind. They had dug into his heart, prodded at the scar his sister's death left behind, and reopened it.

With a tremble, she whispered, "This is not the same as what happened with your sister. You can't let that pain rule your life forever."

His gaze was hard and determined as he met her eye. With a set jaw, he said, "The decision has been made."

She gritted her teeth. Seething head to toe, she took a few steps back. Right out to the terrace.

"My dear wife. Do not do anything stupid." It was meant to be a warning but sounded more like a fearful plea.

It was too late, though. She couldn't let him destroy what they'd built. Spinning on her heel, she grabbed hold of Elettra's side, intending to swing herself onto the dragon and leave her husband to reflect on his own stupidity. But the moment she touched Elettra, his command rang out.

"I, Callum, husband to Adalina the granddaughter of Dragon Rider Calida…"

Adalina gasped, falling back to the floor to find him holding his hand over a burning candle. Blood dripped from his palm, and he dropped the blade he'd used with a clatter.

"No," Adalina growled.

But he continued, "Exercise my authority granted to me by marriage to command you."

The fire flared higher, growing at a controlled rate only magic could influence. Adalina's heart pounded as he reached into his pocket and pulled out the compass that she had given him. It was like he'd plunged the dagger into her heart instead of his hand as he laid it at Elettra's feet.

"With this offering, I call on this bond."

For a moment, she shut her eyes tight and willed with everything she had in her that it would not work. But Elettra side stepped away from her. The dragon's eyes were a fiery glow, like two falling stars, and Adalina's stomach sank.

Conflicted emotions hit her like a tidal wave, and she knew immediately it was what Elettra was feeling. Resentment aimed at Callum, but also resignation. Neither the dragon nor Adalina could deny the authority he was using. The power that flowed in Adalina's veins and the connection shared between her, and Callum was too strong.

Just as Adalina's ancient bond to Elettra extended beyond worldly possibilities—granted by a power that was difficult for even them to understand—so too was Callum's connection to the two of them.

Until now, Adalina had not known the extent of the power that had been granted to him when he lent his magic to hers to wake the dragon. She supposed part of her had always hoped that if he did try to call on his rites, then it would fail. But as Elettra knelt before him, Adalina began to understand all too well. They had no choice but to submit to him.

When he came around to Elettra's side, Adalina wanted nothing more than to claw his eyes out. To tell Elettra to burn the damned marital bed behind them and take her far away from her commanding husband and this war.

But she could do nothing. The dragon had done what the ancient rites demanded. She let Callum climb onto her back, taking Adalina's rightful place. With sorrowful eyes, Elettra projected remorse onto her. With a sniff, Adalina nodded in silent understanding.

Then, to her traitorous husband, she seethed, "I will not forgive you for this."

This time, he didn't bother trying to use a lighthearted facade as he said, "As long as you are still alive *to* hold it against me. I didn't want it to have to be this way, but I can't see any other choice. Not if I want to keep my people safe." His eyes darkened with regret as he added, "Not if I want to keep *you* safe."

Adalina knew she had made mistakes over the last few days. She'd hesitated, allowed herself to lose control at Windshire, and lost her seat at the king's battle. But she never imagined it would be Callum who punished her for these things.

During the king's battle, she had put herself in the frostbitten dragon's sights for fear of what it would do to Callum. She had pushed Elettra to fly at an angle she couldn't handle because she wanted to destroy the dragon before it could destroy someone she cared for. But now Callum was doing the same. Making a poor decision based on emotion. Which was ironic, considering emotion was the one thing the council did not believe belonged on the battlefield.

Adalina turned her back to him and stalked into their room, unable to bear the look of him on her dragon any longer. She couldn't bring herself to watch as he and Elettra left her behind. Couldn't allow herself to stare into his solemn face and risk forgiving him for breaking the trust they'd built. Instead, she clung to the anger, holding it close to her and wrapping it around her foolish heart.

Thirty-Seven

A fever ravaged Adalina's body, but she suspected it was more from fury than from her injuries. Worried healers skittered around her room, shoving concoctions in her face, but she swatted them away.

The guards, who were spread throughout several entry points in her chambers, stayed glued to the walls and out of her way. She paced angrily until Seraphine walked in. She, too, looked ready for battle with leather armor and a whip at her hip in place of a sword.

"Leave us," she commanded the healers, who scrambled out the door in response to the authority she used. She was the queen's niece, after all.

Adalina trembled, her mind going to the worst. Had something happened to Callum? As angry as she was to be left behind, she was still worried for him and Elettra. And after several failed attempts to get past the guards in her room to join them on the battlefield, she'd had nothing else to do but sit and imagine all the horrible things that could go wrong.

"What's happened?"

Seraphine's voice softened as she said, "Nothing. I just wanted to check on you."

"Callum, is he..." Visions of him falling from Elettra's back danced in her mind.

"He's fine. He and Elettra will have reached the camp our men set up on the coast near the mountains by now."

Adalina gritted her teeth. "I should be there with them."

"Yes." Mischief sparkled in her friend's eyes. "You should."

Seraphine tipped her head and her gaze darted past two guards standing at the open terrace doors. Adalina suppressed a smile. Seraphine had a plan. And although she couldn't guess what it might be, considering they were three stories up with no dragon to carry them off the terrace, Adalina was willing to try just about anything her friend suggested.

After a curt nod, Seraphine swung her arms out and a hurricane worthy wind shot at the guards. They shouted as they were knocked from their feet, but the women didn't wait for them to recover. They ran to the terrace. Seraphine climbed onto the railing and reached a hand out to Adalina.

"Do you trust me?"

Adalina smiled ruefully. "You're just about the only one at the moment."

A blush adorned Seraphine's face as she summoned her powers. It was like she was drawing the air, calling it to them. It whipped around them and felt tight, like they were inside a funnel. Then, with an elegant flick of her wrist, Seraphine maneuvered it into a steep slide from the terrace to the ground.

The guards shouted behind them as they regained their composure and Adalina didn't think twice as she clasped hands with her friend and threw herself onto the wind. It was sturdy, and they glided down so quickly that she hardly had time to register the magnificence of it.

Seraphine giggled like a schoolgirl as she waved the wind away, preventing the guards from following them. Then they ran as fast as their legs could carry them. Adalina's injured leg smarted, but the tea the healers had given her for the pain held strong. It would be a shame later when it wore off, and no doubt hurt ten times more thanks to all the exertion.

Taking the stone stairs two at a time to the palace's private dock, the women hurried to a small ship awaiting them. It was no larger than a fisherman's vessel, but its sails were strong and looked as if they were brand new.

Through ragged breaths, Seraphine explained, "I can use the wind to whip us along the coast. The Astarfall army will have a camp there while they prepare for battle. There won't be much they can do or say once we're there, short of sending fighting men away to take us home."

Adalina's heart skipped a beat, and it wasn't from the run. She would be reunited with Elettra. There she would let Callum know that no matter what he did, she wasn't going to let him do this alone. That no matter how afraid he was for her, she was going to stand with them. Even if it meant ruining any chance of having a marriage that extended beyond title. She was his queen. One that would not let her men risk their lives while she stayed hidden.

Seraphine untied the ropes that would release them from the dock.

Adalina followed her to the side of the boat. "Why are you doing this?"

"My cousin is sometimes too concerned with what he believes *others* need, that he forgets to think about his own. Leaving you behind was foolish. A choice pulled from childhood trauma and terrible advice," she said simply, pulling a compass from her pocket.

It was plain and unmemorable compared to the one Adalina had given Callum, but it made her flinch all the same. To give an offering to a dragon was to give them something of value. To *bond* with the dragon meant gifting them something with deep personal meaning and attachment. Just as Adalina had offered the shawl her mother made her to remind her of home. But Callum had given away more than just the compass, hadn't he? He'd given away her trust, laying a broken promise at the dragon's feet. Her chest tightened, and she stifled her tears.

Guards were shouting orders to one another as they scurried down the stairs. Seraphine leapt onto the boat, hands already raised in the air, to summon the winds. Adalina clumsily followed. She landed face first on the polished wood deck and a pair of feet appeared before her. As she raised her head to see who else had joined them, she gasped.

Her grandmother was dressed to match Seraphine. Her mouth had a firm set to it and there was excitement shining in her pale eyes. Adalina couldn't stop the smile spreading wide across her face as the former dragon warrior helped her to her feet.

"I just couldn't resist, Lina. It's been so long since I've been a part of something this thrilling."

Adalina was speechless. This wasn't the grandmother who had made her soup when she was sick. Who had nursed her through the first few times the dragon's magic had awoken inside of her, beckoning her to wake Elettra. It wasn't the woman who had brushed her hair while telling her stories of heroes and dragons.

This was Dragon Warrior Calida. The one who had answered the call when no one else would. The woman who had led her people into battle against men who wanted to take the world by icy storm and bend it to their will. And she was standing here on the ship as proud and courageous as ever.

"You'll need these." Seraphine winked, handing Adalina her riding leathers. They'd been mended and cleaned since the king's battle and looked as new as ever.

Once she changed into them, she felt like herself again. Her heart sped as fast as the boat sailed. It wasn't long before they made it down the coast where the Astarfall camp came into view. A flag flew tall and proud, donning the royal family's insignia, from the largest tent. And beside it was Elettra. Her scales blazed in the sunshine, casting iridescent purples, blues, and greens onto the tents and ground around her.

Adalina clenched her uninjured hand into a fist. The bond she had worked so hard for had been ripped from her with a few simple words and drops of blood. She might not be willing to hate Callum for what he'd done, but he did deserve her ire.

Several soldiers shouted, drawing attention to the small approaching boat. They met the women at the shore, surrounding them with hands drawn and ready to cast their magic in defense.

When Adalina jumped down into the sand, they fell into deep bows of respect. She smirked as she strode past them in her riding leathers without a word, and up to Elettra. The dragon's tail wagged excitedly, and she nuzzled her head into Adalina's side. A sense of regret and relief washed over her.

Adalina suppressed a gasp. The bond between them still held strong, even if Callum had taken the right to command and ride the dragon.

She patted Elettra on the cheek and said, "I know. It's not your fault. He's just afraid."

She wanted to explain away Callum's behavior that morning. To believe that he truly was doing what he thought was best and not simply wielding his power in order to control her. But the scowl on his face as he stepped out of his tent set her teeth on edge.

A crowd gathered. The soldiers were no doubt curious why their queen had arrived after their king on a small vessel without any guards accompanying her. And though Callum smiled broadly when he noticed them watching him, she caught the twitch in his jaw.

He opened his arms to her in a welcoming embrace, and she stepped hesitantly into it.

Angrily, he whispered in her ear, "What the hell are you doing?"

Hissing back, she said, "Whatever the hell I want."

When he drew away, the smile was still in place, but it had tightened. His mask was slipping in front of everyone, and he seemed to realize it. Through clenched teeth, he said, "Let's retire to my tent."

As she brushed by him, she countered, "You mean *our* tent?"

Once they were alone in his quarters, his confident ease faded completely. He plopped onto a leather chair and propped his elbows on the large desk. It was covered in various maps and battle plans. Then firmly he said, "You showing up here changes nothing."

"Doesn't it?" she asked as she fiddled with a tiny structure that resembled a chess piece sitting on the map.

His sigh was strained, but he kept his composure as he said, "You're not coming onto that battlefield."

She swept the piece into her hand and squeezed hard, trying to suppress a grimace that came with the strain she'd put on her wrist by doing so. "You can't stop me."

He raised a knowing eyebrow. "How's the leg?"

"Fine," she said tightly.

"You truly think you can hold your seat on Elettra with an injured thigh?" he narrowed his eyes.

With a tilt of her chin, she said, "I will."

She was stronger than he was giving her credit for. This time she wouldn't push Elettra to do something the dragon knew wasn't safe. She wouldn't let her emotion overrule her sense.

With a shake of his head, he stood, coming around the desk to sit in front of her. He grabbed her firmly by the hips before she could react and drew her in. Unable to move, she simply stared into his face, determined not to balk.

His gaze flitted from her eyes to her lips, and then back again. Then he said with a low husk, "I cannot do what needs to be done if you are out there."

"You think I'm weak." She felt like a building storm. One that might destroy everything in her path if it wasn't contained, and soon.

"I think you are my weakness." He cast his gaze to the ground.

Her heart felt as if it had stopped altogether. Firmly, she removed his hands from her. "How can you say something like that to me after what we've accomplished together?" She stepped back, inching toward the tent's exit. She needed air. Needed space from the cutting edge of his words.

He stood, taking panicked steps toward her. There was no sign of his easy-going mask. Only an openly worried frown as he said, "I didn't mean it like that. You..." He drew in a shaky breath, then said, "You are too valuable to me. I can't risk losing you. And I can't do what I have to out there if I'm worried about your well-being."

She scoffed as she stepped back until she was out of the tent and back in the open camp. He followed swiftly, and all heads whipped in their direction—Seraphine and her grandmother's included.

Adalina ignored the gawking soldiers. Her voice rang out like thunder. "Valuable? Like I am a possession meant to keep in a glass case? I do not belong to you, Callum."

He shook as he cried out, "*You do!* Heart and soul, you are mine and I am *yours*! How is it that you can't see that I'm doing this to give us a future?"

The crowd fell silent. The only sound was a low rumble, like a teapot about to blow out steam. Elettra stood at full height, her eyes filled with wrath as she looked down upon Callum. With each passing second, heat built in Adalina, too. It rose from her chest, flowing through her veins, and piercing her skin. If she looked down, she worried she might actually be visibly smoldering.

But she didn't look down. She didn't take her eyes off her husband for one moment. As she stood with the dragon by her side, she felt more in control than she had in her entire life. Not only was he being unfair to her, but to Elettra as well.

In fact, she herself had been unfair to the dragon. How many times had she thought of what it would be like to command her? To be the one in control, to use the dragon in the ways that she wished to? She recalled the stories of the First Man. He had tended to the dragon, earned its love and respect, and because of that, the dragon had chosen him. Not the other way around. But maybe just as that bond could be formed, so too could it break.

Elettra no more belonged to Adalina than she did to Callum. Binding ritual or not, Elettra should be free to make her own choices. To be unleashed from the magical tethers that trapped her to their words and influence.

Adalina sniffed and turned to the dragon. For years, she had dreamed of meeting her. Of flying on her back and feeling the beating of her wings as they soared through the sky.

Then, with more clarity than she'd ever had, she said, "Callum, I do not want to *own* you. I want to *choose* you and have you choose me in return. I want to know that we stand *together* because we have earned the trust and love that puts us there. Nor does Elettra belong to either of us. And for that..."

She wasn't sure it would actually make a difference, but even if it was only symbolic, she needed to do something to prove her resolve. She drew a dagger from her belt—one her grandmother had armed her with when she'd given her a change of clothes—and pressed the blade against her palm. It was an offering of blood. And it was all Adalina had to give.

She continued, "I release you from your promise to my family. You do not owe me your allegiance or obedience."

Callum, though trying to maintain an air of confidence in front of his men, said with a tremble, "What are you doing?"

Elettra drew a long breath through her nose, pulling Adalina's tangled hair in her direction. An intense sense of gratitude filled Adalina. And then Elettra bowed to her. It was low as she swept her massive head to the ground, dusting her chin along the dirt. And with that gesture, Adalina was filled with something that surprised her. Devotion. It was an overwhelming, blissful feeling that warmed her down to the tips of her toes.

Adalina's grandmother was the first to break the silence. "My girl, I do believe she is telling you that she has *chosen*."

Elettra tilted her head as if to say, *Of course I did*.

Callum dropped all pretense and commanded with a shaking breath, "Take the queen to my quarters. Do not let her out of your sight."

The men froze and looked at each other nervously.

Adalina stared at Callum, dumbfounded. Had he not heard a word she said? Even after all of this, he still refused to trust her? How could he be so oblivious to what was right in front of him? She had come for him. To help him and stand beside him as his equal. As his partner. And he was trying to destroy it all.

She shook her head, tears welling in her eyes. "The only place I'm going to is onto that battlefield."

The guards took an uncertain step toward her. But Elettra was quick. She stepped into their path, using her tail to keep the others from slipping around her to grab Adalina. Fueled with appreciation for Elettra's protection and a determination to prove her husband wrong, Adalina swung herself onto the dragon's back.

"If anything happens to you, I'll never forgive myself." There was sincerity in his eyes, and she could tell he meant it. He thought he was doing right by her.

But did he know her at all? Had he ever? She'd opened up to him. Told him her dreams and hopes and none of that included having a husband who was her master.

"Lina, please," he said tightly.

"Life is full of risks and danger. Especially ours, because of who we are." Adalina settled on Elettra and took hold of the spike closest to her—the very one her grasp had slipped from not so long ago. With a steadying breath, she continued, "You need to decide if you can handle that. If not, you will have to let me go."

He took a step and shook his head. "Adalina—"

"When this is over and all is said and done, we can go our separate ways. Be married only in title. I can go back to Solaris, and you can rule here without being hindered by my presence. But at this moment, right here, right now, you need to *back off*. I will not allow your fears to destroy us all."

His hands went up in an instruction for the guards to back away. They sighed in collective relief and did as he bid. When he lowered his hands, he clenched his fists, making the veins in his arms stand out. And without him saying anything, she knew that he was going against every one of his instincts that screamed at him to make her stay. To do whatever it took to keep her safe.

The weight in Adalina's chest released, and she signaled Elettra sky bound. With a beat of her wings, the dragon ascended. Soldiers stumbled back with grunts of surprise, but no one appeared to be harmed as they dusted themselves off and straightened.

With a plan formulating in her mind, she shared with Elettra, "Take me to the encampment. We'll destroy what we can before our army arrives. Any frost breather who stands in our way has made their choice and will fall by their own poor judgment."

If they burned, then it was their own fault. When they saw the dragon coming, the wise ones would flee over the border as they had done when her grandmother went after their forebears. If they remained to fight, then they would have made their choice, and she would not grieve the lives she took. She would do this for Callum. For Astarfall, and for Solaris. And for herself. She would do this to keep the frost breathers from using their vile beliefs of superiority to harm anyone else. She would burn them all if she had to.

Thirty-Eight

After years of trying to live up to her grandmother's legacy, Adalina finally had her chance. When she departed Callum's camp, she had every intention of proving she was worthy of their trust and of Elettra's loyalty. More than that, she desperately wanted to show everyone they'd made a mistake in doubting her.

The pain in her thigh threatened to return from squeezing her legs together to keep her seat, but she pushed through it. With her uninjured arm, she gripped the dragon's horn tightly. This time, she would listen to Elettra's instincts. As long as they worked as a team, they would be okay.

The frost breathers came into view, but there was no longer thick icy ground separating their camp from the mountains. It was like they had cleared the way for the battle they expected to come. As Elettra dipped lower to release the fire in her belly, Adalina delighted in the sight of men diving from her wrath.

There was no sign of the man with the insignia embroidered on his robes, but she continued to scan the panicked crowd for him. Most of the men had been assembled at the front line, readying themselves for the Astarfall army to march on them. And this time, they were ready for Elettra. The same shields of ice they'd used in the king's battle shimmered above them.

But Elettra's fire had decimated their defenses then, just as it would now. When the blaze hit them, the ice cracked, shattering under the heat of the dragon's flame. Men grunted as the shards scattered and sliced into their skin.

Realization that their ice manipulation was no match for the dragon's wrath spread like wildfire. The frost breathers at the front line pushed and shoved one another to try to get to the rear where the border and vast forest awaited them. On the other side, Adalina would have no power. They could not take their war onto Festiri territory.

She would be forced to wait while Callum delegated with the royal family who ruled those lands. The ones who had been estranged from Astarfall for a long time. Nothing but wilderness awaited the frost breathers and even if Adalina could follow them, it would be fruitless unless she burned the entire forest to the ground. Which was something else that would surely earn them discord with the Festiri.

Frost tipped arrows whipped through the air, falling short of Elettra's belly. Experienced in the art of battle, Elettra navigated the sky above the field with an effortless grace. Adalina trusted her to know what to do and tried to be useful by pointing out weaknesses in the frost breathers' ranks while keeping watch for the leader.

One shot at him and they might solve the issue entirely; ending the war before it went any further. She thought of the men back at the Astarfall camp. They had wives, children, siblings, and parents waiting for them back home in the villages and the city. If she could end this and send them all home, then it would be worth the fight that was surely to come with Callum.

To her dismay, she didn't have long to imagine it. A roar echoed through the valley as Callum and his army charged forward. In chaos, they clashed with the frost breathers. The Astarfall numbers were far greater than the rebellious faction's, but it didn't seem to sway the frost breathers' conviction. They stood their ground, ready to summon the heaven granted magic they wielded.

Adalina shook her head. Astarfall blood ran through their veins and until this moment, she hadn't dwelled much on the matter. The Old King's cruelty must have been unimaginable for them to have turned against their own people in such a violent manner. And for the hatred that one man held half a century ago to still be running rampant within their ranks. Did they even truly know what they were fighting for anymore?

Callum caught her attention, but he wasn't looking at her. His focus belonged only to the frost breathers who continuously tried to tear him down with their magic. His eyes, which she always thought to be beautiful, were filled with a hunger for blood. He sneered at the enemy as he summoned flashes of sunlight and pummeled anyone who dared face him. He was like the avenging heroes in the stories she had read. Fearsome and gorgeous. No longer a man, but a force of nature to be reckoned with.

A storm of emotions beat at her heart like a battering ram. She feared for him, just as he did her, but she wouldn't let it stand in their way. There was no denying she had been falling for him, but right now, the safest thing for them both was to build back the walls around their hearts. Best to be strategic rather than emotional. She steeled herself. Even if it destroyed everything that they had been building between them. Even if it shattered the growing affection that they had for each other.

Callum was busy fending off two attackers from the front and didn't notice as three frost breathers crept up behind him. A strange fog was forming on their lips. When they opened their mouths, it formed into a silver cloud. Adalina grimaced. She vaguely recalled reading about this trick of theirs in the Great War but couldn't remember exactly what it did. But the magic shimmering around it made it clear that they were going to use it as a weapon.

Hoping he would heed her command, she yelled, "Callum! Get down!"

Without even a glance in her direction, he collapsed to the ground on his stomach and Elettra dove, shooting spitfire at each of the men. Before the balls of flames hit them, they released the frosted breath they summoned. As Elettra's fire consumed them, the strange fog tore into their own men—the ones who had been fighting Callum from the front.

The frost spread from one man's chest, up his neck, and over his mouth. Blue crystals formed around his lips and his nose cutting off his oxygen. He writhed, grabbing for his friend beside him, but the man had been hit, too. The frost already coated his face, from the tip of his chin to his hairline. Their bodies writhed wildly until they suffocated completely and collapsed.

Callum pinned her with an alarmed stare, but a grateful smile twitched on his lips and her chest warmed. He'd trusted her at that moment and because of that, she had saved him.

Victory was short-lived, though, as a terrifying crackling sound came from the land below. It was like someone had taken a hammer to ice and the noise reverberated through her. A chill seeped deep into her bones, and it felt as if she would never be warm again as a ghastly beast clawed and skittered its way out of the dark pit.

Elettra shivered, too, and batted her wings desperately to put space between them and the creature that had been summoned from the icy pits of hell.

Adalina quaked, hands shaking so badly she had no choice but to loosen her grip on Elettra's horn. "They've had more than one all along?"

That or they had found a way to summon more. How many did they have access to?

Her gaze whipped toward the army. Time seemed to slow as her husband and his men regrouped. They pressed against one another, raising their hands and summoning their powers in a shield made of light, water, air, and stone. It would have been beautiful in the way the elements rippled together, if not coupled with the appearance of the skeletal creature with rotting flesh whose deadened eyes were pinned on them.

Whatever this thing was... it was a horror. Its very existence was sacrilege. An insult to the proud, beautiful dragons like Elettra, which once roamed the earth by the many.

Its wings creaked as it flew Callum's way in a pained, jagged pattern. Adalina held her breath and gripped Elettra's neck. The promise to trust her held strong. Adalina would allow her to choose how they handled this.

Still, she pleaded, "Stop that thing!"

Elettra wailed so loudly Adalina had to cover her ears. But it seemed to do the trick. The icy dragon's head snapped toward her with a disarming crack. It moved as if every bone in its body was broken.

Like it had been raised from the dead after many years of an eternal slumber.

It stank of rot and the deep, cold earth. Death incarnate. And it was headed her way.

Thirty-Nine

Callum shouted to Adalina. The desperation tore from his throat, but it did nothing to dissuade the beast which was catapulting toward her at a surprising speed. While Elettra's power rumbled in her belly before release, this dragon instead made a strange grating sound. It reminded her of the winters she'd spent skating on the frozen lake in Solaris. Like sharpened blades on thick ice.

And what came from its mouth was even more terrifying. Its blinding blue fire narrowly missed her. But the cold from it sliced into her skin, turning her blood cold, and she choked on the freezing wind that whipped around her as the frostbitten dragon's fire flared by her.

This horrific dragon was stronger than the last, who had relied on venom and teeth. It retreated higher into the sky and then ducked under Elettra when she followed.

Elettra dove and retaliated with a powerful stream of heat that seemed to be made of the same stuff as the sun itself. It warmed her, bringing life back to Adalina's frigid limbs.

While the dragons circled one another in a deadly dance, Adalina made the mistake of looking down below. The army was once again engaged in a relentless battle. It was difficult to see through the shimmering haze of magic. But one thing that was clear was that the frost breathers were pushing back harder than they had during the king's battle. This would be all or nothing for them. Astarfallen soldiers fell to their magic. Their lifeless gray eyes stared up at her with blue, frosted lips.

Desperately, she scanned the field for Callum. When she finally found him, her heart plummeted. He was facing the faceless man who had attacked her at the dock. The self-proclaimed leader of the frost breathers who bore the insignia, declaring his rank.

Her husband glared at the man as his sun-summoned power shielded him from the icy shards being thrown his way. The strain seemed to be too much as Callum fell to his knees, his face hardened and glistening with sweat. His defenses were weakening. And there was nothing Adalina could do for him from where she sat above.

"Callum's in trouble," she hissed at Elettra, who was still battling the hellish beast. Fire and ice clashed as each dragon released their wrath on the other. The frostbitten dragon was a threat, but the army would never survive the loss of yet another king. As his wife and queen her duty was to protect him.

For a moment, she thought maybe Elettra hadn't heard her. Then, suddenly, they were diving. Wind bit Adalina's face from the sudden fall and her stomach felt as if it had leapt into her throat. But she held fast, determined to aid her husband on the ground.

Both Callum and the faceless man craned their necks to see the commotion above. The man's gaze quickly returned to Callum, who was too distracted by Adalina's arrival to notice. Ice shattered the shield he'd been holding, but Elettra shot sparks at it. The frost breather's ice melted from the impact, turning into puddles at Callum's feet.

But the faceless man didn't let it deter him. As Elettra landed and Adalina slipped from her back—ankles jarring from the sudden impact on the hard ground—the faceless man pulled a dagger from his belt. A scream ripped from Adalina's throat as the man grabbed Callum by the collar of his shirt and placed the blade at the base of his throat.

"Stop!" Adalina's command and the ground shaking roar Elettra released made the men around them pause. Both armies froze in their tracks, realizing that their leaders were at a standstill with one dragon on the ground and the other, frostbitten one, hovering uncomfortably close in the air.

Callum fixed her with a frightened gaze. But rather than telling her to go, he said, "It's going to be alright, Lina."

"Shut up," hissed the man as he pressed the steel firmly against Callum's throat.

Taking a page out of her husband's book, she steeled herself. These veiled bastards would not watch her crumble. The grass below was brown and frosted at the tips. Icy wind cut into her like the tip of a blade. Nothing about this was alright. Not the fact that the frostbitten dragon was mere yards away. Or the tired, drawn faces of her army who looked at her with dimming hope as the frost breathers inched around them, hands poised and ready to wield sharpened ice. And certainly not the gut-wrenching pain of seeing the man she was falling for with a blade pressed to his throat.

Callum's voice was soft as he said, "You did well, dear wife."

Adalina smirked at him. "I had an excellent teacher. I only wish we'd had time to get that one twist right," she said, hoping he would take the hint about their defensive classes. It was a move she'd struggled with. But Callum never did have any trouble with it. The irony of him being the one in a situation where *he* would need to use it and not her, would have been laughable had things not been so bleak.

Surprise flickered in his eyes, and he suppressed a smile. *Jackpot,* she thought proudly. Now to distract their opponent.

To the faceless man—the one who dared attack her and the people she cared about, who had set all of this in motion—she said through gritted teeth, "You're nothing but a coward. All of you! Not even brave enough to show your own faces."

Elettra screeched and released a stream of fire into the sky at the frightening beast who threatened to inch closer.

Adalina's lips curled in disgust. "Are you *that* ashamed that you feel you need to hide yourselves from us?"

Something must have hit home, because the frost breather stilled, hesitating just long enough for Callum to twist his arm, forcing him to drop the dagger. They both scrambled for it, but Callum grabbed it first. With his feet parted and ready to attack, he pointed it at the man.

Letting the nerve she'd struck give her courage, she continued, "Remove that mask. Show us your traitorous face. Or I shall have Elettra melt it from your flesh."

The man's head turned to Elettra, then to Callum—who inched closer with his blade—and then back to Adalina. His hands reached gingerly for the silvery veil that had given him anonymity for long enough. The first glimpse was of his mouth, curved in a vicious smile that set her teeth on edge. Then his nose, regal and proud. And last, eyes that smacked her with horrible recognition.

It felt like she'd been punched in the gut. All she could summon was a breathless whisper as she said, "Uthred."

His smile broadened. "Hello, *Your Grace.*"

That vile son of a bitch. He'd been right under their noses. Adalina stumbled back, head spinning. Callum, with his smooth demeanor, sidestepped her way. Uthred watched him with a bored air as Callum placed himself in front of her defensively.

Uthred drawled, "Don't be stupid, Your Majesty. You can't protect her. No more than you could protect your sister. It's a shame, really, that the women in your life meet a tragic end despite your efforts to keep them safe."

Callum tensed and Adalina placed a hand on his shoulder as she warned, "Don't listen to him. He's trying to rattle you."

"I know," he said with a hint of regret. "I've been a coward."

Adalina bit her lip. This wasn't the time nor the place for this conversation. Uthred's men were pressing in on the Astarfallen soldiers. Slick, icy whips formed in their hands, and they began to strike. Men cried out, realizing that the frost breathers were reengaging. Their movements were slow and pained. Every one of them was battle weary. With both sides in such close combat—fighting with both magic and brute strength—there was no way for Adalina to call on Elettra to unleash her fire. Not unless she wanted to sacrifice their men's lives in the process.

The frostbitten dragon hovering above them let out a wicked roar and Elettra grunted. Both Adalina's and Callum's attention landed on her. A blue frost began to spread along her side. She stumbled back a few steps and before Adalina could go to her, Uthred snapped his power at Callum. It cracked like a whip, wrapping around his throat and slamming him into the ground. The blade was thrown from his hands, too far for either him or Adalina to reach.

Her heart broke in two; one piece urging her to go to Elettra, to stop the frost from spreading and hurting her anymore and the other screaming for her to save Callum from the traitor's hold. She cursed herself for freezing up. But she truly didn't know how to get them out of this one.

The frostbitten dragon took to the sky once more, spreading its icy wrath along the battlefield. Agonizing screams slashed through the valley. The sky darkened with an incoming storm and raindrops began to fall.

They ran down Adalina's cheeks like tears, but she wasn't crying. The anger was too strong for that. It was like it was burning her from the inside. She seethed as her eyes met Uthred's. With a deadly calm, she said, "Let. Him. Go."

It took every ounce of strength to keep the rage and power that came with it leashed. The fear of it erupting from her and Elettra and hurting their own men in the process was the only thing keeping it at bay. If they lost control, then everyone—frost breather and Astarfallen alike—would pay the price.

An amused smile spread slowly across Uthred's face, and his eyes sparkled like firecrackers. "Choose," he said with an arched eyebrow. "Your dragon. Or your husband. I'll even throw in your husband's army with him. A safe return home... at least for the time being."

Adalina narrowed her eyes and retorted, "This isn't a game."

"Isn't it?" Uthred asked, tightening his frosted whip around Callum's throat.

Her husband choked, but the fury still blazed in his eyes. He hadn't given up hope, and neither would she.

"Unhand them. Now."

Uthred tutted at her. "Foolish girl. This has always been a game. And it seems you have lost."

She glanced at the frightened faces of those left fighting. Sons, fathers, brothers. Men who had people back home in the city or villages, who waited with breaking hearts for their loved ones to return home.

A pained cry tore from Elettra's throat, shaking the ground beneath Adalina's feet. Uthred's men had surrounded the dragon. They held on to ropes so blue and translucent they looked like they were made of glass. Elettra's skin sizzled where they bound her, pinning her wings down and dragging her belly onto the ground.

"Let them *both* go. Name another price." Adalina turned back to Uthred.

Callum's face was turning blue, and ragged gasps escaped his lips as he struggled for air. If she hesitated for much longer, he would die. But this wasn't supposed to be her decision to make. She was a dragon warrior... A queen, not a king.

Uthred loosened his grip on Callum's throat just enough for a bit of color to seep back into his cheeks. His ragged gasps sent angry goosebumps prickling up her arms.

The traitorous coward struck her with an amused look and said, "I'll call off my frost-wielders and release the men. In exchange for you, your dragon, and your husband."

"You know we can't agree to that," she balked. "We might as well be handing you the keys to the kingdom."

With a wicked laugh, he said, "The keys will be mine, regardless. My men have nothing to lose. They will fight until there is no one left standing. Can your men say the same? Do this and you will spare many lives on this field today. And I will refrain from punishing the entire city for your hesitation at agreeing to my terms."

The pained grunts and dying gasps from their army filled her ears. Uthred still had Callum. If she refused, he might kill him then and there. The army would be without their king. They could lose everything all at once if she didn't agree to Uthred's demands.

When she looked to Callum for answers, he summoned a small nod. He was trusting her to make the decision.

Elettra wailed, sending a bolt of fear up Adalina's spine, and making her muscles seize up. If she didn't stop this, she could lose them both. Uthred was watching her with quiet fascination, as if trying to anticipate her next move.

With their army struggling to stay afoot, there was no fighting her way out of this, no matter how much Callum had tried to teach her. And without Elettra, she had no fire to fight the bitter cold of Uthred's power with.

"How do I know you'll keep your word and not kill the three of us the first chance you get?" Her hands itched to reach for Callum. Her legs longed to race to Elettra. But she was forced to stand her ground, despite the pain lancing up her thigh from the injury that had been overworked.

Uthred looked taken aback. "Why would I want a *dead* dragon when I can have a live one?"

Bile rose in Adalina's throat. He wanted Elettra for himself? It was insanity to believe, even for a second, that she would ever allow him to ride her.

He continued, "And you and Callum are going to see to it that I get precisely what I am owed."

Fire crackled at Adalina's fingertips. She would light him on fire with her bare hands if she had to. But Uthred tightened the silver magic around Callum's throat again and yanked him backwards. Something snapped behind her and Elettra wailed. She spun to find an ugly black whiplash on the dragon's hind leg.

"Okay!" she shouted out of desperation to make it all stop. "Tell your army to stand down. Let our men go. Let Callum *and* Elettra live, and you can have us."

Uthred eyed Elettra hungrily, like he'd been starving all his life and was now being promised a feast. The smile that spread across his face was one of pure glee. One of a man reveling in his victory.

Callum, still struggling for air, choked out the words, "It's going to be alright."

She looked him hard in the eye. It didn't feel like anything would ever be alright again. But she clung to the hope that if they could admit defeat at this moment, then they would live to fight again. It wasn't much, but it was better than watching the two loves of her life die on a frozen battlefield.

Uthred's eyes glittered with victory. "Deal."

Forty

After putting a stop to the battle, Uthred released the Astar-fallen army to return home just as he'd promised. It was the only thing to lift Adalina's spirits as she, Callum, and Elettra were bound with frozen ropes that glistened—slick with magic to keep them in check—and dragged through rows of tents. Once they reached Uthred's quarters—the largest and gaudiest of the bunch with blood red stripes streaking the cream canvas—they descended into the pit beside it.

There was more to the dark, gaping hole in the earth than met the eye. Adalina was grateful Uthred's men had tied their hands in front of them instead of behind. Navigating the decline would have killed her before he ever had the chance. If that was what he was even planning. She glared at the back of his head, wishing she had the ability to burn holes into it with her eyes.

Stairs wound around the perimeter leading into the void. Masked men in front of and behind them carried torches as they forced Adalina and Callum into the dark depths. Elettra, who had been bound tightly with ropes that must have been imbedded with the alarmingly strong, twisted magic, hissed from the center. It took every remaining frost breather who wasn't left to stand guard to lower her down slowly. If Elettra's life hadn't quite literally been hanging in their hands, Adalina would have hoped they'd lose their footing and fall swiftly to their deaths.

It sounded like Callum's throat was full of gravel as he said, "I'm sorry, dear wife—"

"Don't," she insisted with a stern shake of her head. It was impossible to ignore the defeat in his voice. She couldn't allow that. "Don't you dare apologize and say goodbye right now." She wouldn't stand there and listen to him accept a fate she wasn't ready for him to face. For *any* of them to face.

"I should have had more faith in you... in us." He reached for her, but she pulled away.

The pain of watching him claim his rights to Elettra was too fresh. She couldn't yet shake the raw stab of betrayal. The look he gave her was one of heartbreak. Like her grudge hurt him more than anything Uthred and his men could have done to him. Still, she walked on. If he wanted to apologize and make it up to her, then he could use that as motivation to stay alive.

It took nearly an hour to get to the bottom of the pit. By the time her feet hit leveled ground, she couldn't stop trembling. Or shivering. Never in her life had she experienced a cold like this. It was even worse than the blizzards that inevitably came to Solaris in the winter.

Her teeth chattered, and she pressed her bound hands to her chest. Uthred didn't give them so much as a glance as he led the way to a tunnel that was large enough for a man to walk through. She paused, hesitant to go any further. It seemed there was only one way in and out, making their options for escape limited.

A guard shoved her hard in the shoulder and she grunted as she stumbled over her own two feet and hit the frozen ground. Callum swore and elbowed the guard in the face with a crack that echoed through the chamber.

Another masked man came up behind him, bludgeoning him into submission with a massive block of ice he'd summoned from thin air. The blow to Callum's head was hard enough that it knocked him to the ground, but a string of curses coming from his mouth told her it wasn't as bad as it could have been. She screamed, nonetheless, clawing her way toward him and the blood coming from his head. It matted his hair and when he looked at her, his eyes rolled before he collapsed. She fought as someone dragged her back by the ankle.

"We made a deal!" she shrieked at Uthred's back.

He turned slowly, gaze flitting from her to Callum's unconscious body. With a flick of his wrist, he said to his men, "Clean him up. See to it that he does not die. We need him alive if he's going to be of any use to me."

It took two guards to lift Callum's limp body, and they dragged him unceremoniously into a dark alcove. Adalina struggled to follow, but Uthred gripped her arm tightly, targeting the wrist he knew was broken. She swallowed the bile threatening to rise with the pain as he yanked her into him roughly. His fingers dug sharply into her bandages, but it didn't stop her from trying to go with Callum.

She hissed, "Where are they taking him?"

"To his new room." Uthred chuckled. "I admit, it's not likely to be up to his Royal Highness' standards, but it will do for now. Better than a pine box, right?"

Adalina flinched at the blatant threat. *Was* this better? There was no way out of this in sight. They were much further than six feet in the ground. She shoved the fear away, locking it in its own little box in the recesses of her mind. They were still breathing. That meant there was hope.

They continued down the path until they came to a wooden door. At first glance, it was a simple piece of oak, but as the torch light cast a glow onto it, she could see that someone had hand carved it. It depicted a man standing on a mountain with hundreds of smaller people kneeling before him. In his hands he held a snowflake and in the other a bleeding heart.

Uthred's voice made her jump as he said, "A bit dramatic, I know. But it does inspire the spirit, doesn't it?"

She shrugged, channeling the nonchalance she'd seen Callum use a hundred times by now. Maybe the facade did come in handy in certain cases. Lightly, she said, "I've seen better."

Uthred swung the door open and shoved her inside. The guards remained at the threshold, and she wondered how many she would need to get past in order to find Callum and Elettra and escape this hellish pit.

The room they stood in now nearly took her breath away. It was as generously adorned as something inside of the Astarfall palace. Luxurious rugs covered the frozen ground. Leather chairs and sofas were placed neatly around a roaring fireplace. The room itself had been carved into the earth, giving it a musky, rich scent.

There was plenty of space, even enough for a massive oak desk and a four-poster bed. Sickened shivers ran down her spine. Why had Uthred brought her there? What use did he have for a woman who had been royalty for all of one week? She wasn't the important one here. Callum was considering the power he held. And Elettra, of course, who was Astarfall's greatest asset.

Uthred ignored her and walked to his desk, taking a seat, and shuffling through some papers. He licked his thumb and ticked through the pages as if searching for something of importance. Adalina glared at him and sat in the seat across from him. There was no point in standing around wondering. This was her chance to get answers from the source. And then she'd find a way to get them home.

She looked at Uthred as if seeing him truly for the first time. He had planted himself in their lives. Weaseled his way into King Alistair's good graces and made himself an indispensable member of the council. He had pretended to be acting in their best interests. All the while, living a double life. Hating them and everything they stood for from the shadows. He was a monster. A man who could manipulate anyone and everyone around him while pretending to be their best friend and confidant.

He glanced up, eyes roving over her as he said, "I expected you to be hopeless. A lost cause. Unable to handle yourself in battle."

"Sorry to disappoint," she said simply. Then, leaning forward, she tilted her head and asked, "Why does that matter, though? What significance could I possibly have toward your cause?"

If he planned to use her against Callum, he had another thing coming. No matter how angry she was, she wouldn't betray him.

Uthred poured two glasses of amber liquid from a crystal decanter. He shoved one in her direction and nodded for her to drink. As he swirled his own glass in his hand, he asked, "Would you like some pain relief for those injuries?"

She leveled a stony gaze at him. She wouldn't accept a damn thing from him. Not ever. "What I want are answers."

In a detached sort of way, like he was lost in his thoughts, Uthred asked, "Do you have any idea how hard it is to turn an entire kingdom against a royal family that has ruled for centuries?"

She didn't want to play this game. She wasn't there for lessons from a traitor.

He continued as if she'd answered, "You have to strike at the heart if you want to weaken a crown and the people's belief in the one who wears it."

Adalina fought the urge to roll her eyes. So, he wanted to turn the city against Alistair from the start. In his defense, it almost worked. She recalled the whispers she'd heard from the men in the palace. The doubt in their voices had been strong. As much as Alistair tried to make the attacks seem less serious than they were, he was no match for the truth.

"If you wanted us to look bad, then why convince the council to allow me the chance to train? How did me getting stronger benefit you?"

Uthred's sway in the council was undeniable. He could have just as easily convinced them to let her go out there completely unprepared.

"I did what I could, but there was only so far that I could push before they became suspicious. Heely was already a problem; always butting his nose in and standing up for you." His lip curled in disgust, and he took a long drink.

Guilt crept up on her. She'd accused Heely of being the traitor. She'd had him locked away in a cell when she should have seen Uthred for what he was all along. With his charming smiles and easy lies. She expected to feel the prickle of fire that often accompanied her anger nowadays, but instead she felt numbed from the cold. Was that how Elettra was feeling right now trapped down there in the dark when she belonged in the sun?

Uthred finished his drink and poured another, filling it to the brim this time. Then he continued, "I was elated at first, when Callum's magic helped give you enough power to wake the dragon. It was clear from the start that she didn't want to accept him. If we had forced him to invoke his rights earlier, to allow him to ride, then he would have been an easy target. But the council out voted me in the end."

He shook his head and chugged the drink until the last drop. This time, when he poured another, it was with an unsteady hand. Adalina curled her lip in disgust. Was he truly already celebrating his victory?

She left her glass untouched. She needed a clear head if she was going to escape the first chance she got.

She studied him for a moment, then said, "So that's why you pushed the council to change their mind after the king was wounded. It's why you injured me at the dock. It was you who forced their hand and convinced Callum to enforce his rights as my husband. In the hopes that he would ride out and fail."

"Among other reasons." With a sigh, Uthred changed direction. "I've always admired the power a rider is able to take from their dragon."

"It's not taken. It's *given*. The First Man earned that gift."

Uthred swung a finger in her direction, splashing a bit of his drink on the table. "Ah! But that's just it, isn't it? You, a young woman from a nothing village in a forgotten kingdom, *still* claimed that gift. The First Man might have earned it, but after that, it was passed down through generations. Given to snot-nosed brats who had no idea what to do with it."

She raised her chin in defiance. She wouldn't let this son of a bitch make her question her worthiness. Elettra chose her even when Adalina released her from the bond when they were in the Astarfall camp.

Uthred narrowed his eyes. "And just like *that*," he paused, snapping his fingers. "Callum *took* that gift from you."

Adalina's rage took control, and she slammed her uninjured hand on the table. "What do you want from me?" she seethed. "Get on with it, Uthred. My patience is wearing thin, and it's only a matter of time before the council realizes we've been taken. Do you really think they'll wait with open arms for you to arrive in the city?"

It was a dangerous line she was walking. Threats might result in Uthred carrying out whatever plan he had in mind for them. But the waiting was unbearable. She needed to know what was coming if she was going to find a way out of it.

With a reddened face and a lethal tone, he said, "I knew we needed you here in Astarfall if we were to have any chance of waking Elettra. It could only be done with your blood. Your inherited magic."

"Why would you want me to wake her at all?" Her words tasted like ash and her stomach churned. She'd asked for answers, but she didn't like where this was going; couldn't ignore his blatant interest in Elettra.

"I need that dragon."

"You aren't so delusional to think she would ever bond with you." Adalina nearly laughed in his face.

Offense flashed across his features, but he took another drink and said, "After I saw the two of you together, I knew it would never happen. I thought perhaps if I killed you..."

"The assassin on my wedding night," she whispered.

He nodded effortlessly, as if they were talking about him sending her a tea set as a wedding gift and not a painful death.

She pushed away from the desk, but tendrils as sleek as icicles shot from Uthred's free hand. They snapped around the desk, taking hold of the legs of her chair and drew her back in. Forced to remain seated, she bared her teeth.

Another tendril snaked toward her and clasped her chin. The cold burned almost as intensely as the frostbitten dragon's venom. But she didn't fight it. It wouldn't do any good. He was going to make sure she heard every word he said. It felt like he'd been waiting for this moment for a long time.

He sneered. "I realized if I couldn't sway the dragon to forfeit your bond, then I would need to sway you. But the fact that you were actually falling in love with that foolish prince was a problem. I needed you to hate him."

Releasing her chin, he rolled his head, cracking his neck loudly, and continued, "You proved more capable than I gave you credit for. Claiming your victories in battle was counterproductive for me. So, I wounded you, making you look every bit as frail and incapable as the council believed you to be. Showing Callum that you needed to be protected. Controlled. And it worked. Tell me, did it hurt when he forced you to stay behind? Did your heart break just a little watching him ride off on your dragon? Knowing that it was *he* who didn't trust *you*?"

Uthred was the wedge that had shoved itself between her and Callum and she hated him for it; with every fiber of her being. She wanted nothing more in that moment than to see this man burn. But no matter how much she willed it, the fire in her veins would not wake.

She didn't know what to say. Suddenly, the amber drink in front of her looked really tempting. Anything to distract her from the nausea rolling in her stomach. But she resisted, waiting for Uthred to continue. To finally tell her what he intended to do with her, Callum, and Elettra.

"You wanted me to hate Callum so I would fight for you," she guessed. It all made sense now. His manipulations were as fluid as his magic; changing like the frost he morphed into whips and arrows.

"When you turned out to be quite the survivor, I realized if I wanted Elettra, I would have to take you too."

Adalina dug her nails into her palms to keep from climbing over the desk and clawing his eyes out. She'd played right into his hands.

With a slight tremble, she said, "You have to know I would never ride for you. I would never fight for your people."

"Oh, I don't need you to fight for me." An oily smile spread across his face. He stood so abruptly that his chair fell back with a clatter. His eyes, now glazed over from the drinks, glittered with raw excitement as he said, "Let me show you something."

Forty-One

Venturing out of Uthred's personal chambers, and into the rest of the pit was surreal. Adalina couldn't imagine the time and craftsmanship it must have taken to cultivate the underground abode. Tunnels stretched into the darkness, making it impossible to tell how far they went. Or where...

More alert to her surroundings, she scanned each nook and cranny, noticing small alcoves scattered every few yards. Some had wooden doors similar to Uthred's, but they moved too quickly for her to note any of the carved details.

Each door sent a wave of uncertainty through her. Where was Callum? Fear swelled in her stomach and settled at the bottom like molten metal. She felt like a fever was breaking with sweat beading at her temples, but unable to truly get warm. She kept looking as they walked. More rooms. But for what, she couldn't imagine. The only people to be seen down there aside from her were Uthred and a handful of his men. They'd taken to leaving their faces uncovered. Adalina supposed it didn't matter to them anymore whether their identity was revealed or not. Not that she recognized any of them, anyway. They, unlike Uthred, hadn't been right under her nose all along.

She rubbed her arms to rid herself of the goosebumps that didn't seem to want to leave. Something about how ordinary her captors looked shook her. If she had passed them in town, she never would have known who or what they were. Never would have suspected they'd be capable of such upheaval.

Stumbling to keep up with Uthred's gait, she snarled, "What is it that you want to show me?"

"All in good time," he said with a lighthearted singsong voice that made her want to tear his perfectly placed hair from his head.

Had it not been for Callum and Elettra still being trapped down there out of her reach, she would have tried it. But until she found them, she needed to play along with Uthred.

They ducked into a cavern and when they came out into a large opening, blue light twinkled at Adalina so brightly she had to shield her eyes for a moment. As she lowered her hand, her sight adjusted to more than just the dark underground and torches. The blue was coming from gemstones in the walls.

They reminded her of the moonglass in her ring, except for a chill that emanated from them, nipping at her skin. Peering closer, she caught a faint shimmer swirling inside of them like small galaxies. Was that what was giving Uthred the power to wake his dragons? She couldn't wrap her head around it. After all, the only references of dragons they had in the world up above were of her people's bond to them. And none had ever been described as horrific beasts who moved like the undead.

The hairs on her arms rose. Uthred was too quiet. His silence was more unsettling than his ramblings, so she goaded, "What now? You've taken the king and queen of Astarfall as your prisoners. You have Elettra. But as I've said, I will not ride for you. And I think we both know the council will not follow you. Neither will the Astarfallen army or the nobles, after what you've done to the innocent people of this land."

Uthred's laugh was slick and sent shivers down her spine. "*We* are the people of this land. The faceless, nameless men who the Old King cast out."

She scoffed in his face. "Cast out? Maybe the others have a reason to feel that way. But you? You rose in the ranks of court. Became an esteemed member of the council—"

"For them." He pointed to a pair of guards. "For my people."

She narrowed her eyes. "Who are you really?"

At that, a proud smile spread across his face. "Come now, Your Grace. You've spent enough time at court to have heard the rumors. My mother was a member of the queen's court. She served Alistair's mother loyally for years. But her husband was a heavy-handed womanizer."

Adalina crossed her arms, careful not to show any pity for his mother's story. "So, your dad was a son of a bitch. That doesn't explain your connection to the frost breathers."

His smile grew sinister. "I didn't say he was my father." With a laugh, he explained, "My mother had an affair with a man she'd loved when she was young. They conceived me in a western village. Not far from here, actually. Every moment she could get away from the palace was spent there with him. He was a great man. A man who had never once laid an unkind hand on her. And he came from a prominent family."

Seraphine's story at Windshire... The affair. It was true.

With her interest piqued, she asked, "Who was he? If he was of noble blood, then why hadn't she married him instead?"

Uthred's shoulders tensed so quickly it nearly made her shrink back. His birth father may have been a kind man, but she could not let herself forget that Uthred was not. He attacked women, the elderly, and children, all in the name of a cause that had been lost to the world half a century ago.

His voice was as cold as ice as he said, "When King Alistair's father found out what sort of power my father's people wielded, he banished them. Don't you see? What use is an Astarfallen when they cannot be of benefit to this land of eternal summer? My grandfather, Rothin, could have done great things if he'd been given the chance. Instead, your grandmother burned his friends and family alive. It was by the fates' grace that Rothin, his wife and his son escaped. But he and any of his remaining followers were left to fend for themselves in the Festiri wilderness."

Adalina blanched at the admission. Uthred was the grandson of the man her grandmother defeated in battle. The original leader of the frost breathers. A man who slaughtered countless Solarians in his conquest.

"Surely there is a better way to do right by your people. They can't all possibly want to forfeit their lives for this revenge."

Her brows knit together as she came to a halt. For generations, they'd been in hiding. The fact that there were so many of their people left proved that they'd stuck together. Fallen in love, had families of their own. They'd continued their line despite all odds. She didn't know what it was like to be a mother, but she couldn't imagine sending her child to fight a war that their forefathers started.

This time, Uthred showed his temper. With fists clenched tightly, as if ready to strike her, he snarled, "They don't know what's best for them! It falls upon me to tell them."

His words struck too close to home. Legacies were a hard thing to live up to. And the legacy they'd been left with was one filled with generational hate. What if the exiled frost-wielders were given another choice? If they were offered peace and a place where their families could live freely and safely, would they choose not to follow Uthred? What if he was taken out of the equation? If his line ended with him, would Rothin's vile ways die too?

Adalina reached for her power. The guards were too far away to stop her if she went after Uthred. If she was fast and strong enough, then she could try to end this now.

Murderous thoughts were shed when she heard a soft whimper from a dark corner of the cave. She was hit with a sudden rush of both relief and terror that didn't belong to her. She gasped, "Elettra!"

The shout echoed, bouncing loudly off the walls and back to her own ears. She ran for the shadows, but Uthred caught her roughly by the arm and dragged her into his chest. She struggled, but fighting against his hold was useless. After all she'd been through, her body was exhausted. The herbs given to her by the healers had worn off by now and the pain was returning with a vengeance. There was no amount of adrenaline that could make her move the way she would need to in order to escape him.

He hissed lowly in her ear, "You'll get your reunion. But only when I say so."

She glared hard at him, wishing her eyes could burn straight through his very soul.

With a laugh, he said, "I have big plans for our dear Elettra. Big, big, plans." He loosened his grip, but not enough for her to pull away from him.

"She'll never allow you to ride her. And if I won't do it for you, then all this effort is for nothing." Of that, Adalina was certain. No one could force them.

"Stupid girl." His teeth gleamed in the light of the gemstones. It was truly sinister and made her flinch away as he said, "My beasts do not need riders. If I fancy it, I can simply slit Elettra's throat. I can make you watch as I bring her back as something dark and twisted. And then I can order her to tear you apart piece by piece."

Adalina's knees buckled. "You would change her into one of those disgusting creatures."

She could never let that happen. The thought of Elettra coming back as one of those mindless, broken things consumed her with a terror she'd never experienced before.

"I would. You have no power here, *Your Grace*. Long ago, dragons roamed these lands. The Solarian Horned Backs, like your dear Elettra, were few and far between. My men were only able to track down the remains of the far less superior breed of Dagger Heads. Small, squeamish creatures."

Adalina's stomach turned. The Solarian dragons who bonded with her people were buried in reverence throughout her land. But others, who had chosen to remain hidden and live ferally, were scattered through the forests and hills. From what she'd read, their whereabouts were largely unknown. Uthred had found two that she knew of for certain. How many more did he have stowed away?

Wistfully, he continued, "My frost biters, as you've seen, are unreliable. Feral in life and even more so in death. They act on primal instinct. I could only hope that Elettra would be different. I didn't want to have to kill her, but you seem to be intent on forcing my hand."

He wiped a tear from Adalina's cheek, and she jerked away.

With an oily smile he said, "Take comfort in knowing she'll come back in her purest form."

"There is nothing *pure* about the beasts you summon," Adalina spat.

"Is there not purity in death?" There was genuine curiosity in his words. "All life must die and return to the earth. It feeds us. Gives us strength and the ability to create new life. It is what Rothin believed, and it is what Astarfall could not accept."

His icy fingers dug into her chin, forcing her to look at the dark corner. Elettra hissed and the sound of claws scraping against rock bounced off the walls. The men had dragged her into the blue light. Frosted ropes still held her down and, try as she might, Elettra's fire would not come. Instead, the attempts came out in pained gasps. Puffs of steam blew from her nose, only to be swept away by the unbearable chill.

Adalina's knees weakened at the sight of the magnificent creature trapped like a wild beast. But Uthred grabbed her arm with his free hand while still forcing her to look at Elettra with the other.

He spoke soothingly, like he was trying to calm a child, and said, "This is why everyone fears those who bear the magic of the deep. They cannot admit that *we are a necessary balance.* The people of Astarfall boast about the power granted to them by the heavens. But they refuse to admit that my people have also been blessed. We wield the magic of the places down below, where ice and frost and decay reside. The fates know there must always be a balance and that is why they created us."

"Your grandfather destroyed countless lives with his *gifts*. He misled his own people. People who *trusted* him to take care of them. He was wrong. Your power does not make you superior to the rest," she managed to say despite the grip he had on her face.

"That's where you're wrong. All life ends. When all is said and done, it is *my* power that reigns supreme. Magic that claims even that which is considered the most powerful thing of all. I can slay Elettra and then remake her."

She shut her eyes tight, unable to bear the sight of Elettra the way she was. Adalina was furious with herself for not being able to save her. For letting them take Callum away. She hated herself for getting them all into this mess in the first place. If she had just stayed in the palace... She clenched her fists. No. If she had stayed in the palace, then Callum and Elettra could still have fallen in battle.

This moment was the one that mattered. There had to be a way out.

Uthred scoffed. "You probably knew none of this. That's precisely why a Solarian doesn't belong on the Astarfall throne."

"Explain it to me, then. Finish what you have to say." The more he talked, the more time she had to figure a way out of this. She counted the guards. Six. It was more than she cared for, but it wasn't an army, at least. And Callum couldn't have been taken far. If she could just get to those ropes on Elettra...

Uthred continued, "Your husband's magic is connected to nature. It is used to nurture life and make it prosper. Sunlight for the flowers, the trees, for health... But *my* magic—the magic of my forbearers—thrives in the darkness. It rules over everything. No matter how many times the sun rises, the dark will come again. No matter how much something thrives in life, it will eventually wither away and die."

Adalina spotted a sword on one of the men's hips. She needed to get closer to him. Although she'd never disarmed anyone, it was something Callum had shown her in the training yard.

Hoping to make Uthred lower his guard, she stopped struggling against him.

Just as she was about to make her move, he stopped her in her tracks, saying, "*That* is the power I plan to pass off to the next dragon."

Adalina froze. "What is that supposed to mean?"

"You thought I brought you here to see *your* dragon?" he asked mockingly.

He swept his arm to a statue near Elettra. It was as tall as Adalina's hip. A stone column with something shaped like an egg carved on top. Uthred walked toward it, leaving her side. She followed, taking a roundabout way that put her between him and Elettra. It also brought her closer to the guard.

Uthred ran a loving hand over the statue, and it shook slightly. Her heart skipped a beat. As she peered more intently, she realized the egg was not attached to the rest of the stone, but instead balanced on top.

She crept close to it. Then, narrowing her eyes, and praying that Elettra's connection to her wasn't too hindered, she waited for the dragon-enhanced sight to come. The edges in Adalina's peripheral blurred and soon she was looking at the egg with such clarity that she could see it wasn't made of stone at all, but instead, a gray shell. Heat flared in her chest and her fingers tingled like they had little flames dancing across them, and suddenly she saw more than a shell.

Inside, past the hard casing, she saw life. A tiny dragon curled tightly with its tail resting under its head. There was nothing haunting and skeletal about it. It was all growing muscle and soft, baby pink skin. But Adalina sensed its wrongness. Like there was something missing from it. She gasped for air as her throat grew tight, panic rising.

Her voice was small, making her feel frail as she asked, "Where did you get this?"

Uthred raised his eyebrow and followed her as she stumbled back into one of the guards. The frost breathers had their hands on not one healthy dragon, but two now that she'd delivered Elettra to them. If he got the one in the egg to hatch and then bond with him, the havoc he could bring to the world was unthinkable.

She scrambled the recesses of her mind. The history books didn't know much about hatchlings. They were incredibly rare. No human could pinpoint why that was, only that they had seen fewer dragons coming into the world over the years. It was why Elettra was the last of her kind... or so they'd all thought.

Uthred implored her desperately, "What did you see? Tell me! Is it alive and well?"

The only way to hatch an egg was for the mother to breathe life into it. To warm it with her fire until it became strong enough to emerge. But this baby's mother had to have been long gone. Adalina's heart broke for the once noble dragon and what must have become of her. Had she suffered the same fate as the other frostbitten dragons? Forced to wake from her eternal slumber to fight for an unworthy man?

With angry, tear-filled eyes, she seethed at him. "It will never hatch for you. You know that. It needs its mother's fire."

"It needs a female dragon's fire," he countered with a sniff.

It took everything in Adalina to remain on her feet. Deflated, she said, "That's why you risked us waking Elettra. It's why you've only *threatened* to kill her. You need her alive if she's to do this."

Elettra's eyes were filled with dismay; watery and frightened.

But Uthred's blazed brighter, as if hungry for what he had planned. "Think of what might come of it. Mighty Elettra, the strongest and most valiant of her kind, breathing life into the unhatched."

Bile rose in Adalina's throat. She took a horrified step back, but the guard stopped her from going any further.

The hatchling would grow to know only Uthred. It would be too young and inexperienced to win him the throne, but in time, it would be the one thing to make sure he was able to stay in power. And once

Elettra helped him with the hatchling, she'd be of no more use to him. He would kill her. She would be brought back as a mindless thing for him to use however he saw fit.

Without responding to him, Adalina reached behind her, fingers brushing against the guard's side until she found what she needed. Wrapping her hand tightly around the hilt of the sword, she spun on her heel and drew it from the guard's scabbard. Panicked, he released his hold on Elettra's ropes. The other men shouted in terror as Elettra bucked under their desperate hold, but Adalina ignored them.

She turned toward Uthred, intent on plunging the blade into his heart. But he was fast. Face to face with her, he smiled, then smashed her over the head with something hard. White dots blotted her vision before the darkness swept in to claim her.

Forty-Two

When Adalina came to, Uthred was sitting at her bedside. In his thick leather gloved hands was the egg. It wasn't gray like before, but was a deep purple, similar to some of Elettra's scales. There were pin thin lines webbing along the egg's surface in a warm, soft glow. Bile rose in her throat, and she nearly fell off the bed as she spilled the contents of her stomach onto the floor. Uthred didn't so much as move an inch. When she rolled back onto the bed, wiping her mouth indignantly on his expensive blankets, he frowned.

Stroking the egg like it was his own child, he said, "It seems I went through all that trouble of trying to make you understand my side of things for nothing. All it took was a blow to your head for Elettra to see reason."

"What have you done to her?" An unwelcome image of Elettra reanimated with a slit across her throat flashed in Adalina's mind, threatening to make her vomit again.

He swatted at the air, but his other arm pulled the egg close to his chest, careful not to risk dropping it. "She's fine. I've kept her alive for now. As you know, dragon hatching is an incredibly understudied phenomenon. I wouldn't risk killing her before we know for certain that it's worked."

There was a threat laced in that last sentence. Elettra's fate wasn't yet sealed. He could still end her any time he wanted and leave her for dead or bring her back as one of his horrifying *frost biters*.

The egg wobbled in his hands from the baby dragon's movement. Adalina's heart plummeted. Elettra's fire had stirred it from its slumber. The only solace came from seeing that it had not hatched yet. As long as it remained in its egg, then Elettra would stay alive. Long enough for the army to come for them. Or for an escape.

And maybe the baby would never hatch. Not without its own mother breathing life into it...

Shaking in anger, Adalina shouted, "How dare you force her to do this!"

She would kill him. No. Worse. She would destroy everything he cared about, starting with that damned egg.

He shook his head, exasperated. "Elettra was quite willing in order to keep me from killing you both. And now it's done so you can stop giving me that look."

"Where is Callum?" She struggled to maintain a forceful tone. "I want to see my husband."

"In due time. The two of you will be reunited. You've nearly fulfilled your usefulness."

"What more could you possibly want from us?"

This time, malice spread across his face. "What was it that you all wanted to do to me? Oh, that's right. Parade me in the streets as an example of what happens when you stand against the royal family." With a chuckle, he added, "Seems fitting for the two of you, instead. It will be quite a thing to see before you're both beheaded."

Her gaze flitted around her, searching for something to bludgeon him to death with. "You plan to make an example of us."

"You're learning." He stood abruptly, and she partly readied herself for him to hit her again.

With a defiant stare, she spat at him. But he didn't strike. Instead, he tilted his head as if trying to solve a puzzle. "Isn't fate a funny thing? It's like they wove our families together in their grand tapestry. First, your grandmother and my grandfather—sworn enemies. A win for your family that time." He winked. "A now a win for mine." With an amused chuckle, he walked to the door. "I wonder what the tie breaker would have been had there been a new generation to follow." He shrugged. "Guess we'll never know."

Before opening the door, he said, "You know, at our side, you could be magnificent. You and Elettra could live. I could even give you Solaris to rule."

"You're not stupid enough to believe I would ever support you."

"You were stupid enough to come to Callum's aid despite what he did to you."

Adalina clenched her jaw. She and her husband weren't reconciled, and she didn't know if they would ever have that chance. But she wouldn't hide from the feelings that had grown between them. Something like that didn't disappear with a snap of fingers. And nothing Uthred could ever offer would make her betray him or their people.

Even if beating Uthred meant going home to a cold and formal marriage of title only, it was a far better alternative. It was better than being a coward and a traitor. Better than being a widow.

Uthred scowled when the bait didn't seem to work. Then he left with a slam of the door. When he was gone, Adalina sank into the pillows. She grabbed one, pressing it over her face, and she screamed with all her might. When the raging storm inside of her settled, she lifted the pillow from her face with a huff. This wasn't doing her any good.

There was no telling when Uthred would return. She needed to get it together and act. An exit that didn't involve slipping past guards was likely too much to hope for, so she settled to search for a weapon. Something to give her an advantage over their size and their magic.

Her gaze fell to the large hearth. She searched for a fireplace poker or even a log hefty enough to bludgeon someone with. But the only wood to be found was currently burning. It was also the only thing bringing her any relief from the intense chill.

No pokers either. Nothing iron or sharp... She grumbled to herself as she moved to the desk next. Strewn with papers, the surface was an overwhelming mess. It was a wonder Uthred was able to make sense of anything there. The largest drawers were locked, and she searched for something to pick them with.

Clumsily, she bumped into a stack of parchment, and a few pages fluttered to the floor. She bent down to pick them up—the last thing she wanted was for him to return and punish her for snooping—and set them back on the desk. A seal, matching the insignia Uthred wore, caught her eye.

She held the paper up to get a closer look, curiosity getting the better of her. They appeared to be instructions for a coronation ceremony. The paper crumpled at the sides as her fingers dug into it. That son of a bitch was already planning his ascension to the throne. Had likely planned it before she and Callum ever fell into his grasp.

Turning to the next page, her breath caught in her throat when she saw her grandmother's name at the top. She scanned the words quickly. His plans for Adalina and Callum were no surprise. Of course, he would want to make a grand show of the royals' fall from grace. But what he had planned for her grandmother was personal.

Scribbled in Uthred's angry handwriting, it read:

Dragon Warrior Calida - to die by dragon fire.

Adalina let the papers fall from her hands. Hard determination filled her, and she began tearing the room apart. It didn't matter if he found it a mess anymore. No matter what she did, this would end the same way if she didn't get out of there, and fast.

Books were thrown to the floor, trunks upturned. She was ruthless in her pursuit of a weapon to use against her captors. When she came to an armoire, she found it holding nothing but clothing for both a man and a woman, a soft knitted blanket with little blue bows on it, and a large bag for easy packing. She thought of Uthred's wife, Erabelle, and wondered how much she knew about her husband's deceit. Adalina shivered, remembering the way Erabelle had draped herself over Callum at the Winter Solstice ball and wondered if she'd been in on it all along. How many times had she used her charms to sway the royal family's opinion of her and her husband in their favor?

Furious, Adalina kicked the armoire, moving it but a hair from the wall with the impact. Even with her boots on, her foot throbbed. She bent down to rub it and noticed a gentle breeze fluttering her hair. With a furrowed brow, she inspected the source closer to find a dark passageway so narrow only one person could fit through at a time.

It was possible that it led nowhere. But the pit was manmade; carved to Uthred's advantage. There had to be a purpose for this one, right? She grunted softly as she pushed the armoire until there was just enough room for her to slip behind it. When she stepped into the passage, she pulled the dresser back to where it was before. With bated breath, she waited for the sound of guards coming into the room.

When there was none, she started into the darkness. Tiptoeing to prevent any echo, she crept through the winding tunnel. After only a few moments, it came to a fork. In one direction, the ground slanted slightly upward, and a mild breeze blew into her face. It had to lead outside. Instinct told her to take it. To run far and fast. But her heart and head implored her to take the second path. The one that would likely lead her further into the labyrinth of the pit. Somewhere, Callum and Elettra were waiting for her.

Without another thought, she took it. Picking up her pace, she ran despite the cold that still bit into her skin. If only she could use her connection to Elettra down here. But in the hellish pit, there was no warmth. No strength. Only oppressive darkness and decay. She supposed she'd have to do things the old-fashioned way. It was a shame she hadn't had more time to train with Callum.

Trying to quell the urgency that made her tremble, she imagined what would happen once they all got out of there. As much as she longed for a happy ending, she wasn't sure it was in the threads of fate for her. There was no denying her doubts about making her marriage to Callum work after this.

Aside from the fact that he might never forgive her for putting them in this position, she wasn't sure she'd have the ability to forgive him for betraying her trust. Maybe it would be best for her to go back to Solaris. He could rule on his own, since that seemed to be what he was most comfortable with, anyway. She tried to ignore the bitter taste in her mouth and pushed on through the dark passageway.

The further she ventured, the darker her thoughts became, matching that of her current situation. Vicious visions entered her mind as she continued to muse about their future if they survived Uthred's imprisonment. With her in Solaris, Callum would be free to take lovers, while she and Elettra lived out their spinster lives together.

Adalina clenched her fists and ducked under a low dip in the rocky ceiling. Elettra could nap on the hillside while she picked wildflowers in between the hours of working in her mother's shop. A bitter laugh slipped from her lips, echoing louder than she intended. Imagine what people would think of a queen mending the buttons on their shirts.

Her musings were interrupted as she came to a series of alcoves. If she hadn't been horrified at the vast number of them, she would have been awestruck. It was impressive what Uthred and his men had accomplished. And it was clear that they'd been working toward this for years. Perhaps the project had even been started before Uthred's time. He never did mention what had happened to his father. Only that his mother had raised him at court with a nobleman posing as his sire.

Had Rothin's son continued his mission even after he was gone? Or had it been Uthred to take up the mantle? Regardless of who led the charge, they had clawed and raked their way from the western wilderness into the underbelly of Astarfall. She had to give them credit for their patience and perseverance. She supposed a set mind and yearning for revenge would make it quite easy.

She gently pushed open any door she encountered and peeked in to be sure there were no frost breathers lurking inside. After several tries, there was still no sign of Callum. It was likely Elettra was still being kept in the blue lit cavern, but it was impossible to know which entryway would take her there.

She jumped at the echo of footsteps and angry grumblings coming from the dark corridor. The guards must have realized she was gone. She had no intention of being hunted down like a fox in the hills, so she bolted down the winding tunnel. Her hands fumbled for the wall as it was pitch black, with no torch to light her way. Soon she came to the opening with the stairs that led out of the pit.

Pressing herself against the wall and into the shadows, she waited until a few of the frost breathers passed by. They walked toward the cavern that held Elettra. Adalina's nerves crackled like embers in a fire, but she knew she couldn't go to her yet. If she was going to get past the guards, she would need help. She would need her husband.

It wasn't until she came to a door with a guard posted outside of it that she allowed herself to feel hope again. She pressed herself against the frigid rocky wall and tried to think of a way past the man. Her dragon connected magic was dampened in the pit. She wouldn't stand a chance against a frost breather whose power thrived in a place like this.

The man snorted. She breathed a sigh of relief, realizing the big oaf was snoring loud as a boarhound. If he was sleeping heavily enough, then maybe he wouldn't notice when the door clicked open and shut.

As far as she could tell, he was unarmed. Likely because he wouldn't need a steel blade when he could summon an icy one with his magic.

All she had to do was get into the room. Getting out would be easier with Callum by her side. That is, if he was even in there. And if his magic even worked so far down in the deep, stinking earth. After this, she never wanted to smell dirt again, or look at another rock.

She crept lightly on the balls of her feet and held her breath. One misstep and she could find herself right back in Uthred's room, or worse. With her gaze trained on the sleeping guard, she reached for the door. He stirred slightly, but to her immense relief, it was only so he could shift to the other side. She froze, forcing herself to be as still as the stone around her, until the snoring resumed.

Without a moment of hesitation, she turned the latch and slipped into the room. It was so damp that her teeth chattered. There was nothing inside but a small cot in the corner, pushed against the wall.

Callum moaned from the poor excuse for a bed, and she rushed to his side. She dropped to her knees and took his face in both her hands. With nothing to light the room but a sad, dwindling candle, she tried to inspect him for injury, but it was no use. Instead, she closed her eyes and felt, hoping that her sense of touch would improve if she wasn't so focused on trying to see.

Something cold and wet brushed against her fingertips. And she knew it would stain them red. The blow to his head seemed to have stopped bleeding, but only recently. Worry bloomed for him as she patted his cheeks in an attempt to wake him.

There were no other sounds in the room aside from his ragged breathing and dripping water somewhere far off. It was strange that Uthred would leave the King of Astarfall with only one lazy guard attending him. Perhaps he had believed with his injuries there was no chance of escape. Still, it was a surprising oversight.

"Please, you have to wake up," she whispered wildly to him. They were running out of time and needed to get Elettra. If they could break her free of her bonds, it was possible she could fly them out of the pit and back to the city. If Uthred had raised more of his frost biters, then the city was as vulnerable as her husband was as he lay indisposed on the musty cot.

Shuffling in one of the dark corners stole her breath away. She whipped around to see a shadowy figure move. The hair on Adalina's arms rose as she realized they weren't alone after all.

Forty-Three

"Y-you can't be here." A woman's husky stammer had Adalina scrambling to her feet.

The woman was clad in the same black robes as the frost breathers, with a thin silvery veil covering her face. Adalina fell into the familiar defensive stance Callum had taught her.

"I'm not looking to fight you," she warned. "But I am taking my husband and leaving. If that means I have to go through you..."

The woman pushed back the black hood to reveal a head full of tight raven curls. Then she untied the veil, and it dropped gently to the ground. Adalina studied her warily. The woman seemed to be around her age. Her eyes were a deep honey brown and red rimmed, like she'd been crying. They glistened in the torchlight as if she might burst into tears again.

Truthfully, the woman looked terrified as she said, "M-my name is Sage... And I'm not going to stop you."

Adalina narrowed her eyes. "Why would I trust you?"

Sage remained where she was and held her arms stiffly at her sides. But there was a slight tremble in her hands. She was afraid. But she must have known Adalina didn't pose much of a threat down there. So, what had her so shaken?

With a gulp—as if working up her courage—Sage said, "My brother is up there. He was on the battlefield, but I have no idea if he's still alive."

Once again, Adalina was reminded that the frost breathers were people. That they weren't really faceless wraiths without a soul. They had family, too. People who were afraid they would never see their loved ones again.

"There were a lot of casualties," she admitted. "But there will be more if Uthred isn't stopped."

Sage shrank back on unsteady feet. "My brother is a hunter. He learned to track so he could feed our family and friends. He doesn't belong on a battlefield."

"Then why do you follow Uthred? Why fight?"

Sage's face fell with an all-consuming sort of desperation. "And be labeled a traitor by Uthred and his inner circle? They'll kill anyone who gets out of line."

It sounded all too familiar. So similar to Rothin and the way he and only a small group began causing trouble in Astarfall. Trouble that innocent frost-wielders had to pay for with their exile.

Adalina turned, placing herself in front of Callum's unconscious body as Sage finally took a step toward them.

With shaking breath, Sage asked, "Is it true that you refused to burn the men at Windshire?"

Adalina bit her lip. "I didn't want to if I could find another way. But in the end, I did burn them." She cringed at the first memory of cooked flesh. It was something that would be seared into her mind forever.

"Whispers say that you are kind."

"The whispers aren't entirely true," Adalina warned, not wanting Sage to get the wrong idea. If she needed to, she would hurt her. If there was no other way for her and Callum to get out of that room, she would kill the woman donning frost breather robes.

"If I help you and the king out of here, will you do something for me?"

Adalina's pulse jumped. With a frost breather's help, their odds of survival doubled. "If it's within my power."

Sage nodded above, eyes flitting to the ceiling. "Give them one more chance to surrender. My brother, his name is Dane. And he's a good boy who wants to keep his family alive. We all just want to survive."

Adalina's heart broke at Sage's words. She knew she shouldn't let it affect her as much as it did. The council would chide her for being soft. Even Uthred would call her a fool for entertaining the idea that his people might be willing to help her.

But something deep down fought against the doubt. "I will do my best to set everything right."

It was the heaven's honest truth. She would do everything within her power to end this. She just didn't know if Callum would trust her to do it her way. In a way they could all live with.

That seemed to be enough for Sage, though. She placed the hood back on her head and said, "If you can wake the king, I can escort you out, making it look like I'm under orders from Uthred." She slipped the veil back on, but Adalina concentrated on the face that had been revealed underneath, reminding herself that this woman was not a monster.

Turning back to Callum, Adalina dropped to her knees and shook him with fervor.

"Wake up."

Nothing.

"Callum, wake up," she begged, heart sinking a little lower each time.

Still nothing.

"Please, wake up. I can't do this without you." She slumped to the floor and stifled a cry against her hand. "I was wrong, okay? Is that what you want to hear? Damn you. I was wrong about being able to handle all of this on my own. I should have trusted you more. Should have been working *with* you instead of against you. I was so busy trying to prove myself to the council, to you... And even to myself, that I wasn't thinking clearly."

She sank into his bedside. "We've made such a mess of everything, and I need you to help me get us out of it."

A soft chuckle came from Callum in a breathy sort of way, and for a moment, she wondered if it was her imagination.

That is, until he said, "Would you mind repeating that one more time?"

Although she couldn't see his smile, she could hear it in his voice and picture the dimple that was no doubt making its appearance.

With a sniffle, she asked, "Which part? That I wasn't strong enough to handle things on my own?"

"No. Not that. Never that. You're the strongest, most capable woman I know." He sighed. "Just repeat the bit where you said you need me."

A broken laugh escaped her, and she wiped her tears away with the back of her hand. "I need you, Callum. And I would very much like for us to leave this place behind."

"Then what are we waiting for?" He groaned as he attempted to sit up on his own and she was quick to offer him assistance.

Leaning on her shoulder, the two of them stood together. He cursed under his breath, though she wasn't sure if it was for his own lack of strength at the moment, or for the men who had put him in that cot to begin with.

When he spotted the female frost breather, he tensed.

Quickly, Adalina explained, "Sage is here to help. She says that not everyone believes in Uthred."

Callum shook his head vehemently. "Absolutely not. I won't put my faith in someone like her."

He sneered in Sage's direction, forcing her to wither under his gaze.

Adalina argued, "I believe what she's told me. I think we can still get through to some of the frost breathers. Maybe not all, but if she is willing to help us, then others might follow."

The buzz of magic coming from Callum made Adalina's stomach sink. It prickled across her skin but did not manifest before them. Perhaps because of where they were? Or that he was too injured?

Her words were rushed as she insisted, "Listen to me. Our chances of getting out of here are better with her."

Sucking in a breath through his teeth, he turned to look at Adalina. His gaze was frightened and searching. Wide, open eyes bore into her, making her cling to him tighter, hoping he wouldn't let his fear control him.

His fingers wove into her hair, touching the strands as if they were a lifeline he was clinging to. Then his hand found her face. He cupped her cheek and breathed deeply, as if the touch alone might give him strength.

There was no argument in his voice, only fear, as he said, "She can't be trusted."

"You don't have to trust her. You only have to trust *me*."

The fear retreated from his eyes, and something seemed to register as he softened. He tipped his forehead until it met hers and their noses touched lightly."I do, dear wife. Lead the way."

Adalina kissed him. It was so fast and fleeting, she hardly even registered what she'd just done. A flicker of surprise crossed Callum's face, but she didn't dare give them a moment to dwell on what the kiss meant.

He seemed to sense her reluctance and grunted as he tried to take a step. He was still unsteady on his feet, but with Sage's assistance, they led him to the door. One thing that was clear was he needed a healer. The chill of the room no longer bothered Adalina. For her blood was so unbelievably heated by the memory of the frost breathers daring to put their hands on the man she loved... Her train of thought broke. The man she *loved*. He had broken her trust, and yet, she could not ignore the way her heart felt fuller in his presence.

She gritted her teeth and focused on putting one foot in front of the other. Though little by little, he seemed to be trying to prove to her that he was willing to put his trust in her, it didn't mean they could go back to the way things were. She couldn't afford the distraction of trying to figure out what sort of future she wanted with him when they weren't even certain they would survive the next hour.

They stumbled a few steps before finding a way to walk comfortably with one another. Callum, still weakened from the hit he'd taken, leaned on her and the female guard. And although it would have made their lives much easier if he found his strength again, it did make her feel good that he was ready and willing to take her helping hand.

As they walked to the door, Adalina quickly apprised him of everything she'd learned. From Uthred's plans for them, to the dragon egg. When she finished, he hummed quietly. With bated breath, she waited for his response, but none came. She decided not to press. It was a lot to take in, and she wouldn't blame him for needing the space to process it.

Snoring still filled the narrow passageway when the three of them slipped from the room. Sage stared down at the man in disgust. Adalina couldn't imagine what their life must have been like living in the wilderness for so long or scurrying below ground in the tunnels. But she sensed the tension rolling from Sage as they snuck away.

To Adalina's relief, the guard didn't stir as they crept along the wall and up to the larger clearing of the pit. Smoothly, Sage fell into step behind Adalina and Callum, taking a gentle hold of their elbows like a guard escorting prisoners.

The moment they stepped into the opening that was lit by the sun which had risen above the pit's gaping mouth, Callum pulled away from her and Sage. He turned Adalina to face him and his gaze was searching as he said, "I thought I would never look upon your sunlit face again. That, more than anything, filled me with despair."

Sage took a step back, looking down at her boots.

A blush bloomed across the bridge of Adalina's nose. Surprising, since she was sure such a thing was impossible down where death and despair dwelled. Choked up, she said, "I'm relieved to see you as well."

Callum's eyes dimmed. "I thought you would never want to see my face again."

Her gaze fell away from his, unable to hold it any longer. Anger still stirred in her chest, but part of her wanted nothing more than for him to take her in his arms. He had failed her, but there were moments when she had failed, too. At Windshire, and the king's battle...

Callum's voice was hoarse. "I can't begin to tell you how sorry I am, Lina."

"This isn't the place, nor the time. Who knows how long we have before Uthred's men find us?"

Callum nodded and spoke faster. "I just need you to know. I was an idiot. A complete and utter jackass and I intend to make it up to you. If you'll let me, I'd like to earn back your trust."

"One step at a time," she said, pulling away from him.

Sage stepped forward and took them both by the arms again. As Adalina's nerves returned, she instinctually reached for Callum's hand, and held it tight as they inched along the perimeter toward Elettra's makeshift jail cell.

"I'm sorry, too," she whispered. "I was so intent on fulfilling my grandmother's legacy that I didn't think—"

"You don't owe me an apology. All you've done since coming to Astarfall is what you felt was right." He tipped his head toward her chest and said, "You have a heart that burns brighter than any fire this world has ever seen. Your spirit and your courage are two of *many* things I love about you."

Love. It was one word. But it held more weight than any he had ever said to her before. And she wasn't sure yet what to do with it.

"Still, we've both made mistakes." It felt good to acknowledge it out loud. Like she was releasing something she'd been holding on to for too long.

"What I did was a betrayal to you and what we built. Your mistakes pale in comparison."

"I almost fell to my death," she pointed out.

"Yes," he chuckled tightly. "There was that. But those are moments you can learn from."

It was far from the time for smiles, but she couldn't stop the one tugging at her lips. "I also got us imprisoned." She nodded to the rocky passageway they were walking down.

Sage snorted behind her.

"Only after *I* got bested by that self-righteous asshole." Callum nudged Adalina playfully in the ribs and added, "We'll have better luck next time. After all, you could barely swing a punch until the fourth or fifth try. My nose is a testament to that. But eventually you figured it out. So, you lost your first negotiation—"

"By the heavens, I hope there's not a *next time*," she huffed.

There was a squeak of a laugh from Sage as she guided them to the passageway's opening.

Callum simply shrugged, and Adalina peeked at him to find a dimpled smirk. Normally that small carefree gesture in such a dire situation would have gotten under her skin. But she could see now that it was how Callum coped. It wasn't meant to offend. He was simply protecting himself. Just as he had tried to protect her with his decision to take Elettra—misguided as it was.

As they approached the path that Uthred had led her down when he took her to see Elettra, Callum lowered his voice. "Even so, I'm sorry for not giving you more credit for how far you've come since you arrived. I couldn't have possibly expected you to get any of this right the first time. And I honestly don't believe I could have done any better. Riding Elettra without you was easily the most nauseating experience of my life."

Adalina delighted at the thought of his discomfort for a moment.

Sage's voice was low as she interrupted. "Your dragon is in here. There will be guards, though. And they're not likely to believe that I brought you here as prisoners."

Adalina turned to her and placed a hand on her shoulder. "Thank you for getting us this far. You should find someplace safe to hide until it's all over."

"No way." Sage shook her head fiercely. "I said I wanted to help, and my job isn't done until the two of you are safely on that dragon's back."

With sincerity, Callum said, "Thank you, Sage. Truly."

With his fingers intertwined with Adalina's, he leapt through the opening that led to the blue lit cavern. She followed hurriedly with Sage at her other side.

Sage's voice was laced with skepticism as she leaned in and whispered to Adalina, "He's not at all what I expected from the way Uthred described him."

Apparently over hearing them, Callum boasted, "I get that a lot."

Adalina rolled her eyes. "Let's not boost his ego. He's already..." She trailed off as Elettra came into view.

Still trapped by the ropes, she appeared to be sleeping. The only thing that told Adalina that she was remotely aware of what was going on around her was the fact that a wave of barely contained anger hit her. It was as if Elettra was biding her time; drawing her guards into a false sense of calm, so that she could unleash the whole of her wrath on them when they least expected it.

Adalina buzzed with adrenaline. *Smart girl*, she thought, hoping Elettra would sense her through the bond. Because that was precisely what they were going to do.

Forty-Four

Adalina gasped as Sage shoved her and Callum into a divot in the wall. Shadows were their savior for once as they shielded them from the view of the guards. Sage crouched, drawing a chill to them all as she summoned her icy power.

Adalina, however, was too distracted by the heat of Callum's body to mind. Having him pressed against her brought about a familiar longing. Her heart ached. There was so much she wanted to say to him when they got out of this. So many questions about their life and what it would be. Even though he had apologized, he still hadn't answered her question from back at their army's camp. Would he be able to handle a lifetime of worry and fear that something might happen to them without breaking the trust between them again?

All the heartfelt things he had said since their reunion made her think that maybe there was a chance for them still. But what if something bad happened again? Would he shut her out? Lock her away because he was afraid for her? She couldn't live like a dragon with one clipped wing, only able to fly when given aid by her master.

Callum's firm voice broke through her thoughts as he said, "Stay here."

She had half a mind to ram her knee into his balls.

Sage—who had abandoned her veil once again—stood abruptly with her eyebrows raised. It looked like she wanted to steer clear of the upcoming argument.

Callum was so close to Adalina that she had to crane her neck to look him in the face. She hoped he felt the fury rolling off her in waves.

"Are you *seriously* telling me what to do right now? You're trying to leave me behind again?"

With an instant look of panic, he shook his head. "No, I wouldn't dream of it." He nodded to the gemstones embedded in the earthy walls. "I just meant, if you're going to get to Elettra, you'll need a distraction."

She raised a skeptical eyebrow. "You're volunteering?"

His hot breath tickled her neck as he leaned in close. "I've always thought myself to be a *delightful* distraction, dear wife."

"I'll go with him," Sage offered quickly. "Maybe I can make it look as if I'm here to recapture him."

In the blink of an eye, both Sage and Callum had left her. Callum skipped into the middle of the cavern with his arms spread out wide in a grand show. "Hello, gentlemen. Fancy seeing you here."

Sage shouted, acting like she'd been chasing the unruly king. "Get back here!"

The guards, struck with confusion, grappled to summon their magic, dropping Elettra's ropes in the process. But before they launched an icy attack on Callum, he tore the light from the gemstones. They flickered wildly as blue streams met his hands. The power shimmered, and he gave a hard shiver.

Adalina ran to Elettra. She was afraid of what that sort of power—magic that formed in the dark and did not come blessed by the sun—would do to him if he used it for too long.

There were roars of confusion as one of the guards fell to Sage's silvery power. It shimmered in the form of a whip, tied tightly around his neck. Which was fitting, considering what they'd been holding Elettra with.

Adalina slid to a stop at the dragon. Callum's distraction and Sage's betrayal to her own men had done the trick. With the guards focused on fending off their attack, Adalina tore the icy ropes from Elettra's body. They were so cold that they burned her hands, leaving behind angry red marks.

Elettra peeked one eye open, and relief flooded Adalina as the dragon realized it was time to go. Quieter than would have been expected, Elettra snaked behind the frost breathers' backs like a serpent preparing to strike its prey. Adalina kept in careful step with her, moving just as the dragon did. Shouts echoed outside of the chamber. More men were coming. They needed to act fast. Even with Sage on their side, and Callum having access to magic, it wouldn't matter if they were vastly outnumbered.

One set of footsteps reached the pathway's entrance first and Adalina whipped around to see a boar of a man blocking their only way out. He seemed to take inventory of the scene before him. When his attention settled on Callum, Adalina's heart leapt into her throat.

The frost breather lifted his veil and a wintery cloud formed from his lips. The same one she'd witnessed in the battle. The one that would snake along Callum's face, covering his mouth, nose, and eyes until he could no longer breathe. She shouted for him to move, but it was too late. The frost breather blew, releasing the horrific power in Callum's direction.

Sage shoved Callum to the side so hard he slammed into the ground. In the same instance, one of the guards fired a frosted arrow. It plunged into Sage's chest with a sickening crack. Adalina screamed for the woman as she fell to the ground not far from Callum. With a grunt, he rolled over and snapped his power at the attackers. Blinding blue light burst through the room, knocking the frost breather's back.

Adalina scrambled to Sage's side and tried to shake her awake. "Can you hear me?"

The woman didn't respond. She didn't move. The frost had missed her face but covered her neck and chest. Adalina reached for it. If she could heat it and the arrow, then maybe she could save her. She held Sage with one arm and pressed her other hand to the woman's icy skin, willing the dragon fire touch to come.

Callum inched close to them and placed two fingers against Sage's neck. Sorrowfully, he said, "She's gone, Lina. There's nothing you can do."

The guards were shouting again. Once recovered from the impact of Callum's blast of power, they snarled threats and curses. But Adalina couldn't move. She couldn't leave Sage. Not like this.

"She saved us," she said with a sob.

"We have to go," Callum urged breathlessly.

She clung to Sage, blood from the arrow wound soaking her and blending into the dark leather.

With a more intense sob, she argued, "We can't leave her here like this."

"We'll be back for her. I promise you, we'll give her a proper burial, but right now, we need to go."

Through the tears, Adalina whispered to the woman who had given up everything to help them, "I'll find your brother. I'll do as I promised and try to help him."

Reluctantly, she allowed Callum to pull her to her feet.

He began raging at the men again with any bit of power he could summon from the dimming gemstones. With sweat beading his brow from the exertion, he slammed it into them with every ounce of power he could muster. But there was fatigue in his eyes and his movements slowed as his body seemed to grow heavier in betrayal.

Suddenly, an intense hunger rumbled deep in Adalina's belly. She knew at once it didn't belong to her. Elettra snapped her jaws as she slinked along the shadows. Her beautiful iridescent scales did not glitter. Instead, they were sleek and deadly with their razor-sharp ends. Darkened by the shadows and her hatred for the men who had trapped her there.

With one last teary glance at Sage, Adalina said to Elettra, "If you want them, you can have them."

For the briefest moment, Adalina could have sworn the dragon *smiled* at her. A quick and terrifying movement as vicious as any she'd ever seen. The world seemed to still—rock and sediment and trickling water frozen in time. Even the sounds of fighting no longer filled her ears. Instead, all she heard was Elettra's steady heartbeat. All she could see was the dragon's daggered teeth, blindingly white like the first snowfall in winter.

And then she struck. Elettra moved like rapids in a river. Fluid and deadly. With jaws extended, the dragon fed. Each man's cry for help was cut off before it could even begin. It didn't even seem to take

Elettra any effort as she threw each one back, swallowing them like they were nothing more than roasted pigs on a spit.

Callum blanched but recovered quickly when Elettra finished with the last one. Sound returned to Adalina's ears once more and her heart raced. Shouts outside the chamber grew louder and now footsteps accompanied them. Elettra knelt low enough for Adalina and Callum to swing themselves on her back.

At a gallop, the dragon ran full force out of the cavern. Adalina closed her eyes, but it did nothing to drown out the sounds of bones being crunched beneath Elettra's feet. She trampled the frost breathers heading their way and soon the darkness was replaced with a few rays of light.

"Wait!" Adalina cried. "The egg. We need to get the egg. Uthred cannot have it. We'll never be safe."

Callum argued, "Uthred will be dealt with."

She tensed in preparation for the argument that was coming. That he or someone else would take care of the egg and the traitor.

But instead, he gave a resigned sigh and said, "Okay, let's go."

Something fluttered in the pit of her stomach. His tension made it clear that giving in was a struggle. But she was proud of the effort he was already putting forth to prove he was trying to keep his instinct to protect her from getting in their way.

Elettra danced around nervously as he slipped from her and patted her on the side, "Wait here for us. If anyone else comes, consider it an open buffet."

The dragon gave a curt nod, then settled on her haunches like a wolfhound waiting to pounce. Satisfied that Elettra could handle herself now that she was unbound by the frost breather ropes, Adalina showed Callum the way to Uthred's quarters.

Speaking low, she said, "You could have stayed with her, you know. You're the king. If anything happens to you—"

"I'm flattered to hear genuine concern coming from you, dear wife. But I assure you, we are better off doing this together."

Adalina didn't argue. It was what she'd been asking for all along. And it wasn't her place to try to push him to stay behind when that was exactly what she'd asked him not to do to her. Besides, if the last few days had shown her anything, it was that they stood a far better chance beside each other. She longed to go home and curl up in their big bed. The best shot they had at that was by grabbing the egg together and getting the hell out of Uthred's bizarre home. She knew they were running out of time. Going back for the egg might have been foolish, but she couldn't risk him keeping his hands on it.

She pressed on, trusting her instincts. Callum grew uncommonly quiet, and she knew he wanted to get up to the surface. There was no telling what was happening up there. They could only hope for the best; that the army had made it back to the palace and that they were regrouping under the council and Gwendolyn's guidance. Surely with them, her grandmother, and so many others, they could hold things down until she and Callum returned.

A skittering sound above them made her stumble into Callum. With firm hands, he grabbed her and pulled her into the side of the tunnel wall with him. Rocks hurdled down, crashing into smaller pieces on the frozen ground. Callum's hand went to her mouth, stifling a scream.

The skittering creature moved down the wall and stopped directly across from them. Adalina held her breath. Shrinking against Callum, she found that every muscle in his body had grown taut. Frozen with fear, they could do nothing but watch as the creature sniffed around. It helped calm Adalina's racing heart to realize it couldn't see them in the dark any better than they could see it.

She bit her lip as she tried to think of a way out of this one. They couldn't call for Elettra. She'd never fit down the tunnel, nor could she use her fire without harming them. And as for Callum... there was no light for him to draw from. No star or moonlight to strengthen him. Nothing but the darkness. She gritted her teeth. She still had fire running in her veins. A connection to the dragon. She'd burned hot before when she scalded the man who tried to assassinate her in her room.

It would be foolish to attempt now. Even if she was sure it would work, it would mean getting close enough to whatever it was that was attempting to hunt them. It gave a low whine and then something clacked together like teeth snapping softly. Or nails tapping on rock. Adalina couldn't tell. And if she had to spend one more moment guessing, she would go mad.

Craning her neck to whisper into Callum's ear, she said, "I need you to trust me."

His fingers grazed along her arms, sending goosebumps up and down them. Then, in answer, he dropped his hold on her, releasing her to do what she needed to.

Again, she whispered, more urgently this time, "Run."

Callum hesitated, but ultimately did as she said. His feet clattered against the ground, sending an echo through the tunnel. The beast chattered again and took off behind him. Adalina raced after them. Her legs burned as she forced herself to catch up to the monster.

The light nearly blinded her as they came to the mouth of the tunnel. Callum halted just as he reached Elettra, nearly slamming into her. The skittering creature was visible now, too. Its skeletal frame wasn't as large as its brother, whom she'd seen on the battlefield mere hours before. It moved like a newborn colt, unsteady but eager.

But one look at Elettra and it backtracked, moving into the tunnel once more. Elettra growled. A flash of Callum's magic narrowly missed the beast. Desperate to take cover, the frostbitten dragon nearly crashed into Adalina.

A scream tore from her throat as she shoved it away defensively. But the frostbitten dragon was stronger than it looked. It pummeled her and her head slammed against the ground. The headache was immediate, splitting her thoughts. But one thing that did not falter was the fire building in her chest. She welcomed it like an old friend as it spread down her arms to her fingertips. She inhaled deeply and did not fight it. She didn't even try to fight the undead dragon. Instead, she closed her eyes as it snapped at her face.

Then, focusing only on the blazing heat, she called on her connection to Elettra. She grabbed the beast by the neck, drawing him close to her. He continued to snap but couldn't get a good shot at her. *Burn*, was all she thought. Callum's shouts became urgent as he hurdled her way. She couldn't let him get hurt. So, a second time, and with more fury. *Burn*. Then out loud she screamed, "Burn!"

The beast screeched, and steam rose from its neck where she was holding it. Power granted through the dragon bond sizzled and popped against the icy creature's skin. Its wail was ear piercing, but Adalina didn't stop until the cries died out completely; until she was sure the frost dragon was no more.

She remained where she was for a moment. The heat died down in her hands and the chill from the pit returned. Shock radiated through her. The frost dragon had collapsed at her feet, but she didn't dare move. The realization of what she'd just done sank in and as Callum reached for her, she flinched away. Too afraid of hurting him, she stepped aside. Seeming to understand her reluctance, he simply walked beside her until they reached the pit's opening.

Concern clouded his beautiful eyes as he asked, "Are you okay with riding?"

She sidestepped bodies on her way to Elettra. The remaining frost breathers who had come for them were nothing more than melted flesh and charred bone now. Elettra's handiwork, no doubt.

Adalina only nodded before mounting.

Seemingly unworried about what he'd just witnessed, Callum slipped confidently behind her and rested his hands gently on her hips. As Elettra's wings beat excitedly, lifting them off the frozen ground to take them far away from the depths of Uthred's manmade hellscape, Callum leaned in and whispered, "Let's go home."

She leaned back, resting her head on his chest, practically melding into the contours of his body. As wonderful as it was to see green grass and feel the sun on her face, she couldn't help but feel that there, in Callum's arms, she already *was* home.

Forty-Five

The symphony of war drums was head splitting. As the palace came into view, Adalina expected a rush of relief, but instead she was met with utter dread. The frost breathers—though far fewer in numbers after the recent battles—pounded at the city gates.

Callum's grip on her tightened as she leaned too far forward to try to get a glimpse below for any sign of Uthred. Surely, he wouldn't have brought the egg to a palace scourge, but if they could get their hands on him, then they could go back for the hatchling later. To her dismay, there was no sign of the wretched man below.

Elettra kept to the clouds, well out of the frost breathers' reach. Snowflakes settled into Adalina's hair, and she shivered. When they passed the archers on the city walls, there were hoots and hollers. As they soared over the streets, the people of Astarfall cried out and rejoiced with one another. Callum's fingers tightened on her thighs, and she smiled to herself.

"They're happy to see you, Your Majesty," she said hoping to lighten the dread she knew they were both feeling.

"They're happy to see *us*, Your Grace." He forced a chuckle.

The palace looked grander than Adalina ever dreamed as Elettra circled it and prepared to land in the courtyard. Courtiers gathered around. Their frightened faces turned to bright smiles as they realized who had come home at last.

Callum helped Adalina down. Her wrist and leg ached, and she looked forward to getting a chance to ask for some clean dressings for her injuries. The last thing she needed was an infection.

A warm breeze danced around them. It was as if the sea itself was embracing her and she reveled in it. One night beneath the cold, dreary ground was enough for her liking. She never again wanted to feel that sort of frost nip at her skin.

Seraphine was the first to greet them.

Alfie lingered close and clapped Callum on the back as he said, "You gave us one hell of a scare."

Laughter sparkled in Callum's eyes. "You want a scare? Remind me to show you what those bastards have dug right under our noses when this is all over."

He gave an exaggerated shiver, which earned laughs from everyone but Adalina. Part of her knew he wasn't wholly pretending. That he, too, would dream of the bitter cold and suffocating darkness for years to come.

Her grandmother was the next one to take hold of her and that was when the tears began to fall. It was like opening a damn as she buried her face in her grandmother's hair and let all the anguish out. Every ounce of fear she would have felt if she'd had the time for it while she was under Uthred's imprisonment released with that embrace. And the grief of losing Sage—a woman who gave her life protecting a king and queen she barely knew. Adalina was glad to have held it together for as long as she had. It was something she didn't know she was capable of doing.

A hush fell over the joyous reunion when the councilmen arrived. They bowed and greeted both the king and queen. Heely was there with them. He stood front and center. Something was different about him. There was a firmness in the way he held himself and showed no emotion. To her surprise, it made her a little sad to not see his familiar, easy smiles. This war was costing them all.

Callum raised his chin as he stepped to Adalina's side. He placed an arm around her waist and said, "Tell us what we've missed."

Heely spoke quietly. "We thought you were both dead."

With a shrug, Callum replied, "Well, we're not. We're here and we want to know what's going on. What are we doing to fortify the defenses? How are our supplies in the city if we are to hold them off for some time?"

Adalina's mother-in-law stepped forward and gave them both a soft smile before speaking. "Every able-bodied man and woman have formed a perimeter within the city walls. In the event of a breach, they will be the first line of defense. And as for supplies, thank the fates that Astarfall has always enjoyed an abundance. We will be fine, should the siege take longer than we anticipate."

Callum scratched the back of his neck uncomfortably. "We had a run in with another one of Uthred's frostbitten dragons. There may be more coming. Our men need to know."

Gwendolyn's face blanched and everyone fell into horrified silence. None of the frost biters had followed them, and Adalina was determined to take that as a good sign. Maybe Uthred hadn't had the time to reanimate any more of them. Or maybe he was finished with all of that now that Elettra had breathed life into the dragon egg.

Her gaze fell on the archers standing on the battlements. They were working tirelessly to hold off the frost breathers below the wall. Adalina knew firsthand how skilled the Astarfallen were with a bow and arrow thanks to their ability to manipulate the wind and aim true. Worry gnawed at her for all the lives hanging in the balance. Was Sage's brother, Dane, down there? What about the others who fought only to avoid Uthred's wrath?

Adalina made a promise to Sage and now, more than ever, she owed it to the woman to keep it.

"Tell the archers to stand down while Callum and I take Elettra up," she interrupted, drawing wide-eyed stares. "We will give them one last chance for surrender. Should they refuse, then it will be an easy feat if Elettra's fire takes the enemy out before they can damage the gate."

Several of the councilmen exchanged appalled looks. By now, she would have thought they'd have gotten used to her butting her nose where they believed it didn't belong. But this was war. It was more serious than anything they had faced in centuries. And she supposed they weren't ready to take orders from a woman yet. Or perhaps they just weren't prepared to believe her offer to burn men alive in one fell swoop.

Seraphine's eyes brightened. "I say it's a damn good plan, *Queen* Adalina." She shot a pointed look at the men as she spoke the title.

Callum clapped his hands together, making several people in the crowd jump. "You heard her. Send word to the archers."

A royal messenger skidded in the dirt as he ran toward the battlements. Adalina mounted Elettra and cringed in pain from her unhealed wounds. Callum's eyes clouded with worry, and he frowned but said nothing.

She reached a hand down to pull him up, but he shook his head in refusal. With a half smile, he said, "You go."

"You're not coming with me?" She furrowed her brow. Going alone wasn't a problem, but she hadn't expected him to be the one to suggest it.

"I've seen what you can do on this beast." He patted Elettra affectionately when she grumbled in response to the term he'd used. "I'm going to join them on the battlements and see if I can't spot Uthred from there."

Seraphine tapped Callum on the shoulder. "If you're not going to use the extra seat, think maybe I could?"

Adalina smirked at her. "You feel like riding?"

Seraphine gave her a dazzling smile in return. "It's a nice day for it, don't you think?"

Adalina grinned and helped her friend onto the dragon's back. Seraphine was practically buzzing with excitement. "I've always wanted to feel the wind up there."

Elettra bounded from the ground and into the air at a jarring speed. They whipped around until they faced the small army of rogue men. The sight of the dragon gave them pause. It was their one chance to make them listen.

Callum's voice boomed from the battlement, "Surrender. Lay down your arms and you will have a fair trial."

With Elettra hovering low enough for them to hear Adalina's words, she warned, "Refuse, and you will burn!"

A blue haze crackled between the enemy ranks—evidence of the magic they were holding back as they listened. Still, there was no sign of Uthred. Many of the men didn't even bother to be masked any more.

Now that the games were over and the real fight had begun, there was no reason for anonymity.

Some of the men huddled together with their heads down. The frost breathers who were left out of the discussion fidgeted nervously. Were they hoping their leaders would do right by them? Did they want to give up and go home to their loved ones?

It felt like a lifetime as she waited for their answer. When they drew away from each other, she sucked in a sharp breath. Giving them this chance fulfilled her promise to Sage. She didn't want to take their lives. But if she had to choose between them and the safety of Astarfall and Solaris, then she would have no other option.

Rather than answer her with words, the men signaled to those around them. One by one, each man knelt to the ground, hands raised high above their heads. Some trembled. Others had their fists clenched. It might not have been a majority decision, but it had been made, nonetheless. And Adalina intended to honor her word.

Callum walked along the parapet and caught her eye. Opening the gates was an enormous risk. But how else would they arrest the men? They couldn't just let them walk away without knowing for sure that they were going to give up on their revenge.

He gave her a confident, encouraging smile and nodded his head. They were in this together. And together they were making the decision.

He shouted to the Astarfallen who were standing by the gates inside of the city, "Bind them quickly. If any show resistance, kill them."

He once again nodded to Adalina, giving her the encouragement she needed to command, "Open the gates. Arrest the men and take them to the council and my husband for judgment."

The gates creaked loudly as they opened. Astarfall soldiers marched out to take the frost breathers and she inhaled fully for the first time in what seemed like forever. Generals barked commands as the soldiers approached the kneeling men.

Seraphine tensed behind her. "Something is off. The winds have changed."

A jolt of adrenaline coursed through Adalina. Fire rumbled in Elettra's belly, but it was too late to fire on the men. Astarfallen soldiers wove around the frost breathers. If Elettra attempted to burn them, then the Astarfallen would be caught in the crossfire.

Before any of the frost breathers could be bound, they jumped Callum's men. Clouds of frost were released on them. Cries of combat filled the air and Elettra roared. Instant regret and fury overtook Adalina. Fire flared in her veins, begging for release. Those bastards had taken their mercy and thrown it back in their faces. Because of her promise to Sage, the city was going to fall.

Forty-Six

Devastation rocked Adalina as men poured from the gates in defense of the city. The frost breathers pushed against them, forcing their way in, and scurrying through the gates like rats. The army did their best to hold them off, but even one frost breather within the city walls was too many.

Callum shouted from the battlements, "Close the gate!"

The gate creaked in resistance. One of the frost breathers was coating the hinges with ice, hindering it. Adalina's first instinct was to have Elettra melt it, but what sort of damage would the fire do to the gate's integrity? She couldn't risk it.

Instead, she commanded, "Stop that man!"

She hissed through her teeth and a crackling erupted from Elettra's throat as she released a fiery shot at him. Flames licked up his robes, engulfing him until there was nothing left.

The ice on the gate melted simultaneously with the frost breather's death, but too many of his people had already gotten through. Adalina cursed under her breath and searched for Callum. Try as she might, she couldn't find him anywhere in the chaos. Not on the battlements where he'd stood before and not on the ground with his army.

"We need to get down there and help them," she insisted, as memories of the little girl she had protected in the tavern swirled in her mind's eye. There were countless innocents there. People who—despite their power—did not know how to defend themselves.

Astarfall had known only peace for many generations. They had refused to engage the last time the frost breathers tried their hand at power. But now there was no ignoring the threat; for it was knocking at their front door.

Seraphine pointed to the Dew Drop Inn. "There's an opening there on the street for Elettra to land. Alfie's there searching the streets for anyone who can't fight."

Elettra didn't need any instruction. She swooped back to the city, dropping Adalina and Seraphine on the cobblestone street. They were far enough from the gate that no frost breathers had reached them yet. Citizens hurried around seeking shelter or running to the gate to do what they could to stop the invasion.

Seraphine ran off. It was like the wind carried her. But Adalina turned to the dragon. "Elettra, can you go back up? Watch for an opening. Any clear shot you get, take it."

Elettra snarled, revealing her razor-sharp teeth. If she couldn't use fire, she would use other means to stop the bastards. Adalina hugged her tightly and ran a loving hand over the dragon's smooth scales. They were like stones in a riverbed. It reminded her of home. And of everything they were fighting for.

Wordlessly, Adalina turned and headed toward the Dew Drop. It was well within the heart of the city and away from the bulk of the fighting. When she reached the front of the inn, she found Seraphine and Alfie ushering stragglers inside. Nerves twisted in the pit of her stomach as she searched fruitlessly for Callum.

"Where is he?" she asked breathlessly.

"He wasn't on the battlements?" Alfie's face paled with fear as he held the hand of an elderly woman trying to take the stairs carefully.

Seraphine calmly said, "I don't imagine he'd have strayed far from the gate."

The end of the street erupted. Rocks flung in every direction and sent a cloud of dust up in the air. When it cleared, an Astarfallen woman—an earth-wielder judging by the wreckage—raised her chin proudly. Beneath several large boulders were four frost breathers.

Seraphine spoke low. "We're winning, Adalina. Their numbers are too few and they're no match for the people in this city when we work together."

Alfie was steering more frightened citizens into the Dew Drop Inn with his bright hair matted with sweat and a determined glint in his eye. He shouted to Seraphine, "Help her find Callum! I'll handle things here."

"Are you sure?" Seraphine bit her lip with worry.

Adalina assured her, "I can find him on my own."

Alfie interjected. "It's safer if the two of you go together."

Elettra's wings continuously bobbed in and out of view and Adalina knew the frost breathers were being held off in large part to her. But it was the screaming that dug into her like a thousand tiny needles. Each cry could belong to a friend, a neighbor, or even Callum. Rather than allow her mind to go to the dark place, she focused on Seraphine's steady presence beside her. It wasn't just her and Callum who were stronger together. It was all of them.

With the threat of tears stinging her eyes, she gestured for Seraphine to follow, and they headed for the gate. If her husband wasn't on the battlements, then she would take to the streets. The crowds were growing, congesting the main roads, so they veered into an alley Seraphine claimed would lead back out to the gate. It was as quiet as a tomb, and it sent an unsteady shiver up Adalina's spine.

Before they could reach the end of it, soft approaching footsteps caught their attention. Adalina stopped in her tracks, fearing a frost breather might be rounding the corner, and gasped when she saw Erabelle. Uthred's beautifully polished wife was nearly unrecognizable. Her hair was matted and dirty. caked to her face with a coat of sweat. Her eyes were bright, though. Alert and ready for a fight.

Seraphine turned, pressing her back against Adalina's as if to keep watch on the other end of the alley. Erabelle halted and Adalina glanced down at the bags in her hands. A knitted blanket with bows stuck out of one.

Gently, as if speaking to a frightened doe in the forest, Adalina asked, "What are you doing here?"

Her gaze followed Erabelle's hand which went to her belly. The last time Adalina had seen her, they'd been dressed in fine gowns for the dinner at Windshire. There had been plenty of layers to hide Erabelle's secret. But there was no hiding it now. Adalina couldn't take her eyes off the swell showing in the silk dress. Her own stomach churned at the realization. Uthred's wife was carrying his heir.

Uthred would not be the last of his line. Another generation would be born into a world of hate, nurtured by vengeance. The child's very existence would be a danger to all of Astarfall if Uthred had his way. But the babe was innocent. And the innocent shouldn't be punished for the sins of their forbearers. Allowing their enemy's wife to flee was a great risk. But if Erabelle fought back, the unborn baby could be hurt.

The woman tilted her chin defiantly. "There was something I needed to get." She clutched a velvet bag to her stomach and her knuckles were white from the grip she had on it.

"What's in the bag?" Adalina asked cautiously.

"Nothing that belongs to you," Erabelle spat.

Seraphine, turned and leaned in to whisper, "I can kill her."

"No," Adalina whispered back in a panic. "She's pregnant."

Seraphine sucked in a sharp breath.

Erabelle was watching them with darting eyes, as if trying to calculate a way to get past them.

Adalina asked her, "What now? You'll slip away through your tunnels and hope that your husband will return for you?"

After witnessing the vast tunnel system in the pit, she wouldn't be surprised if there were entrances scattered all throughout the city. It would explain how the assassin had gotten into the palace on her wedding night. And how Uthred got in and out of the city without being missed.

When Erabelle didn't answer, Adalina implored, "Where is he? I can promise you mercy if you'll just—"

"Betray him?" She hissed, "You little bitch. How dare you come into *my* home and threaten me?"

Adalina raised her nose in the air. "If you cared so much about your home, then you wouldn't have sent men to destroy it. Listen closely. Do you hear what's happening out there?" She pointed to the main streets. "Or perhaps you'd like to see it with your own eyes?" With a pause, she shook her head ruefully. "Judging by the looks of those bags in your hands, you don't want to hear or see any of it. You're just going to run away and hope that your husband's men prevail. Isn't that right? Let them do all the dirty work so you can come back to reap the rewards later."

Erabelle simply glared at her.

"Think of your child. What if the council doesn't agree to put Uthred on the throne? You need to do what's best for that baby. To keep him or her safe."

Erabelle hissed like the snake that she was as she said, "You have no idea the things I've done to ensure that my child is safe. To make certain that he inherits *everything* he deserves and more."

"A throne bathed in blood," Adalina countered. "*That* is what he will inherit if your husband doesn't stop. The people of Astarfall will never trust him, especially not now. They will never accept you or your son. Fear is not a weapon to wield.'

"That is where you're wrong. When they see how much power we hold, and when the unhatched dragon is born, they will fall to their knees in the face of its glory. They will see how wrong they've been about my husband and the power he and his men possess."

Erabelle inched around, sticking to the buildings.

Seraphine tensed, but Adalina was determined to make the mother-to-be see sense. "What if we found a way to allow people with your husband's abilities back into Astarfall? Callum's not a cruel man. We can help him see the reason in it."

Erabelle stopped and barked with laughter. "Was stealing what was rightfully yours and locking you up not cruel? Face it. He's just like the others. If you came out of today as the victor, you would go back to living a meaningless existence of tea parties and balls. Never for a moment did he really intend to let you help him rule. You're nothing more than a pretty doll with a dragon for an accessory."

An intense buzzing swept across Adalina's arms. The heat spread, and it was as if Erabelle's words had put a match to her. Like she was a tinder just waiting for the right spark to catch. But she doused it quickly, reminding herself that despite his betrayal when he took Elettra, he hadn't pursued her when she took the dragon back.

Instead, he stood by and watched her fly ahead to the frost breather camp. He'd trusted her on the battlefield regardless of his instinct to protect her at all costs. They'd both made mistakes, but what mattered most was what they did to keep from making those same mistakes again.

Rather than let Erabelle use Callum against her, Adalina shook her head and snapped back. "You're no better. You think Uthred will treat you any differently as his queen? From what I've seen, the only benefit you pose to him are your looks and charms."

Erabelle balled her hands into fists and took a fierce step toward her and Seraphine.

Adalina stood her ground. "I saw you at the Winter Solstice ball. I know exactly what you are. But what happens when your beauty fades? You've already given him an heir... if it's a boy, then you'll have fulfilled that usefulness. Then what?"

Erabelle narrowed her eyes and took another bold step. "I should have slit your throat myself. I told my husband not to send one of his men into your room that night. Assured him that I would be better suited for the job. Men are always so eager to prove their strength. They don't take the time that's needed for such an art."

"Killing is an art to you, is it?" Adalina glanced down sadly at the woman's rounded belly. "I suppose that is what you intend to teach your child?"

With unadulterated hatred, Erabelle snapped, "I will teach him to take what is rightfully his, damned the cost."

"Then you will damn his soul." Adalina dug her nails into the palms of her hands. More than anything, she wished to wipe the sneer off the awful woman's face, but she resisted. No matter the child's parentage, they did not deserve any ill will to befall them.

Erabelle must have noticed Adalina's hesitation. She dropped her bags, lunging across the gap between them. The wind was knocked from her as she fell under the woman's weight. Nails met flesh as Erabelle tore into her in a fury. Adalina shielded her face with her arms, but it didn't do much good.

Seraphine's winds picked up, but Adalina wheezed, "No!"

She'd seen how powerful Seraphine was and she didn't want Erabelle gravely injured.

Adalina gasped for air, unable to breathe beneath the crazed woman. No matter how much she attempted to push her off, Erabelle would not relent. When Seraphine grabbed the woman by the shoulders, trying to pull her off Adalina, the ground shifted under them.

Seraphine was thrown back into the wall of one of the shops. Rocks began pelting Adalina, aiming for her face. She'd never witnessed Erabelle's magic, but it was clear now that she was an earth-wielder.

The only thing for Adalina to do was defend herself. But to do so without hurting the baby was difficult. The hesitation cost her dearly as Erabelle straddled her and took hold of her throat. The alley became an array of white spots, like stars twinkling in the night sky. It reminded her of Callum's eyes when he was truly happy. Not the moments where he was being the great pretender to make everyone else feel at ease, but the ones where he was utterly and completely content.

The memories of their time as husband and wife and of the night they'd been together at the Dew Drop Inn danced in her mind. It brought a sense of happiness, wrapping around her like a heavy wool blanket on a cold winter's night in Solaris.

Erabelle screeched loudly and released the hold on her throat. It burned as Adalina gasped, filling her lungs with air once more. When she sat up, Erabelle had already scrambled away with hands so red, it took a second to realize it was from a burn and not blood.

Erabelle opened and closed her mouth as if grappling for what to say. Tears streaked down her cheeks, but Adalina suspected it was from the pain and not because she felt sorry for trying to kill her.

Adalina got to her feet and thought about grabbing the woman. She could stop her from running. Lock her up in the dungeons and allow the council to deal with her. But the idea of a baby being born in such a dank, dark place... of feeling the shame as they were raised in a community that their own parents had tried to destroy, gave Adalina pause.

There was only one option. She could let Erabelle go and pray that she never showed her face in Astarfall again. Through clenched teeth, Adalina commanded, "Run. Do not return. Do not go looking for your husband. I swear to you I will not show him the same mercy. He is ours. But you are free. Think of your child and take them far away from here. This is no longer your home."

Seraphine warned, "That's a dangerous risk to take."

Adalina ignored her, waiting for Erabelle's answer.

The woman's jaw ticked. For a moment, Adalina thought she might challenge her again. But instead, she took the bags with a pained groan and ran. Adalina watched until she was gone. Then, with a frustrated curse, she too, left the solitary alley.

Erabelle had used up all the good faith Adalina had. She would not extend the same courtesy to the next frost breather she came across. And she most certainly had no compassion to extend toward Uthred. For him, she had something special planned.

Forty-Seven

There was still no sign of Callum when Adalina and Seraphine arrived at the city's gate. The Astarfallen were holding the frost breathers off with a ferocity that made her proud. Callum's men seemed to have fallen into a comfortable dance with Elettra. They drew frost breathers away from the group to give the dragon a clear shot of them. Small balls of fire rained down, taking out the frost breathers one by one.

Adalina could stay there and fight, but she had no weapon. And the use of dragon magic at her own hands was too unreliable. The uncertainty of what to do next was overwhelming, so she let her instincts take over.

She reached for her connection to Elettra and summoned the enhanced senses. This time, using the dragon abilities was like slamming into a brick wall. One that was putrid with the scent of sweat, blood, and death. The burning corpses from Elettra's attacks nearly knocked her off her feet. But she pushed past it, trying to find Callum. She thought back to their moments together. And of the fresh, inviting scent of him.

When that didn't work, she strained her ears, hoping to hear his gruff, familiar voice.

Seraphine's power lashed out at a frost breather headed their way. Wind blew him off his course before he could reach them.

With a sneer, Seraphine said, "The next man who approaches us is getting flung out to sea."

Despite their precarious position, Adalina smiled gratefully at her friend's ferocity.

Suddenly, lean, confident shoulders, and a wild grin, caught her eye. Only Callum could summon a dimpled smile in the middle of a fight. There were bruises forming on his face, but other than that, he appeared unharmed.

Longing stirred within her, and she wanted to run to him, but was stopped when Elettra screeched from up above. She was circling a clearing beside the gate where a community garden had once been. There were too many men in the way as they fought, and Adalina couldn't get a clear line of sight at what Elettra had found.

The dragon screeched again, this time with steam streaming from her nose and mouth. There was something—or someone—there that she wanted to burn. As she snapped her teeth, Adalina's adrenaline spiked. Her vision sharpened, and she gasped as her eyes became unfocused.

Callum's worried voice rang in her ears. "Lina, Seraphine, are you two alright?"

Adalina couldn't focus on anything but the sharpening vision.

Seraphine answered for them, "We're fine. We were searching for you but then... I don't know what's happening to her."

Worry was laced in Seraphine's words, but Callum was as calm as ever as he said, "Elettra. She's sharing something with her."

Adalina saw through the dragon's eyes as if she was flying above the gardens with her. It was obvious now what had Elettra ready to pounce, and the thing that was holding her back. Uthred had an icy blue dagger pressed against Gwendolyn's throat.

Adalina blinked and her vision returned to normal. Callum was staring intently at her with worry creasing his forehead. Nervously, he asked, "What is it?"

She buzzed with urgency. "It's your mother. Uthred has her."

The gust of wind Seraphine summoned was one for the history books. Adalina couldn't imagine the amount of power it took to throw hordes of men out of the way with a simple flick of the wrist. Pushing past the awe she felt toward her friend, she ran for the community garden. It was trampled now, with bodies littered all around it.

Elettra calmed at the sight of Adalina and the others. They halted a few feet away from where her grandparents were trying to persuade Uthred to release the Queen Mother. Callum breathed erratically. Fury radiated from him like heat when a dragon's belly filled with fire.

Uthred's gaze bounced to each of them, but finally settled on Adalina. With malice he said, "You think you've won, but you haven't."

The grip he had on Gwendolyn tightened and a trickle of blood dripped down her throat where the dagger pressed into it. Callum balled his fists and took a step forward, but Uthred clucked his tongue at him in warning.

Adalina gritted her teeth. There was a chill in the air. It reminded her of the pit and the frosty dragon's breath as it attacked them. She shivered as she said, "Your men will lose today."

Pained cries of death echoed off the stone walls surrounding the city. She gestured to the frost breathers slain behind her at the garden's edge.

"It's over. Let the Queen Mother go, and we can be finished with it all. Aren't you tired of this, Uthred?"

"Tired?" he snarled. "For half a century, my people have done nothing but work toward this one thing."

Callum's lip curled in disgust. "Revenge is not the path to happiness. The people of Astarfall were never going to accept you on the throne."

"They won't have had a choice," Uthred countered.

Callum's face smoothed as his indifferent facade took over. "Then let's just end this, shall we? You want your revenge? You want to rip the Astarfall King from his throne? Go ahead." His grin was wicked as he shrugged his jacket off.

A handful of frost breathers who had strayed from the bulk of the fighting inched closer. Seraphine lifted her hands in their direction in a clear warning not to come any further.

Surprise flashed across Uthred's face, and he loosened his grip on Gwendolyn. He shoved her aside and began to circle the garden. He and Callum faced each other like wild beasts. Each with hunger in their eyes and determination in the sets of their mouths.

Adalina didn't want this. She couldn't stand by while her husband engaged in a battle to the death. She moved forward, but her grandfather caught her arm. With a curt shake of his head, she settled beside him.

It was her turn to trust that Callum could handle himself.

The sounds of battle lessened, coming to an eerie hush as Elettra landed with a powerful thud. The frost breathers flinched away from her and didn't dare step in to stop the two leaders from the standoff that was about to happen.

Uthred made the first move. It was sloppy and showed his arrogance as he lashed out with shards of ice. Callum dodged them with grace and closed the gap between them, striking Uthred in the jaw. Stunned, he stumbled back and then dove for Callum's waist.

They hit the ground with pained grunts, drawing more attention from outliers in the fight by the gate. Adalina tensed as blows were thrown between the two men. It was hard to keep track of who was landing them and who was receiving the brunt of it.

Callum rolled away, allowing him the distance to get back to his feet. Uthred followed suit, and the two began the dance once again. There was a grunt as Callum took a hit to his brow. Blood dripped into his eye and Adalina feared it would hinder his ability to see Uthred's next punch coming.

But Callum side stepped him, backhanding Uthred in the mouth like he was nothing more than a nuisance. Uthred tried again to summon his frosty power, but Callum was faster. The remaining sunlight answered his call. With expertise, he guided it into Uthred's eyes. The traitor screamed in frustration as it blinded him long enough for Callum to land another blow. This time in his stomach.

Uthred doubled over, but when he looked back up, there was still a glimmer of determination in his eyes. "My legacy does not end here," he spat, and blood trickled from his mouth. "One year, ten, even fifty years from now, you will see. When the Old King expelled my kind, he sealed the fate of Astarfall and the rest of the living world. We will rise again."

Uthred's men made no sound of agreement. Instead, it seemed like there was a deep sense of dread spreading through the crowd that had gathered. They were tired—frost breathers and Astarfallen alike. It appeared the armies were placing their fates solely in their leaders' hands. The outcome of this would determine the victor of the war.

With pursed lips, Uthred summoned the dangerous frost his people were so well known for. The one that breathed death upon its victims. Panicked, Adalina leapt to Callum's side. Uthred had done a number on his face, which was so bruised it was becoming nearly unrecognizable. Her fury burned so hot that she could barely focus on Uthred as he braced to release the lethal frost breather ability.

With a roar, she pounced on him. She and Uthred landed on the ground. It was like she'd forgotten every single thing Callum taught her in the training arena. Instead, she acted on pure rage and instinct. Uthred yelped when she took hold of his wrist. She rolled, wrapping her legs around his arm, and pulled until she heard a pop. Heavy footsteps approached and she jerked away to find Elettra. The dragon paced back and forth, watching them intently and snapping with drool dripping from her lips.

Pain lanced through Adalina's head as Uthred struck her. But all it did was make her more furious. Channeling all her rage, she allowed the heat to flow to her hands, turning them into something akin to branding irons. She ignored the rocks that tore at her legs through her ripped pants and Uthred's attempts to strike her again.

When she reached him, she latched onto his face. She thought of the helplessness she'd felt at being attacked again and again. The frustration of not being respected by the council. And the regret for letting her fears stop her from admitting her feelings for Callum. She gathered those emotions and let them turn into a bonfire. Each feeling was thrown into it like kindling, making it rise higher and higher.

Uthred's muffled screams made it feel like she wasn't connected to the world around her. Like she wasn't in her body, but instead, was watching from above. Skin crackled under her touch and there was a popping noise as the blood bubbled in his veins. Soon there was no more struggling from the man. He went limp in her hands and as she let go, his head dropped to the ground with a thud.

The world came back into focus like a tidal wave. It was so overwhelming that she fell to the ground and tried to catch her breath. Callum was beside her within seconds. He smoothed down her hair and spoke so gently she couldn't comprehend the words.

It didn't matter, though. Drained of energy, she rested her head on his lap and let him brush the tangled hair from her shoulders. The shouts of the Astarfallen were ones of triumph. Adalina struggled to find the ability to stand again. She'd killed a man with her bare hands. And although she knew she had done the right thing, she never wanted to experience that sort of thing again. Nor did she ever want to allow her rage to consume her until she lost herself.

Sitting up slowly and trying to quell the nausea burning in her stomach, she turned to face Callum. Blood, sweat, and dirt coated his beautiful face, and despite Uthred's death, he frowned.

"It's not over yet, dear wife. Can you stand?"

She nodded and allowed him to help her up. Elettra was still blocking the path of the remaining frost breathers. There were far fewer than she expected to see. Their ranks had been relentlessly thinned out by the Astarfallen army and citizens who rose to the fight.

The mere mention of frost breathers had once haunted her. They had seemed like an unstoppable force. Their veiled faces made it hard to remember they were even human. But she'd just killed their leader. Had shown them that even the grandson of the great Rothin could be slain. She held tight to Callum with bated breath and prayed to the fates that the rebels would accept this as their end.

Forty-Eight

Elettra stood as still as a statue, poised and ready to snap at any frost breather who might have a little fight left in them. Seraphine nudged Adalina and pointed to three men who had their heads bowed as they took a step toward the dragon. Their black cloaks were worn and tattered. Blood streaked their faces, which were free of the veiled masks they used to hide their identities.

Wind whipped wildly around them, and she caught sight of Seraphine's hands. Her fingers made elegant circles in the air, keeping the men from moving any closer. Callum's firm hand found the small of Adalina's back, filling her with the strength to face what might come next.

"Let them pass," he commanded.

Elettra refrained from snapping at them, and Seraphine's winds slowed to a steady breeze.

The youngest, who looked more like a boy than a man, and had a ghastly wound on his cheek, folded his hands. There was a look of resignation on his face. The two beside him followed suit and together they knelt in front of Adalina and Callum.

As she stepped forward, she realized that all three of the men were young. They were practically boys, with plump cheeks and a smooth youthfulness around their eyes.

The youngest spoke. "We surrender to your mercy, King Callum and Queen Adalina."

"You've surrendered once. Look where that got us." She gestured to the gates where the injured were groaning and crying in pain.

The crowd of Astarfallen fell into a fit of rage.

One shouted, "Burn them all!"

Another agreed. "They don't deserve any more chances."

Dread consumed her. The people of Astarfall—the ones who had welcomed her there, whose smiles so often came easily and freely—were calling for blood. She couldn't blame them. Looking around at the wreckage and lives lost, her stomach sank deeper. But amongst their own people were the frost breathers. Their hoods and masks had slipped from their heads and faces, revealing the living souls underneath.

In front of her, the boys' eyes welled with tears and panic. They were just as afraid as her own people were. Except, if Sage's words rang true, then these boys had been *raised* in fear. While the Astarfallen were going about their lives, enjoying the safety and prosperity of their kingdom, the young frost breathers were being terrorized by Uthred and those closest to him—his inner circle, as Sage had called it.

Callum caressed her back, and it lent a bit of courage to her. Her words came out quieter than she intended as she said, "Please, every-one, let them speak."

Angry murmurs spread through the crowd. She needed to make them see past their fear. But how?

The boy shook his head sadly. "We only ever wanted to keep our families safe."

Other frost breathers who were nearest to them tipped their heads in agreement. Adalina felt the weight of their stares. Callum shifted uncomfortably, but still held onto her. Perhaps he was trying to draw strength from her just as she was from him.

With a gulp, she asked, "At what cost? You've caused nothing but destruction."

Even if she wanted to help them, she needed her own people to see that the boys and the others willing to surrender understood the severity of what they'd done. That it would not be so easy for the Astarfallen to forget, even if they could forgive.

Tears streamed down the boy's face. "We have known nothing else. My sisters and I were raised in the western wilderness. All we ever heard was how unfairly the royal family treated their subjects. How they wanted us dead because we were different... *useless* to them and the land."

He reminded her so much of Sage with his large, earnest eyes. It sent a pang of guilt digging into her chest. She didn't know what to say. She was a newcomer to Astarfall. The Old King, Alistair's father, had expelled them before she was born. It would be ridiculous for her to pretend that she understood what it was like to be cast out of her home. Especially when she had *two* homes of her own. Born and raised with love in Solaris and accepted into Astarfall despite being an outsider.

What she did understand was the pain of having power that didn't quite meet expectations. It had taken marriage to a stranger to get her magic to work. Up until that moment, it had been useless. *She* had felt useless. She supposed in a way, these young men felt the same after being shunned for a power they had not chosen and told that they weren't good enough if they couldn't benefit society.

Trying to hold her head high like the queen that she was, she said, "If you surrender now, you understand that you will still be tried?"

The boy's frightened eyes flitted between her and Callum. "I-I understand. We will accept any mercy you see fit to grant us. You could have burned us all alive and have been done with it, but instead, you offered us a fair deal."

Adalina glanced at Callum, wishing she could read his mind or that she had the ability to sense his emotions like she could with Elettra. There was no way to predict his response. The only hint was the draw of his lips and brow. Was he thinking of Sage and the way she had thrown herself in front of him to save his life? Or was he only remembering the lives of his men—men he'd grown up with, trained with, and trusted—dying at the icy hands of these boys and the others?

There was no conviction in his voice as he said, "My grandfather would say they should all burn." Then, with a painful pause, he turned to Adalina. "It's why we wanted Elettra here. Dragon fire to end the threat." His gaze was intense and searching. It seemed like he was begging her to give him a solution.

Adalina laced her fingers with his. "Is a crown truly worth having if it has been forged in flame?"

His thumb brushed against her knuckles. He spoke low as he asked, "What do you want to do?"

"Me?" She furrowed her brow.

"You are Queen of Astarfall, dear wife, and I trust you more than any other—more than even myself—to make the choice."

The crowd fell into silence, as if straining to hear their king and queen. It was stifling as everyone waited with anticipation. Frost breathers inched closer to watch the exchange, but the Astarfall soldiers followed closely behind, ready to reengage in battle if they needed to.

Adalina laced her fingers through Callum's. The boys were so young. They hadn't had the chance to experience life. Not really. Instead, how long had they spent digging Uthred's tunnels? When they should have been reading bedtime stories about grand adventures and the wonders of the world, they were only given horror stories about a place that didn't want them. One that thought they were disposable and useless. A blight on their society and their land. There would be nothing just or right about taking their lives because of that.

Softly, she said, "We make the decision together. If you can promise me that they will be tried fairly, then I believe we should accept their surrender."

The boy's voice broke as he said, "We only want a chance."

Callum looked between her and the boy. Then around at the tired men—king's men and frost breathers alike who were worn and battle weary. Adalina stared at them, too, and it broke her heart.

Finally, Callum asked, "What is your name, boy?"

"Dane," he said, with some returning courage.

Adalina staggered into Callum slightly. Sage's brother. The one she had renounced the frost breathers to save. Sage gave her life in order to give him a chance at his. Adalina's hand trembled and Callum tightened his grip, though he was shaking too.

She glanced up at the sky and willed her tears not to fall. Not yet. Not until Dane was declared safe. She wondered if his sister was watching from the veil beyond the living. Had she risen to the heavens yet or was she lingering there, waiting to see if Adalina would fulfill her promise?

Finally, Callum said, "Dane, you have your chance. You all do." To his men, he said, "Bind their hands. We can't risk another trick."

Dane held his hands out first. "You will have no tricks from me and my friends."

With his promise, the cool nip in the air was replaced with the familiar warmth Astarfall was known for. The frost that coated the ground and the gate melted into water like the first melt of spring. The frost breathers were releasing any hold they had left on the city.

The other young men offered their hands to be bound, too. They stilled as the king's guard moved in on them, wrapping their wrists with rope that was so thin it looked more like thread. The silvery strands shimmered much like Elettra's bindings had. But there was no sign of pain from the boys. Rather, their faces softened, as if relieved that it was all over.

More frost breathers followed suit, kneeling with their hands clasped in front of them. A few shifted nervously. Adalina wondered if they would try to run or put up a fight. This wouldn't work if they didn't come willingly. How many of them were engrained with the same ideals as Uthred? The boys in front of her were young, but what of the older ones? Their minds might be harder to shift.

Only one man openly resisted. He snarled curses at her and Callum. To her surprise, it was Heely who dealt with him. Rearing back, he punched the man in the face. The resister fell to the ground spitting blood. Heely bound his wrists himself and said with a lopsided smile, "I've always wanted to do that."

Callum chuckled and nudged Adalina in her side. "Better than your first time, huh?"

She rolled her eyes. "Careful, my aim has improved."

In the end, any frost breathers left standing from the battle allowed themselves and their magic to be bound. It would take time to figure out which men were members of Uthred's inner circle. Adalina suspected they had surrendered peacefully with the others in order to save themselves. But with Dane's help, perhaps they could easily weed them out. They could build a list with the names of those who organized and led the rebellion with Uthred. Those were the true threats. And if this was going to work, they needed to do their best to minimize the risks. To keep those who remained loyal to Uthred from walking free amongst them.

The guards took every frost breather to the jail to await trial, leaving Adalina and Callum to stand amidst the ruins of battle. Bodies—Astarfallen and frost breather alike—littered the ground. It made her sick to her stomach, and she had to cling tightly to Callum in an effort to keep her balance.

The dead would be taken to pyres so their ashes could be returned to the earth. Even the frost breathers would be given a proper burial. Uthred's body would be amongst theirs. Even though he didn't deserve the honor in the majority's eyes, Adalina and Callum couldn't bring themselves to waste another moment of hatred on him.

"You did well, dear wife," Callum whispered in her ear.

"With you by my side, how could I not?" She nuzzled into him, breathing in his familiar scent. The sounds of the city coming back to life filled her with comfort.

Callum spoke so low, she almost missed it as he said, "About that apology I owe you."

"You already apologized." In truth, it was his actions since then—his faith in her—that had worked its way through that wall she'd begun to reconstruct around her heart. It slipped through the cracks, reminding her that he was trying to make things right again.

His chest rose and fell heavily, with her head pressed against it. Then, more confidently, he said, "I let the grief for my father rule me. I never should have taken your choices away. Rather than face my heartache, I channeled it into fear for you. It festered into something ugly and I'm sorry."

He drew back with his hands gripping her shoulders firmly. With his mouth pressed into a hard line, she sensed he was struggling with what he wanted to say next. Patiently, she waited.

"You said you could return to Solaris so that your presence doesn't hinder my rule. But I don't want you to leave. You make me a better king. I'm a better man when I'm with you." He gestured to the few remaining frost breathers who were being escorted away peacefully. "I never would have had the courage to do what we did just now if it weren't for you."

Something stirred in her heart. "Callum, I—"

"I will get on my knees if it will convince you to stay. Not just as my queen, but as my wife. A true wife." He blew out a heavy breath and said, "If you want to go back to Solaris... If it will make you happy, then I'll understand. I won't press you on the matter again. But please know that a moment won't go by, that I don't treat you as my equal in every way. Damn the council and what anyone else says."

Adalina watched in awe as the words tumbled out of him, leaving him breathless and red in the face. It was a rare sight to see him tripping over himself like this, and she had to admit that she was enjoying how flustered he seemed.

At her silence, he added quickly, "We can even build a new council. One that includes women. Seraphine!" He snapped his fingers as if the ideas were pouring into his head faster than he could get them out.

Adalina glanced at the citizens who had come out of hiding so they could help carry the dead into the great hall to be prepared for the pyres. Families reunited and embraced one another with such fervor that it brought tears to her eyes.

Solaris still was and always would be her home. But going back would mean leaving Astarfall and Callum behind. Already, he had shown that he was willing to learn from his mistakes. It didn't mean he wouldn't allow his fear to impact their relationship again, but wasn't it something worth exploring?

Before she answered, Callum said, "I love you, Lina. And I can live with whatever life throws my way—danger and all—if you are by my side."

She placed her hand on his chest to stop him. "I..." His declaration took her breath away. "I do want to stay," she said with more certainty than she realized she had.

His face was still swollen, and he likely needed to see a healer, but he flashed her a stunning smile. Only he could summon something as dazzling as that after being beaten and battered.

She laughed softly at herself. If anyone had asked her on her way to Solaris if she imagined falling in love with a man who brightened the world with a single smile, she'd have said they were crazy. Callum had never been part of her dream. She never imagined anyone other than her and Elettra flying through life together. But she'd been wrong. He was the greatest dream come true for her. A man who was swearing to not only stand up for her but stand *by* her.

Finally, she allowed herself to be brave; to say what she'd known deep down but hadn't had enough trust to say out loud. "I love you, too, Callum."

He cupped her face in his hands, wiping away her tears. With a touch of good humor, he said, "Dear wife, I do believe that's the nicest thing you've ever said to me."

Elettra danced around, pawing at the ground eagerly. Something glinted in her mouth. Moonstone. Callum reached out his hand and the dragon dropped the compass into it. His fingers closed around it tightly as he said, "I'm sorry, Elettra. I truly am."

She snorted and shot him a haughty look.

Adalina chuckled. "I do believe she's saying you'll have to make it up to her as well."

Callum nodded and patted the dragon's cheek. "Let's start with a nice big dinner for you, eh?"

As he called over a few of the king's guards to give them directions on Elettra's post battle feast, Adalina gazed out at the mountains in the distance. They'd captured a good portion of the frost breathers. Others were slain. But she thought of the underground tunnels. Of the mothers and children who had survived to carry on the legacy once before. She shivered violently, unsure if it was shock setting in from everything they'd gone through or if it was something more than that. Despite her desperation to celebrate their victory, something in her gut told her that the people who had endured half a century in the wild forest to the west were still out there.

But she didn't want to dwell on any of that. Not now. Instead, when Callum returned to her, she leaned into him and rested her forehead against his. Nose to nose, she closed her eyes and imagined what would come next if she let it.

A life together. Ruling side by side on the Astarfall throne. Prosperity and peace between them and Solaris. A world where the sun shined, and she could smile freely. Where Elettra would no longer have to fight but could instead enjoy her time basking in the sunshine while she lazed about or played ball with the children in the city.

They could have a home together—the three of them—filled with love and laughter. So, shoving her doubts and fears aside and tucking them into a deep pocket of her mind, she tilted her head to kiss her husband.

Their lips brushed together softly at first, but then it turned fierce. Hungry for one another, they embraced and only broke away when they heard the voices around them. The council had gathered and waited with red faces for their king to address them.

Callum took Adalina's hand, drawing her close. Then he announced, "My wife and I are going to retire to our room for the night. We'll reconvene tomorrow."

"But Sire," one of the elders objected.

Adalina's grandmother chuckled with a hand on her hip. "Give it a rest, you old dolt. They just saved your asses. Let them celebrate.

There will be time for talking tomorrow." She winked at them as they swept past the stunned councilmen and headed up to the palace.

Walking into their bedroom was strange. Not one thing had changed about it. Gauzy curtains blew inward from the open terrace where Elettra was already laying. Her eyes were shut and Adalina sensed contentment from her. The dragon had earned a peaceful night's rest, so Adalina closed the doors, leaving them open only a crack. Then she drew the curtains and joined Callum.

He was already undressed. His body was bruised and there was still blood on his face, so she went to the basin in their washroom. She filled a large white bowl with fresh water and grabbed a bar of sandalwood soap.

With him sitting up, she dipped a rag into the water, rubbed soap on it and began to clean his wounds. Using a gentle touch, she cleared away the grime and blood until his incredibly handsome face was visible once more. With the help of some salve left by the healers, the swelling would soon go down.

When she was done, her hand lingered near his cheek, and he took hold of it. Shivers ran down her spine as he planted a kiss on her palm and then on the inside of her wrist. A sea breeze drifted through the crack in the terrace doors, filling the room with the familiar salty scent she was beginning to adore.

She shivered in delight as he worked his way up to her neck. Between kisses, he muttered declarations about how much he admired and loved her. He rolled over top of her, bracing himself with the headboard as they fell back into the cloud-like blankets.

His gaze bore into hers, and she swore he was looking into her very soul. The pressure of his body against hers anchored her to the moment, leaving no room for all the ache and pain of what they'd been through.

Strong fingers brushed her slip up her thigh and tickled her bare skin. She shuddered with building anticipation. Moonlight wafted through the split in the curtains and enveloped them as if blessing their love. She moaned as his touch inched up her inner thigh. She wanted this man to utterly consume her. But there was something she needed to say first.

With a gentle touch, she grabbed his chin and turned his gaze to her. Warmth blossomed in her chest as she said, "I want us to do this right, Callum. If you meant everything you said out there, then I want to be here with you and be by your side. But it won't be easy. This isn't like the storybooks I read as a child. What comes after the happy ending will not be all sunshine and rainbows..."

He jerked his chin slightly and made a sound as if to stop her from continuing, but she shifted until he had no choice but to look at her.

She continued, "Trust takes time to build. I can admit that I should have given us the chance to know each other before assuming the things you were doing—bossing me and pretending things weren't a big deal—weren't because you wanted to control me. Now I know it was deep-seated fear underneath all of it. I know *you*. And I need you to know that I choose *you* and everything that comes with it."

With a boyish smirk, he said, "So what you're saying is you love me and can't live without me?"

She rolled her eyes playfully. Then, slipping from under him and pushing him down until she was straddling him, she said, "Exactly. Now, I'd like to *show* you."

She ran her lips down past his naval and watched hungrily as he bit his lip. When she inched lower, the guttural growl that rumbled from him made her ravenous. All her life she only ever wanted to belong to herself. But she had a new dream now. There was no denying that their hearts belonged to one another. And there was no one else in the world that she wanted to experience the highs and lows of life with.

Sixteen Years Later

Callum kicked his feet unceremoniously up onto the table. The Dew Drop Inn was exceptionally busy with troves of people coming in for the blessing of his new ship, *Alistair's Prize*.

Adalina swatted at his boots and shot him with a scolding look. Sixteen years of marriage and he still hadn't learned any manners. She smirked and shook her head as she sipped her refreshing, fruity ale. All this time in Astarfall and still her Solarian blood struggled to adapt to the humidity.

With a chuckle, he filled both their glasses from the pitcher that Alfie's new waitress had brought them. Seraphine was busy with the council as they prepared for a visit from the Festiri emissary to talk about possible trade agreements. The wilderness remained between Astarfall and their western neighbor, but perhaps there were ways around that.

Cheerfully, Callum said, "Relax, dear wife. This is meant to be a celebration."

She fidgeted with the moonglass ring on her finger. It still sparkled as brightly as it had when he first gave it to her. She sighed and said, "I know…"

Things had been going so well for such a long time. Astarfall and Solaris were both more prosperous than ever. Their families were happy and healthy. But she couldn't get the nagging suspicion to go away. The one that had been eating at her since builders from a western village brought back a piece of broken shell two nights ago. It was gray and worn, buried beneath dirt and sediment. It was weather-beaten and everyone agreed it must have been there for some time.

She did her best to push down the lump in her throat. "What if it's what I think it is? If the dragon egg—"

"If a dragon has hatched, we would have known." Callum reached across the table to take her hands. "There's been no sign or word of Erabelle or the egg for sixteen years. The trail has gone colder than cold. It's downright frigid." He shrugged and tilted his head toward the beach. "Just look at everything we have to be thankful for. That daughter of ours, for starters."

Adalina's heart instantly swelled with contentment. Skipping through the sand, Elettra's glittering scales caught her eye first. In recent years they had dulled slightly, but when the sun was at its highest, the purples, blues, and greens still dazzled the eye.

On her back, Kenna's dark auburn hair caught the light, reminding Adalina of the sweet baby she had been. Through the years, her hair had darkened, making the likeness to Callum nearly uncanny, save for the wild curls that refused to stay in place no matter how much Gwendolyn tried to tame them under a tiara.

Laughter bubbled up from Adalina's throat as she watched their daughter, who was no longer a tottering child, but a girl of fifteen, taunt her friend who was trying to get on Elettra. Seraphine and Alfie's son, Gustave, attempted to climb onto the dragon's back, only to slip into the sand again and again.

Kenna's laughter filled the whole beach, drawing amused smiles from each passerby. Meanwhile, Adalina's grandparents chased after the unruly teenagers. It only seemed to egg the two on as they tried to escape their lessons.

As usual, Adalina and Callum's youngest, Alistair—an eight-year-old boy with a penchant for mischief—was in tow.

Adalina's grandfather shouted at Gustave, "How are you ever going to be a swordsman if you keep running off?"

Her grandmother, with hands on her hips, shook her head in disapproval, though her smile revealed how much she was enjoying herself. With laughter in her voice, she yelled, "If you're going to run off on a dragon's back, you should at least do it right! Kenna, help that boy up there properly!"

Kenna gave the same charming grin her father so often used. With a flick of her wrist, she called on the sunlight to whip her friend up behind her like a person giving someone a leg up on a horse. Her Astarfallen magic was yet another gift inherited from her father.

Gustave yelped, then raised his chin proudly as the three of them finally took off into the sky. They whooped and hollered until they were soaring high above the water. Alistair ran after them, shouting about the unfairness of being left behind, as per usual.

Adalina laughed until her side cramped as she watched her grandparents arguing about how they were too old to be dealing with childish antics. She knew they would continue to do it, though. Her grandmother claimed Kenna, Alistair, and Gustave kept them young.

The nagging feeling quelled slightly. When she turned back to the table, her stomach fluttered. Callum's dark blue eyes sparkled with pride as he watched their daughter fly away. He was as lighthearted as ever. And by now, she could see the signs of whether he was faking it or not. In this case, he was being truthful.

And maybe he was right. There had been no mention of frost breathers to the west or anywhere else, for that matter. Those who surrendered and were not found to be part of Uthred's inner circle had been reintegrated into society. They'd worked hard to start a program that allowed them to utilize their skills for good. Helping to enrich the soil for crops, to help sailors navigate the cold treacherous waters in the far south, or to work the icehouses. The young had been eager to accept the proposal. Though, the older generations were harder to convince. For that reason, they were still treated with extreme caution.

As for those who remained loyal to Uthred's cause, Callum had seen to it that they were humanely treated, but it seemed there wouldn't be any hope of reintegrating them. Some wounds just ran too deep.

Otherwise, it was quiet and peaceful in their land. She and Callum had joined their people to sweep Uthred's tunnels before caving in the passageways to prevent anyone from using them ever again.

But every so often, Adalina would get a chill deep in her bones, reminding her of the woman she allowed to escape. The woman who they believed had taken the dragon egg with her in a velvety bag. As much as Adalina prayed that Erabelle would do the right thing and raise her child somewhere peacefully, a pestering voice inside her head told her she was too spiteful for such a thing.

She sighed as Callum took the seat beside her and stroked her hair away from her face. His fingers inched to her lips, and he brushed a thumb softly over them. This time, his smile was not taunting or playful. It was one he reserved for just her. One that accompanied a look in his eyes that made her feel like she was the only woman in the world. Like she was the most dazzling creature he'd ever seen.

His fingers dropped to her chin, and he tilted her head up. As he pressed a firm kiss to her mouth, her heart soared. Regardless of what came their way, these were the moments she would cling to. The quiet ones like sitting side by side with a husband who loved her wholeheartedly while the sunshine warmed their skin. This was true happiness.

Acknowledgments

This story began with a wine bottle. No, seriously. In my usual fashion, I picked a bottle of white wine off the shelf because it had a pretty label. Three years later, a story grew from that girl with a dragon standing behind her. But more importantly, through it all, I couldn't have created this new fantastical world without the love and support of those in the real world.

First, to my patient and supportive husband, Zach. Thank you so much for loving me through my stress. I'm not exaggerating when I say that none of this would be possible without you. You're my best friend and I'm so lucky to have you in my corner, always.

Next to Emily Fluke. When I say I couldn't have gotten through the last few weeks of working on this book without you, I'm not even kidding. Thank you for holding me accountable especially during my "I'm tired of this, Grandpa!" moments.

To the rest of my Chaos Corner: Danielle, Samantha, Jes, Kate, and Emily H. You truly make me a better writer and push me to grow. Thank you for sticking with me through the first version of Callum. I know it was rough!

To my Cozy Club. Thank you, Stephanie, Justice, and Nicolle for reminding me to come up for air every once in a while. And for letting me send you six too many Tom Hardy tiktok edits.

A special thank you to Ardena and Chase for cheering me on even when I hand you the roughest of drafts to beta read. That's true friendship.

To my street team, Beth, Kassie, CJ, Jessica, Annika, Kelsey, Lisa, Amber, Ardena, and Chase. Thank you all for being there for me when I finally pop my head out of my writing hole like a groundhog. And thank you for loving on my books as if they were your own.

To my babies and to my friends and family. I love you with all my heart. I am incredibly blessed to be surrounded by so much love and encouragement. Thank you for making me who I am today.

And finally, to my readers. Without you, stories of villains and monsters would be trapped in my head. Thank you for the opportunity to share these stories and characters with all of you. You will forever have a special place in my heart.

About the Author

J.M. has spent much of her adult life moving around with her husband and their two children, making stories of their own. As a young girl, she always dreamed of fantastical worlds. Even when horseback riding, she was never in her own yard; instead, she was in an enchanted forest or riding into battle alongside brave knights. Today, she puts those stories to paper.

Local to Eastern NC, she does this in the little pockets of her day between giving her kids snacks, exploring local cafes and bookstores, and crafting with her cozy club.